For a moment the two women regarded each other without speaking. The gipsy stood still, her face impassive. The mistress of Foxearth was obviously ill at ease, but trying hard to conceal her nervousness. In contrast to Lavinia's obvious agitation, the gipsy stood in the middle of the unfamiliar room with an air of calm composure. Only her eyes moved – straying to the three shillings which lay on the table nearby.

'Do you have some news for me?'

The gipsy nodded and held out her hand. Abruptly she said, 'What am I to call you? I remember you when you was Vinnie Harris, but now you've come up in the world.'

The words were accusing and Vinnie's cheeks burned with a mixture of confusion and resentment. A phrase came back into her mind – 'You're Vinnie Harris from the London slums and don't you forget it.' She would not, could not, forget it, but all that had ended three years ago. The woman was being impertinent.

'You should call me "ma'am",' she said. 'But now your news, please.'

'Well, *ma'am*.' There was a hint of sarcasm in the gipsy's voice. 'They're as well as can be expected, though the Westlands cottage is poky.'

Unconsciously, Vinnie lowered her voice. 'And Tom Bryce?' she ventured.

Summer Song

PAMELA OLDFIELD

SPHERE BOOKS LIMITED
London and Sydney

First published in Great Britain by
Century Publishing Co. Ltd 1984
Copyright © 1984 by Pamela Oldfield
Published by Sphere Books Ltd 1985
30–32 Gray's Inn Road, London WC1X 8JL

TRADE
MARK

Printed and bound in Great Britain by
Collins, Glasgow

For Dick and Barbara

CHAPTER ONE

Lavinia Lawrence, mistress of Foxearth, sat in the drawing room with a book open in her lap, but she was not reading it. Her hands were folded over the book and she stared into the log fire with unseeing eyes. It was not officially a moment of leisure or relaxation, for the book was a leather-bound ledger in which the household accounts were recorded and a forgotten pencil was held lightly in her right hand. Something was wrong with her calculations, however, and she was trying to discover the error before Julian, her husband, checked them. It shamed her that she did not manage her household more efficiently, but she had assumed the responsibility on her marriage to Julian at the early age of sixteen, with no previous experience to prepare her for such a task.

During the first months of their marriage Julian had found her inexperience appealing and had tried to teach her, but gradually his other duties had demanded his attention, the lessons had lapsed and she suspected that nowadays her inefficiency irritated him. Now with an effort her fingers tightened on the pencil and she frowned with concentration at the neat columns of words and figures which she had pencilled in the previous day. Once they were correct, she would take the ledger upstairs to the study and ink them in. The study belonged to the master of the house and nominally this was still Colonel Henry Lawrence, her father-in-law, but he had relegated the position to his only son when a riding accident had confined him to bed and failing health and old age made it impossible for him to continue.

Now Lavinia pressed the blunt end of the pencil into her chin and sighed deeply as she stared at the figures which obstinately refused to balance. The amount spent did not tally with the items purchased, so obviously she had forgotten to record something – an item of food, perhaps – but no, she had totalled the bills three

times and they matched the entries in the ledger. She smiled
faintly to herself as she recalled her attempts, many years ago, to
act as the Lawrences' temporary 'booker'. Then she had toured
the extensive hop gardens with the 'measurer', pencil and notebook in hand, earnestly recording the number of bushels in each
bin. Those days were indelibly stamped on her memory. Then
she was only Vinnie Harris, a poor girl from the East End of
London, brought up by Mrs Bryce in the village and desperately
in love with Julian, the Lawrences' golden-haired son. Her eyes
softened at the memory and she sighed again, absent-mindedly
pressing the pencil point into the page and working it round.
When a small hole appeared she withdrew the pencil guiltily and
rubbed at the offending mark, only to make it worse. She merely
said, 'Drat it!' however, for Mrs Bryce had been very strict and
had not allowed her to use any of 'that dreadful London language'.

Vinnie had shared life at the cottage with Mrs Bryce and Tom,
her grown-up son. Tom had later married Rose Tully and Vinnie,
with her generous heart, had loved them both and extended her
affections to encompass their children as each one came along.
She loved them still and indeed it was the Bryce family who now
distracted her thoughts from the pressing matter of the accounts,
for their present situation was not a happy one and Vinnie lived
with the knowledge that she was partly to blame.

A log shifted and she jumped as a shower of sparks rose into the
chimney. With a muttered cry of irritation she threw down the
pencil, closed the ledger and rested her head in her hands. It was
no good – the Bryces, or her conscience, would not let her be.
The accounts were dry as dust and boring, but the Bryces were
alive and crying out for help. To nineteen-year-old Vinnie it was
an appeal she could not refuse.

'I'm so sorry!' she whispered despairingly. 'So very sorry.' With
a weary movement, she lifted her head and stared once more into
the flames. 'I'm sorry for you and I'm sorry for me. It's all going
wrong and I don't know what to do. I don't even know who I am!'
She leaned forward to pick up the pencil, blinking her eyes to
discourage any tears that might be gathering. 'I'm not Vinnie
Harris and I don't feel at all like Lavinia Lawrence.' Reluctantly,
she opened the ledger again and struggled to regain her composure. There must have been an extra expense which she had
overlooked . . . Ah! Of course! The cotton sheeting – five yards of

best cotton. She had given the parcel to Mrs Tallant, the housekeeper, and no doubt the invoice was still inside the brown wrapping paper. Her success briefly chased away the gloomy thoughts and the shadow left her eyes. Licking the pencil, she bent her head and began to write.

*

Upstairs the Colonel lowered his paper as the door opened and Janet bustled into the room.

'She's going, Janet!' he told her triumphantly. 'The old girl's going at last!'

His face broke into a broad grin and Janet tried to look disapproving. 'That's not a very nice thing to say, sir,' she told him as she began to plump up the pillows and straighten the bed. 'That's not kind at all, sir. Poor old lady!'

'Kind or not, Janet, I tell you I've done it. I have outlived her.'

'Ah, but she's not dead yet, sir. Only sinking.'

'She's sinking *fast*, Janet, not just sinking.' He began to turn the pages of the paper, still smiling broadly, then put out a hand to take hold of Janet's apron and tug her towards him. Janet leaned over good-naturedly.

'I did it!' he whispered and at last she relaxed and smiled with him.

Colonel Henry Lawrence had been born on the same day as Queen Victoria and although bedridden for several years, was determined to outlive the small, spritely lady who had ruled England for so long. Almost eighty-two years old, the Queen had suffered from rheumatism and her failing sight had given cause for concern, but now suddenly she lay at Osborne on the Isle of Wight with her life drawing to a close. Janet looked down at the bony fingers which held her apron and wondered with dismay how much longer the Colonel would be with them. He, too, was growing frail and the doctor visited him twice weekly. She could not imagine Foxearth without the old man.

'Cook says we shall have a king before the week's out,' she said. 'That will seem strange, won't it, sir? England's never had a king, leastways not as far as I can remember.'

He became aware suddenly that she was prettying the bed. 'Why are you fussing so?' he demanded.

'I want you to look your best for the doctor, sir.'

'Doctor? Janet, he isn't coming today surely – he has only just been.'

'No, sir, that was three days ago. You are getting in a bit of a muddle.'

'Three days ago?' He frowned, vexed at his confusion.

'He told the mistress how well you looked, sir. He is very pleased with you.'

This was a small white lie, for the doctor had said no such thing.

'Pleased with me?' said the Colonel. 'I should hope he is pleased with me. I shall live a long time yet. I shall see ninety.'

'I certainly hope so, sir. Whatever would I do without you? Now I think you look tidy. I will just comb your hair, sir.'

The Colonel tutted impatiently. 'You know very well I have little or no hair to comb. You mollycoddle me, Janet. Did you know that? You're a mollycoddler!'

Janet laughed. 'It's my job, sir. "Mollycoddle the Colonel", the mistress told me.'

'I'm sure Vinnie didn't tell you to cluck over me like an old hen!' Janet was not deceived by his grumbling, however. She spent more time with him than anyone else in the household and a strong bond of affection had sprung up between them during the past few years. The Colonel returned once more to his newspaper.

'The Duke of Connaught is on his way over and they say the Kaiser is expected in London shortly. It's serious, Janet, there's no doubt about that.'

Janet produced a small cloth from the pocket of her apron and began to wipe over the table which stood beside the Colonel's bed. She wiped the neck and stopper of each medicine bottle and rearranged them to her greater satisfaction. Then she fiddled with the magazines, arranging them neatly so that the spines of the books were parallel to the edge of the table.

'England without Queen Victoria!' said the Colonel. 'It's going to take a bit of getting used to, but she's had a damned good innings.'

'You make her sound like a cricketer,' Janet laughed, 'batting for England.'

'Well, that's not so far out. But a new king . . .' He pursed his lips.

'Will we call him King Albert, sir?'

'Possibly, or King Edward.'

'They can hardly call him King Teddy!' she laughed.

'He'll make a good king, you know, Janet. Oh, I know there are some who will wag their finger at him. He's no saint and he hasn't always been discreet, but he's a man's man, Janet, and there's nothing wrong with that.'

'Certainly not, sir,' said Janet taking her cue. 'You're a man's man, sir, by all accounts.'

The Colonel was pleased by her remark but made no comment.

'Have you ever seen him, sir? The Prince of Wales?' Janet glanced round the room with a practised eye. She took satisfaction in its appearance, regarding the Colonel's bedroom as her sole responsibility.

'Several times, Janet, but the last time – let me think – it was at Evans' just off Covent Garden. He took a group of his friends there to hear Victor Liston sing "Shabby Genteel". I was there with one or two chaps from the regiment. Best supper room in London, was Evans'.'

' "Shabby Genteel", sir?'

The Colonel nodded and began to sing:

> Too proud to beg, too honest to steal,
> Something, something, dum de dum,
> My tatters and rags I try to conceal,
> I'm one of the shabby genteel.

Janet regarded him humorously. 'I didn't know you could sing, sir.'

'Well, now you know I *can't*! Funny thing, Janet – I can remember that evening as though it were yesterday, but you ask me when the doctor last called and I can't tell you.'

'It's your memory, sir. It plays tricks now and again. Nothing to worry about.'

'I remember that evening so clearly, Janet. Of course the Prince was younger then, but he knew how to enjoy himself and so did we when we got a spot of leave. I loved the music halls, but Marie Lloyd was my favourite. I can see her now – a big grin on her face and *such* a naughty wink. She could be very naughty, you know. Oh, she was always in trouble. She used to do a bit of patter with an umbrella.' The Colonel's eyes gleamed. 'She used to hold it out in front of her, trying to open it, you see, and rolling her eyes and smiling that saucy smile of hers. No one could smile like

Marie. Then she would get it undone and hold it up over her head. "My goodness", she would say, "what a relief, haven't had it up for weeks!" '

The old man threw back his head and chuckled at the memory, while Janet struggled to keep her face straight.

'Haven't had it up for weeks!' he repeated and then glanced anxiously towards the maid. 'You wouldn't understand that, Janet.'

'No, sir.'

'At least, I hope you wouldn't.'

'I don't understand it, sir.' She managed to look suitably puzzled and the Colonel threw back his head and laughed again.

'No, you wouldn't, Janet, if you are a good girl. Ah me! We knew how to enjoy ourselves in those days.'

'I am sure you did.'

'But they are gone and now the old Queen's going with them.' He sighed, his mood changing suddenly. 'The old girl really is dying at last and we shall have a king.'

Janet made no answer and for a moment he was lost in thought, then he shrugged and glanced up.

'And what time is the doctor coming?'

'Any moment, I should think, sir, and I had best be on my way downstairs again or Mrs Tallant will be after me.'

Mrs Tallant was the housekeeper, who ruled the kitchen staff with the proverbial rod of iron.

'Off with you, then!' said the Colonel and Janet left the room, closing the door quietly behind her. She stood at the top of the stairs for a moment, rehearsing the scene with the umbrella – which she understood only too well – then, putting her hand to her mouth to stifle a giggle, she hurried downstairs, eager to pass it on.

*

As Janet hurried into the kitchen, the back door closed behind the two men – Tim Bilton, the groom, nearing fifty and 'Young Harry', twenty-seven years old, who helped him in the stables and also tended the garden. Only the women remained to hear her story. Cook, in her sixties, was slow and stolid but extremely capable; Edie Bilton, the groom's daughter – a large, slow-witted girl who could be entrusted with only the most menial tasks; and Mrs Tallant. As Janet entered the room, Edie – who stood at one

end of the large scrubbed table ironing handkerchiefs – returned
one flat-iron to the fire and took up the other, spitting on to its
surface to test the heat. She took a handkerchief from the pile,
spread it out, eased it into shape and began to iron it with
elaborate care. Janet, disappointed at the disappearance of the
men, nevertheless recounted her story and was gratified by its
reception. Mrs Tallant laughed; Cook pretended to be shocked;
Edie, however, stared at Janet with a frown on her face.

'But what's the joke?' she demanded. 'What's funny about an
umbrella?'

Janet giggled. 'If you don't know, Edie, then I'm not going to
tell you.'

Edie appealed to the others. 'But what's funny about it?
What—'

'Never you mind!' said Cook. 'It's best you shouldn't know –
and watch what you are doing, girl!'

With a squeal, Edie lifted the flat-iron, her expression dismayed at the sight of the scorched handkerchief.

'Now you've done it!' said Cook.

'It wasn't my fault,' Edie began. 'It's her fault.' She glared at
Janet.

'Don't blame me,' said Janet. 'I was only telling a joke. No law
against that!'

'You had best run it under the tap straight away,' said Mrs
Tallant. 'Give it a good rub with soap and if that doesn't work,
soak it in lemon juice – and next time, watch what you're doing.'

As Edie obeyed, a frantic expression on her face, there was a
knock at the back door. Cook, her hands white with flour, waved
them helplessly and Janet opened the door to find a young gipsy
woman on the doorstep, her weather-beaten face impassive. On
her back she carried a young baby in a shawl; a large apron made
of sacking was tied round her waist and her dark hair was tied
back with a ribbon.

'Tell your fortune, lady!' she began in a monotone. 'Cross my
palm with silver and learn what the future has in store for you?'

Janet had a natural distrust of strangers and pressed her foot
against the door. 'No, thank you,' she said sharply.

She began to close the door, but now the gipsy's foot was
pressed against it from outside. 'Read your teacup, love,' she
continued. 'Discover your future in the cards—'

'I've told you, no.'

The woman remained undeterred. 'Buy a few pegs, lady.' She fumbled in her apron pocket and produced a handful of pegs for Janet to inspect.

Mrs Tallant called out to her. 'She's told you no. Now you be off,' she said, but although her voice had the authority that Janet's lacked, the gipsy continued as though she had not spoken.

'Rabbit's fur?' She took out a soft pelt from her pocket and held it up. 'Make a nice hat, that would. Or a pheasant's egg, maybe?'

It was Cook's turn to look up sharply. 'Pheasant's eggs? You've no business with pheasant's eggs. Stolen, I don't doubt!'

The woman shook her head. 'I found them by the roadside.' She held one out to show them.

'Roadside, my foot!' said Cook, although they both knew nothing could be proved. Fascinated, Janet had relaxed the pressure of her foot and the door had opened a little wider. The baby on the gipsy's back stirred in its sleep and whimpered.

'Then buy a bit of mandrake, love,' the woman persisted, returning the controversial egg to its former hiding place. She pulled forth a handful of dried root chopped into inch-long pieces and began her spiel.

'Genuine mandrake, the human herb cures most ills.' She saw that Janet hesitated, aware of the properties claimed for the plant. 'Dug that himself, my husband did – and a full day's work it was. The sweat poured off him and that's the truth. Four feet down he went for that root and that wasn't enough, for when he got it up one leg was shorter than the other. I was there and heard it groan.'

'Groan?' repeated Edie, abandoning the soapy handkerchief and joining Janet at the door. 'Roots don't groan,' she said.

'Oh, the mandrake does, love,' the gipsy told her. 'Because the mandrake is a *human* herb. Four feet high this one was and shaped like a man, arms, legs, head, everything.'

'She's right,' said Janet. 'They are human. I have been told that they do really groan, though I've never heard one myself.'

Cook made a wry face.

'Groan?' said Edie and her disbelief was apparent to them all.

'Weighed nearly a stone, that one did,' the gipsy told them, 'and it's been drying this past month. I could sell this mandrake to a herbalist and get a good price, but I'm offering it to you. Put it into a glass of wine and there's nothing better for the blood. Good for your chest, too, if you're a bit wheezy. Do the old Colonel the world of good.'

'What do *you* know about the Colonel?' Mrs Tallant asked her.

The gipsy shrugged. 'Only that he's a good age. I'll be drinking mandrake when I'm his age, I can tell you.' She looked at Cook. 'It's wonderful stuff. Look here, I'll give you a handful for a shilling. How's that?'

'Sixpence,' said Cook.

'Ninepence.'

The deal was settled and money and goods exchanged. Still the gipsy made no move to go.

'I have to see the mistress now,' she told them.

'You will do no such thing,' said Mrs Tallant. 'The mistress has no wish to be bothered by the likes of you, so take your money and off you go.'

The baby wailed, suddenly fretful, but received no attention from its mother.

'Last time I came,' the gipsy insisted, 'I passed the mistress at the gate as I was leaving. "Next time you come this way", she told me, "ask for me".'

'What would she want with you?' asked Janet.

The woman shrugged her shoulders carelessly. 'That's between her and me, love,' she said.

Mrs Tallant hesitated. 'If you're lying—' she began.

'It's no lie.'

The housekeeper sighed. 'You had best tell the mistress, Janet,' she said. 'She's in the drawing room.'

Edie rinsed out the scorched handkerchief, which looked no better than it had before, and hung it over the stove to dry. By this time the iron had cooled, so she exchanged it for a heated one and applied herself once more to her task.

*

For a moment the two women regarded each other without speaking. The gipsy stood still, her face impassive. The mistress of Foxearth was obviously ill at ease, but trying hard to conceal her nervousness. The fingers of her right hand strayed to the heavy gold hair which was piled on top of her head in an impeccable arrangement which framed her oval face and large grey eyes to perfection. She was not a beauty – her bone structure was not delicate enough to be fashionable. Nor was she sufficiently tall or slender for the role in which she was now cast as wife of Julian Lawrence, the Colonel's only son. When the Colonel died, Julian would inherit Foxearth and the extensive hop gardens and Lavinia would then be mistress in her own right. At present she held that position only because the Colonel's wife had died several years earlier.

However, if Lavinia Lawrence was not a beauty, she was certainly more than presentable. She wore a gown of grey silk, high-necked and with long sleeves. A long rope of pearls and pearl earrings were her only adornment; she wore neither powder nor perfume. The fingers of her right hand moved to the wedding ring on her left and she turned it with nervous movements.

In contrast to Lavinia's obvious agitation, the gipsy stood in the middle of the unfamiliar room with an air of calm composure. Only her eyes moved – straying to the three shillings which lay on the table nearby.

'Do you have some news for me?'

The gipsy nodded and held out her hand. She was given one of the shillings, which she slipped immediately into the pocket of her apron.

'Have you seen them?' Vinnie asked.

The woman nodded but volunteered no information. Abruptly, she said, 'What am I to call you? I remember you when you was Vinnie Harris, but now you've come up in the world.'

The words were accusing and Vinnie's cheeks burned with a mixture of confusion and resentment. A phrase came back into her mind – 'You're Vinnie Harris from the London slums and don't you forget it.' She would not, could not, forget it, but all that had ended three years ago. The woman was being impertinent. Drawing herself up, she assumed a cold and distant manner.

'You should call me "ma'am",' she said. 'But now your news, please.'

'Well, *ma'am*.' There was a hint of sarcasm in the gipsy's voice. 'They're as well as can be expected, though the Westlands cottage is poky.'

'And Rose Bryce – is she well? Is she happy?'

The gipsy shrugged. 'Well enough, but does not smile much.'

'Oh!' Vinnie half turned and stared out of the window. 'And the children?' she asked.

'As well as can be expected.'

'And the new baby?' continued Vinnie.

'Dead,' said the gipsy. 'Born dead.'

'Oh, poor Rose!' For a moment she was silent, digesting this information. 'And the others?' she went on. 'Tom, Bertha, Jim?'

The gipsy shrugged. 'What can I say about a brood of young 'uns?'

Unconsciously, Vinnie lowered her voice. 'And Tom Bryce?' she ventured.

'He's drinking.'

Vinnie turned sharply, her distant manner forgotten. 'Tom's drinking? That he never did – at least, hardly.'

'Well, he is now and a sight too much for his own good, so they say. There's talk about him in the village.'

'What sort of talk?'

'That he'll lose his job before long.'

The gipsy stared at Vinnie curiously as the girl made an ineffectual attempt to hide the extent of her concern. Oblivious of the scrutiny, Vinnie clenched her hands until the knuckles became pale, then abruptly she turned and walked to the window, staring out with unseeing eyes.

'And you're sure of these facts?' she said.

'I'm quite sure. Why should I bother to lie to you?'

Vinnie turned hastily. 'Please!' she stammered. 'I am not suggesting that you're lying. Rather, I was hoping that you might have been mistaken. If he loses his job—'

'He won't be the first that's lost his job through drink,' the gipsy told her. 'The master there is a very firm man, strong teetotal and even frowns on the odd pint or two. The men all curse him. There was a young man there last year, just wed he was, and had a few too many one Saturday night. Reeled out of the pub and straight into the side of this trap which just happened to be passing. He was lucky to get away as lightly as he did – he could have been killed.'

'What happened to him?' Vinnie asked.

'Two black eyes, a broken collar-bone and the sack. Mr Lidden fired him on the spot. They say Bryce has only lasted this long because he's so good at his job.'

'And that's all you know about them?'

'Isn't that enough?'

'Yes, of course it is,' said Vinnie.

She returned to the table, picked up the rest of the coins and handed them to the gipsy who pocketed them without thanks.

'Tell your fortune?' she offered.

'No, thank you,' said Vinnie.

'Have a glimpse into the future?'

Vinnie hesitated. 'Another sixpence,' said the gipsy, quick to take advantage; without waiting for an answer, she took hold of Vinnie's hand.

'A good life line,' she murmured, glancing up at Vinnie, 'but disappointment here and here.'

'What sort of disappointment?'

'That I can't tell you.'

Vinnie made as though to withdraw her hand, but the gipsy's grip on her wrist tightened. There was a further sixpence involved and she did not intend to relinquish her opportunity. 'There's good health here,' she said. 'You have a strong constitution . . . and there's a surprise, a pleasant surprise, in the not-too-distant future. I see changes in your life, but they come later. Do you want to ask me any questions? Do you understand all that I've said?'

'No,' said Vinnie. 'I mean, yes, I do want to ask a question. At least—' She faltered and stopped. The question uppermost in her mind was of such importance to her that she wondered if she dared voice it to another. How discreet was this gipsy woman, she wondered.

'You have a question for me?'

Reluctantly Vinnie shook her head. 'No,' she said. Afraid that she might weaken and change her mind, she snatched back her hand and reached for her purse.

'That's enough,' she said quickly. 'I don't want to hear any more. Take the sixpence and tell me your name.'

'Lotty.'

'Is that all?'

'Lotty Hearn.'

'Thank you, Lotty. You'd better go now.'

'Thank you, ma'am.'

Vinnie waited for her to leave, but to her surprise the woman lingered. 'You have a hard row to hoe,' she told Vinnie.

'I know,' said Vinnie, her tone sharp.

As the woman still made no move, Vinnie crossed to the bell-pull and rang for Janet, waiting in silence for her to appear.

The gipsy watched her with a strange smile on her face.

'And you *will* come again?' Vinnie asked her. 'If ever you have any more news?'

'I will.'

Vinnie nodded as the door opened. 'Lotty Hearn is leaving,' she said to Janet.

'This way,' said Janet and with relief Vinnie watched them both leave the room. Only then did she give way to her emotions, sinking down on to a chair and covering her face with trembling hands.

'Poor Rose,' she whispered and again, 'poor little Rose! What's to be done?' She thought of Tom Bryce drinking heavily, threatened with the loss of his livelihood; tears welled in her eyes, but she made no effort to wipe them away. 'There must be something I can do,' she thought desperately. 'I will help them somehow, I swear I will!'

That afternoon Vinnie walked in the hop-garden, rehearsing the speech she intended to make to her husband when he returned from the solicitor. She would ask him to offer Tom Bryce work at Foxearth, although she knew he would be unwilling to do so. Tom had worked in the hop-fields for many years as the Colonel's chief pole-puller, but certain events had led to his dismissal and the job was now held by Ned Berry. Although not as experienced as Tom, Ned was nevertheless hard-working and reliable; he was also a comparatively young man, still not yet thirty and the job of chief pole-puller could never again be offered to Tom. Vinnie proposed suggesting to Julian that they should find other work for him to do – even general handyman would be better than nothing, and if Rose had finished child-bearing there might possibly be work for her also.

There was a small cottage on the far edge of the estate which had stood empty for some years. At least it would be a roof over their heads, but would Julian agree to it? Vinnie thought this unlikely and knew that the way in which she couched her appeal to Julian's better nature would be all-important.

Vinnie loved the hop-gardens with an intensity which was lacking in her husband. Julian had been born to Foxearth and knew no other way of life, therefore hop-growing to him was a business matter which he saw as a means to an end. Hops gave the Lawrence family their income and Julian's interest was mainly financial. For Vinnie, however, the hop-gardens held still the magical quality of her childhood when as a young girl she had left the squalor and ugliness of the London slums to wander among the green and leafy aisles in a transport of delight. To the young Vinnie the gardens were fairyland and for her that essential quality had never quite disappeared.

She wandered among the bare hop-poles which reared up on every side of her, gaunt and grey in their serried ranks, row on row as far as the eye could see. The gardens covered the sloping sides of the Medway valley, from the road which ran along the top boundary down almost to the river bank itself. In summer the hop-bines would provide lush green cover, clinging tenaciously to the twelve-foot-high poles and casting a green shadow over the earth. But now it was January and the plants lay dormant, hidden beneath the soil at the base of each pole, waiting for the spring sunshine to warm them into life. In September the greeny-yellow hops would hang heavily upon the plants and the field would echo to the sound of the hop-pickers harvesting the crop, but in a winter landscape the gardens were mainly empty and lifeless. Occasionally casual labour would be taken on. Women from the village would be hired to weed between the rows – a little extra money was always useful – and men would loosen the soil around the dormant bines.

But this afternoon there was no one working in the gardens and no one to observe Vinnie's distracted wanderings as she made her way to and fro across the hard cold ground, her fur-trimmed hood held close round her face, her buttoned boots protecting feet and ankles from the cold wind that blew along the valley with the ever present threat of snow.

From the top of one of the poles a magpie watched her warily until she came too close. Then he startled her with the fierce flutter of his wing-beat and the flash of white from beneath his wings. Vinnie sighed deeply, then raised her head and looked around. The trees that edged the field swayed with the force of the wind and a few dead leaves whirled past her. A movement in the ash tree caught her eye and she smiled faintly at the antics of a squirrel which clung tenaciously to one of the lower branches, chattering furiously, its fluffy grey tail arched over its back. From the other side of the river came the crack of a shotgun. Someone was rabbiting.

From the road above her came the creak and rattle of wheels and the rapid clip-clop of hooves. Her heart pounded a little faster. It might be Julian returning, in which case there was little time left for deliberation. Finding her absent from the house, she knew he would come in search of her, so she must be ready for him with all her arguments prepared. She *must* convince him. Once more she bowed her head and her lips moved over the familiar words of her speech.

When in due course she saw him striding across the grass, her heart sank. There was no welcoming smile on his face and when he realized that she had seen him, he beckoned peremptorily. Dismayed, Vinnie gathered up her skirts and hurried towards her husband.

'What the devil are you doing out here?' he called. 'It's freezing! Do you want to go down with pneumonia?'

'I'm not cold, darling,' she assured him. 'You can see I'm well wrapped up. I wanted to think and you know I always think better in the garden.'

She attempted a light laugh and as she reached him, caught hold of his hand. He was bareheaded and the wind dishevelled his fair hair. As he bent to give her a brief kiss her heart, as always, leapt at the sight of his soft mouth and blue-grey eyes. He wore a warm tweed suit, the trousers of which reached just below the knee. Stout leather shoes and long, thick wool socks completed his outfit, but he shivered in the keen wind and immediately turned back towards the house.

'You are earlier than I expected,' she said, the opening line of her speech having momentarily deserted her.

'Thompson insisted on bringing me home,' said Julian, 'in that infernal machine of his.'

Vinnie's eyes widened. 'In his motor car? Oh, Julian, you lucky—'

'Damned noisy things! I protested that the carriage was waiting for me, but he would have none of it, silly old devil. Nothing would satisfy him but that he should bring me home to demonstrate his new toy. *He* may choose to be rattled and bumped at an unholy speed, but I really do not see why *I* should also be forced to endure such discomfort. I had to close my eyes for the last few miles because the cold was making them water.'

'My poor dear,' said Vinnie, almost running to keep pace with his long determined stride. 'You just were not dressed for it, Julian!'

'I certainly was not. I have no desire to dress up in an enormous fur coat and parade through the streets looking like a bear on wheels.'

Vinnie laughed. 'But you had a ride in a motor car,' she said. 'I envy you, Julian.'

'There is nothing to envy,' he told her. 'Be thankful that you missed it.'

'Poor darling,' she said. 'And then when you got home you had to come searching for me. I am sorry.'

She was trying hard to restore his good humour. The distance between them and the house was decreasing rapidly and if she did not broach the subject soon, it would be too late.

'Julian,' she began, 'there is something I want to ask you before we get to the house.'

He glanced at her in astonishment. 'Out here, do you mean?'

'Yes. Please, Julian, do stop for a moment. Look, we can stand in the shelter of that chestnut tree.'

'Are you mad? Why can't you ask me whatever it is in the comfort of our own drawing room?'

'Because I don't want to be overheard. Oh, Julian, do wait!'

'Absolutely not,' said Julian. 'Whatever it is that you want to discuss must wait until I have thawed out.'

They had reached the edge of the field and now passed through the gate and up into the garden which surrounded the house.

In the dining room there was a roaring log fire and while Vinnie took off her cloak, Julian warmed himself before its comforting blaze. He rang for a brandy and Vinnie waited until Janet brought it up. When at last they were alone, she stood beside him.

'I have a favour to ask you,' she began.

'Ask away.'

It might have been the old Colonel talking, Vinnie thought – like father, like son. Now that Julian had grown a moustache, the likeness between them was stronger than ever. The only difference lay in their life-style, for at twenty-three Julian was virtually master in his own home. At the same age, his father had already embarked upon a military career.

'I'm afraid you will be angry, but please do hear me out. It's about Tom Bryce.'

She saw the muscles in his face tighten but hurried on, averting her eyes from his face so that she would not be distracted by his expression.

'He is in such dreadful trouble, Julian. The whole family is in a bad way. Oh darling, please don't interrupt. Let me have my say.' She swallowed and continued, picking her words as carefully as she could.

'I heard today that he has started to drink heavily and they have given him a warning that he may lose his job. If he does, then the family will lose the cottage as well. I know you don't like him and for my part he is nothing to me—'

'You can't say that.' Julian's voice was ominously low and she looked up at him fearfully.

'But I do say it, Julian, and I mean it with all my heart. Rose was my closest friend and the little ones—'

'You are sorry for him and you want me to help him,' said Julian coldly. 'The answer, of course, is no.'

'Oh, you're wrong, Julian. I don't want to help Tom – I want to help Rose and the children.'

'It amounts to the same thing. As far as I am concerned, he can drink himself to death and the world will be well rid of him.'

'But Rose and the children! Darling, please! It's not like you to be so hard and unfeeling.'

'I am not unfeeling, Vinnie. Quite the opposite. I feel too much. The man is an absolute blackguard and treated you most shamefully. He used you most cruelly—'

'Julian, I don't want to talk about that,' cried Vinnie. 'It all happened so long ago. Please try to understand. I'm not asking for Tom's sake, but for theirs. I want you to give him work, Julian. You could find him something!'

'I tell you no, Vinnie. He doesn't deserve your pity, nor can he expect my help. He had no right to ask you.'

He turned away from her, finished his brandy in one mouthful and set down the glass upon the mantelpiece. Vinnie said nothing. Slowly he turned to face her.

'I'm not unfeeling, Vinnie. I am not cold or hard, but towards Tom Bryce I feel nothing but hate. How can you expect me to tolerate him? I don't wish ever to set eyes on him again and I am surprised and hurt that you so obviously do. How can you love *me* and still feel anything for *him*?'

'Julian, I have told you, he means nothing to me, nothing – and he didn't ask; it was my own idea.'

'It makes no difference, Vinnie,' said Julian. 'You bore him a child. He was nothing to you, but you bore him a son. I am your husband, but you have not done as much for me.'

'Julian!'

She stepped back, horrified at the passion in his voice; her mind reeled with the shock, for her childlessness was a subject which had never before been mentioned by either of them. By tacit agreement, they had continued to wait hopefully for the welcome signs that Vinnie was with child. Now, seeing Vinnie's pain, Julian half regretted his words, but not entirely. The sad but unspoken truth was that the ghost of her stillborn child haunted their marriage. The pain in Vinnie's eyes mirrored the agony which Julian had borne in silence since he had first learned of her tragedy.

'Vinnie!' he began. She was shaking her head like a dazed animal. 'Stop thinking about Rose, Vinnie, and think about us for a change. Think what it would do to us to have him near! If Tom Bryce drinks, it is no concern of yours. If he has been given fair warning and continues to drink, then he will bring about his own downfall. Rose married him for better or worse and she must take the consequences. I can't bear it, Vinnie, if you go on seeing him – and if he's right on our doorstep, how could you help doing so? Please, darling, you ask too much of me! I'm only human and I cannot bear to see that man and think what you once were to each other.'

'I'm sorry,' said Vinnie dully, defeated by his obvious wretchedness.

'And you will forgive me, Vinnie, for saying what I did?'

'Of course I will – and I will give you a son, Julian. I promise I will.'

Her thoughts flashed back suddenly to the gipsy's reading of her hand, for Vinnie had waited in vain to hear her mention a child. No, resolutely she put the thought from her. Of course she would have a child! She would give Julian the son he craved and then another and another. As many as he wished! All she wanted was to be a good wife to him. Nothing else mattered, she told herself. Perhaps he was right. Maybe Tom Bryce should fend for himself and Rose must make the best of a bad business. She forced a smile as he pulled her gently into his arms and kissed the tip of her nose.

'You have not said you love me,' she whispered. 'Not for a long time.'

'Have you ever really doubted it?' She laughed shakily as she shook her head in denial.

'Then enough of this sad talk! I shall ring for another brandy – no, *two* brandies – and we shall sit comfortably beside the fire and talk of other things.'

For a moment he held her close and kissed her, then he stood back, smiling. 'And I will tell you the awful details of my uncomfortable ride in Mr Thompson's bone-shaker. Believe me, it is *not* a pretty tale!'

CHAPTER TWO

Soon after noon on the 21st of January, 1901, Queen Victoria called for her eldest son and held out her arms to embrace him. The future King sobbed as he held his mother in his arms for the last time; his name was the last word she spoke. The following day, at half-past six in the evening, she died in the arms of her favourite grandson, the Kaiser Wilhelm. She was not quite eighty-two years of age.

The coffin in which the Queen's body lay was guarded by Grenadiers and England plunged into mourning for the loss of a well-loved and deeply respected sovereign. Her body was brought from Osborne and taken direct to Windsor, where preparations were made for the funeral procession. From there the gun-carriage with a Naval guard of honour was drawn into London. On a grey day Queen Victoria was once more united with her husband Albert in the Frogmore mausoleum, watched by the Emperor of Germany, the Kings of Belgium, Portugal and Greece and many other heads of state, as well as the grieving members of her own large family. 'Bertie' meanwhile had attended the Accession Council at St James's Palace, where he had chosen the name of Edward for his kingship and, speaking without notes, had made a stirring speech in which he promised to be 'a constitutional sovereign in the strictest sense of the word'. The Coronation was planned for the summer of the following year.

Mary Bellweather's grief for the loss of England's Queen, however, was overshadowed by the recent loss of her own mother and the black hat which she pinned so purposefully to her dark hair had been purchased on the occasion of her own bereavement. Six weeks had passed, but although Mary had resumed the normal round of her activities, her pale face still retained a measure of shock and reddened eyes often testified to her unhappiness. The absence of her mother's affectionate and familiar company was hard to bear now that Mary was entirely alone. As the only child she had inherited a considerable amount of money, as well as her home where she continued to live in solitary splendour, ministered to by Mrs Markham, the housekeeper. This capable lady had been with the Bellweathers for more than ten years and she too found the house a lonely place without Mrs Bellweather's bustling presence. Mary was rarely in, concerning herself as always with the poor of the neighbourhood and even – much to Mrs Markham's dismay – following them into the country when they departed every September for their annual 'holiday' in the hop-gardens of Kent.

Since her mother's death Mary had devoted more and more time to charitable causes, as a way of filling her days. Mrs Markham was mortified that there still seemed no hint of romance in the air. All that good lady's hopes that the house would once more become a family home seemed unlikely to be realized.

Mary considered her reflection carefully in the small hall-stand mirror. Her pale face was striking, but there was a firmness about it which hardened the line of her jaw and her dark eyes were disconcertingly shrewd for a young woman in her mid-twenties. Good breeding showed in the neat contours of her face and her skin was perfect. She dressed with simple good taste and the knowledge that – with a little more effort – she might be considered a beauty did not interest her.

Now, she thought, Princess Alexandra would become Queen. That pleased Mary very much, for she greatly admired the Princess and to some extent, like many other women, had modelled herself upon her. Mary's own hair was swept up severely on top of her head in the style that Alexandra had made so popular.

'I am leaving now,' she called, making a final adjustment to the collar of her warm black coat. She glanced at her boots and reflected that the shine so lovingly produced by Mrs Markham's efforts would vanish as soon as she set foot outside the house. Mrs Markham hurried into the hall, a look of concern on her face.

'You are never going out in this weather, Miss Mary. It's raining cats and dogs! You'll get a real drenching.'

'I shall take the umbrella, Mrs Markham. I am not quite the scatterbrain you think me.'

'But even with the umbrella – oh, don't open it in the house, madam!' she cried, as Mary took the large black umbrella from its stand and released the first clip.

Mary laughed good-naturedly. 'Don't worry, I should not dare to do anything so rash! I am merely preparing it so that I can raise it more quickly when I am outside. Now, I think I have everything.'

The housekeeper regarded her despairingly. It seemed to her that Mary Bellweather carried her good work to excess, but it was not her business to say so. Even Mary's own mother would have protested at the number of hours her daughter devoted to the rejects of London's society.

'Will you be home for lunch, madam?'

'I hope so,' said Mary. 'But please don't prepare anything until I arrive. Steamed fish will do me very well. We are distributing clothes this morning and hopefully an hour or two should see it through. And remember, please, that if anyone should telephone me, you are to ask them to leave a number. Then I can return the call.'

'Yes, madam, I will try to remember.'

Mary smiled at her encouragingly. 'I am away then,' she said and was gone, struggling to put up the umbrella as the housekeeper closed the door behind her.

She could have taken a hansom cab, but it would have been against her principles, aware as she was of the vast difference between the lives of the rich and the poor. Instead she walked, away from the respectable area in which she lived, towards the hovel of mean streets that was Whitechapel. Passing a horse trough where a group of grubby children surrounded the drinking fountain, she turned into the next road where a group of men – obviously unemployed – had spilled over into the road from the public house on the corner. She hurried past them and turned yet another corner where here she was brought up sharply by a scene which shocked her – a group of children dancing to the strains of music from a barrel-organ. For a moment Mary watched as the children dipped and swayed, the boys flinging out their arms, the girls holding out the tattered garments which served as coats. One or two were barefooted and Mary shuddered involuntarily at the thought of their tender feet upon the cold, wet pavement. In spite of the rain their faces glowed with excitement, but Mary could not approve. She stopped beside the man who was turning the handle of the barrel-organ.

'What are you thinking of?' she asked him. 'Dancing in the street, and so soon after the Queen's death! Have you no finer feelings at all?'

His hand did not falter on the handle. 'Oh, I've plenty of feelings,' he told her. 'One of them is hunger. I've got a living to earn, same as the next man, and a family to feed – Queen or no Queen.'

Mary hesitated. 'Well, as you say, Queen or no Queen, but it's still most unsuitable in this dreadful weather. Look at them – they will be wet through.'

'Missus, they was wet through before they started,' he told her, 'and a lot less cheerful. A bit of music cheers them up.'

'They should be at school.'

He shrugged. 'Should be, but they aren't. What am I supposed to do about it? Drag them along by the hair and shove 'em in at the school gate? I'm an organ-grinder; I don't work miracles.' With his free hand he took off his cap, shook the surplus water from it and settled it firmly once more on his head. 'It's not as if they have money,' he said, ' 'cos they don't. I make no profit out of this lot. I make my profit from folks like you.'

Mary sighed and felt in her pocket for sixpence which she dropped on to the tin plate in which several pennies lay already.

'See what I mean?' he said and Mary, feeling herself finally ousted, lowered her eyes and walked on.

The Brothers in Jesus met in a small shed in a narrow back alley. Here they dispensed breakfast seven days a week to any man, woman or child who was in obvious need. That service was one of many provided by this small group of well-intentioned people who had come together five years earlier as a result of the efforts of Roland Fry.

This handsome young man with his startling blue eyes and black hair held views very akin to those of Mary Bellweather, being devoted to the task of ameliorating the lot of some of the most unfortunate rejects of London society. Roland also came from a wealthy family and had no need to work on his own behalf; he had founded the Brothers in Jesus as a way of bringing together those with aims and aspirations similar to his own. During the past five years the numbers had dwindled and although there were others who could be called on in an emergency, only five people remained faithful to the group's original aims: Roland Fry himself and his wife, Emily; Gareth Brooks, Lydia Grant and

Mary Bellweather. They took it in turn to serve the breakfasts and today it was the task of Roland and Emily. When Mary tugged open the door, they were just finishing the washing-up.

'Ah, there you are!' cried Roland. 'We were just talking about you. Were your ears burning?'

'Hardly, in this weather,' Mary replied with a laugh.

'We were discussing September,' said Emily, 'and wondered if you would be free to go down to Kent with the hoppers.'

Mary said quickly, 'Of course I will, but I thought you two—'

Emily blushed faintly. 'I shall not be able to go,' she said, with a glance at Roland.

He put an arm round her and smiled at Mary. 'You are the first to hear our news,' he said. 'We are expecting our first child in August. I know you will be pleased for us.'

'Pleased? I am *delighted* for you,' said Mary. 'That's wonderful news. My very sincere congratulations!'

'Thank you,' he said.

'So you see,' said Emily, 'I shall have to miss this year's hop-picking.'

'Do say you will come instead,' said Roland. 'If you can bear it, that is! It's hardly a picnic and in no way could it be called a holiday!'

They all laughed, for during almost the entire month of September, the streets of Whitechapel would be half-empty and the schools would be closed. Thousands of people from the East End of London would migrate to the Weald of Kent, there to work as casual labour among the vast area of hop-gardens. Those not fortunate enough to hold down a regular job would make their way on foot, or by the special trains provided, to the many farms who welcomed their annual invasion with mixed feelings. Every available pair of hands would be needed to harvest the crop and without the Londoners it would prove an impossible task. The Brothers in Jesus followed their own 'flock' from the mean streets of London to the wide green gardens of Foxearth Farm; there they set up a small mission tent and tried to alleviate some of the Londoners' worst discomforts and in a small way to minister to their spiritual welfare.

Mary smiled. 'Don't worry,' she assured them, 'I know exactly what I am letting myself in for and of course I will come with you. I shall look forward to it. As you say, it is no picnic but it looks as if I missed all the excitement last year.'

Emily put out a hand and patted her arm. 'Poor Mary,' she said. 'You had your own difficulties. Your poor mother—'

Mary nodded. Her mother's fall several days before the planned departure to Kent had eventually led to her death. It was during that same September that Roland's relationship with Emily had suddenly blossomed and they had married at Christmas.

The door opened and Gareth Brooks came in, brushing the rain from his clothes and grumbling about the weather. They all exchanged greetings, but Roland's and Emily's news was not repeated. The next twenty minutes were spent sorting out a vast pile of clothing which was stored in boxes in one corner of the room. It was divided up into four separate sacks – men's, women's and children's clothing, and footwear of all kinds. When at last it was arranged to their mutual satisfaction, Gareth smiled at Mary.

'Are you ready, then?' he asked and she nodded. He pulled out the hand-cart they had recently acquired and hoisted the sacks on to it, covering them with a tarpaulin sheet. Roland and Emily held open the two doors, while the others trundled the cart out into the alley and made their farewells; then Roland and his wife went home, leaving Mary and Gareth to their task.

They each took a handle and made their way slowly along Whitechapel High Street, turning right into Osborne Street and left into Wentworth Street, ignoring the curious looks and occasional jeers. The back streets between Whitechapel and Spitalfields were notoriously rough and each was glad of the other's company and moral support. Toynbee Street was their first port of call, where Mary consulted a small pocket book. The Brothers in Jesus had compiled a list of families in dire need and were methodically working through it.

Today it was Mary's turn to call on the various families and give them whatever clothing or footwear seemed reasonable. While she made the actual call, Gareth remained in the road with the cart, for bitter experience had shown that it should never be left unattended. There were four families in Toynbee Street and the first two made Mary welcome. Various items were handed over, with a stern reminder from Mary that they were *not* to be pawned. At the third house she met suspicion amounting to hostility and retreated hastily with as much dignity as she could muster. With burning cheeks, they hurried away, while a fat unshaven man continued to shout after them so that all the street could hear.

'We want no truck with the likes of you!' he shouted. 'Meddling, interfering busybodies! If my kids want clothes, *I'll* buy them. Bloody snoopers, that's what you are. You don't fool me with your lah-di-dah talk and your free bloody hand-outs. You know what you can do with 'em!'

Mary marched on, her eyes fixed straight ahead, trying to ignore the mocking glances cast in their direction by the people they passed. She was thankful when they turned the corner into Brune Street and stopped once more.

She looked at Gareth ruefully. 'I do hate it when they're like that,' she said.

Gareth consoled her. 'Take no notice, Mary. There's nothing personal in it, really. They are just ignorant.'

'I know,' said Mary, 'but I feel for them. It is such an awful way to live. I saw his wife behind him in the hallway – a poor, shrunken thing with a baby in her arms; it was wrapped in an old towel and its little bare feet were sticking out.' She sighed.

'We can't help them unless they want to be helped,' said Gareth, 'and there's plenty who do, so let's get on to the next one and forget about him. Would you like *me* to make the next call?'

She smiled at him gratefully, but shook her head. 'I'd rather risk the insults,' she said. 'I hate to stand guard over the cart.' She ran her finger down the page of her notebook. 'Number 19 – Cyril and Annie Wallbridge. I remember them; they are an elderly couple.'

Mary walked up to the front door and rapped sharply on it. There was a long pause and then she heard footsteps shuffling along the passage towards the door. It was finally opened by a small and very dirty old woman who peered out shortsightedly.

'Good morning, Mrs Wallbridge! Remember me? I am Mary Bellweather.'

'Mary who?' The old woman cupped a hand to her ear.

'Bellweather!'

'The lady from the free breakfasts?'

'That's right,' said Mary, smiling. 'I said we would bring you some clothes.'

The old woman looked at the bundle of garments in Mary's arms. 'That them?' she asked.

Mary nodded.

'You'd best come in, then.'

Mary took a deep breath of fresh air and stepped inside. The

passage reeked of stale urine and cooking smells; the woodwork
was rotten and the paintwork faded and peeling. As they passed a
door on the right, the old woman gave a jerk of her head. 'He's
laid out with his back,' she said, 'and he don't want to see nobody,
but he *did* say he was promised a shirt and a pair of boots.'

Unable to hold her breath any longer, Mary took a few quick
breaths and nodded. They went down two steps into a small
scullery where the walls and windows ran with condensation. In
one corner of the room stood a small copper in which clothes were
obviously boiling. The old woman began to clear a space on the
cluttered table.

'Nice bit of heat that copper gives off,' she told Mary. 'Warms
up the room a treat, that does. I always look forward to wash-day.'

'It does indeed,' said Mary, spreading the clothes on the table.
'I brought some things for you and your husband,' she said. 'You
have a look and see if you can find anything that suits you –
anything that you like.'

'Anything that suits my complexion, you mean?' Mrs Wallbridge chuckled, and Mary smiled without answering as the old
woman snatched up various garments and held them up for quick
appraisal. From the bedroom they had passed came the sound of
raucous coughing.

'Let's 'ave a look now. Cyril's got to 'ave a shirt. I reckon this
one will do for his lordship. Bit frayed round the cuffs, but
beggars can't be choosers.' She held it up to the window and with
a quick nod threw it over the back of a chair.

'That one's too small, dear. Pity! He's big, my old man. Always
been big, he 'as. Same size now as when I married him.'

'Really?' said Mary.

'Oh, yes, 'asn't lost or gained a single pound. A very big man.
What's these trousers?'

She rubbed the cloth between her fingers. 'Not bad! Still a
good bit of wear in them.' They joined the shirts hanging over the
back of the chair.

'And boots, let's 'ave a look at them. Oh, very nice,' she nodded
approvingly. '*Very*, very nice, but will they fit him? He's a big man
and he's got big feet.'

'They are the biggest pair we've got,' said Mary. 'They are a
size eleven.'

'Well, they don't look it but if you say so, they should fit him all
right. If not, we'll 'ave to chop his toes off!'

Cackling with laughter at this sally, she gathered up shirt, trousers and boots.

'I'll take these into 'im and let him 'ave a look,' she said and Mary was left alone. Immediately she crossed to the back door, opened it and breathed deeply for a moment or two. The dingy back-yard was as depressing as the scullery. A small brown mongrel dog, tied to a ring in the wall, regarded her listlessly and made no effort to bark. A rusty dustbin overflowed with rubbish and behind it a rusting bedspring was propped against the wall. There was a tea-chest half-full of coke and a round wooden tub contained the remains of what had once been a plant.

Hastily, Mary closed the door on this dreary sight and turned back to the scullery which apparently doubled as a kitchen. Recently washed clothing hung from a string which stretched from one wall to the other and the small iron fireplace contained the ashes of a fire. There were two battered armchairs and on the floor between them a newish rug made from woven strips of various materials. The lino was cracked and worn and the deep china sink was full of half-rinsed washing. Newly-rinsed clothes had been wrung out and piled on the draining board.

Mary resisted the temptation to peer into the half-open cupboard. She was oppressed by the obvious poverty of the Wallbridges and the lack of home comforts. At that moment the old woman returned and catching sight of the rug, nodded towards it.

'Salvation Army give us that,' she told Mary proudly. 'Brand new, that was. Made by some ladies' group and give to the Army. Never been used!'

'It's most attractive,' said Mary. 'That was a nice present.'

'A very nice present. And my hubby said to thank you for them things.'

'They all fit him, then?'

'Like they was made for him – and he's that pleased. So that's 'im settled.'

Her small hands began to dart once more among the pile of clothing that remained, but at that moment there came the thin wail of a child from the room above them. The old woman tutted irritably.

'Don't you start,' she muttered with a glance at the ceiling. 'Had enough of you last night, bawling your head off till the early hours.' She nodded disparagingly. 'Still, what can you expect, poor little beggars? Probably hungry! It's disgraceful. There's no other word for it. Call yourself a mother, I said. Leaving them kids all on their own! I told her straight – don't expect me to run up and down stairs after them with *my* legs. Not that I would if I could. I've done my bit; raised seven children, I did, and only lost two.'

She held up a long flannelette nightdress. 'There's a button missing,' she said sharply. 'But I expect I can find one.' She shook it out and held it up against her small frame. It swamped her but she appeared satisfied.

'Isn't it a bit long?' said Mary.

Mrs Wallbridge shook her head. 'I like 'em long. Tucks up round your feet nicely. Nothing worse than cold feet in bed. Rather too long than too short.'

She folded it neatly. Upstairs the child's fretful wail had developed into loud screaming.

Mary frowned. 'Do you mean the children up there are on their own?' she asked.

'That's exactly what I do mean. On their own from seven in the morning until seven or eight at night. Disgraceful, I told her! You should have the law on you. That's neglect, that is!'

'But where is their mother?'

'Gone to work,' said the old woman.

She sat down in the chair, kicked off her slippers and pushed her feet into a pair of shoes.

'I'm not struck on laces,' she said. 'I've always preferred buttons. Still,' she shrugged, 'they are a nice enough fit and if they last me the winter I shan't grumble.'

Mary was finding it harder and harder to ignore the sounds from upstairs.

'Should I just take a look at them,' she suggested, 'in case something has happened? There may have been an accident of some kind.'

'Accident?'

'Well, they might have hurt themselves.'

'They're hungry,' said the old woman. 'That's what's wrong with them, but you can take a look if you want to. It's no skin off my nose. First on the right, it is.'

Reluctantly, Mary made her way up the narrow stairs. Reaching the landing she glanced in at the half-open door on her right, but at first could see no sign of the children. There was very little furniture in the room, but two tea-chests stood beside the bed and this was where the noise seemed to be coming from.

Uncomfortably aware that she was trespassing, Mary crossed the room to investigate and to her dismay, she found a child in each chest. In one a very young child slept, whilst in the other a red-faced toddler screamed hysterically.

'Dear God!' whispered Mary. After a moment's hesitation, she picked up the screaming child and held it awkwardly in her arms. Its clothing was saturated, but for a moment Mary tried to comfort it; then she rested it against her shoulder, but the attention seemed to increase the child's distress and she was forced to return it to the chest. Turning her attention to the baby, she wondered how it could possibly sleep through the noise. She thought it was a girl, for the upturned face was delicately coloured and the blonde lashes curled. Mary felt sick with pity and helplessness as she made her way downstairs again, where she found that none of the clothing remained.

'It was all very suitable,' the old woman told her firmly. 'It all fits a real treat.'

Mary's thoughts were still on the children upstairs. 'I beg your pardon?'

'I said everything fits a treat and thank you kindly.'

'Oh, the clothing.'

Mary glanced round the scullery. 'But the shirt,' she said. 'The one that was too small for your husband?'

'I can let it out for him.'

'Let it out, but—'

'Or put a gusset in it. That might be best.'

The old woman stared at her, defying her to argue the point and weakly Mary gave in. The shirt would no doubt appear at the pawn-shop before the day was out, along with the second pair of shoes, but suddenly she no longer cared.

'Those children upstairs,' she said, 'where does their mother work?'

'Works for a tailor, but don't ask me where, dear. I wouldn't begin to know.'

'Is it near here, do you think?'

The old woman shrugged. 'Might be Casson Street,' she said, 'and there again, it might not.'

'But she definitely works for a tailor?'

'She definitely works somewhere. Leastways, I hope so. Seven shillings a week, she told me, and if she's lying I don't get the rent.'

'And her husband?'

Mrs Wallbridge laughed. 'Well, if there is one, I haven't seen him. Her sort don't get husbands, only kids.'

In the next room her husband began to cough again and then he called out to her.

'Well,' the old woman hinted, 'I suppose you'll be getting along. More important things to do than hang about 'ere.'

'Yes, I must go,' Mary agreed, 'but if you could find out where the mother works, I would be very grateful. I could call round again.'

'How grateful?'

'How – oh! a shilling,' Mary nodded. 'And look, give the mother this,' – she pressed a shilling into the old woman's hand – 'and tell her to buy the children milk and eggs and say that I shall call again soon with some children's clothing.'

A sullen look settled on the old woman's face. 'It's putting me to a great deal of trouble—' she began.

Mary found a sixpence and handed it to her.

'Now remember,' she insisted. 'Eggs and milk for the children and find out where the mother works.'

'I 'eard you.' She raised her voice suddenly. 'All right, Cyril, I'm coming!'

Mary followed her along the passage, where Mrs Wallbridge held open the front door. 'Well, thanks again for them things. They'll come in very handy.'

'I hope so,' said Mary as she went back to join Gareth, her face set in unusually thoughtful lines.

CHAPTER THREE

The meeting on the twelfth of February was held in a small church hall in Maidstone. When Julian arrived, a quarter of an hour late, it had already started. He nodded apologetically towards the platform and sat down in the back row as quietly as he could. One or two heads turned, but no more. The matter under discussion was far too important.

There were three men on the platform around a small table and one of them was on his feet addressing the audience of between eighty and a hundred men; they had filled the middle of the hall, leaving the first half-dozen rows empty, so the speaker – with no microphone – had to raise his voice in order to be heard by everyone present. He was a thickset man wearing a well-cut tweed suit and his general manner was confident. Julian smiled to himself; he had known Daniel Hicks a long time and knew that he was enjoying the limelight.

'—and it can't be allowed to go on,' Daniel declared, jabbing the air with a meaty fist to underline his words. 'Let's admit it – we have been misled!' The audience murmured. 'What happened next? I'll tell you what happened. All the time we were grubbing up *our* hops, those damned foreigners were planting more and now where are we? We are losing money on the hops we *do* grow because they are sending them over here cheaper than we can grow them. They're stealing our markets!' He waited until the clamour subsided, then continued, 'How can we get a good price for our Goldings when they are flooding the country with cheap, poor quality rubbish? The United States of America are making fools of us and we are letting them do it! I tell you, my friends, we have got to stop the foreign hops coming in free of tax. We *must* pressurize the Government until something is done! If they don't tax the foreign hops, then the English hop industry is on the way out.'

There was a murmur of approval in which Julian joined.

'Don't fool yourselves,, Daniel Hicks continued, 'that it's going to be easy, because it *isn't*. No one is going to put out a hand to help us, so we must help ourselves. We've got to organize – to close ranks against the foreign competition – to act in such a way that the Government is forced to take notice. This is no time for divisions between workers and bosses. We're not on different sides of the fence; we're all on the same side and we *all* stand to lose: the growers, the factors, the labourers, the carters, we are *all* in it together. Because if we don't stay together and pull together, I tell you, my friends, we're lost!'

He sat down to loud applause, shouts of, 'Hear, hear!' and, 'That's told them!'

Glancing round, Julian saw a number of familiar faces. A few rows in front of him were Clive le Brun and his son William, hop factors from Tunbridge Wells. There were several others from his own neighbourhood and many more whom he did not know, presumably from the other side of Maidstone. A large proportion of the audience was made up of labourers from the hop-gardens and as the audience began to chatter, he caught sight of his own dryer Steven Pitt, and Pitt's right-hand man John Burrows. He recognized also several men from Merryon Farm, three or four of the leading carters and even one or two railwaymen. The presence of the latter surprised him, but then he reminded himself that hops were sometimes carried by rail. Indeed, in the Weald of Kent hops formed a major part of the area's economy and the threats to the industry were being felt by a variety of allied trades. Only the brewers were complacent, he reflected bitterly. They could make their beer more cheaply than before, although the quality was not the same.

The second speaker, a grower from Paddock Wood, rose to his feet and echoed Julian's thoughts.

'Now we all know how to make beer,' he began and the audience laughed obligingly. 'It's very simple. All we want is first-class hops, malt and water.' He paused for dramatic effect and stared round at his audience. 'We *don't* want cheap foreign hops, chemical preservatives, flavourings, drugs or headings – because with all that lot we have a drink that may look like beer and may smell like beer – but by God, it isn't beer! A man could poison himself drinking that lot!'

Cheers and thunderous stamping of feet greeted his words.

'Now five years ago, I had sixty acres under hops,' he went on. 'Eastwells they were and I was a proud man; I don't mind admitting it. Last year it was forty-four acres, this year it's down to forty. Well, you might say, I have a very nice orchard of Cox's apples instead – but I don't want to grow apples, I want to grow hops. I want to grow Eastwells or Early Birds and I want to keep my staff in work. I have a sound experienced team – a good pole-puller, a good dryer and I want to keep them. I also have a good crowd of pickers who come down from London regular as clockwork, year after year, to pick my hops. Now I don't want to turn any of them away – they rely on me for that extra bit of money and a man has to be responsible for his work force . . .'

Looking round the hall, Julian noted with relief that there was no sign of Tom Bryce. In fact, he had almost hesitated to attend the meeting for fear of meeting him, but Vinnie had insisted that Foxearth should be represented and he had allowed himself to be persuaded.

All was not well in the hop industry. There was great anxiety and a feeling of impending disaster among those involved, for the over-production of hops at the end of the nineteenth century had led to a reduction in the acreage of hop-growing, on the assumption that a smaller harvest would maintain prices at a reasonable level. But this had not happened. Instead, growers on the continent and in the United States had seized the opportunity to corner part of the market. For a variety of reasons they could grow the crops more cheaply than the English farmers and – with the absence of an import tax on hops – could transport them to this country and still sell at a price which equalled or even undercut the English growers.

After the hop-picking month of September, English hops were sold through factors and merchants – the 'middle men' – to be stored. They were then sold off throughout the year and, as prices varied from week to week, it was usual for the grower to wait for a favourable price if he could afford to do so. As more and more foreign hops arrived, so the price of English hops was depressed proportionately. Many growers had been forced to reduce their areas under hops already and the situation could no longer be ignored. All over Kent and indeed in other parts of the country where hops were grown, the problem was being discussed informally at markets and public houses and more formally in church halls. Some thought it was already too late to arrest the flow of incoming hops. Others considered the imports should be stopped altogether. If, as was feared, the latter was not possible, then all were agreed upon the sole remedy: the Government must pass legislation to tax all foreign hops, so that prices would be competitive and the quality English hops would once more come into their own.

The last speaker rose and addressed them along similar lines to those already taken. When he had finished, they asked for questions from the floor and a young labourer stood up nervously, his cap twisting in his hands.

'All I want to say,' he began, 'is – well, it's just that I think the Government should tell us where we stand, one way or the other. I work for Mr Blackwell at Wateringbury and me and my wife and two kids have got a tied cottage there. My father and my grandfather worked for Mr Blackwell and he's only just given up because of his health. He's been a good boss to us and I've no wish to leave, but – well, if, as they say, the industry is dying, then I'm young enough to get out and look elsewhere, though God knows I don't want to. The Government should tell us what they're up to – are they trying to squeeze us out or not?'

The audience murmured approvingly.

'Well, all I want to say is, let's ask the Government outright and then we shall know what to expect. A man with a wife and kids has got to earn a living and I'll turn my hand to anything to see my family don't go hungry. But we must know where we stand.'

He sat down abruptly and was rewarded with a round of applause for his courage. Other people rose to express very similar views and finally, on a show of hands, it was agreed that 'something must be done'. The meeting was then declared closed.

A buzz of conversation followed as the men, singly and in groups, made their way up the gangways and out into the night. Clive le Brun and his son William joined Julian and they stood just inside the door while everyone else filed past. William le Brun was eighteen years old, broad-shouldered, with a pleasant open face and unruly red hair.

'We looked for you,' he said. 'We thought you weren't coming.'

'I am sorry,' said Julian. 'I was delayed and arrived later than I intended, but I think I heard most of it.'

'You didn't speak,' said Clive. 'You should have done!'

Clive le Brun, unlike his son, was tall and slimly built with a

serious expression and keen grey eyes. He was sparing with his
words and some people found him unapproachable.

'I did wonder whether to speak,' Julian confessed. 'But as one
of the few growers unaffected – I haven't reduced my acreage, you
see – I felt I might not be accepted.'

'I think you were wrong,' Clive said bluntly. 'They would have
welcomed a few words of support from you. Do them good to
know that even people like yourself, who aren't losing ground, are
still concerned with the general trend and are in favour of the tax.'

'Oh, I am certainly in favour,' Julian assured him. 'I am losing
money on the price, of course.'

'But you have not had to cut back your acreage?' William asked.

Julian gave a slightly embarrassed laugh. 'I daren't,' he said.
'Vinnie would never forgive me! She is so concerned for the
pickers that she cannot bear the thought that we might have to
turn some of them away and refuse them work.'

The other two nodded understandingly.

Vinnie's marriage into the Lawrence family had not gone
unremarked by the local farmers. The news had been greeted
with incredulity – even some hostility – for the hop-garden
fraternity was a closed one and marriage between members was
common. The son of Colonel Lawrence had been considered a
most eligible bachelor and there was great disappointment among
several families who had secretly hoped for a union between
Julian and one of their daughters. The fact that he had married
outside the circle was shock enough, but to marry a girl like Vinnie
Harris was almost an affront and Julian at least had been aware of
the general disapproval.

For Vinnie it had been easier. For instance, she was quite
unaware of the number of functions to which they were *not* invited
and her tough upbringing made her impervious to slights which a
more refined girl would have felt keenly. Her immediate problems had been with the management of Foxearth and all her
energies had been directed towards fulfilling her new role as
mistress. The organization of a large household had absorbed all
her attention and even on her home ground she had met resentment and difficulties, but to Julian's relief she had dealt with them
with unquenchable optimism. She was determined to succeed as
Julian's wife and her sincerity and enthusiasm had finally won
over all but her sharpest critics. With her rough London accent
and lack of breeding, she would never pass for a lady and was the

first to admit it. She neither pretended nor aspired to gentility; she remained essentially the same Vinnie Harris, but inevitably some of the rough edges were being smoothed off and her confidence was growing with each passing year.

'You've heard about Matthews?' said Clive, and Julian shook his head.

'Poor devil's bankrupt!'

Shock showed in Julian's eyes. 'Good God!'

'It's a terrible thing for a man of his age. Of course they're keeping it as quiet as possible, but my wife's cousin married into the family. They went down for £900.'

Julian whistled.

'And they seized all his hops –' said William, '– at least they're trying to. One hundred and eighty-five pockets. All that he had left in store. Matthews wanted to sell it to pay off his creditors, but if the bank gets it . . .' He spread his hands in a helpless gesture and the other two men shook their heads, their expressions grim.

'Poor old Matthews!' said Julian. 'He must be seventy if he's a day.'

'All of that,' agreed William. 'Just when a man is thinking of getting out and putting his feet up, something like that happens. I don't know where it's all leading, but it makes me very nervous about the future.'

As they talked, the last few people came through the doorway and the three of them were about to follow when a dishevelled man arrived on the steps, steadying himself with a hand on the door jamb to heave himself into the hall. It was Tom Bryce, very much the worse for drink. He swayed unsteadily on his feet and his brown eyes blinked owlishly at them.

'The meeting . . . there's a meeting here,' he said. 'Is it here, the meeting?'

William and his father regarded Tom with distaste and Julian hastily averted his head, hoping that Bryce would not recognize him.

'The meeting is over,' Clive told him. 'You've missed it. You had best get off home now.'

Tom Bryce regarded him without understanding, his eyes roaming over the empty hall. Only the three speakers remained, chatting on the platform.

'What time is the meeting?' he insisted. 'There's going to be a meeting!'

Clive put a firm hand on his shoulder. 'There has been a meeting here, but it's over,' he said loudly. 'Now, be a sensible chap and get off home. Bed's the best place for you.'

'But the meeting—'

Clive was losing patience. 'I tell you it's over,' he said sharply. 'There will be other meetings later. Now get off home.'

But Tom Bryce seemed disinclined to take this advice and clung tenaciously to the jamb of the door. Julian glanced at him again, his curiosity getting the better of him. What he saw shocked him, for the man was only a shadow of his former self. He had lost a great deal of weight and his clothes hung loosely on him – his baggy trousers held up by a broad belt. His skin had an almost yellow pallor and his eyes, sunken in their sockets, gave his head a skull-like appearance. All that remained of the fine looking man he had once been was the thatch of curly brown hair, although even this – neglected and tousled – seemed in need of a good wash. He had drunk too much, as his blurred speech and unsteady gait proclaimed only too well, and there were damp stains down the front of his shirt which looked like spilt beer.

'I don't want to go home,' he said suddenly. 'I don't—' He swayed and would have fallen if William had not put out a restraining hand to save him.

'I don't want to go home . . .' he protested. 'I've come to the meeting.'

Clive and William each took an arm and tried to guide the drunken man outside but Julian could not bring himself to touch him and watched helplessly as they marched Tom a few yards down the road in the direction of Laddingford. Then, leaving him to his own devices, William and Clive returned to Julian who now waited outside the hall. Behind him the caretaker, grumbling at the late hour, was locking up the building.

'I can't imagine how he will get home in that state,' said William. 'God knows how he got here if he has no transport.'

'Unless he was drinking with friends in Maidstone,' Julian suggested.

'That's about it,' said William, 'and now they've gone home to bed and he's on his own. A good man wasted,' he went on. 'He was one of the best and look at him now.'

Julian recalled uncomfortably his earlier conversation with Vinnie and for the first time a small doubt arose in his mind, but then he shrugged the thought away. Whatever the rights and wrongs of the matter, he was not Tom Bryce's keeper. If the fellow didn't reach Laddingford he would no doubt sleep under a hedge and be none the worse for his adventure in the morning.

For a while the three men continued talking, but eventually they went their various ways. Julian collected the trap from the stables and set off along Week Street and down the High Street towards the river. At the bottom of the hill, as he was turning left, he saw Tom Bryce sprawled on the ground in the doorway of a shop and his conscience pricked him once again. With a muttered oath, he reined in the horse and pulled over to the kerb-side. With the help of a passer-by, he managed to get the drunken man into the trap. As he was unable to sit upright, they left him to lie on the floor and in that condition Julian drove him home to Laddingford.

Once there, Julian was forced to knock at a house where the windows were still lit and ask for the Bryces' exact address. He arrived at the cottage soon after eleven o'clock, by which time Tom was snoring heavily, oblivious to his surroundings. After a moment's initial hesitation, Julian made his way up the narrow path and tapped sharply on the door. The cottage was in darkness, but almost immediately an upstairs window opened and Rose Bryce leaned out.

'Is that you, Tom?'

'I've brought him home,' said Julian.

'Brought him home? Dear God, he's not hurt, is he?'

'Not hurt. Drunk!' Julian's tone was brusque.

'Oh no! I'll be right down. Give me a moment.'

The window closed, a light was lit and there were footsteps on the stairs. The door opened and Rose stood before him with a candle in her hand, a shawl wrapped round her shoulders.

'Mr Lawrence!'

But Julian was already striding back towards the trap.

'Give me a hand,' he called to her over his shoulder.

She set down the candle on a small table and ran after him, barefooted. Somehow they managed to rouse the sleeping man and lift him down from the trap. It was very dark and Julian could not see her expression, but he could hear the agitation in her voice as she coaxed her husband along the path with a mixture of mild curses and endearments that was strangely moving. When they reached the door Rose turned to Julian.

'I can't thank you enough, I'm that grateful!' she told him. 'Don't think too badly of him, Mr Lawrence. I don't know what's got into him this last year, but at heart he's a good man. Deep down, he's the man he always was. Nobody's perfect and he's got faults enough, God knows, but he's never raised a hand to me and I've always loved him—' Here her voice broke suddenly and Julian heard the sharp intake of breath that heralded tears. Hastily, he propped the half-unconscious man against the door, where he slid down at once into a sitting position.

'I'm glad I could be of help,' said Julian stiffly.

Rose was on the verge of tears now, a hand held up to shield her face. Then she dropped to her knees beside her husband.

'Tom! It's Mr Lawrence. He brought you home. You must thank him!' Tom Bryce only groaned and Julian could bear no more.

'There's no need for thanks,' he said. 'You'll be able to manage now?'

Without waiting for her answer, he almost ran down the path, pausing only to close the rickety gate behind him. Then he climbed back into the trap, turned it and urged his horse away from the unhappy scene. He tried to put the incident out of mind, but the image of Tom Bryce as he had first seen him in the doorway of the meeting hall returned again and again. Julian was puzzled. What was wrong with the man? He had a good job, a good wife, a family. What had wrought this dreadful change on him? Was it only his banishment from Foxearth, or was there another reason? The rumours about his drinking excesses were obviously true, but that could not entirely account for his ravaged looks. The wretched man looked very sick indeed. Perhaps he was ill – perhaps, thought Julian, he was *very* ill. He was ashamed that the thought gave him some comfort, but try as he would his jealousy outweighed any sympathy he might feel. He knew that while Tom Bryce lived Vinnie, with her infinite capacity for forgiveness, would always keep a small corner in her heart for him.

Julian decided he would not tell Vinnie of the night's encounter. Tom Bryce had not actually attended the meeting, so it would be possible to answer her inevitable questions without referring to his belated appearance. It would be a lie, he reflected, but a lie by omission only and one for which he thought he might be forgiven. With a slight lightening of his mood, he whipped up the horse and made good time over the last four miles to Foxearth.

*

Tom Bryce slept restlessly all night. He did not wake at all but frequently threw himself from side to side and snored loudly, disturbing Rose's uneasy sleep. When dawn began to brighten the room, she welcomed it thankfully and slipped out of bed into the warmest clothes she could find. On a mattress at the foot of the bed, their youngest child slept soundly and there was no sound from the adjoining room where the other children slept together in a large bed. Tom's mother also was still asleep, Rose noted, as she rubbed a damp flannel over her face, willing herself into a proper wakefulness. Then she tiptoed downstairs, seeking a few moments privacy and time to think and promising herself a comforting cup of tea.

The small kitchen range kept the kitchen warm overnight and when she opened it she was relieved to see a few glowing embers. From the cupboard beside the fire she took out a box and from it drew out a few twists of newspaper. On top of those she laid a handful of kindling wood and then a shovel full of coal. Almost immediately flames flared up and she watched for a moment with a satisfied expression on her face. Then, setting a kettle to boil above, she took a small pail from beneath the dresser and went out into the back garden to fetch the morning's milk.

In the shed the goat greeted her with a friendly flick of her tail and a playful butt of her dainty head. Normally Rose would have petted her but on this morning she attended to the milking in silence, her thoughts elsewhere as the white liquid frothed into the pail. With a disconsolate shake of its head, the goat watched her return to the house.

At the back door the goose demanded attention with a raucous honking, but Rose put a finger to her lips. 'Hush, you silly creature! You'll wake the whole house with your noise,' she whispered. 'You'll get your food at the proper time and not before.'

Quickly Rose went inside and closed the door, knowing that her disappearance would silence the goose. The last thing she wanted was to disturb her mother-in-law, who would join her in the kitchen and demand to know the reason for her early rising and obvious preoccupation. Rose spooned tea from the Jubilee caddy into the old brown teapot and added the boiling water. The milk she strained through a muslin square into a jug. Soon she was hunched beside the newly awakened fire, a mug of hot tea warming her hands.

Tom, she knew, would wake up with a head as clear as a bell, remembering nothing of the previous night's escapade. If she told him what had happened he would believe her and be mortified to learn of Julian's part in it – but would it make him mend his ways? Rose doubted it. He was letting himself go physically and mentally and the terrible thing was that he did not seem to care. He seemed almost determined to destroy himself or at least to remove for ever the man he had once been. Rose wanted desperately to help him, but so far had been quite powerless to do so. Now she felt that perhaps fate had played into her hands and that it might be possible to shock him out of his decline.

She took a sip of her tea, revelling in its warmth, and wondered whether she and Tom would quarrel. If they did, she would lose her temper and say spiteful, bitter things which she would prefer left unsaid. She sighed. What was it, she wondered, that drove him to such reckless behaviour? If only he would talk to her! But her husband was a proud, stubborn man and she knew that this was unlikely. So far, her few attempts to win his confidence had failed miserably, but Rose was not a girl to give up so easily. She had made up her mind during the long wakeful night that she would try again and somehow turn this present situation to her advantage. For some time she sat debating ways in which she could approach the subject without inviting an angry retort, but had reached no firm conclusions when the floor-boards creaked overhead and she knew that Tom's mother was on her way downstairs. She was adding more hot water to the teapot when Mrs Bryce came into the room, huddled as usual in an old coat which had once belonged to her husband.

'I thought someone was up,' she said, accepting the mug of tea which Rose poured for her and settling in the chair which her daughter-in-law had just vacated. Rose poured herself another and for a few moments the two women stared at the fire without speaking to each other.

'It's Tom,' Rose began.

Mrs Bryce nodded without looking up. 'What happened last night?' she asked. 'I heard the commotion and I was on my way down when I heard another voice. Sounded like Mr Lawrence?'

'It *was* Mr Lawrence,' said Rose, 'and Tom – out cold! He brought him home in a trap. I don't know how it came about. He didn't stay long and I don't remember if I spoke to him or not. I was so put out.'

'Julian Lawrence, eh, after all these years. How did he look, Rose?'

'It was difficult to tell. I only had the candle, but he seemed well enough. He was polite. It was good of him but . . .'

'But you would rather he hadn't seen Tom like that?'

'That's right,' said Rose. 'I would rather it had been anyone but him. I was so ashamed, I can't tell you. I wanted the ground to swallow me up.'

Mrs Bryce leaned forward and patted her knee. 'I know, dear,' she said. 'It's a bad business. I've been meaning to talk to him about it, but I don't like to interfere . . . then again, he *is* my son.'

Rose sighed. 'I don't know what's got into him,' she said, 'but I *do* know he'll kill himself if he goes on like this. He looks like death.'

'Drink won't kill him,' said Mrs Bryce. 'He's tough, Tom is, like his father. So don't worry on *that* score.'

'But it's not only how he looks,' continued Rose desperately. 'He's so changed in his ways. I just wish I knew what was going through his mind.'

'Well, he's never settled here,' said Mrs Bryce. 'I mean, it has always been second-best for him, hasn't it? His heart's at Foxearth and always will be. I know he was grateful for a job and a roof over his head, but it'll never be the same for him, will it?'

Rose did not answer.

'Folk talk about him in the village, you know,' said Mrs Bryce. 'They ask me what's up with him. It's his health, I tell them. What else can I say? I don't think they're fooled anyway. It isn't difficult to spot a man who's had too much to drink, but if they think I'm going to admit it, they've got another think coming!'

'I know, Ma. Tom's a good son, a good husband and a good father but if he doesn't stop drinking, he won't be any of those things. We've got to do something, but I don't know what.'

'Would you like me to talk to him?'

'Thanks, but no,' said Rose. 'If there is anything to be said, it will have to be me that says it. Somehow I'll have to get it into that head of his that he must call a halt before it's too late.'

Rose got up and filled a larger kettle for the early morning washing.

'I'll go up right now and talk to him,' she said, suddenly making up her mind. 'The longer I put it off, the more nervous I get.'

'Oh, I do hope he sees reason, dear. It's so hard for you. I am so terribly sorry; I would never have thought to see Tom in this state and that's the truth. What his father would say if he could see him, I shudder to think!'

Rose rinsed her mug and up-turned it on the draining-board. As she passed her mother-in-law, she bent to give her a quick hug and then made her way up the stairs to the bedroom.

Tom had struggled to a sitting position by the time Rose reached him. He stretched and yawned blearily and Rose noticed – not for the first time – that the once brawny arms had lost their firmness.

'Is it Tuesday?' he asked. 'Because if so, we have a tree to fell and it's going to be a swine. I'm not looking forward to that at all!'

He threw back the clothes and made to get out of bed, but Rose drew the covers over him again and sat down facing him, her expression as stern as she could manage.

'You're not going anywhere, Tom Bryce!' she said. 'Not until I've spoken to you.'

He looked at her uneasily. 'What about a cup of tea?' he asked.

'There'll be a cup of tea all in good time,' she said, 'and it will be downstairs on the kitchen table same as usual. But right now, Tom, I have something to say and you've got to listen.'

He opened his mouth to protest but she rushed on. 'No, Tom, I mean it, you have *got* to hear me out. Something happened last night. A shameful thing . . .'

'Last night?' He was immediately wary.

'Yes, Tom, you know what I mean. You got drunk last night. Don't shake your head at me like that – I know you did, because I saw you when you came home and a fine state you were in too.'

'Well, a man's got a right to a few drinks with his mates—'

'A *few* drinks is one thing, Tom. When you're brought home in a drunken stupor, that's something else and there's no way you're going to tell me that's a good thing. You told me you were going to a meeting and you said you'd be straight home. You promised me, Tom!'

'I might have had a drink or two—'

'I reckon they could have floated a battleship on what you drank last night, Tom Bryce! After all your fine promises! And if that's not bad enough, you had to be brought home in a pony and trap because you couldn't walk.'

A sullen look was settling over Tom Bryce's face and Rose's

heart sank, but she forced herself to finish what she had intended to say.

'You were out like a light, Tom, and that's the truth of it. You had to be *carried* up the path. And d'you know who by? Me and Mr Lawrence! Oh, yes, you can look at me like that. It was Julian Lawrence brought you home last night, Tom – I thought that would make you sit up and take notice. Now you know why I'm so upset.'

'Julian Lawrence? I don't believe it!'

'Oh yes you do, Tom, I can see it written in your eyes. You know I wouldn't lie to you about a thing like that. Mr Lawrence brought you home and you were too drunk to recognize him. We dragged you up the path and I have never been so ashamed in all my life. Can you imagine how I felt? Gone eleven at night and me in my old nightgown. What he must have thought I can't imagine and what he said when he got back to Foxearth . . . Oh, Tom, I can't bear it! I hate you to be thought of so badly. Where's your pride?'

Tom would not look at her. 'I'm sorry, Rose,' he said at last. 'I wouldn't have had that happen for anything.'

'But it *did* happen, Tom and you let it happen!' she said. 'I just don't understand you any more. It's as though you don't care. Where's the Tom I married, that's what I want to know? There was a time when folk respected you, but not any more.'

'Folk can think what they like.'

'Oh, they will, Tom! They'll think that you are a ruined man. You've got to pull yourself together. I don't like talking to you like this and I know you don't like hearing it, but what's to be done? Someone has got to get some sense into that head of yours.'

'You just don't understand, Rose,' he said with a deep sigh.

'But I'd like to understand, Tom. If you could try to explain why you have changed, then I'd try to understand.'

But he was shaking his head. 'It's no good, Rose, I don't want to talk about it.'

'But Tom—'

'I said that's enough!' He pushed the bedclothes aside and swung his legs out of the other side of the bed.

'But Julian Lawrence of all people!' said Rose helplessly.

'Well, it's done and there's no undoing it. Maybe I have changed . . .'

'Oh, you have, Tom. Your mother has noticed it as well.'

He began to pull on his shirt. 'Oh, I see it! The two of you have been getting your heads together, is that it? Tongues wagging at my expense?'

'Tom, she's as worried as I am, poor soul. And what about the children? Goodness knows what they hear at school from the other kids. I've seen them look at you lately – they don't know what to make of it, bless them.'

'That's enough!' he said and now his voice was edged with anger. 'You've had your say and I've said I'm sorry. If I'm not the man you married, it is because . . .' His voice faltered and she waited but he broke off abruptly, thrusting his legs into his breeches and refusing to say any more on the subject.

Nevertheless her words had depressed him and after a hasty breakfast, Tom left for work in a sombre mood. The tree that was to be felled was a crack willow which grew between the pond and the house. Already it was higher than the roof and a high wind from the north-east could bring it down at any time. The wood would be useful for firewood and the base that remained could be pollarded.

He met up with the two farm-hands and collected a big saw and an extending ladder. One of the men carried a coil of rope over one shoulder. First Tom trimmed off some of the thinner lower branches, then he set the ladder against the willow and lashed it fast at the top. From there he climbed higher into the tree in order to tie a second rope round the trunk. His movements were smooth and assured, but the men noticed that once or twice he paused for a few seconds and closed his eyes. When the main rope was firm, he unlashed the top of the ladder and then climbed down to the ground. One of the men went back to the house with the ladder while the other was given the rope which was now fastened near the top of the willow. Tom directed him to a position at right-angles to a line running from the tree to the corner of the house; a steady pull in that direction would be necessary if the tree was to fall safely. Then he took up the saw and when the first man returned, told him to help with the rope.

'Don't pull till I tell you,' he told them, 'and don't twist the rope around your hand. Let it run freely through your fingers or it will take off your finger. Remember you're not there to bring it down but to direct the line of fall. If anything goes wrong and it looks as though it's coming down on top of you, drop the rope and get out of the way as fast as you can. It may not look much from here, but that tree is going to look much bigger when it hits the ground!'

The men nodded. 'Remember, don't pull till I give you the word and don't take your eyes off the bloody thing until it's safely down!'

Tom cut a notch four inches wide in the side of the tree which faced them and then moved round to the other side. He began to saw, with a firm, steady action, through the tree-trunk which was almost eighteen inches in diameter. He worked till the sweat ran down his face, brushing it away with his forearm. Once or twice he paused, bowed his head and screwed up his eyes with pain, cursing roundly as he did so, but at last the tall willow surrendered. He shouted and the two men, eyeing the tree apprehensively, pulled as hard as they could. With a splintering sound and a rush of air through the branches it toppled slowly to the ground, sending up a shower of earth and dead leaves. The two men, safely out of reach, breathed sighs of relief.

'She's down!' one of them called.

Tom shouted, 'Well done!' and put down the saw. Then with a muffled groan, he doubled up once more with the sickening knowledge that the pain in his stomach was growing worse.

CHAPTER FOUR

'A letter from Eva!' cried Vinnie, hurrying into Colonel Lawrence's bedroom. 'I know you cannot read it, but I felt sure you would like to open the letter yourself and then I can read it for you.'

The old man allowed himself to be tugged into an upright position with the pillows plumped around him for support. When at last Vinnie was satisfied, the precious letter from India was placed in his hand and she stood back to watch the excitement on his face which almost matched her own. Eva, the Colonel's only daughter, had married Gerald Cottingham, a railway engineer, and the two of them had travelled to India soon after their wedding. They had resided there for four years now and when Eva had last written to her father she had told him that their second child was expected in January.

'I expect you are a grandfather twice now,' Vinnie told him, stifling her impatience as his frail fingers fumbled with the envelope.

'Here, you take it,' the Colonel said, returning the letter to Vinnie's eager hands. 'I think she has sealed it with a new and invincible glue, which certainly defies my feeble efforts.'

Vinnie had already slit the envelope and was drawing out the familiar notepaper covered in Eva's small, neat handwriting.

'Sit yourself on the bed, Vinnie,' the Colonel told her, 'and don't gabble. I like to take it in slowly and you race away and leave me behind!'

Vinnie laughed. 'I'm sorry,' she said. 'It's dated the eighteenth of January and it's now . . .'

'Don't ask *me*,' said the Colonel. 'I can't tell one day from the other any more.'

'It's March the tenth,' she said. 'It has taken seven weeks to reach us.'

'Read the letter, Vinnie!'

'I'm sorry, I will. She says, "Dearest Papa, Julian and Vinnie, At last the promised letter. Please forgive the delay, but the latest Cottingham is another little boy. We call him Lucian." '

'Another boy!' cried the Colonel. 'Well done, Eva! Two grandsons, Vinnie. What do you think of that, eh?'

'I think it's splendid,' she told him.

'Splendid? That's an understatement if ever I heard one. Why isn't Janet here? I want Janet to hear the news. Ring for her, Vinnie, there's a good girl!'

Obediently Vinnie rang the bell and waited patiently until Janet appeared. Then she waved the letter.

'I know, ma'am,' said Janet. 'We all saw the stamp!'

'I wanted you to hear it, Janet,' said the Colonel. 'Read it again, Vinnie!'

Vinnie did so and Janet's congratulations were both generous and sincere. 'That's marvellous, sir, wonderful news!' she cried. 'I must tell the others.'

'Wait a moment,' said Vinnie. 'Listen to the next bit.' She read on: ' "Lucian is very demanding. *So* like his grandfather! He likes to have his own way." '

The Colonel chuckled delightedly while Vinnie and Janet laughed. ' "He's also like his brother Francis and won't sleep at night. He is always hungry, but Calcutta obviously suits him. He grows daily stronger and the doctor is very pleased with us both. We all thank God for a safe delivery. A sad thought, though, that while he was being born our dear Queen Victoria was dying." '

The Colonel punched the air with a frail but triumphant fist. 'So!' he said. 'Tell Cook to open a bottle of wine, so you can all wet the new baby's head. Perhaps you should make it two bottles, then you can send one up to us. Oh, I know it's not allowed, Vinnie, but it's not every day that I get news of a grandson. Very demanding, is he, like his old grandfather?' He chuckled again. 'My lovely little Eva, she's a good girl. A good daughter. She was always my favourite, you know.' Vinnie nodded. 'And now she's the mother of two! Amazing! Incredible! But go on, read the rest of the letter.'

Janet departed and Vinnie continued to read out news of Gerald, including a glowing account of his cleverness which did not impress the Colonel, who had secretly hoped that his only daughter would marry into the Army.

Then she went on, ' "I was surprised two weeks ago to receive a visit from Louise Tarlton, who you will no doubt remember as one of my oldest friends. She married a young Army officer but as yet they have no family which, I think, is causing her some concern." '

Here Vinnie's voice faltered slightly, but the Colonel pretended not to notice.

' "She brought some news," ' Vinnie continued, ' "which I am reluctant to pass on, although Gerald says I must. I am so afraid of raising Vinnie's hopes as it concerns – or possibly concerns – her brother Bertie." '

Vinnie gave a gasp and her shocked eyes met those of the Colonel, who nodded slowly. 'Go on, my dear,' he said.

' "Louise's husband, Rupert, recalls a trooper in his Regiment by the name of Robert Harris. He came from Whitechapel." '

Vinnie closed her eyes. 'But his name is Bertram,' she whispered. 'It can't be him!'

' "When I questioned him that perhaps the name was Bertram and not Robert, he could not say for sure, but had heard him described only as Bert and assumed his name to be Robert . . ." '

Her voice trailed into silence and the Colonel, knowing her history, waited for her to finish. He had, he told himself, done his best by Vinnie's family when their mother drowned. The baby girl Emmeline had been packed off back to London with kindly neighbours; Bertie, her older brother, had been settled on a nearby farm, while Vinnie herself had moved in with Mrs Bryce. He was satisfied that the Lawrences had fully met their obligations in that direction – more than met them, he reminded himself, for there was a Stanley Harris still living somewhere who should have resumed responsibility but had never been traced. Emmeline had subsequently contracted an unnamed fever which had killed her, so only Bertie remained; he had joined the Army and had last been heard of in India. The Colonel knew how much it would mean to Vinnie to be reunited with him.

At last Vinnie looked up from the letter. 'She says this man was injured in an accident and has lost his right eye. He was moved to a military hospital and from there he was expected to return to England. Oh, I wonder if it's Bertie! But to lose an eye! Could it be him, Colonel? What do you think?'

The Colonel hesitated. 'It seems very possible, my dear,' he said. 'But I beg you not to raise your hopes too high. There must be more than one Bertie Harris.'

'But he comes from Whitechapel,' said Vinnie eagerly.

The Colonel nodded again. 'Let's hope it is him.'

'But his poor eye—'

The Colonel shrugged. 'A soldier is a fighter,' he reminded her. 'A man who takes the Queen's shilling – King's, rather – lays his life on the line for his country. To lose a leg, an eye or an arm – that's the risk he takes as part of his duty.'

Vinnie was silent. For a moment her thoughts whirled chaotically. Then she looked up. 'I *want* it to be him,' she said, 'but I don't want him to have lost an eye.'

Tears sprang into her eyes and the Colonel put out a hand and clasped hers. 'Don't cry, Vinnie,' he implored. 'Let us pray that Bertie is found. If it *is* Bertie, he will soon be home and Julian can take you to visit him in hospital. You would like that, my dear, so cheer up! Better a brother with one eye than no brother at all.'

She laughed shakily.

'That's my girl! Let's see a smile on that pretty face of yours. If it is Bertie, we shall have something else to celebrate. Another excuse for a bottle of wine!'

Vinnie laughed. 'You are a terrible man, Colonel,' she told him. 'The doctor will be so cross if he finds out.'

'The doctor is an old fool,' said the Colonel. 'Ring the bell again, Vinnie, and find out what has happened to our wine. We will drink a toast, my dear, to your news and mine. But while we're waiting, read me the rest of the letter.'

*

Later that day, while Vinnie was still pondering the contents of Eva's letter, Clive le Brun arrived and was shown into the drawing room. He had been both factor and friend to the Lawrences for a long time and was always very welcome. Since his wife had died giving birth to her second child, he and William had lived alone except for the servants.

Clive le Brun was well respected as a factor and his advice was frequently sought. His role was that of 'middle man' – or more correctly, one of two 'middle men'. In his capacity as factor he would assess the value of the crop, negotiate a price and sell the hops to a merchant who would in turn sell to a brewer. The factor was the growers' man, while the merchant's loyalties lay with the brewers. As well as buying and selling, the factor would advise clients on various matters, from the extent of a hop disease in the surrounding area to the current market price of hops in the international market. The firm of le Brun had fifteen clients scattered throughout the Weald of Kent and therefore had a valuable overall knowledge of the state of the industry. A good factor could save the grower a great deal of money in one way and another.

Vinnie joined Clive in the drawing room, her hand outstretched and a welcoming smile on her face.

'Mr le Brun,' she said, 'how nice to see you again after all this time.'

He laughed briefly and shook her hand. 'Whenever I call you seem to be busy, but at last I am in luck.'

'And so am I,' said Vinnie, 'but sit down and Janet shall bring us some refreshment. Will you take some wine or something stronger – or we could share a pot of tea and some of cook's delicious sandwiches.'

'That sounds tempting,' he said, settling himself into a chair. Vinnie watched him with pleasure, seeing a tall lean man whose dark hair was barely touched with grey. His face was angular and his grey eyes seemed cold, but a humorous mouth softened the overall impression. She rang the bell for Janet and when she looked up saw that he was regarding her with apparent amusement. Seeing her puzzled look, he laughed softly.

'Forgive me,' he said. 'I was just thinking how different you are today from the young bride who threw us all into such a state of excitement.'

Vinnie laughed. 'I don't think *I* ever saw anyone in a state of great excitement,' she said.

'Ah, they hid their feelings in your presence, but I can assure you the whole of Kent was bubbling with news of the Lawrence boy's untimely marriage.'

'And disapproving, no doubt?' said Vinnie.

'Of course!'

'It was natural enough,' said Vinnie, 'but no one snubbed me – at least, I don't think they did.'

'I am sure no one would be so unkind. After all, the deed was done and the Lawrences are a highly respected family. An engagement might have been quite bearable, but a secret wedding! A *fait accompli*, wasn't it?'

Vinnie laughed. 'How strange that I didn't really notice,' she said. 'I've often tried to ask Julian about it, but he won't talk about those difficult early days.'

'I should hope not,' said Clive. 'That would be most ungentlemanly! But I am only teasing you. Of course it wasn't a scandal, but a great many eyebrows were raised and a lot of whispered comments were exchanged behind raised hands. You have to remember, Mrs Lawrence, that Julian was a very eligible bachelor.'

Just then Janet arrived and was sent downstairs again for tea and sandwiches.

'You have come a long way from those early days,' Clive told her. 'I heard from a most reliable source,' he continued, 'that you refuse to allow your husband to grub up any of his hops.'

'I haven't refused,' Vinnie protested with a laugh, 'but I have begged him not to do so. So many people depend on us for work in September and I couldn't bear to turn any of them away. Julian has been very understanding, but it really is the most awful problem.'

'Politics and farming don't mix,' he said. 'They never have done. Yes, it *is* a difficult problem and it will grow worse.'

Vinnie frowned. 'Julian tells me "not to bother my pretty head" about such matters, but I can't just do nothing and hope the problem will go away.'

She stood up abruptly and crossed to the window. 'Look,' she said, 'the young bines are just beginning to show above the ground and then in a month or so they will need tying, washing and dusting.'

He moved to stand beside her and together they looked out on the broad expanse of hop-poles which stretched away in all directions like a petrified forest.

'But this won't do,' said Vinnie, turning to face him. 'I am not doing my job as a good hostess. Instead of talking hops, I should be amusing you with tittle-tattle or entertaining you with a story. When Julian returns, the two of you will no doubt have this conversation all over again.'

Janet came in and set down the tray on the table and Clive le Brun sat down opposite Vinnie as she busied herself pouring the tea.

'Do have one of cook's potted beef sandwiches,' she said. 'I dare not send the tray back with the food untouched.'

'I have no intention of leaving it untouched,' he assured her. 'I had no lunch and very little breakfast.' He tasted a sandwich. 'They are delicious.'

'I shall tell her you said so. So what are you advising Julian about today?'

He seemed about to reply humorously, then changed his mind. 'I am recommending the Fuggle hops,' he told her, 'or at least pointing out the advantages to my clients. It is easier to grow and more resistant to disease.'

'But does it smell as good?'

'Maybe not, but it is a very reliable crop and the grower is more likely to see a proper reward from his year's labours. The Golding has more aroma, but it needs constant nursing.'

'Well, I would rather nurse them,' said Vinnie.

'No doubt Julian will be guided by you,' he said with a smile.

Vinnie laughed. 'I don't *always* get my own way.'

'You surprise me, Mrs Lawrence,' he said. 'It must be difficult to resist you when you plead your cause so passionately. No wonder my son was so loud in your praise.'

'William was?' Vinnie was surprised, for she rarely saw the young man.

'Oh yes. He told me what a fortunate man Julian is – and he did not exaggerate.'

His steady gaze disconcerted Vinnie and, slightly embarrassed, she wanted to look away but his eyes held hers. There was no challenge in them and no pretence – it was simply a look of admiration which Vinnie appreciated for its obvious sincerity.

Clive le Brun also wanted to look away, fearing that his long stare would be misinterpreted, but there was something in Vinnie's wide and still innocent eyes that moved him. At length it was Vinnie who turned her head and the fingers of her left hand strayed to tidy away an imaginary strand of hair. It was a gesture which she made when she was nervous. He saw it almost immediately and then he laughed.

'Forgive me! I am an old fool,' he said.

'You are not old,' Vinnie protested, then added hastily, 'Nor a fool!'

Then they were both laughing, glad of an excuse to relax the sudden slight tension which had arisen between them. To make amends for her lack of tact, Vinnie said, 'I wish you would call me Vinnie. "Mrs Lawrence" is too formal.'

'I would deem it an honour and a privilege,' he answered with a slightly mocking bow. 'I trust you will call me Clive?'

As she nodded, they heard the front door open and close.

'That will be Julian,' said Vinnie. 'Janet will tell him you are here, but I always like to greet him. Will you help yourself to another sandwich and excuse me for a moment?'

He nodded and Vinnie made her way to the door and outside on to the landing, where she closed the door behind her and leaned back against it for a moment. Then she took a deep breath, straightened her back and ran downstairs to greet her husband.

*

Later that evening, as they sat on at the table after their meal was finished, Vinnie sought for an opening to the subject which had worried her ever since her conversation with Clive le Brun. Several times she saw a chance but each time her courage failed her until at last she could wait no longer.

'Mr le Brun said something . . .' she began.

'He's a good man,' said Julian. 'They are a nice family, the le Bruns. A very well respected family. He seems to have enjoyed your company and spoke very highly of you.'

'That was kind of him,' said Vinnie. She was slightly disconcerted by the turn of the conversation but Julian went on speaking.

'He should have married again. He is a lonely man and at the moment his work is all he lives for. That and his bees. He is quite an expert, I hear.'

Vinnie fiddled with the stem of her wine-glass, not meeting his eyes. 'He said something that worried me,' she said at last.

It was Julian's turn to look surprised. 'He shouldn't have done that,' he said. 'I have told you before, I don't want you to worry your head about business matters. You have quite enough to do in managing the house.'

'No, it wasn't about business,' said Vinnie. 'It was about me. He said – oh, it doesn't matter, Julian.'

'Darling, of course it matters, if you are worried. It matters very much. What did he say to you?'

She took a deep breath. 'He said that everyone was shocked when you married me. That they disapproved.'

His face relaxed. 'Not that old worry again,' he protested. 'I told you at the time it was quite inevitable and that you were not to worry about it. I thought you had forgotten it all long since. You are my wife and mistress of Foxearth – and a very pretty one, if I may say so.'

'Of course you may,' Vinnie laughed, 'but you are changing the subject.' Her expression grew serious once more. 'I sometimes wonder if you have ever regretted marrying me. I haven't regretted marrying you, but—'

'Vinnie! We've been over this ground so many times. How can I convince you?'

'I don't know,' she said, 'but I wish you could. Oh darling, I couldn't bear it if you were sorry that you married me. I do my best, Julian, and sometimes I think I'm succeeding – then something happens that makes me uncertain. Like Clive—'

Julian raised his eyebrows. 'Oh? Is it "Clive" now? What happened to "Mr le Brun"?'

Vinnie shrugged. 'I suggested he called me Vinnie, so he said I should call him Clive. You don't mind, do you? Or was that another mistake? Oh Julian! You see, I'm not succeeding at all. I don't understand these things – to me, they don't matter.'

'"Lavinia" would have been more suitable,' he said and she was aware of his disapproval.

'I don't feel like a Lavinia,' she said slowly. 'Maybe that's what's wrong. Maybe after all this time I ought to *feel* different.'

Julian sighed and Vinnie felt a chill of fear sweep through her. He *was* sorry – she was *not* making him a good wife. He was looking at her with an expression which was hard to read although she searched his eyes desperately.

'Please, Vinnie!' he said. 'Once and for all, can we stop going over this question? If I cannot reassure you, then there is no point in these dreary discussions. You ask me if I regret our marriage. I say "No". What more can I say?'

'You could say it in a different way!' cried Vinnie. 'You always sound so cross.'

She immediately wished the words unsaid but it was too late. Now he would become sarcastic and she dreaded that. His eyes narrowed and her heart sank.

'Oh, it's *my* fault!' he said. 'I should have known. Now it's my fault for not expressing myself properly.'

'I didn't say that,' said Vinnie quietly. 'I'm sorry. I shouldn't have brought up the subject again. It matters dreadfully to me, but you never understand.'

He was looking at her coldly. 'Vinnie, it was years ago. Could we please stop talking about it?'

She was silent for a moment, earnestly studying the empty glass which twirled busily between her fingers, then she took her courage in both hands. 'I've asked you before if I am making you a good wife,' she said, 'but now I want to ask you something else. Then I swear I won't talk about it again. I have always wondered whether you would have wed me if you had known I wasn't going to die.'

He hesitated for a second or two before saying brusquely, 'Of course I would! That's a terrible thing to suggest.'

The glass slipped suddenly from Vinnie's fingers and rolled on the table. They both watched it without speaking.

'I love you, Vinnie,' said Julian. 'And surely that's all that matters!'

'But it *isn't*!' she cried. 'It matters to me to know the truth. How it really was. I was ill and delirious and I can't remember. I have to rely on you to tell me and if you don't tell it the right way—' she broke off and picked up the glass.

Julian sighed wearily. 'You might not have accepted me!' He was trying to lighten the tenor of the conversation and she recognized the ploy. Again she felt the coldness and her heart raced in panic.

'Swear on your mother's grave, Julian,' she begged. 'Then I will believe it! Can you do that, Julian?'

Julian stared at his wife. He had asked himself that question many times and would never know the answer.

'Of course I can say it,' he said, 'and I *do* say it. Now, will that do?'

Vinnie continued to stare at him with a stricken look on her face and his mood softened. He had married her for better or worse and he loved her in spite of her failings.

'Come here, you silly goose,' he said, holding out his arms, but Vinnie shook her head.

'What's this, then?' he teased. 'A mutiny? You shake your head at your lord and master?'

'Don't mock me,' she whispered, her eyes dark.

'I'm not mocking you, Vinnie,' he said, his voice gentle. 'I'm asking you to come to me and sit on my knee. Most women would—'

'I'm not most women,' she broke in dully. 'I'm Vinnie Harris from the London slums.'

'You're Lavinia Lawrence and I love you, so come here and be hugged.'

'It's the letter, isn't it?' said Vinnie suddenly. 'Eva's letter? It's the baby.'

'What on earth are you talking about?'

She jumped up from the table and faced him wildly. 'It's Eva's son! You're jealous,' she cried. 'It's because I haven't given you a son. Everything would be all right if only I could give you a son. Oh Julian, I want to *so* much!'

He got up from the table and walked round to her. Without speaking, he put his arms round her and held her in a fierce embrace, burying his face against her hair as they clung together in agonized silence.

'I *do* want a son,' he whispered at last. 'I won't deny it, darling. But we shall have one, I am sure of it. Maybe this month or next. Soon, I swear it.'

'Oh, dearest Julian!' She kissed him. 'I don't know why . . . The doctor says there's nothing wrong—'

'I know he does, I know it. Please, Vinnie, I'm not blaming you. No one is to blame. We *will* have a child—'

'A little boy!'

'Yes.'

'James Henry Lawrence,' she whispered shakily as tears welled in her eyes.

'Yes! Oh Vinnie, please don't cry. My poor little Vinnie, I do love you. I swear it on my mother's grave. There! I love you and we will be happy. We shall have a son and everything will be the way we want it.'

Vinnie took out a handkerchief and dabbed at her eyes. 'And a girl, Julian, remember? James Henry for you and Lorna Jane for me. Or we could have another son and call him Edward James after the new King.'

'Everyone's son will be an Edward!'

'Oh, that's right, they will. Oh, Julian, I don't mean to make you wretched. I'm so sorry, my love!'

'I know,' he told her. 'But we have so much. We have each other and Foxearth. So much to be thankful for.'

'I have a loving husband—'

'And I have a loving, dutiful wife.'

She laughed.

'That's better,' he said. 'I hate to see you cry. I have an idea. Let's go to bed, Vinnie!'

'To bed? So early?'

'A *dutiful* wife, remember?'

'Julian!'

'It's nearly nine o'clock.'

'But what will the servants think?'

'Damn the servants! We want a son and sons don't grow on trees.' Her mood was changing, he saw thankfully as she began to laugh.

'An early night,' he whispered, 'and no arguments.'

With his arm round her, he rang the bell for Janet to clear the table, then led Vinnie out of the dining room and up the stairs.

*

The following evening Janet changed the Colonel's bed for the second time that week. She rolled the old man back into place on the clean sheet and pulled the other covers over him, tucking him in gently.

'Now then, sir, you'll feel better now and no one the wiser.'

'Thank you, Janet, you're a good girl. I know I am a fool but I just can't bring myself to say anything to Vinnie.'

'You ought to tell the doctor, sir. He might be able to help.'

'How can he help me, Janet? He can't make me young again. I am just an old man and old men wet the bed.'

'You must not worry about it, sir. Everyone gets old. It will happen to us all in time. You are not to go upsetting yourself, do you hear me?'

'I hear you.' He shook his head miserably.

'Now you promise me, sir. When I go out of this room I don't want you brooding over things that can't be helped. If I was you, I'd tell the doctor when there's nobody else around. He will understand – that's what doctors are for, sir, to help us.'

'I know, Janet. I think I will do that and thank you again.'

'It's nothing, sir. I will pop this sheet into the laundry and no one will be any the wiser.' She paused at the door to wag an admonitory finger at him. 'And remember, sir, you are *not* to fret about it. I will come up later if I can. If not, I shall see you in the morning.'

She closed the door quietly behind her, hurried along the passage to deposit the sheet in the large laundry basket and then made her way downstairs with a sinking heart. Mrs Tallant, she knew, would be very displeased by her prolonged absence.

'Janet!' called Mrs Tallant the moment she stood inside the kitchen. 'Where on earth have you been all this time? I have had to lay the table myself and that is not my job and never has been.'

'I'm sorry, Mrs Tallant. I got held up a bit.'

'Held up a bit? You've been gone nearly twenty minutes. It doesn't take that long to take a bit of supper up to an old man.'

'I'm sorry, Mrs Tallant. I was as quick as I could be.' She was uncomfortably aware that Edie was watching her with a look of malicious triumph on her face. Cook was busying herself with the soup tureen and pretending not to notice the altercation. 'Young Harry' watched the argument with undisguised interest.

'It's no good, Janet,' Mrs Tallant continued angrily. 'I've warned you before and this time I'm going to speak to the mistress about it. I am not prepared to do your job while you sit around upstairs chattering with the Colonel.'

'I wasn't chattering,' said Janet. 'The old man needs a bit of nursing, that's all.'

'Well, he should have a nurse then. You are not a nurse; you are a parlourmaid and one of your duties is to set table. Now this is the second time this week I have had to do it.'

'Couldn't Edie—' Janet began.

Now it was Edie's turn. 'Why me?' she wailed. 'Why should I do it? I don't know how; I'm not a parlourmaid.'

'You mind your own business, Edie, and speak when you're spoken to,' Mrs Tallant told her. 'Of course you couldn't set table. You hardly know your right from your left, so get on with those pans or I will have a word with the mistress about you too.'

Hastily Edie returned to the job of washing up the pans that had already been used and discarded by Cook.

'I promise it won't happen again, Mrs Tallant,' said Janet, but the housekeeper was not to be mollified.

'It's no good, Janet,' she said. 'You said that the last time and the time before. Now it's gone too far and it's got to stop.'

She turned on her heels and marched out of the kitchen, her back straight, her head held high.

'Now you've done it,' said Edie.

'You hold your tongue!' snapped Cook. 'Anyone would think you were perfect.' She jerked her head towards the tray piled high with china. 'You'd better take that lot in, Janet, and hope to goodness the mistress is in a good mood.'

*

Vinnie *was* in a good mood and listened patiently while Mrs Tallant told her side of the story. Janet wasted too much time chattering to the Colonel and was neglecting her work, 'and it's not fair on the rest of us,' she concluded. 'I certainly don't intend to do her work any more. So I would be glad if you would have a word with her, ma'am.'

'I certainly will,' said Vinnie, 'and I'm sorry you have had to complain about her. She has always been a very good worker.'

The words, as always, sat uneasily on Vinnie's tongue. Even after nearly four years there were times when the role of mistress of Foxearth felt unreal. She could put herself so easily into Janet's shoes or Edie's. To discipline any of the servants was one of the least pleasant parts of her duties as Julian's wife.

'Send Janet up to me,' she said and waited uncomfortably for the maid to appear. She could still see herself very clearly as a child of five, being led into the very room where she now stood, after a scrimmage in the hop-gardens. Janet, a very new house-maid, had been kind to her then. Vinnie sighed. Those days seemed so far away. A few moments later Janet appeared, looking mildly rebellious.

'Mrs Tallant's a bit upset,' Vinnie began and saw Janet's scowl deepen. 'It is so unlike you, Janet, that I am sure you have a perfectly good reason for your absences. Mrs Tallant feels that you are wasting time and naturally she objects to setting the table herself.'

Janet's mouth settled into a tight line and Vinnie's heart sank. How did people deal with difficult servants, she wondered. 'Would you like to tell me your side of the problem?' she suggested.

Janet stared fixedly at the carpet, but said nothing.

'Please, Janet, you must understand that I need to know. I'm sure it is nothing terrible. Can't you just tell me,' said Vinnie, 'because if you don't I shall not know what to do next!'

Janet looked up, surprised by the change in Vinnie's manner, and her face relaxed. 'Well, if you promise not to breathe a word to anyone. I promised the Colonel and I don't want to go back on my word.'

'What did you promise him?'

Janet took a deep breath. 'He's had a couple of little accidents – you know.' Vinnie looked at her blankly. 'The *bed*, ma'am, I told him that we shall all be old one day and it's nothing to worry about.'

'You mean he—'

'He wet the bed and I changed the sheet for him, that's all. But I can't go telling them all in the kitchen, because I promised him. I have asked him to tell the doctor, but he won't. He says he will, but he doesn't.'

'I see. Poor Janet.'

'Oh, I don't mind, ma'am. I'd do anything for the old man, I'm that fond of him.'

'I ought to speak to the doctor. I'll have a word with him in confidence.'

'Mrs Tallant says that he ought to have a nurse if he needs so much attention,' said Janet.

'We have talked about that,' said Vinnie, 'and I feel, now you have told me this, that it might be necessary. It's not fair on you and there is no one else to do it. But I don't think the Colonel will like it one bit.'

Vinnie bit her lip, considering the problem, and Janet took a deep breath.

'The Colonel wouldn't mind so much if it were me, ma'am,' she said. 'I mean, if I was his nurse. What I mean is, I don't know what nurses have to do, but perhaps I could learn. We get on well together and he's used to me. I know it isn't my place to say this, but . . .' She hesitated.

'Go on,' said Vinnie encouragingly.

'Well, how would it be if you got another parlourmaid and I learned how to be his nurse?'

Vinnie stared at her, astonished. 'That's a very good idea, Janet! It might be the answer. I will talk to the doctor about it. Perhaps we could have a nurse in for a few weeks in order to show you how things should be done and then you could take over. Are you sure you would like to do that, Janet? It is quite a responsibility.'

'I'm quite sure, ma'am. I like looking after the Colonel.'

'I know you do, Janet, and he *is* very fond of you. I shall speak to my husband about it and see what he thinks of the idea. I will also have a word with Mrs Tallant and in the meantime if you need to spend time upstairs you may do so. But, Janet—'

'Yes, ma'am.'

'You must remember that it won't always be as easy as it is now. The Colonel may live for another five or ten years, and I hope he will because we are all very fond of him, but the various problems may get worse. Would you still want to nurse him then?'

'Yes, I would, ma'am, as long as it's not an injection. I don't know if I could do that.' She shuddered.

Vinnie nodded. 'I'm sure if anything like that were necessary, the doctor would do it. Don't worry, Janet, we will talk it over and I will send for you again. And, Janet, keep the plan secret for the time being.'

'Of course I will, ma'am.'

CHAPTER FIVE

Sammy Tulson ran what he liked to describe as 'a tight ship'. There were no slackers in his establishment and at the first misdemeanour, out they went. It was not a ship, in fact: it was a tailoring business, one of the many small private enterprises which flourished in London's East End at that time. To Sammy Tulson it was a tailoring business, but to the growing number of social workers it was yet another 'sweat shop' where women were employed in appalling conditions for long hours and low wages. It was precisely this type of establishment, as well as the larger factories, which had nudged into being the early Suffrage movement. Only when women were given the vote could they fight against the exploitation which now crushed them.

This particular establishment was no worse and no better than hundreds of others. It was situated in Cobb Street and was reached by three flights of dirty stairs and broken banisters. The room was small, but seemed even smaller than it was because so many tables, boxes and chairs were crammed into it that very little of the bare boarded floor was visible. Paint was peeling from the yellow walls and in part the brickwork showed through. The only window was permanently closed, but fresh air entered through a broken pane. A gaslight hung from the middle of the ceiling and in winter this also provided the only source of warmth. Large hooks protruded from the walls and on these the finished garments were hung.

Sammy Tulson provided ready-made dresses and coats to a large store in Kensington, but he was not a rich man, as he frequently reminded his 'girls'. He and his wife lived on the top floor of the building and the workroom doubled also as their bedroom. There were times when his wife Lena, a sickly woman, slept in late or was confined to bed for the whole day. On these occasions, work continued around her as though she did not exist.

The Tulsons were in their late fifties and their grown-up family had all fled the nest.

The small work force consisted of four women. Three of them laboured over machines all day, while the fourth sewed button-holes by hand for which she was paid by the dozen. They were Mollie Pett, the mother of three children; Meg Wilson, a single girl of seventeen; Dulcie Webb, a widow in her fifties; and elderly Sarah Nott who went by the nickname of 'Snotty' for obvious reasons.

The thirteenth of June was another humid day and by mid-morning the women were already sweating. The window faced out on to a brick wall which reflected very little light but the gas-lamp, permanently on, hissed as a background to their conversation. Mollie Pett bit off a thread, pulled the fabric from beneath the needle of the machine, turned it round and rein-serted it. She was twenty-three, with a thin freckled face and untidy ginger hair. Mollie looked across the room to the elderly woman who sat with head bent, watching the smooth progress of her needle through the material.

'How's your boy then, Snotty?' she asked. 'When's he coming out?'

The old woman shrugged. 'Maybe next month,' she said, 'if he gets remission. They promised remission, you know, and he's a good boy.'

Meg Wilson giggled. 'How can he be a good boy if he's in the nick?' she asked.

Mollie gave her a warning look. The old woman was easily upset.

'Snotty means he's been a good boy while he's been in there, don't you, Snotty?' she said. 'If he's good enough, he gets out early.'

'That's right,' said the old woman, 'and he's made me a promise not never to pinch nothing else.'

Mollie rolled her eyes in disbelief but said nothing. Dulcie's foot slowed on the treadle of the machine and she straightened her back wearily.

'Isn't it about time for a cup of tea?' she said. They all looked hopefully in the direction of the kitchen where Lena Tulson was clattering cups. Meg raised her voice. 'I said, isn't it about time for a cup of tea?'

A voice answered her from the kitchen. 'I heard you the first time. You'll get it when it's ready.'

'Miserable cow,' muttered Meg.

Dulcie was easing a sleeve into a bodice. 'Your Alex got over his cold?' she asked Mollie, who nodded.

'Always going down with colds, that boy of yours.'

'You don't have to tell me,' said Mollie. 'He's got a weak chest.'

Meg giggled again. 'Take after his father, does he, or don't you remember?'

Mollie did not take offence at this remark, but put out her tongue. 'Jealous, are you?' she asked the girl, ' 'cos I can get a chap and you can't?'

Meg snorted indignantly at this slur on her physical attractions. 'I don't want the sort of chap you get,' she said. 'Love you and leave you, that's the sort you get!'

'Vic's not left me,' Mollie protested. 'Bert did, but only 'cos he's a soldier. He *had* to go.'

'Well, Vic hasn't married you either, has he – and you have got *two* of his kids.'

'How can he marry me? He's only an apprentice, he can't afford to get married.'

'Perhaps you should have thought of that before,' said Meg.

'I did,' said Mollie calmly. 'I thought, here's a nice chap as'll make me a good husband one of these days. He's worth waiting for.'

Dulcie glanced up. 'But you liked the other one better,' she reminded her, 'the soldier. You liked him best – you said so.'

Mollie shrugged. 'What if I did? It was just one of those things. He would have married me if he could, but he got sent abroad.'

Snotty said, 'Supposing he comes back and you've married the other one?'

'Be just too bad, then, wouldn't it?' said Molly. 'I'll take whichever one asks me first.'

Meg giggled. 'Supposing neither of 'em asks you?' she said.

'Well, then, I will wait for someone else, clever-clogs! At least I'm not short of offers, like some people I could mention. I've kept my looks in spite of having three kids. Men find me attractive, you see, Meg Wilson.'

'They find you easy, you mean!'

Molly snatched up a reel of cotton and threw it the length of the table. By a lucky or unlucky chance it caught Meg on the chin and she squealed, partly in pain, partly in anger. Lena Tulson chose that moment to come into the room with a trayful of steaming mugs.

'You can pack that up,' she said sharply. 'My husband isn't paying you to lark about. You're here to work and if you can't work, we'll find someone else who can.'

Behind her back, Dulcie Webb moved her thumb and fingers together in a chattering motion.

'Is that a piece of pattern on the floor there?' Lena pointed under the table and Molly hastily retrieved the paper, reaching behind her to place it in a box full of similar pieces. She then pushed aside the cloth that lay on the table, making enough room for the tray. Noticing that there were only four mugs, she said hopefully, 'Not joining us then, Mrs Tulson?'

'No, I'm not,' said Lena. 'I'm off shopping and then I'm round to see my mother-in-law, but that's not to say you can all stop work the minute my back's turned. Sammy will be back in a few minutes, so drink up your tea and get on with your work.'

The women exchanged meaningful glances, because in spite of this obvious bluff they knew that as soon as the pubs opened, Sammy would be in the 'Bull and Bush'. They would very probably be left to their own devices until closing time, which was a welcome thought.

When at last the door closed behind Lena, Meg drew her material out from underneath the needle but continued to work the machine with her foot so that Lena, if she paused on the landing as she sometimes did, would assume they were still working. At the same time, Meg put a thumb to her nose and waggled her fingers in the direction of the stairs.

'Old bitch,' she said conversationally. 'I'll be right glad to see the back of her if I get them flowers to do. Eleven shillings a week, I'll make then.'

'*If* you get them to do,' said Snotty. 'You've been telling us about them flowers for months now.'

'I'll get them, don't you worry!' said Meg. 'Just as soon as someone drops out. My sister's had a word with the guv'nor and he's as good as promised me a job.'

'But *you* won't never make eleven shillings,' said Dulcie, 'because you're new to the work. You'll be all fingers and thumbs at the beginning, and be lucky if you make as much as we do.'

'Jealous, are we?' sneered Meg. 'Just because you'll all be stuck in this hole for the rest of your lives and I'll be in the comfort of me own home making flowers?'

'Don't torment the poor kid, Dulcie,' said Mollie. 'Perhaps she *will* get the job and then you'll look a bit sick.'

'Oh, I shan't look sick,' said Dulcie. 'Because *I* don't want to sit at home all on my own making silly little flowers. I like a bit of company and someone to have a laugh with.'

By this time they had all stopped work and were leaning back in their chairs. Snotty fanned herself with what had once been an expensive feather fan. Dulcie stood up, stretched her back and rubbed her red-rimmed eyes; then she moved over to the window and stood looking down into the alley below.

Without turning, she said, 'You want to boil up a cupful of vinegar, a chopped onion, a spoonful of honey and a drop of water. Simmer it, then mash it all up together. My Gran used to swear by that for her chest. Do your Alex good, that would, Mollie.'

Mollie pulled a face. 'Vinegar and honey,' she said. 'Ugh! I don't want to poison the poor kid.'

'You won't poison him – you'll cure his cough.'

'He hasn't got a cough; he's got a cold.'

'Same difference,' said Dulcie. Suddenly she craned her neck. 'Here, there's a motor car pulling up outside with a lady driver!'

'A motor car?'

'Here, let's have a look!'

All of them except Snotty rushed to the window and stared down.

'Crikey Moses! That's a beauty,' whistled Meg.

'Nice for some folk, isn't it?'

'I could just fancy myself in one of them,' said Dulcie, 'bowling along, terrifying the poor old horses. I'd let 'em know it, if ever I had a car.'

Snotty sniffed. 'Trust you! What have horses ever done to you, Dulcie Webb? No one wouldn't get *me* in a motor car. Death traps, they are. Not even the King himself. I'd decline his offer.'

Mollie giggled. 'Oh, you'd *decline* it, would you? How very posh of you. Hear that, girls? Snotty's going to *decline* a ride in the King's car.'

Meg laughed. 'Don't worry, Snotty! He's not likely to offer you a ride. Not his type, dear, see?'

She made an ineffectual attempt to push up the window but

failing, pressed her nose to the pane in order to get a better view.

'Oh, doesn't she look lovely, whoever she is? That'd suit me, that colour.'

'She's never coming in here!' said Meg, but as though to prove her wrong, they heard a rap downstairs on the street door. Mollie left the other two admiring the car and rushed to open the door to the workroom. She stood listening on the landing as below them they heard footsteps ascending the stairs.

Mollie rushed back inside. 'She's coming up!' she cried, and they all took up their work again in case the visitor should find them idle.

Outside, Mary Bellweather straightened her hat and knocked on the door.

'Come in!'

Inside the dingy room she found the four women bent industriously over their work.

'Is one of you ladies Mollie Pett?' she asked.

Three heads turned towards Mollie, who rose self-consciously to her feet.

'I am,' she said, 'but I ain't done nothing.'

'I'd like to talk to you,' said Mary. 'Could we talk outside, perhaps?' She indicated the landing and Mollie hesitated.

'What's it about? I don't know you. Who sent you here? I haven't—'

'Please!' said Mary, successfully hiding her own nervousness. She held the door open and reluctantly Mollie followed her outside. Mary spoke in a low voice so that their conversation could not be overheard by the women in the room.

'I've called at your home three times,' she began, 'and each time I have found your two children unattended and—'

'That's a damned lie!' cried Mollie. 'The old girl below gives an eye to them.'

'She says she doesn't,' said Mary gently. 'I understand she can't manage the stairs. She told me so herself and—'

Mollie's eyes blazed. 'What? Can't manage the stairs!' Her rage was genuine. 'I'm paying her a shilling a week to mind those kids! She never said nothing to me about not managing the stairs. The evil old cow! You wait 'till I get home tonight. She won't manage the stairs when I've done with her! For weeks now I've been paying her. For months!'

'I'm very sorry,' said Mary, 'but you really should be aware of what's happening—'

'Who the hell are you, anyway?' Mollie demanded, anger making her brave. 'Snooping into people's homes and spying! Accusing people of neglecting their kids! I'll have you know I'm a good mother to my three. Oh yes, I've got a son and all – Alexander, his name is. He gets a few hours work sometimes round the slaughter-house, washing down floors.'

'How old is he?'

'Eight, but he looks older – nearer ten, really.'

'He should be at school, then.'

'I know he *should* be at school,' retorted Mollie, 'and I *should* be at home with the two girls and my husband *should* be out earning good money to keep us all in luxury, only it's not quite like that.' She glared furiously at Mary. 'It's me on me own, with nine shillings a week for working my guts out in this hell-hole. If the boy didn't bring in a few coppers we'd be a damned sight worse off than we are now.'

She stood with her hands clenched by her sides, her head tilted defiantly. 'If you know a better way to earn a few bob, I'd be glad to hear it. Unless you'd like me to go on the streets? I've not sunk that low yet, but there's plenty of time!'

'Of course I wouldn't,' said Mary hurriedly. 'I know you've got a lot of problems and I want to help you. I represent a group of people called the Brothers in Jesus and we are a . . .' She stopped suddenly, biting back the word 'charitable'.

'Then you're not from the courts or nowhere like that?'

'The courts? No, certainly not! I'm one of a group of people who try to help wherever we can.'

Mollie frowned suddenly. 'I've seen you somewhere before,' she said. 'I thought there was something familiar about your voice. Brothers in Jesus? Don't they go down to Kent with the hoppers?'

'That's right. We do.'

'But you wasn't there last year?'

'No. My mother was ill and then she died. There was so much to do.'

Mollie's expression softened. 'I'm sorry. My Ma's dead, too. Heart, two years ago. She used to mind the kids for me; she was only fifty.' They looked at each other warily, somehow brought closer by this mutual loss.

'I have a little money,' said Mary. 'I mean, *we* have a little money . . .' She did not intend to reveal that the money she was proposing to spend was her own. 'We want to help one or two needy families until they can get back on their feet.'

Mary was picking her words carefully. 'What we propose is to give you a small regular sum each week. Enough to pay a baby-minder perhaps, so that the children would be properly cared for while you are working.'

Mollie's suspicion was giving way to incredulity. She stared at Mary, her jaw slack. 'No catch?' she asked.

'No catch,' Mary assured her.

'But why? And why us?'

Mary shrugged. 'Why not? It had to be someone. Not that you're the only ones, of course. There are other deserving families.'

'Like who?'

'I'm not at liberty to disclose names, I'm afraid,' said Mary, 'and I shall not disclose yours to anyone, except the committee. No one needs to know that I'm helping you.'

'You keep saying "I".'

'I mean "we".' Mary searched hurriedly for a reason for her slip. 'You are the family *I* have nominated for help.'

Mollie drew in a deep breath and let out a low whistle. Then an unwelcome thought occurred to her.

'It's not that my chap's mean,' she said. 'He'd give me money if he had any and he'll marry me as soon as he can. He's that fond of the girls. Always larking about with them, he is, and giving 'em sweets and everything.'

'That's very nice to hear,' said Mary. 'They certainly are lovely children. Well, I'm glad you will let us help out for a while.'

Mollie looked slightly chastened. 'How long is "for a while"?' she asked.

'Er . . . I'm not sure,' Mary improvised. 'It will be reviewed at intervals.'

'And there are lots of other families?'

'Not many. A few others.'

'Well,' said Mollie, 'I don't know what else to say really. It'll be a load off my mind to know the girls are safe and it's very kind of the Brothers in – what was it?'

'Jesus.'

'Oh, yes. Very kind. You'll bring some money each week, will you?'

'Probably. We haven't finalized all the details. We will write to you. You can read, I take it?'

'Oh yes, I'm a good reader. Top of the class I used to be – not that it did me much good. Don't need to read in this game.' She jerked her head towards the closed door.

'No, I dare say not. We will write to you then, very soon. My name's Bellweather, by the way. Mary Bellweather.'

She held out her hand and after a second's hesitation, Mollie grasped it.

'Thank you kindly, Mrs Bellweather,' she said.

'It's Miss Bellweather.'

'Miss, then.'

After the handshake neither knew what else to say, but at last Mary smiled shyly. 'I mustn't keep you from your work,' she said. 'I must be going now.'

'And I'll hear from you soon?'

'Yes, I promise. Within a week, most likely.'

'And I can tell them in there?'

Mary hesitated. 'Perhaps, but I think you should keep the name of our group a secret. Otherwise we shall be besieged by people wanting money, and we only have limited funds at our disposal.'

Mollie beamed. 'Don't you worry. I won't let on,' she said and Mary realized with a shock that in spite of her having three children Mollie Pett was little more than a child herself.

'Ooh, I can't wait to see their faces!' cried Mollie. She snatched up Mary's hand and kissed it before rushing back into the workroom. As the door closed in her face, Mary paused for a moment, listening to the buzz of excited chatter, then she made her way carefully down the stairs with the satisfying feeling that at last she was doing something really worth-while.

*

Where the grass verge widened on the right-hand side of the road between Teesbury and Farleigh, two caravans were parked and beside them a rod tent. One caravan was a simple affair, a wooden cart with a curved top made of canvas – almost a covered wagon. Beside it a heavy black horse grazed, tethered to a stake. The other was more firmly constructed, with a curved wooden roof and four large wheels. The entire vehicle was covered in an intricate design of red and yellow on a green background and there were two vents at the front which could be closed in winter or half-opened if the weather was kind enough. The windows sparkled and even the axles had been washed free of mud. This was the home of Sebastian and Amy Hearn, both now in their sixties. Their son Nation and his wife Lotty lived in the other wagon with their three children.

Behind the rod tent two more horses grazed, a large blue roan and a chestnut gelding. A dark-haired man in his thirties was washing the hooves of the roan. This was Amos, one of Nation's distant cousins whose wife had recently died. When they travelled, the tent would be folded up and stowed in one of the caravans, ready to be erected at the next stopping place. It was well designed to keep out the worst of the weather, made of willow rods set into the ground and joined together at the top; at each end the framework resembled a pumpkin. The two round ends were joined by a ridge pole and thick blankets were thrown over all but one end – here a fire would be lit and the kettles would stand on a large stone slab nearby. Orange boxes served as furniture and more orange boxes were used for storage. At the far end of the tent a thick layer of straw was spread and this, covered by a carpet, made a very satisfactory bed.

When Amos was 'on his feet again' financially he would buy another caravan. In the meantime he was content to accept the hospitality of his family which was offered willingly. It was June and hop-tying was in progress in the surrounding gardens, but the Hearns did not take advantage of this work. In September they would move to Foxearth, where they would be joined by many other Romany families and would stay for the whole of the hop-picking season. The money would be welcome, but for the rest of the year they were self-sufficient. The men would trade horses, buying where they could and grazing the animals until they came to a horse fair or made a private sale with a farmer. Lotty would make her way through the villages selling whatever knick-knacks she had accumulated. Sometimes she would sell lace which Amy had made. In the spring when the primroses were out, the children would make small baskets of twigs and line them with moss. A primrose plant would go into each basket and these sold well as Easter presents. Sometimes the men wove baskets with dyed peeled willow or found work putting new cane seats into old chairs.

The life of the Romanys was not idyllic, but whatever the hardships they were compensated for by the sense of freedom. If they met hostility, they could move on. If there was no work in one place, they could look elsewhere for it. The children's schooling was rough and ready; if there was a school in the neighbourhood they were sent to it, but these educational sessions rarely lasted more than a month or two.

Lotty was baking a large sultana pancake in the Dutch oven inside her mother-in-law's caravan. Outside on the fire a stew simmered, an aromatic mixture of vegetables, rabbit and pigeon. Tomorrow, she thought, she would send the children fishing. Eleven-year-old Seth was handy with a rod and could be relied upon to bring home a few eels and maybe a perch or mullet. She was wiping her floury hands on her apron when a pony and trap drew up and the driver, an elderly man, cracked the whip to attract her attention.

'Are you looking for work?' he cried.

'I reckon we have work enough,' she said. 'What sort of work is it?'

'My stable lad's sick and I need someone to muck down the horses. There's a shilling a day in it.'

Lotty shook her head.

'You answering for your menfolk, then?' he asked.

'They'll not work for a shilling a day,' she answered.

'There's plenty as would!' he blustered.

'Then they're welcome to it,' she responded calmly.

Lotty knew how to drive a bargain; she also knew that this man would not have approached them if there were labour to be had from any other source.

'A shilling a day,' he repeated, 'and that's not a full day's work.'

'How long, then?'

'Four hours,' he told her.

'Make it one and sixpence and they might be willing.'

He blustered a great deal more, as she had known he would. Then he offered one and threepence. She had known *that* also.

'One and threepence a day,' she said, 'for four hours work for seven days. I'll tell them.'

'To start today,' he said. 'Merryon Farm. Ask for Mr Meddows, that's me.'

She nodded.

'Only one man, mind,' he told her.

She nodded again. He gathered up the reins and then paused.

'There's a pigeon shoot Sunday week,' he said, 'on my place. We want plenty of live pigeons.'

'How much?' she asked.

'Twopence a bird to reach me by noon.'

'I will tell them. Any limit?'

'No limit. We want as many birds as we can get – and watch that fire! We don't want the grass set alight.'

Lotty smothered an angry retort. She had been tending fires all her life without mishap and anyway, the grass was too green, for May had been a rainy month.

'Want any chairs mended?' she asked. 'Any lace for your wife? Any horses for sale, sick or lame. We'll cure them.'

He gave a dismissive wave of his hand and whipped up his horse. Lotty pulled a face at his retreating back, but she knew Nation would be pleased when he got home. She was a shrewd businesswoman and he would praise her. She would never conclude a bargain unless she had to, for the sealing of bargains was men's work. Nation, she knew, would be paid one and *six*pence an hour for his work. She put her head in at the door of the caravan and the old lady grinned at her toothlessly.

'You did well,' she mumbled. 'You should have been a man.'

Lotty smiled. 'Keep an eye on that pancake, mother,' she reminded the old lady and went outside to add a few potatoes to the stew.

*

'I'll have to go the other way,' said Vinnie. 'I'm getting dizzy.' She was standing on a stool while Madeline Bressemer crouched beside her, making last-minute adjustments to the hem of her new gown made of apricot taffeta.

'It is nearly done,' the woman told her. 'One moment more and it will be finished.'

'I hope so,' said Vinnie. 'I seem to have been standing on this chair for ever!'

Madeline laughed. 'But we must get it right,' she insisted, 'and we have only a few hours because your visitors arrive tomorrow morning and you will wear the dress in the evening. The hostess must look perfect.'

'I won't look perfect,' said Vinnie, 'because I'm not tall enough.'

'Ah, but you will look tall in this gown,' Madeline told her. 'I have shaped in it in such a way – and with the little heeled shoes . . .'

Vinnie remained unconvinced. The little heeled shoes pinched her feet and the stays which went beneath the new gown stifled her. She was, however, quite determined to wear both, for tomorrow was a big occasion – the first time since their marriage that they had given a week-end house party. Vinnie had always fought shy of such occasions, maintaining that she did not have enough experience to cope with the various problems which an overnight stay involved. Finally, however, Julian had insisted and Saturday morning would see the arrival of Mary Bellweather, who would travel back to London on Sunday night; they had also invited the le Bruns. To this end, Cook had been busy all week. Vinnie, in an agony of indecision, had changed the menu twice and Cook's temper had grown very short indeed over the preceding days.

Madeline stood up and stepped back several paces. Obligingly, Vinnie began to rotate once more.

'At last we have it,' the dressmaker told her. 'Let me help you down and you can see for yourself.'

There was a large swing mirror in the corner of the room and Madeline took Vinnie's hand and led her towards it with the air of an escort leading his partner into the ball. Vinnie stared at herself in the long oval mirror and decided that she did not look at all like a successful hostess. Her hair was dishevelled from pulling the gown over her head and there was panic in her eyes. The collar, with its white lace frill, tickled her chin and she thought it made her neck look shorter than it was. The long slim sleeves bothered her and she plucked at them nervously.

'I think they are too tight,' she told the dressmaker and began to wave her arms about.

'But madame will be keeping her arms by her sides,' the dressmaker protested.

'But I might have to stretch my arms,' Vinnie insisted.

'But not like that! It is not seemly.'

Vinnie sighed as Madeline tugged down each sleeve to its proper place.

'And with the head-dress,' she promised, 'madame will look very beautiful.'

Vinnie doubted it, but she had to confess that the dress suited her. The warm colour flattered her. The front of the dress was pin-tucked and fastened with a row of tiny covered buttons which were repeated on the inside of each cuff. From the waist it fell straight at the front, while the back was carefully padded to emphasize the smallness of her waist.

'Move about in it, madame,' the dressmaker suggested. 'See how it feels. Turn and sit. You might even dance in it.'

'Not in these terrible stays,' said Vinnie and Madeline laughed again, a trilling sound. Vinnie watched her own reflection for a while longer, then gave a resigned nod. 'Yes, it will do very well, Madeline,' she told the delighted dressmaker. 'Perhaps you will stay on here and finish the hem? There is no need to go home – you may use our sewing room.'

'Thank you very much, madame. I am glad you are pleased with the gown.'

'I am *very* pleased with it,' said Vinnie, 'but now there is so much to do before tomorrow, you must excuse me. If you will just help me out of the dress?'

She glanced at the clock on the mantelpiece. She was going out and had chosen the time carefully so that Julian would not know.

*

Twenty minutes later she was on her way to collect a small posy of rosebuds. Emerging from the florist, she made her way to the churchyard and walked quickly along the path between the gravestones, then left the path and crossed the grass. The Lawrence family grave was an imposing affair of grey marble which was never allowed to become stained or dirty. Here Vinnie's small son was buried. The family gravestone bore the additional words 'Bertram Harris died at birth', for Vinnie's child had been named after her brother. Since the death of her child she had made frequent visits to the grave to replenish the flowers in the small copper vase. Today, within yards of the tombstone, she suddenly stopped and stared, for the copper vase already contained a bunch of bright orange marigolds which lent a splash of colour to the grey marble. For a moment Vinnie gazed at the simple orange flowers, then she turned and looked all around her in case the anonymous donor was nearby. She saw no one, however, except the grave-digger and with the posy of rosebuds still in her hand, she approached him. Straightening his back, he touched his forehead respectfully and leaned on his shovel. 'Nice drop of sunshine, Mrs Lawrence, ma'am,' he said.

Vinnie nodded.

'Nice weather for a funeral,' he added.

'I suppose it is.'

'Old Mrs Sampson, this is.' He jerked his head in the direction of the grave he was digging. 'Ninety-one she was, when she was took. That's how I want to go – nice and peaceful at a ripe old age. Found her with her hands clasped together, they did. Just like she was praying right up to the end. Nice touch, that.'

'Very nice,' Vinnie agreed.

'A proper God-fearing woman, was Mrs Sampson. They say she never missed a day's church except when she was child-bearing.'

Vinnie nodded.

'Though mind you, she had eleven children, so I reckon she missed eleven times.' He gave Vinnie a wink and laughed. 'But not a bad record, that. Not bad at all. Something to be proud of, that is.'

'Yes, it is.'

He took off his battered cap and fanned himself with it. 'Hot work in this sunshine,' he told her, 'and come August 'tis something cruel. I always say to my old wife, I wish folks would die from September onwards when it's more comfortable for digging!' He laughed heartily and was obviously disappointed when she did not join him.

'Those marigolds,' said Vinnie, 'on the Lawrence grave. Did you see who brought them?'

'I did. Woman it was. Put me in mind of little Rose Tully that wed Tom Bryce.'

Vinnie's eyes widened with shock. 'When did you see her?'

'Not long since. Half an hour, maybe more.'

'And it was definitely Rose Bryce?'

He shook his head. 'I wouldn't swear to it,' he told her. 'People change, but that's who she put me in mind of. Not that I've seen her for some time but it could have been her.'

'Did she say anything to you?'

'*I* said something to *her*. I said, "Here, what are you doing there? Them's not your folks".'

Vinnie swallowed. 'What did she say?' she prompted.

He returned his battered cap to his head and frowned. 'Told

me to mind my own business,' he said. ' "But it *is* my business," I told her. "That grave you are digging is your business," she says to me, "so you get on with it and stop spying on folks." "Spying," I said, "that's not a nice thing to say, not nice at all." '

Vinnie waited for him to go on, but he seemed to have come to the end of his story.

'Did she say anything else?' she urged.

'Not a bloomin' word. Not one more word!' He shrugged. 'So I thought it was best to just leave her be.'

'Yes, that was best. You did right.'

'Well, if it isn't my business, whose is it? Am I or am I not the grave-digger? Whose business is it, if it isn't mine?'

Vinnie nodded. 'Thank you,' she said and was just turning away when suddenly a thought occurred to her. 'Have you seen her before, this woman?'

He shook his head.

'So you don't know for sure who it was?'

'I think it was little Rose Tully, like I said.'

'I don't want you to tell anyone else what you have told me,' said Vinnie. 'Whoever it was, it was a private matter and I don't want you to gossip about it.'

She fumbled in her purse and held out a sixpence and his eyes gleamed. He touched his forehead twice in quick succession. 'I'm not one to gossip, ma'am, and not a word shall pass my lips. Not one word!'

'Thank you.'

'But between you and me, ma'am, it was a rum do.'

'In what way?'

'Well, I watched her, ma'am, out of the corner of my eye like. Went down on her knees, she did, and was whispering away to herself. When she got up to go, there was tears on her face, though she wiped them away so I wouldn't see 'em, but I did.'

Hastily Vinnie closed her eyes to hide the anguish she felt at this piece of news. When she opened them, he was watching her curiously.

'Remember,' she said, 'you must speak of this to nobody. I have paid you well.'

'You have that, ma'am, and I will remember.'

'You had best get on with your work, then,' Vinnie told him and he obeyed without argument.

Vinnie looked at the posy in her hands and then at the

marigolds. With trembling fingers, she lifted out the marigolds and laid them on the grave, then knelt to unwind the raffia holding the rosebuds together to arrange all the flowers carefully in the copper vase before returning it to its former position. With a few words of her own to her departed child, she turned and hurried away. The grave-digger, pausing again in his work, shook his head in bewilderment at her retreating figure. He took out the sixpence, flicked it into the air, caught it neatly and returned it to his pocket. Then he took up his spade again and began to dig.

*

The weekend entertainment started unexpectedly when Mary Bellweather drove up to the front door of Foxearth in a maroon Wolseley car. It was the first time that any motor vehicle had been parked outside the house and the word soon spread, bringing Vinnie and Julian hurrying down the steps, closely followed by the household staff. They clustered round eagerly while Mary, resplendent in hat, swathes of veiling, a long motoring coat and long gauntlet gloves, proudly displayed her knowledge. With the air of a conjurer about to perform a new trick, she drew their attention to the three-and-a-half horsepower engine with its three-speed gearbox, transmission and suspension. None of this meant much to any of her listeners, but her enthusiasm was infectious and, invited to examine it for themselves, they were soon exclaiming over the delights of the dark red paintwork edged with gold and the dark brown leather upholstery. Edie squeezed the bulb which sounded the horn and made them all jump. Mary demonstrated the twin brass carriage lamps and the steering wheel which had replaced the earlier tiller.

After a while Julian observed loudly, for the benefit of the kitchen staff, that no work was being done, but nobody heeded this remark. Mary then offered to give Vinnie a ride in the motor car, but just as they took their places side by side the le Bruns arrived in their brougham, and the idea had to be temporarily abandoned, for it was almost certain that the unfamiliar noise of the car's engine would terrify the horses. Introductions were made all round while the staff reluctantly returned to their duties, then Tim Bilton led away the horses and the guests were taken indoors for refreshments. Their luggage was taken up to their rooms. Mary, as the only owner of a motor car, became the centre of attention, a fact which suited Vinnie very well.

Later on they all strolled in the garden in the June sunshine, Mary accompanied by Julian on one side and by William le Brun on the other. Vinnie found herself escorted by Clive and the two of them conversed very agreeably on a number of subjects. She found him an interesting person to talk to; he had travelled extensively in Europe as a young man and did his best to convince her that without a trip to France – to Paris, at least – her education would not be complete. After a light lunch, the guests were taken upstairs to pay a brief courtesy visit to the Colonel – visitors tired him – and then the party split up once again. Mary, who had learned to ride as a child, seized the opportunity to explore the surrounding countryside from the broad back of Bracken, the Lawrences' elderly but good-natured carriage horse. As earlier she was accompanied by Julian and William, who rode the other two horses and Vinnie – by now feeling more confident and at ease – was piqued to note their obvious admiration for her. She thus found herself again in the company of Clive le Brun, who openly endorsed her own private opinion that horse riding was a 'very overrated pastime'. Given the chance to choose an afternoon's entertainment, he told Vinnie, he elected to play chess and was appalled to learn that she knew nothing of the game. To her dismay he immediately decided to teach her and a small table and two chairs were carried out on to a shady part of the terrace. The chessmen were set out, the intricacies of the game carefully and clearly explained and, much to Vinnie's surprise, she at once grasped the basic moves and actually began to enjoy herself. When, two hours later, the others arrived back from their ride they found Vinnie and Clive engrossed in their game and reluctant to abandon it.

Dinner was to be served at eight o'clock and the guests went into the dining room promptly at five minutes to the hour. They seated themselves at the table which glittered with silver and glass, all of which reflected the light of candles in the four matching pairs of candelabra gracing the white damask cloth. Vinnie tried hard to appear relaxed, but as Janet brought in the turtle soup anxiety showed in her eyes and her smile was forced. She had worried needlessly, however, for it was delicious and everyone was obviously enjoying it. As the conversation began to flow, her apprehension gradually evaporated and she was able to meet Julian's triumphant smile, from the far end of the table, with one of heartfelt thankfulness.

The talk turned inevitably to the war and Clive le Brun put forward the view that Kitchener was not necessarily the best man for the job.

'Roberts was doing a reasonable job under difficult circumstances,' he said. 'But now it's a different war altogether. The Boers are born guerrillas and they're on their home ground, so to speak. When you think of the vast areas involved, fifteen thousand men are a drop in the ocean. Take Byng for instance – back in February he had twenty-five miles of front to cover and only two hundred men! They can do what they please, the Boers, which is exactly what they are doing. They laugh at us – and they can go on laughing for as long as we stay in their Godforsaken country.'

'The Free Staters will never give up until we capture de Wet,' commented William.

'None of the blighters will ever give up,' said Julian. 'The Middleburg Conference established that, if it did nothing else.'

'I don't understand what went wrong,' said Mary. 'I thought last October that the war was as good as finished.'

'You weren't alone in that thought,' responded Clive. 'I believe most of the Boers thought so too.'

'Probably hoped so,' said Mary. 'It has gone on for far too long. Neither side can win and the whole war has become impossible.'

Vinnie offered no opinions. She understood little of the situation and was afraid of revealing her ignorance, but her admiration for Mary grew as she watched and listened. But at least, she thought, the turtle soup was a success and was then ashamed of her concern for such mundane matters. Next week, she decided, she would make a sustained effort to improve her mind. She would read more books – there were plenty to choose from in the library – and she would study the editorial columns of *The Times*. Next time they had guests, she too would enter into the conversation and would astonish them all with her keen grasp of any subject which came under discussion. Her recent success at chess had given her new confidence and she glanced at Clive, recalling his patience and unexpected tact throughout the 'lesson'. She thought guiltily that she had considered him rather taciturn on earlier acquaintance, but recently had cause to revise her earlier judgement of him.

'We've always been deficient in horse power,' William was saying. 'The Boers are natural horsemen and they are nearly all mounted. These guerrilla raids – they ride in, demolish a stretch of railway or a bridge and ride off again in a cloud of dust! Only cavalry can hope to follow – let alone catch – the beggars, and we don't even have enough good horses.'

Julian shrugged. 'If we had the horses we wouldn't have enough trained riders. No, it's a hopeless task and I wouldn't be in Kitchener's shoes. Roberts is well out of it, in my opinion.'

Seeing that everyone had finished the soup, Vinnie gave Janet a nod and the dishes were quickly cleared. The next course consisted of salmon steaks in a cream sauce and Vinnie watched this being served with her fingers crossed under the napkin which lay across her lap. However, her luck was holding and that dish, too, was perfectly prepared – the fish hot and the sauce smooth and delicately flavoured. Vinnie wondered gratefully if Julian would agree to give Cook a small rise in salary, and made up her mind to talk to him about it later.

Soon talk turned to Mary's new motor car and then to cars in general. Mary had strong views about the new Daimler.

'They say it is to be named after a little girl,' she said. 'The daughter of the Daimler agent – or is it the designer? I forget. I must say that to me Mercedes doesn't sound much like a motor car; it is far too feminine.'

'It's a very pretty name though,' protested Vinnie, 'but not English, surely?'

'Austrian,' Mary told her. 'Mercedes Jellinek, to be precise!'

'We must be thankful that they didn't call it the Daimler Jellinek!' laughed Julian. 'But do you really believe it will catch on – motoring, I mean?'

'It already *has* caught on,' said Mary, a trace of indignation in her voice. 'The King himself is said to be interested and Queen Alexandra has a small electric car of her own which she drives around the grounds of Sandringham.'

'But only for fun,' said Clive. 'Surely she doesn't go anywhere in it?'

Mary had to admit the truth of this remark. 'But she will do, you'll see. It's early days yet and the sport is in its infancy.'

William seized on her unfortunate turn of phrase. 'So you admit it *is* a sport and does not constitute a serious challenge to the horse carriage?'

Mary had the grace to laugh at her own slip and while she searched for an answer, Julian came to her rescue.

'I imagine man once regarded the riding of horses merely as a sport,' he said. 'Maybe it was only later that it was decided to use them as beasts of burden.'

Mary looked at him gratefully and Vinnie thought she saw a spark of sympathy leap between them. Beside her, Clive leaned back in his chair and gave one of his rare smiles.

'This salmon is very good,' he said. 'Your cook is to be congratulated, Vinnie. I must say it is pleasant to dine out and be feasted so royally.'

'We rarely entertain,' William admitted. 'We are just two dull bachelors and food is not high on our list of priorities.'

The two women at once protested, as he had hoped they would, that he and his father were not in the least dull.

Vinnie was drinking more than she usually did. She had hired an extra manservant for the occasion (as well as an extra pair of hands for the washing-up), and he was performing his duties a little too well, for her wineglass was never allowed to remain even half-empty and she was unable to judge how much she was actually drinking. As the meal progressed, a claret was served and later a monbazillac. By the time they reached the port, Vinnie's mind was delightfully hazy and she had relaxed to the point of complete insouciance and was quite oblivious of the severe glances Julian was casting in her direction.

Mary was holding everyone enthralled with an account of her work in Whitechapel. There was nothing patronizing in her attitude, but Vinnie nevertheless felt a prickle of resentment at her description of a community to which Vinnie had once belonged. She sat forward, her elbows on the table, chin on her clasped hands and allowed a scowl to darken her face.

'The saddest thing is that we know we cannot win,' Mary told them. 'The squalor and the degradation can never be wholly removed, only alleviated. Groups like ours do what they can all over London, but this can only brush the surface of the problem . . . We cannot feed all the hungry nor house all the homeless, nor can we convert all the criminals to the straight and narrow. All we *can* do is help a few individuals as best we can with the meagre means at our disposal. We can buy a few medicines for the sick and distribute a few second-hand clothes – but the chances are that the wretches will sell or pawn what we have given them the moment our backs are turned.'

Mary held out her hands in an elegant gesture of helplessness. 'What is the point,' she demanded, 'of buying cough syrup for a bronchitic mother who sells it in order to buy food for her children? It is a quite hopeless situation!'

'What would *you* do then?' said Vinnie. 'If you were a mother and your children were starving? Could you swallow the syrup?' All eyes were turned on her, but suddenly she was not embarrassed by the attention.

'Well, I—' Mary stammered slightly, taken aback by the interruption. 'I really don't know. I . . .'

'You would be a funny sort of mother if you could,' said Vinnie. 'You see, poor people are funny like that. They put their children first. When there is not much to eat, the mothers pretend they have had their meal and share whatever food there is among the others. Oh yes, husbands included! They reckon the man has got to keep fit in order to do his work, you see.'

'Mary didn't mean to suggest—' began Julian.

'How do you know what she meant?' said Vinnie. She sat upright now, her back stiff and her face flushed with unnatural courage. 'She can talk for herself, can't she?'

'Of course I can,' said Mary hastily, giving Julian a warning look. 'I didn't intend to cast a slur of any kind on these people. I am sure they do what they do from the best of motives, but it still makes it difficult for us to help them.'

'Perhaps they don't want to be helped,' said Vinnie, growing terribly reckless. She sensed that already she had said too much and gone too far and that Julian would be furious with her. She knew that the best thing would be to remain silent, yet some dreadful perversity drove her on. 'Perhaps they like being poor and dirty and horrible,' she said. 'Perhaps they don't want rich folk turning up in their expensive cars to give them a shabby old coat two sizes too big—'

'Vinnie, stop it!' cried Julian, horrified at the turn of events. 'You don't know what you are saying!'

'Of course I do!' cried Vinnie. 'I know what it's like, remember? Poor people have got feelings, you know. Poor people have pride just the same as you and Mary and others like you. It's not easy accepting charity – did you ever think of that, Mary? It's hard to admit that you can't care properly for those you love. I'm sure you mean well—'

'Well, *thank* you!' said Mary icily, her face scarlet.

'—but sometimes it makes things a whole lot worse,' Vinnie went on. 'My Mum once accepted a coat for me from the "Sally

Ally" and my Dad went mad when he came home. Gave my Mum
hell, he did. Snatched the coat off me and slung it out of the back
door into the rain. I can see it now – my Mum crying because he'd
hit her and my brother Bertie yelling at him—'

She choked over the name and stopped abruptly. Having
half-risen from her seat in her indignation, she now subsided,
shattered by the sudden silence which had fallen over the room.
She dared not look at her husband and was ashamed to look at
anyone else.

'I didn't know you had a brother,' said Clive calmly. 'You are
full of surprises, Vinnie! Do you have any other family?'

Vinnie stared at him while she tried to gather her confused
thoughts. He seemed unaware of the fact that she had made an
exhibition of herself and she was dimly aware that he was trying to
avert total disaster.

'A sister,' she whispered. 'I had a sister called Emmeline, but
she died.'

'I'm so sorry. And Bertie? Is he still alive?'

Tears filled her eyes and threatened to spill down her cheeks.
Then she raised her eyes to Clive's face and read there, as clearly
as though he had spoken, a demand that she control herself. He
was willing her to respond and with a tremendous effort, she
forced back the tears and steadied her voice.

'My brother is with the Army in India,' she told him. 'At least,
we believe so. There is a chance that he may have been wounded,
but we don't know anything for certain yet.'

'India is a long way away,' he said. 'Communications are still
most unsatisfactory. I hope you hear better news of him eventually.'

'Thank you.'

They stared at each other, seemingly unaware of the rest of the
table where Julian was recovering from shock, Mary was trying to
disguise the extent of her anger and William was searching his
mind desperately for a new and innocuous topic of conversation.
Then Clive beckoned the stricken manservant, who hurried
forward with the coffee pot.

'A little more coffee, Vinnie?' asked Clive and she nodded
gratefully. The manservant moved round the table and they all
accepted more coffee, but as they sipped it, another long silence
fell. Again it was Clive who broke it, turning to Vinnie with a
deceptively innocent smile.

'Could I talk about bees,' he asked, 'without risk of retaliation?'

After a stunned silence, Vinnie burst out laughing and following a moment's hesitation, everyone laughed with her. Miraculously, the evening was saved.

*

The following morning Vinnie apologized to Mary for her behaviour at dinner and Mary accepted the apology most charmingly.

The little house party spent an agreeable morning playing croquet and the exercise sharpened their appetites. Lunch was a picnic, served beside the river in the Lawrences' favourite spot below the lock. They made a delightful picture, the ladies in their pastel dresses (Vinnie in primrose and Mary in lavender) and the men resplendent in white flannels, striped blazers and boaters. The sun was very hot and the ladies were grateful for the shade of their parasols. The water glinted and sparkled and occasionally a fish jumped after a fly.

The weekend's entertainment concluded with a leisurely stroll along the river bank and on this occasion Vinnie did at least start out in the company of her husband, while Mary walked with the le Bruns. Before long, however, Mary had called back to Julian to see a clump of forget-me-nots and then again to note the cuckoo's cry which was lengthening with the summer.

'Don't you know the old superstition?' she teased him. 'If we run now until we cannot hear him, counting the calls as we go, we shall live that many years longer!'

Julian, Vinnie noted, made no protest as Mary took his hand and made him run along the river bank, with William in pursuit, until they were out of sight round a bend in the river. The sight of her husband holding hands with another woman shocked her.

'High spirits, nothing more,' said Clive, as though reading her mind. They began to walk on in the direction taken by the others.

'Mary is charming, isn't she?' said Vinnie, without quite knowing why.

'Very charming and very independent.'

Vinnie had hoped for a compliment for herself but she was disappointed.

'My wife was a very independent woman,' Clive said suddenly. 'She became involved in this question of Women's Suffrage and attended that fateful Trafalgar Day free speech meeting – quite

without my knowledge or approval, I may say – and was lucky to
escape serious injury. I doubt if you are old enough to remember
it? It was in eighty-six.'

Vinnie shook her head. 'I was only four then,' she told him.

He looked at her in surprise. 'So young! I had not realized.
Foxearth must have been quite a responsibility to take over at
sixteen.' He plucked a stem of 'ragged robin' and presented it to
her. 'A token of my esteem and admiration for a gracious – though
very young – hostess!'

'Thank you, kind sir!' she said with a laugh and a small mocking
curtsey.

They soon caught up with the rest of their little party and then
all turned back in the direction of Foxearth.

'There's a pigeon shoot at Merryon next week,' Clive told
Julian. 'I can get you an invitation if you would care to come
along.'

Julian explained that he would be away on business – investi-
gating a new strain of hops being developed in Hertfordshire – so
must turn down the invitation. William, it seemed, was also
otherwise engaged and Mary, of course, would be in London.

'Vinnie might care to join me then?' Clive suggested, but she
shook her head.

'I don't think I could actually shoot at a bird,' she confessed. 'I
should feel so terribly sorry if I killed it.'

To Vinnie's surprise, Julian slipped an arm round her waist
with a gesture of great affection. 'My wife has a very soft heart,' he
said.

'And probably a very poor aim!' Vinnie added. 'If I did shoot a
pigeon, it would only be by mistake!'

Julian's arm tightened round her and he kissed her lightly. He
was not normally at all demonstrative in company and Vinnie
knew with sickening certainty that he was doing it to arouse
Mary's interest. As he did so, Mary turned her head away, but not
before Vinnie had caught sight of her expression and read the
pain glittering in the dark eyes. Mary and Julian? thought Vinnie
frantically. Oh no, it could not, *must* not, be so.

*

That night when the guests had gone home, Vinnie lay silent in
bed beside her husband until at last she could bear it no longer.

'Did you enjoy the weekend, Julian?' she asked.

'Some of it was pleasant enough,' he said. 'I thought the staff did very well and the food was excellent.'

Vinnie took a deep breath. 'You and Mary seemed to get on very well together,' she said.

'She's a charming and refined woman,' said Julian.

Vinnie sensed that he stressed the word 'refined', though she could not be certain. 'I thought William seemed very attracted to her,' she suggested.

'Most men would find her attractive.'

'Then Mary must have enjoyed herself very much with two handsome men in attendance.'

'I hope she did,' said Julian. 'Perhaps it made up to her for your bad behaviour.'

Vinnie had been expecting this attack, yet it still hurt her, for the fact that it was well deserved did not make it any easier to bear.

'I apologized to Mary for my outburst,' she said. 'I am sure someone as good as she is would find it in her heart to forgive me.'

'Now you're sneering at her,' said Julian. 'Perhaps you are jealous of her?'

Vinnie felt a flutter of anxiety. 'Should I be?' she asked.

'Of course not. Anyway, you had Clive to keep you company.'

'Yes. He was *very* good company,' Vinnie told him. 'And he managed to teach me to play chess.'

She wondered if she could make Julian jealous and added, 'It's easy to see the attraction an older man holds for a younger woman.'

Hopefully she glanced at his face, but it was too dark to see him properly although the comment did seem to have silenced him. Serve him right, she thought miserably. She was aware that a growing anger simmered dangerously a little way below the surface and tried again.

'Clive suggested that we shall be receiving an invitation from the le Bruns before long. That will be pleasant, won't it?'

'If we are able to accept the invitation of course it will be pleasant,' he corrected her. 'But we are approaching the busiest time of the year.'

'Well, if you can't go,' said Vinnie, 'I will.'

'You will do no such thing.' His voice hardened and he half sat up in bed. She knew he was glaring at her in the darkness. 'It would be quite improper for you to accept the invitation on your own.'

'I don't see why,' argued Vinnie. She knew, of course, that what he said was perfectly true and she certainly had no real intention of going alone. She also knew that she was behaving rather childishly, but she now felt committed to her line of argument.

'You don't see why?' said Julian. 'That's because you don't see a number of things you should. You don't see, perhaps, that it was wrong of you to hang back whenever we went out so that you could be with Clive le Brun.'

Vinnie gasped at this patent distortion of the facts, but before she could rally her thoughts he went on, 'You don't see that you should have accompanied us on our ride—'

'But you know I hate riding,' said Vinnie. 'I can never keep up. It would have spoilt the ride for everyone else.'

'That's beside the point. You are the hostess and if your guests want to go riding, you should be prepared to accompany them.'

'One of the guests did not want to go riding,' Vinnie retorted. 'Clive was obviously not very enthusiastic about the idea. Surely, if I had insisted on accompanying you, he would have been bound to come with us too. That is not a very considerate way to treat a guest, is it?'

The conversation was becoming a mere battle of words between them and with a sudden movement, Julian turned over in the bed and lay facing away from her.

'I don't want to talk about it any longer,' he said. 'I didn't enjoy it very much, thanks to you, and I shall think very carefully before we invite anyone over again.'

Vinnie could think of no answer and for a few minutes said nothing. Stubbornly she sought in her mind for a way to prolong the argument, however.

'I do wish we could have a car, Julian,' she said. 'I thought Mary's Wolseley quite charming.'

'For heaven's sake, Vinnie, we don't *need* a motor car,' cried Julian. 'We have plenty of horses and a brougham that's still in perfect working order. Besides, you know what I think of motor cars. They are noisy, smelly and dangerous!'

'You didn't say that to Mary,' Vinnie persisted. 'You admired it with the rest of us and pretended to like it.'

'That,' he said cuttingly, 'is because, unlike you, I do not choose to offend my guests. Now, Vinnie, I would like to get some sleep. Is this conversation over, do you think?'

'I suppose so,' she said sulkily.

'Thank you. Then I shall wish you goodnight.'

There was another pause while Vinnie wondered whether to provoke a full-scale row between them. Such a confrontation might 'clear the air', but she was afraid she might say something she would later regret. Quarrels were a part of every marriage, she knew, but theirs were becoming more frequent and they no longer came together again with tears and kisses. The hostility lingered, faded and was finally forgotten – it was never resolved.

Vinnie felt frustrated, helpless and utterly out of her depth. Her memories of her parents' quarrels were crystal clear – a violent, physical struggle with screaming and abuse, followed by a slamming door as her father left for the 'Jug and Bottle'. Later there would be recriminations of a quieter nature and sometimes an apology or even an embarrassed hug. That way did not solve anything either, Vinnie reflected, but at least her parents had expressed their feelings in a direct and honest way. Her confrontations with Julian seemed no more than wordy games and since he had a superior way with words, she was invariably routed. She resented the fact that, with so much still needing to be said, he could now turn over and go to sleep, while she would lie awake for hours, unable to reach a merciful oblivion. I hate you, Julian Lawrence, she thought, but knew it to be untrue. If she really hated him, it would be so much easier to bear his disapproval. Perhaps *he* hated *her*! Vinnie sighed deeply and wished Mary had not been included in the house party. Turning on her side, she said hopefully, 'Goodnight, Julian,' but there was no reply.

CHAPTER SIX

A crow flying from Maidstone to Wateringbury at the end of June would have seen very little of the sun-baked earth below, through the high rows of hops which all but covered the entire area, stretching acre upon acre over the undulating Weald. The hop-gardens edged each road and grew down the lush slopes of the valley through which the river Medway flowed. From his vantage point, forty to fifty feet in the air, the crow might be forgiven for assuming the crop to be a good one. Some of the twelve-foot poles were already hidden by the vigorous plants which had reached the top and continued on their way along the linking wires. But all was not well, as Vinnie knew. The dense green foliage was the result of too much rain earlier in the year and the plants had reached the tops of the poles too early. To have one or two plants per acre in that position by the end of June was considered a good sign. More than that and the growers became anxious as the plants themselves became 'owzy'. Owzy hops were small hops well hidden by the dense leaves which surrounded them. They were difficult to pick, weighed light and were not at all popular with the pickers whose wages would suffer and who would grumble accordingly. Now the very warm weather had brought about an infestation of vermin – flies and lice – which required frequent applications of Dyseleine. All over Kent the hop-growers prayed for warmer nights and a few heavy showers of rain. And at Foxearth, if nowhere else, a few traces of downy mildew had been discovered, so half-a-dozen schoolgirls had been recruited to walk along the rows after school and pluck off any of the leaves on which the dark spores had appeared.

However, these were the hazards of a normal farming year and Vinnie knew that Julian was not unduly dismayed. What did concern him, however, was the lower price he might receive for his final crop. That, she knew, was the real threat and she wondered how many more seasons must pass before he would be forced to follow the example of other farmers and grub up some of the hops. Vinnie could not imagine Foxearth without hops. Would the time ever come when the industry was dead, as many people prophesied?

With an effort she put the idea behind her, for she had other worries of her own. She was on her way to see Rose Bryce and was not looking forward to the meeting at all. She had pretended to Julian that she was going into Maidstone on a shopping expedition and had in fact set off that way, but had then cut back through the lanes and was now heading in the opposite direction. She carried a light whip, but did not use it on the horses for she was in no hurry to reach her destination. She hoped that Tom Bryce would not be around – he should in fact be working. Vinnie had only a vague idea of what she hoped to say to Rose; she wanted to help in some way, but did not know how. Whatever she did, it would have to be done in secret and Julian must not know about it. Their relationship was already suffering because of her childlessness and she had no wish to put a further strain on it.

Vinnie followed the Tonbridge road to Wateringbury and then turned left down the hill. At the bottom she was delayed for a while by a motor car which had broken down. A growing crowd of onlookers was enjoying the discomfiture of an elderly man, who sat in the car staring straight ahead of him while his young chauffeur-mechanic struggled with the intricacies of the internal combustion engine. Several carts and carriages were held up in both directions, but at last Vinnie was able to pass them and be on her way once more. When she reached the village, she made enquiries as to the Bryces' whereabouts and was soon dismounting outside their cottage. She tethered the horse, opened the rickety gate and walked up to the front door. It was Mrs Bryce who opened to her knock and Vinnie stared at her speechlessly. The old woman had hardly changed at all and Vinnie's first instinct was to fling herself into her arms. Mrs Bryce had brought her up from the age of five and although she had never called her anything but 'Mrs Bryce', she was the only 'mother' Vinnie could really remember.

'Please,' Vinnie began, 'I must see Rose! Is she there, Mrs Bryce? Will she speak to me?'

The older woman's expression changed from delighted recognition to suspicion. 'She's not here,' she said. 'What do you want with her?'

'I want to talk to her,' said Vinnie, 'on an important matter which I cannot discuss with anyone else. When will she be back? Can you tell me that?'

'I wish I knew,' said the old woman with a sigh. 'I really don't know.'

'Mrs Bryce, I want to help!' Vinnie burst out. 'I have heard rumours – I don't want to talk about them – and I want to help. I know Tom won't listen so I thought I could talk to Rose. I dare not be away from home too long, however. Do you know where Rose has gone?'

'I don't,' said Mrs Bryce. She hesitated. 'Do you want to come in? I don't know if I should ask you or not.' She looked helplessly at Vinnie, who was equally at a loss.

'These rumours,' said Mrs Bryce. 'They're about Tom, I suppose? About his drinking?'

'Yes, I am afraid so. I just don't understand it,' said Vinnie.

The older woman opened the door wider. Vinnie ducked her head and went in to the low-ceilinged room that served as both kitchen and living room. A small scullery led off it. Vinnie's glance took in the faded curtains and threadbare linoleum. There were no cushions on the chairs, no bird in the window and no cat on the hearth. Altogether it was a cheerless room. Mrs Bryce, seeing her expression, shrugged.

'It's a roof over our heads,' she said, 'if nothing more. Poor Rose, she has almost given up and you can't blame her, poor lass. If only Tom—' She stopped and pressed her lips firmly against the temptation to blurt out what was in her heart, then motioned to a chair and Vinnie sat down.

'You are looking very grand, Vinnie,' said Mrs Bryce. 'Very elegant. The grand life suits you.' Vinnie forgave the trace of bitterness in her voice. 'Are you happy, Vinnie?'

Vinnie hesitated, then nodded. 'But I would be much happier,' she said, 'if you and Rose and Tom and—' She could not go on, unable to put into words the overwhelming despair which she felt.

'I know, I know,' said Mrs Bryce. 'But what's to be done, Vinnie? He's my own son, but I can't do anything with him. I am that ashamed of the way he's carrying on. If his father were alive today, he would die of shame, I know he would.'

'It isn't your fault,' said Vinnie. 'You must not blame yourself.'

'Then who is to blame?' cried the old woman. 'That's what I

would like to know. He was a good boy, a good son and a good husband.'

'I know,' agreed Vinnie. 'He was all those things.'

'But not any more!' cried Mrs Bryce. 'He's a different person altogether, even a stranger to me. Rose has gone to look for him now – I wake up every morning and wonder what terrible things the day will bring.'

Vinnie looked at her in alarm. 'Oh yes,' Tom's mother said. 'You can look at me like that! I tell you he's a changed man. He drinks that heavily, there's no talking to him, no reasoning with him at all and these last few weeks' – she lowered her voice a little – 'he's been violent.'

'Violent?' Vinnie could not hide her shock.

'Yes, there's no other word for it. He thrashed poor little Tom until he was black and blue. If we had anywhere to go to, we would have gone and taken the children with us, but there's nowhere.'

'But that doesn't sound like Tom!' cried Vinnie. 'He's not a violent man.'

'The drink has changed him,' Mrs Bryce told her. 'He hit Rose the other day and broke one of her teeth. She won't tell you though – she's that loyal and she's a plucky girl, but my heart bleeds for this little family and I feel so helpless.' She sat down wearily.

Vinnie sat opposite for a while, deep in thought, digesting this new and terrible information. Then she said, 'Mrs Bryce, where exactly has Rose gone?'

'She's gone out to look for him. He didn't come home last night; went out trapping pigeons for this shoot on Sunday. Poor Rose, she sat up all night waiting for him and this morning at first light she went out to look for him. She hasn't come back yet. I sent the children off to school and I've been here ever since waiting . . . It's the waiting that gets me down. The "knowing" I can cope with, but the waiting frightens me. Supposing—' she shrugged her shoulders. 'He could even be dead for all we know.'

'Please!' cried Vinnie. 'Don't talk that way.' She stood up and clumsily put her arms round the old woman's shoulders and hugged her. 'You must not think such dreadful things – I'm sure Tom isn't dead.'

'Oh, Vinnie, sometimes I almost hope—'

'Hush, don't say it!' said Vinnie. 'You know you don't mean it.'

The old woman burst into tears, threw her apron over her face and began to sob. Vinnie knelt on the floor beside her. 'Don't give up,' she begged. 'I am sure there is something we can do to save him. That's why I'm here. I want to give Rose some money – it's all I can think of. I have some jewellery I can sell – presents to me from Julian.'

The old woman continued to sob. 'Rose will never take it,' she cried. 'Never! I know her as well as I know myself and she's a proud girl. She blames you, you know, says it was as much your fault as Tom's.'

'She's quite right,' said Vinnie. 'I *am* as much to blame, and I have never pretended otherwise. But there is no turning back the clock, Mrs Bryce, and neither I nor Tom can undo what happened. All I can do is try to help in some way. You must try to persuade Rose to take the money – or perhaps I could give it to you?'

The old woman jerked up her head in alarm. 'No, no!' she protested. 'I wouldn't dare to take it. Rose would never forgive me, nor Tom either!'

'But what will become of you all?' cried Vinnie, anguished. 'If Tom loses his job, you will lose this cottage.'

'I know.' Mrs Bryce fumbled for a handkerchief and blew her nose. 'But we must trust in God. I never thought to say it, for I was never much of a churchgoer, but now I feel He is our only hope. Trust in the Lord, they say. Well that's what we shall have to do; it's all we have left, Vinnie.'

Her sobs gradually lessened, much to Vinnie's relief and when she had composed herself a little, Vinnie said lamely, 'And Tommy and Bertha and the others? How are they all?'

'Well enough, I dare say,' said Mrs Bryce, 'though little Sam, bless him, will never be very strong. It's his lungs.'

Vinnie nodded. 'Are they doing well at school?' she asked, hoping to steer the old woman on to a more cheerful topic of conversation.

'Yes, they're doing very well. That is, all but little Sam. He is away so much, you see and misses so much schooling. The teacher says he may never catch up.'

Vinnie nodded. 'Is it a good school? Are they happy?'

'Happy enough, I think, bless them! I think they are happier at school than they are at home just now.'

Vinnie frowned suddenly. 'How is it that Tom was out trapping pigeons yesterday? Wasn't he at work?'

'He's off sick,' said his mother. 'He collapsed at work three days ago and they took him to the doctor. Two days rest, the doctor said, but would not say what was wrong with him. They don't know, you see, Vinnie. These doctors aren't as clever as they pretend.'

'Is he ill, do you mean?'

Mrs Bryce shrugged. 'The doctor didn't say. Didn't give him any medicine; no tablets, nothing. And Mr Lidden paid the doctor, you know. Tom's guv'nor paid him out of his own money! Surprised everyone, that did, because Lidden's a God-fearing man and can't stand drunkenness.'

Vinnie stared into the grate where the ashes of the last winter fire still lay. 'Perhaps I ought not to wait,' she said. 'If Rose has found him and brings him back – they won't want me to be here.'

'Perhaps not,' said Mrs Bryce reluctantly. 'Maybe you should go, Vinnie. Perhaps I'd best say nothing about you coming.'

Vinnie hesitated. 'But then how can I help you?' she said. 'I must talk to Rose. Perhaps you could ask her to get in touch with me somehow? To come to Foxearth, maybe, but tell her not to let Julian see her. No, better still, tell her to send me a note. Lotty Hearn could bring it.'

The old woman looked puzzled. 'The gipsy woman?'

Vinnie nodded. 'She is very discreet,' she said. She stood up and straightened her dress with small nervous movements, for now that she had decided to go she suddenly wanted to be out of the cottage as quickly as possible.

'And you will tell her?' she asked. 'You promise me? You will tell her that I came and ask her to get in touch?'

'I will.'

They went out of the cottage and along the path, where Vinnie unhitched the horse and turned the trap round. Then she came back to the gate where Mrs Bryce still waited and impulsively she leaned forward to kiss the old woman. 'I still love you,' she whispered suddenly, 'and I am so sorry I have caused all this heartache.'

They clung together for a moment and the old woman said, 'Vinnie, the baby, Tom's baby? I'd never say anything to Rose, but what was it like?'

'A little boy,' said Vinnie, 'with golden hair.'

'Ah. He took after you then, Vinnie?'

Vinnie nodded. 'He never did open his eyes,' she said, 'so I don't know what colour they were.'

'Never mind,' said Mrs Bryce. 'Maybe it's best not to know these things when you lose them. I lost a little girl before I had Tom. You never really know them, yet you never forget them, do you?'

Vinnie swallowed hard and turned abruptly to climb back into the driving seat and pick up the reins. 'No, you don't forget them,' she replied.

Mrs Bryce nodded and waved a hand in farewell as the pony leaned into the harness and the trap rolled away.

'I just wondered,' she said.

*

The day of the shoot dawned bright and clear and at half-past nine the long meadow below Merryon Farm was dotted with people preparing for the day's event. A hay wagon stood in one corner of the field just inside the gate, and from this bales of hay were being taken to various points along the field where they would provide hides and windbreaks for those taking part in the shoot. In front of the line of windbreaks was a dense hedge and on the other side of this wicker traps containing the birds would be set. Beyond the hedge, the ground ran level again until it reached a small wood. This was the haven to which the freed pigeons would inevitably fly and thus the line of their flight was predetermined.

Along the hedge which ran from the gate trestle tables were being set up; later, barrels of beer and cider would stand side by side along their length. Glasses had been hired from the 'Barley Mow' in the village and members of their staff would be on hand during the day. Still further over the bonfire was being prepared and a side of beef had been ordered from the best butcher in Tunbridge Wells. Mr Meddows was a generous host and no expense had been spared to make the day a success. At intervals the Merryon gardeners appeared carrying chairs which they arranged in semi-circles for the use of the ladies; above these brightly coloured awnings of red, white and blue were erected to provide shade for them, for the hot sun must not be allowed to colour their pale complexions. A small handcart arrived, loaded with charcoal and beside the grill a large iron spit was being hammered into place.

The day promised to be even hotter than the preceding week and the field, bordered by the wood on one side and hop-gardens on the other three, would become a veritable sun-trap. Already sweat glistened on the faces of the men as they toiled about their various duties. A small table stood in the shade of the hedge just inside the gate and here a member of Mr Meddows' staff received the pigeons which were being brought in for the shoot and paid over whatever money was due for them. Two or three gipsies had already deposited baskets and sacks full of live birds which fluttered and murmured protestingly beneath the small table. Money changed hands and business was conducted with the minimum of words – the tug of a cap brim and the nod of a head proving sufficient most of the time. Mr Meddows himself strode up and down with his walking stick poised, ready to point out anything of which he disapproved.

Above all this activity the sky was a clear blue, studded with the occasional lark contributing its musical offering to the day's festivities. A little girl made her way along the hedge behind the table, picking wild flowers – selecting with fastidious eyes from the profusion, choosing the foxglove, honeysuckle and dainty yellow vetch, rejecting the dog rose and black bryony. This was Mr Meddows' grand-daughter, Eleanor. She added a handful of heavy-headed grasses to her posy and one or two stems of pink clover. Totally absorbed in her self-imposed task, she remained oblivious of the other children who dodged in and out among the men, screaming and shouting with excitement, tumbling and rolling together with a fine disregard for themselves or anyone else who happened in their way. Mr Meddows, despite the heat, wore stout brogues, thick woollen socks, plus-fours and a Norfolk jacket. He carried a gun in the crook of his arm – a muzzle loader without which he was rarely seen. A snappy deerstalker hat covered his bald head and he wore a moustache in the style which Lieutenant-Colonel Haig had made popular at the beginning of the Boer War. Slowly now he made his way up to the man at the gate. 'How many birds so far?' he demanded. The man consulted a small notebook. 'About sixty-four, sir.'

'Hmm.'

The man took this as a mark of his master's disapproval and amended hastily, 'But it's early yet, sir. Only a few have checked in so far.

'We were promised nearly four hundred,' Meddows grunted.

As he turned away without further comment, the man hid his relief in a pretended perusal of his notebook.

Just then a small elderly man hurried up.

'Mr Meddows, sir!' he called. 'About the extra ammunition – should I fetch it down now, sir?'

'Certainly not!' cried Mr Meddows. 'What are you thinking of, Bingham? It would not last long unsupervised. Too many light fingers around at an event like this. You should know better than to ask such a question. Didn't Shaw brief you?'

The old man shook his head. 'He's sick, sir. I haven't seen him.'

'Oh, that's different then. No, Bingham, the ammunition stays in the house until the last moment. I will give you the word as the day wears on. We shall have some idea then as to how much we are likely to need.'

'Right, sir. Thank you, sir.' The little man touched his forehead and hurried away.

Mr Meddows moved across to the trestle table where one of the kitchen-maids was setting out the tankards, turning them upside down on the scrubbed wooden surface to keep out the dust.

'There will be wine later,' he said, 'so don't forget the glasses.'

'I won't, sir. How many, sir?'

'Four or five dozen should do and I will get the wine sent down some time after three o'clock. Should be drawing to a close by then.'

'Right you are, sir.'

He looked at her for a moment. 'What's your name?'

'Meg Barker, sir. I've been with you a long time now, sir. Nearly seven years.'

He was mortified that he had not recognized her. 'Have you now?' he said. 'Well, that's well done.'

Satisfied at last that all was proceeding in a proper manner, he called to his grand-daughter and admired her posy. Then together they began to walk back to the house.

*

Nurse Ramsay had taken up temporary residence at Foxearth. She was a small woman with greying hair and a face full of broken veins which gave her a permanently intoxicated appearance. She disregarded this handicap as of no consequence, however, holding to the adage that inside every plain woman there is a beauty trying to get out. Her bedside manner was brisk and she was undeniably efficient, but Colonel Lawrence was not impressed and by the second week of her stay a state of unarmed hostility had developed between them. She was, however, a good teacher – even the Colonel could not deny that. At eight o'clock each morning she stood beside the bed with a thermometer in her hand and on this particular morning Janet was instructed to stand beside her.

'Not that damned thing again,' grumbled the Colonel. 'I am not running a damned fever, woman. What's the matter with you?'

'It is merely part of the day's routine, Mr Lawrence,' said the nurse briskly. She steadfastly refused to accord him his military title, knowing how much this irritated him. 'If we don't take your temperature in the morning, then we shan't know if it's gone up or down by the evening.'

She held up the thermometer so that Janet could see it. 'You will note,' she said, 'the small and large gradations marked in black along one side.' Janet peered at it solemnly and then nodded. 'If we rotate it slowly, a set of red figures comes into view. These numbers register the degrees fahrenheit and you know, no doubt, the normal temperature of the blood?' Janet looked stricken but said nothing.

'There is a small arrow which points to the figure you are searching for,' the nurse prompted her.

'Oh, do get on with it, Janet!' said the Colonel. 'Even I know that.' She looked at him hopefully, but he merely winked an eye. 'My lips are sealed,' he said. 'If you are going to receive an extra £4 a year, then you must earn it!'

Janet screwed up her face, then a look of triumph spread over it. 'Ninety-eight point four!' she said.

'Right!' said Nurse Ramsay. 'Ninety-eight point four – and what is it reading now, pray?'

Janet turned her head still further, but could not see. The nurse's large fingers were obscuring the silver mercury.

'Perhaps if I could hold it?' she suggested.

By way of answer, the nurse moved the thermometer nearer to Janet's face whilst still retaining a firm grip on it. 'You will see that I rotate it backwards and forwards until the mercury comes into full view. Now can you read the figure?'

'It is just over one hundred,' said Janet.

'Right again,' said the nurse. 'Now we shake the thermometer,

so, keeping a firm hold on the end furthest from the mercury.'
With a practised flick of her wrist, she shook the thermometer
until the mercury level had dropped to her satisfaction.

'Now,' she said, 'it is below the normal figure. Can you read
what it says now, Janet?'

'Just after ninety-four,' said Janet finally and the Colonel
groaned with impatience.

'You are like two vultures hovering over me,' he grumbled.
'Where's Vinnie? I want to see Vinnie. I have had enough of this
masquerade. I don't need a nurse.'

The two women ignored him and the nurse handed the
thermometer to Janet.

'Now, Janet, you take Mr Lawrence's temperature,' she said.
'*Me?*'

'Your name's Janet, isn't it?' said the Colonel. 'Get on with it,
girl!'

'Oh, very well, sir . . . Open your mouth, please.'

Janet adopted as brisk an attitude as she could and waited for
the Colonel to open his mouth, but his lips remained firmly closed
and he stared at her defiantly, the beginnings of a smile on his
face.

'Oh, please, sir!' said Janet. But very gently he shook his head
and his faded blue eyes crinkled in a smile.

'Colonel, *please!*' she begged, but his mouth remained closed.
Janet looked appealingly at the nurse.

'No matter,' said the nurse. 'There are always some patients
who will not co-operate, and there are alternative ways to measure
the temperature of the body. The thermometer can be placed
under the arm or in the—' She paused, fixing the Colonel with a
steely look.

'The what?' asked Janet, truly innocently.

'—rectum!' said the nurse. 'Ah, I thought you would change
your mind, Mr Lawrence. Thank you!'

The Colonel had opened his mouth and Janet took the opportunity to slip in the thermometer.

'Two minutes is the normal time it takes for the correct blood
temperature to register,' Nurse Ramsey continued, 'and while
that is taking place we take the patient's pulse – so.'

Before the Colonel knew what was happening, she had taken
hold of his wrist and was showing Janet how to find the artery and
how to place her fingers when she had found it. When two

minutes had elapsed, Janet removed the thermometer and studied it anxiously.

'It *is* ninety-eight point four,' she cried. 'Look, sir, it is! Ninety-eight point four exactly. You're *normal*, sir!'

The old man groaned. 'Of course I am normal, girl. I keep telling you there is no need for all this fussing and I shall tell Vinnie so myself. Where is the girl?'

'I told you this morning, sir,' said Janet, 'that she's gone to the Merryon shoot with Mr le Brun.'

'Vinnie has?'

'Yes, sir.'

'She doesn't shoot, does she?'

'Oh no, sir, she has gone as Mr le Brun's guest.'

'That's damned funny,' said the Colonel. 'Vinnie with William le Brun—'

'Not *William* le Brun. His father, sir.'

'Ah, that explains it!' The Colonel nodded. 'Capital fellow, Clive le Brun! A damned shame, losing his wife like that. I don't know why he never married again, but I suppose he's got enough on his hands with— What the devil are you up to now, dammit?'

The nurse had pulled up the bedclothes to reveal the lower part of the Colonel's legs. She ignored him completely and, beckoning Janet forward, produced a small pair of scissors from one of the many pockets in her apron.

'There's a right and a wrong way to clip the toenails,' she began and the Colonel, with a loud groan, gave up the unequal struggle and closed his eyes.

*

The Merryon shoot was not simply a shoot in the strictest sense of the word. Mr Meddows prided himself that his annual 'day' brought together most of the hunting fraternity in the neighbourhood, their 'lady wives' and children. The pigeon shoot always took place in the morning between eleven and one, watched by the admiring womenfolk, while the children were entertained on the lawn at Merryon by a Punch-and-Judy show. A light lunch was then served consisting of small savouries, accompanied by wine, and the afternoon was given over to a number of activities which year by year grew in variety until it had become close to being a fair. Races were organized for the children, there were pony rides through the hop-gardens, and in the drawing room at Merryon a magic lantern show was provided.

Promptly at eleven o'clock the shoot began and for a while Vinnie and Clive watched as the men took it in turn to try their skill. Then it was Clive's turn and Vinnie put her hands to her ears as he raised his gun and shouted 'Pull.' From the far side of the hedge one of the traps was pulled open and a pigeon was released. It swooped up through the blue air towards the safety of the trees.

Bang! Vinnie opened her eyes in time to see a small shape plummet to the ground, followed by a burst of feathers which drifted gracefully downward.

Clive turned to her. 'Clean as a whistle!' he said.

Vinnie nodded as the ripple of applause died.

He called again and brought down another pigeon.

'Pull!' Bang!

Clive brought down nine out of ten birds and there were shouts of approval from all around them. He turned to Vinnie. 'I think you should try.'

He brushed aside her protestations and placed the shotgun in her unwilling hands.

'It's too heavy,' said Vinnie. 'I can't even hold it.' It was one of the new breech-loaders which the English gunsmiths were beginning to copy from the models coming in from abroad.

'It's very simple,' Clive told her. 'Hold it at an angle, like this. Now I am going to "break" it and the cartridge will fly out – you see?'

Vinnie jumped as the spent cartridge ejected and then Clive withdrew another from his pocket and slipped it into the breech for her.

'Now, put one hand here and one on the butt,' he told her, 'and we bring the two halves up together to snap them shut.'

'I don't think I can,' she protested. But he helped her and to Vinnie's gratification, barrel and stock fused once more.

'Now, lean forward,' he went on, 'left foot in front, back straight, shoulders relaxed.

Vinnie felt perspiration break out on her skin, partly with the novelty of the situation and partly with embarrassment, for she was now the centre of attention and felt sure she would make a complete fool of herself. She could already visualize the disappointment on Clive's face.

'It's too heavy,' she protested again, but Clive laughed. 'Nearly ten pounds,' he admitted, 'but you're a big strong girl.'

'I *thought* I was,' said Vinnie and there was some laughter.

The crowd began to urge her on, insisting that she try. Vinnie found it difficult to refuse and in the excitement quite forgot that she was aiming at a live bird, or she might never have pulled the trigger. As it was, she gave the command on Clive's instructions and then squeezed the trigger. To her relief, the shot whistled harmlessly through the air and the freed pigeon flew safely into the trees. Vinnie smiled shakily as she accepted the crowd's commiserations. The gun's recoil had driven the butt painfully against her shoulder but she made no mention of it.

'Now have another try,' said Clive and the little ritual was repeated – spent cartridge ejected, new shell inserted, barrel and stock snapped together.

'You know what to do,' he said. 'Try it on your own. I will try to borrow a lighter gun for you. There are usually a few spares.'

As he left her, Vinnie felt instinctively that the interest of the crowd had grown. She knew, without looking, that all eyes were turned in her direction.

'I mustn't hit it,' she thought desperately. 'Whatever happens, I mustn't hit it!'

With an effort, she raised the heavy gun to her shoulder. Somebody in the crowd shouted, 'Lean forward Mrs Lawrence!' and she hastily altered her position.

Suddenly she felt someone's arms enclose her and strong hands covered her own, grasping the gun with her. When a voice called 'Pull!' she recognized it instantly and was almost paralysed with shock. She made no effort to sight the gun and Tom Bryce lifted it for her as another pigeon darted skywards. His face brushed hers as he leaned foward; his finger, over hers, squeezed the trigger and she watched in horror as the shot found its mark and the bird's grey form spiralled to earth.

The crowd showed its delight with a spontaneous burst of cheering as Tom's hold on the gun slackened. Vinnie was acutely aware of the nearness of his body and conscious of the smell of alcohol on his breath, but strangely was not repelled by it. She was shocked to discover that something in her own body was responding to the nearness of his. Suddenly, she forgot the crowd of onlookers, forgot the fact that she had just killed a living creature which even at that moment was being retrieved by an eager cocker spaniel. She only knew that Tom Bryce had his arms round her and that she wanted more than anything to turn and look into his eyes – but it was not possible. His hands still covered hers and it was his hand which 'broke' the gun and snapped it shut again. She held it awkwardly by the barrel, letting the stock swing down and only then did she turn to face him.

'Oh, Tom!' she gasped, for the once handsome face was haggard but the dark hair that she remembered so well still curled untidily around his face and the brown eyes were as dark as ever, darker perhaps.

'Vinnie Harris,' he murmured and without glancing up, Vinnie knew that the crowd around them had averted their eyes out of respect for something which they did not quite understand. She could not take her eyes from his face, helplessly trying to convey with her own eyes all that she had longed to say over the past five years. This man had been her first lover. This man had given her a child. There was a bond between them which nothing and no one could break. Yet he had never loved her. There had been nothing but desire and the satisfaction of that brief desire had led to tragedy. Now was her chance to tell him she was sorry, but she could find no words. She could only look into the brown eyes with a passionate, unspoken plea for forgiveness. A loud sob startled her and she realized she was crying. Tom drew her gently towards him as he had done just once before and patted her clumsily in an effort to comfort her.

'Vinnie Harris,' he whispered. 'Don't cry, Vinnie Harris,' but her sobs only grew louder. Just for a moment she was four years old and her father held her in his arms. The smell was so familiar, of sweat and whisky, and she remembered one of her father's rare smiles. Her lips framed the word 'Pa', but she did not utter it.

'Forgive me!' she whispered but was it to her father she spoke, or Tom? She wondered why her father had gone away.

For a second she felt Tom's lips pressed against her hair, then suddenly he was gone and she saw him stumbling unevenly away through the crowd which parted to let him go. Then suddenly Clive le Brun was beside her and although she did not look at his face, she knew by the tone of his voice that he was angry.

'Come away!' he snapped. His hand closed on her elbow and he steered her, still sobbing, through the curious crowd. She had to run to keep up with him and several times would have fallen without his support. As he went, he called out to a gipsy lad to fetch his carriage and bring it round to the gate and the boy sped off.

'Where are we going?' cried Vinnie. 'You're hurting my arm.'

'I am taking you home,' he said. 'You cannot possibly go back to Foxearth in that state. Whatever were you thinking of? I should never have left you. It will be round the village like wildfire!'

Vinnie cried anew under this threat, but Clive made no effort to console her. When they reached the carriage, he merely said, 'Get in!' and strode round to the other side to climb up into the driving seat. She realized with a sinking heart that she had made a terrible mistake for, as Clive predicted, her encounter with Tom Bryce would make rich pickings for village gossip and Julian would inevitably hear of it.

'But I don't care,' she whispered. 'I don't *care* what happens!' and with those words she succumbed once more to a bout of uncontrollable weeping.

CHAPTER SEVEN

Mollie, Dulcie and Meg sat on the edge of Dora's bed and waited impatiently for her to pin up her hair. Dora's room was at the top of five flights of stairs and looked out over the gasometer; it was a dingy room, with stained wallpaper and a bare board floor. The gas-mantle in the centre of the ceiling was broken and the lace curtain was grey with age and dirt. The table was covered with brown paper and a bluebottle buzzed eagerly over the remains of a frugal meal which had not been cleared away. Unwashed clothes and old newspapers littered the room and some dead flowers in a jam jar stood on the window sill.

'For crying out loud, Dora!' cried Dulcie. 'How much longer are you going to be jabbing pins into that scrawny stuff you call hair? You're never ready on time!'

'I've got things to do,' Dora told her, not in the least put out by this criticism. 'Not like some I could mention.'

'Things to do? Like what?' Dulcie demanded.

Meg giggled. 'She's been spring cleaning, haven't you, love?'

The three on the bed screeched with laughter and Dora tried to look offended, but failed.

Mollie said, 'Oh leave her be, you lot! Five minutes isn't going to make much difference. They're not open yet, anyway.'

'At least someone's on my side,' said Dora. She licked her fingers and smoothed up a few straggly hairs which clung to her forehead.

'Give us me hat then,' she demanded, 'and stop gawking. How'd you like to get dolled up with three pairs of eyes watching?' She accepted the ancient straw hat from Mollie and surveyed it critically, turning it round on the point of a finger. 'Tatty old thing!' she said.

'Oh, you're not that bad!' said Meg innocently. 'Not tatty, exactly – just 'orrible!'

There was more laughter as Dora began to belabour Meg with the unfortunate hat. Mollie slid off the bed to avoid the scrimmage as Meg fought back and Dulcie hastily retreated to the far side of the bed.

'Oh, pack it up, you two!' cried Mollie. 'Or else you'll look like a couple of bleedin' scarecrows. Dora, stop it! And you shouldn't rile her, Meg. You know what she's like.'

Dora did not work for Sammy Tulson, but was employed in Bryant and May's match factory. She did, however, live in the house next door to Mollie and the two women had been friends for a long time. Dora was the same age as Mollie, unmarried and aiming to remain so. She was startlingly pretty, with child-like blue eyes in a round face surrounded by an untidy mass of curly blonde hair which all the others secretly envied. If Dora had worn an old sack she would still have drawn the men's glances, but she was not vain. She accepted her good looks as a sign that heaven smiled on her. Her nature was a sunny one, but she was also bold and promiscuous and the fact that she remained childless was a source of wonder to all who knew her. She and Mollie usually went out together as a twosome, but tonight it was Mollie's birthday and she had suggested that the girls from Tulsons join them for a celebratory drink.

Meg still giggled hysterically while Dora frowned upon her hat which had not survived unscathed.

'Look at that bloomin' rose!' she grumbled. 'Half the petals have come off. That's your fault, Meg Wilson. I'm going to look a proper sight with this stuck on me head. Oh well, who cares? Worse troubles at sea, I suppose.' She put it on and studied her reflection in the small swing mirror, then, catching sight of Mollie's reflection also, turned to look at her friend. 'That's a new shawl!' she exclaimed. 'Mollie Pett, you sly piece! Last week it was a new hat, now the shawl. You got a rich old man tucked away somewhere?'

'I told you,' said Mollie. 'These people keep giving me money. What am I supposed to do, say "no thank you"?'

Dora whistled enviously. 'Wish they'd give me some,' she said.

'Ah, but you've got no kids,' said Mollie triumphantly. 'That's where you made your big mistake, Dora Wilks.'

'That was no mistake,' grinned Dora. 'That was me being smart. Only careless girls like you get lumbered with three kids.'

'How *do* you do it?' Meg asked Dora curiously. 'My sister's only been married four years and she's got four kids already. At that rate she'll have ten by the time she's thirty. If you know anything we don't . . .'

'I don't,' said Dora, 'I'm just lucky. I jump off a table, drink a bottle of gin and then stew in a hot tub.' She shrugged. 'That shakes 'em loose.'

'My sister tried all that and it never worked.'

'She wants to try saying "No",' said Mollie.

Dulcie stared. 'Look who's talking!' she said. 'I bet you've never said "No".'

''Course I haven't,' said Mollie. 'Much more fun saying "Yes".' Amid more laughter she continued, 'It's part of my philosophy. You only live once. Say "No" and it gets you nowhere. Say "Yes" and you get to see—' She stopped.

'Oh, we know what you get to see!' said Dulcie, but Mollie assumed a superior manner. 'I was going to say – you get to see more of the world!'

'The world? Oh, that's what you call it!'

'Pretty small world!' said Dulcie with a snigger, which set Meg off into peals of laughter.

'You'd be surprised,' said Mollie. 'Some worlds are bigger than others – *and* a lot more fun! And on top of that, the Brothers in Jesus give me—' She clapped a hand to her mouth as the words slipped out.

'Brothers in Jesus?' cried Dora. 'It's never that lot giving you the money?'

'Hell!' said Mollie. 'Forget I said that; I'm not supposed to say. Miss B. will have my guts for garters if she finds out I've told you.'

'Well!' exclaimed Dulcie. 'That's a turn-up. I thought they was only breakfasts and old clothes. Can anyone get money off 'em?'

'I told you, you haven't got any kids,' said Mollie, deciding that since the secret was out she might as well tell it all.

While Dora searched in the chest of drawers for another flower with which to replace the damaged rose, Mollie told them of her earlier meeting with Mary Bellweather and the generosity of the Brothers in Jesus.

'So it's for the kids,' said Dulcie. 'The money's meant for the kids.'

'That's right. And yours are grown-up and Dora and Meg haven't got any.'

'So it's not for buying new clobber,' Dulcie persisted.

Mollie scowled. 'They're not to know,' she defended herself. 'As long as the kids don't go short, who's to know? Or care? They give me the money and that makes *them* feel good. I buy a new hat and then *I* feel good. So don't poke your rotten oar in, Dulcie Webb, because it's none of your business.'

'It *is* my business,' said Dulcie. 'If you're getting money to buy new shawls, then why shouldn't I? And Dora and Meg?'

'Oh, shut up about it, Dulcie!' said Dora mildly. 'You're only jealous. Now girls, what d'you think of this instead of the rose?' She held up a rather faded imitation bird.

Meg threw back her head and laughed. 'It's a bloody parrot!' she snorted. 'We're not going to the zoo, love. We're going to the pub!'

'Pretty Polly!' Dulcie croaked in a fair imitation.

'Oh, very funny!' said Mollie, still smarting from the sting of Dulcie's criticism. 'Well, I say it looks fine. Stitch it on your hat, Dora, and let's get going, for God's sake, before I say something I shouldn't to someone here who shall be nameless.'

'Meaning me, I suppose?' said Dulcie. 'Well, if it's going to be like that all evening, I shall be sorry I came.'

'Go home then – no one's stopping you.'

'I'll go when I'm ready, thank you, Mollie Pett.'

'That's right,' said Dora, 'keep arguing. Mollie'll have a lovely birthday. There, I think that'll stay on. What d'you think?'

Dulcie forbore to make any comment and Meg was making ineffectual attempts to swat the bluebottle. Only Mollie assured her friend that the bird looked fine.

'*Is* it a parrot?' she asked. 'It's a bit small.'

Dora shrugged and picked up her purse. 'I think it's a canary,' she said.

'Canaries are yellow.'

'Not all of them,' said Dora and still arguing amiably, the little party clattered down the stairs.

'And remember,' said Mollie. 'If we find any nice young lads with money to burn, I'm the one with the birthday, so I get first pick!'

*

After an unrewarding visit to the 'King's Head' and an unpleasant encounter with a drunken sailor in the 'Five Bells', they ended up in the 'Swan', a little the worse for drink but still without escorts.

Here their luck remained unchanged at first, for the saloon bar seemed to be full of fat ladies and old men, apart from the three sailors leaning on the bar and gulping down pints of porter.

'Would you credit it?' muttered Dulcie. 'Four of us and three of them.'

Mollie winked at one sailor, a lanky young man with bristly hair. 'Perhaps they've got a mate outside in the khasi,' she muttered.

They found a corner seat and squashed into it, their bright faces turned in the direction of the Navy.

'Bit young for Dulcie,' said Meg. 'They don't look a day over eighteen.'

'Probably need mothering, then,' Dulcie giggled, 'which makes you lot too young.'

'I'm a mother too,' Mollie protested, arranging her legs so that one ankle showed beyond the table leg. She hitched up her skirt and smiled broadly in their direction, determined that if one of them was going to go without a man it wouldn't be her.

The three sailors nudged each other, blushing and laughing, obviously delighted to see the four new arrivals. The bristly-haired sailor winked at Mollie and pursed his lips into a kiss.

'*He* looks as though he wants more than mothering,' Mollie grinned, with a provocative toss of her head in his direction.

'You mind he doesn't "mother" you!' warned Dulcie. 'You've been mothered three times already, love, so watch your step or it'll be four times.'

A few winks later all seven of them were snugly esconced in the corner of the room. Meg sat on the lap of a shy young man who blushed furiously; Dora's catch was stocky and bearded, with a twinkle in his eye and easy manners; the bristly-haired youth sat between Mollie and Dulcie with an arm round each, entertaining them all with an endless succession of bawdy jokes. Half an hour later saw Dulcie on her feet, singing and swaying, and Mollie had seized the opportunity to climb into the third lap and snuggle drowsily into his arms.

This was how Mary Bellweather discovered them when she pushed her way through the crowd that slouched in the doorway and stared furiously round the room. Her angry gaze took in the children who crawled among the sawdust on the floor, and the mainly drunken men and women who sat or stood around, peering at each other through the smoke of a dozen pipes and countless cigarettes. Her ears were assailed by a variety of sounds

– a group laughing, a couple quarrelling, the landlord remonstrating with an awkward customer and above it all the jangle of a pianola.

'Oh Christ!' muttered Mollie and she hid her face against the sailor's dark blue tunic.

Mary Bellweather was attracting attention.

'What's up, my duck? Lost your old man, have you?'

There was loud laughter which Mary ignored. Normally the situation would have caused her grave embarrassment but now, buttressed by righteous indignation, it passed her by. Finally her sharp eyes spotted Mollie's bright red hair and she marched across the room to tap her on the shoulder. Reluctantly Mollie turned round.

'I thought it was you,' said Mary, her tone low but vehement. 'Please come outside with me for a moment, I have something to say to you which you will not want your friends to hear.'

Meg and Dora exchanged startled looks. 'It's her, from the breakfasts,' Dora hissed.

Mollie tried to collect her thoughts. The sailor, momentarily awed by Mary's air of authority, opened his mouth to make a rude remark, then thought better of it and remained silent.

'Let her go!' said Mary, as the sailor's arms closed round Mollie protectively. 'I have something to say to her and if she chooses to come back to you afterwards, then she can. I'm waiting, Mollie, and I won't wait long. If you know what's good for you, you will follow me outside without any fuss and without delay.'

Turning on her heel, she marched out of the room and after a moment's hesitation, Mollie struggled to her feet.

'I'd better go and see what she wants,' she said.

'I wouldn't,' said Dora. 'I'd let her go hang.'

'Who does she think she is?' Meg demanded. 'Lady Muck?'

Mollie looked down at the sailor whose arms were still round her waist. She ran a hand through the spiky hair and frowned.

'What did you say your name was?' she asked him.

'Owen.'

'Owen? Are you a foreigner?'

'No.'

'Well, Owen, will you wait for me?'

'Of course I will – if you give me a kiss.'

She leaned down and kissed the top of his head. 'A proper one later,' she promised, 'when I've got rid of her outside,' then she made her way unsteadily to the door.

As soon as Mollie set foot on the pavement Mary Bellweather pounced, catching hold of her arm and dragging her some yards along the road so that their conversation would not be overheard.

'Now, Mollie Pett!' she demanded, her eyes flashing fire. 'You will please explain why your two little girls are left unattended and your son is playing in the street. Do we or do we not give you money, so that you can pay someone to mind the children when you have to be away? Did you, or did you not, promise that you would not leave them unattended? Did you or—'

'Her downstairs is looking after the little ones—' Mollie began defensively.

'Her downstairs is *not* downstairs, for your information,' cried Mary, 'and according to your next-door-neighbour she hasn't been there for at least a week! Because, Mollie Pett, if you had bothered to find out, she's away nursing a consumptive sister in Shoreditch. And this looks like a new shawl . . .' She snatched it from Mollie's shoulders.

'And that, your neighbour tells me, is a new hat!' She reached for that, too, but Mollie had taken a step backwards and the hat remained on her head.

'Here! You give me that shawl!' she wailed. 'You've no right to take that.'

'I have every right,' snapped Mary. 'That money is given to you in good faith and now I discover you have been spending it on yourself. Have the children been getting extra food and milk? Has your son been attending school regularly? Mollie Pett, you don't deserve another penny!'

Now Mollie began to be really alarmed. Mary's wrath she could survive – even a few cuffs or a kick – but to lose her money!

'I never meant no harm,' she cried, turning on the tears. 'I did buy them some food. Honest to God I did! And Alex has been to school. Cross my heart, he has!'

'That's not what I heard at the school,' cried Mary, 'and do stop bellowing like that, or I shall walk away and leave you here and you will not get another penny. I mean it, Mollie. Stop that racket at once and listen to me! I shall tell you once and once only. This is your last chance – and you don't deserve it – to keep your allowance. Extra milk, eggs and bread – do you understand?'

Mollie nodded. Her head was beginning to ache and she felt sick.

'No more new hats. No more shawls or shoes, or finery or any clothes. That money is for the *children*. Do you understand? Because I shall keep my eye on you, Mollie, and I shall call on you when you least expect it and I shall ask questions. Oh, don't bother to protest, it will do you no good at all. Your choice is clear. If you don't care for these children, the allowance stops. For good, mind – there will be no second chance. I shall find someone who really deserves it – someone who cares enough about her children to be grateful for the money and to use it properly. Now, are you going back to your friends or are you going home to look after your children?'

Desperately Mollie hesitated, reluctant to give up the evening's entertainment and the promise of the young sailor's lively and amorous company. She had hoped to take him home with her to share the night, for she was young and lonely and a man's body was a joy and a comfort.

'You're a miserable cow!' she muttered rashly, but Mary chose to ignore the remark.

'I'll go home, then,' said Mollie, her voice sullen with defeat, 'but I'll have to go back in and say goodnight to the others.'

'I'll wait here for you,' said Mary, 'and see you home.'

'Oh, Christ!'

Mollie went back inside and told the others that she had to go home with Mary Bellweather.

'But why?' asked Dora.

'I just do,' said Mollie. 'I can't explain. It's a secret.'

No one felt inclined to argue the matter and Dulcie saw a chance to keep the sailor to herself. Meg had knocked over her drink and was trying to scoop it off the table and back into her glass.

Dora shrugged and watched Mollie go – then she raised her glass.

'Happy bloody birthday!' she said.

*

The 'Horse and Cart' at Teesbury had undergone extensive and long overdue renovations. The exterior walls had been rendered a muddy pink and the window frames and doors gleamed whitely in the sunshine. The thatched roof had been patched and the large central chimney repointed. A cowl had been fitted to the latter to stop it smoking, but although it failed to do so nobody could blame Ted Hunter for that. Inside, the pub had also been transformed, with new brown linoleum, six pictures of hunting scenes in ornate black frames and a newly papered wall in red and gold on which to hang them. The old rickety tables and high-backed chairs remained unchanged, but the long wooden bench which ran along the wall gleamed with a coat of varnish.

Generations of Hunters had seen no reason to waste money on refurbishing the pub and Ted and Maisie had been equally indolent. Even while the rival 'Blue Fox' flourished the 'Horse and Cart' had kept its regular customers, but when the 'Blue Fox' burned down, they had assimilated the influx with quiet thankfulness. Suddenly, however, early in 1900, the 'Blue Fox' had been rebuilt by a family from Tonbridge and the population of Teesbury was once more divided in loyalties. In ones and twos the customers had drifted to the other end of the village, curious to sample the delights of the 'Blue Fox'. Some of them had stayed there and Ted and Maisie were forced to consider ways of winning them back, hence the reluctant expenditure in the late spring of 1901. By the end of July work was almost finished and on 18th August the last ladder was removed from outside and the interior varnish was officially declared dry.

Andy Roberts, the blacksmith, as first customer to step inside the bar that night, was offered an evening of free drinks by way of celebration.

'Free drinks? By Christ, I'll have a whisky for starters then, Maisie, my dear! And to think I nearly stopped by at my mother's place. Good job I didn't!' His good-natured face beamed with pleasure as Maisie handed him his drink. 'Well, here's to you both and to the old "Horse and Cart",' he chuckled, 'and God bless all who sail in her!' He downed the whisky in one quick gulp and wiped his hand over his lips, then took a long look round and nodded his approval.

'You've made a good job of it,' he told them. 'A right good job! Tasteful without being vulgar.' He crossed the room and considered the wallpaper. 'A tasteful design, that,' he said.

'That's what we hoped,' purred Maisie. 'It's so easy to be flashy and we wanted to avoid that. We leave *that* to others,' she added pointedly.

Andy nodded, taking her meaning. 'It makes a nice warm

background,' he said. 'Who chose it, eh? You or your old man?'

'I did,' said Maisie. 'I always have had good taste for furnishings and suchlike.'

'And husbands?' said Andy with his usual cunning.

'Good taste in husbands? I don't know about that,' said Maisie, but Ted – preening himself – held out a hand for Andy's empty glass.

'Oh, I won't say "No",' said Andy happily.

Just then the door opened and Jarvis and Joan Tupp entered the bar. Jarvis had recently taken over the village store from his father, Will, who had retired early and gone to live with his sister in Margate. Joan was older than her husband, but they had been married for nearly three years now and the match had proved to be a happy one to date.

'Evening Andy, Maisie, Ted!' cried Joan.

Maisie's face stiffened slightly, for the Tupps had been two of the first to move to the 'Blue Fox'.

Jarvis grinned sheepishly. 'We're back with the old "H" and "C",' he said, 'and it's good to see it looking so smart.'

He and Joan gazed round with exaggerated admiration until Maisie rewarded them with a smile and Ted said, 'They'll all come back, you'll see! But what's it going to be?'

While he was drawing a beer for Jarvis and a port and lemon for Joan, Andy told them about his good fortune.

'Free drinks all evening!' he told them. 'Isn't that so, Maisie?'

'That's right,' she agreed. 'When it's finally finished, we said, the first person in here will have drinks on the house. That's what we decided and it turned out to be Andy here.'

Jarvis and Joan congratulated him and then all three retired with their drinks to a favourite corner to chat. Slowly but surely the room began to fill up; an hour later it buzzed cheerfully with conversation and laughter and Maisie and Ted exchanged occasional satisfied glances. Tim Bilton, from Foxearth, came in with Young Harry and immediately they began their weekly game of shove-halfpenny.

Liz Parsloe arrived just before nine for her usual two bottles of stout and three bottles of beer, which she stowed away in her basket. She was a dull-looking young woman with few charms, but her marriage to Joshua Parsloe – an unpopular man – had earned her a certain amount of attention and not a little sympathy.

'Evening, Liz!' Jarvis called to her. 'How's things with you and Josh? Treating you all right, is he?'

'He's treating me fine,' she said with a toss of her head. 'I'm not as daft as some folk think and me Ma told me a thing or two.'

Heads turned in her direction. 'What sort of things, Liz?'

She gave a sly smile. 'Just things! I'm bigger than him and he doesn't scare me. If he lays a finger on me, I'll know where to hit him.'

There were a few guffaws at this. 'Where's that then, Liz?' cried Andy.

'Never you mind! But *I* know and what's more he *knows* I know.' More laughter followed.

'You keep him in order then, do you, Liz?' laughed Joan.

'I do.'

Maisie snorted. 'It's more than his first wife could do, poor soul. Right bully he was to poor old Maude. Do him good if the boot's on the other foot.'

'You keep him under your thumb, love,' said Andy.

'Letting you come hopping this year, is he, Liz?' Tim asked.

'He'd better,' said Liz. 'I shall raise Cain if he doesn't.'

'One of our best pickers, is Liz,' said Tim. 'Made a tidy little sum last year, didn't you?'

'I did. 'Cos I get on with the job,' she told them. 'I don't waste time flirting, like some I could mention.'

There was a delighted roar at this sally. 'Mention no names, but watch where my eyes roll!' cried Andy. 'Is that how it is then, Liz?'

'Something of the sort.' She went on her way with a farewell wave of the hand, allowing the door to slam behind her.

Andy stared after her. 'What a change in that girl these last few years,' he said. 'Proper little mouse she was, before she got wed. I felt real sorry for her when I heard the news, but she's come up trumps, no doubt about it.'

'I bet Josh wonders what's hit him!' Jarvis grimaced. 'One false move and she'll have him over her knee!'

There was further merriment at Joshua's expense and then the talk turned to more general topics – the new riverside malt-house being planned for Maidstone by the Whitbread brewers; the death of a Laddingford brewer who had left over £30,000; the state of the Hunton apple crop. The women discussed the appointment of a new teacher at the village school, then inevitably the condition of the hops was argued and the imminent influx of Londoners lamented.

'You ready for them, then, Ted?' asked Tim. 'Letting them in here, are you?'

Ted took up a mug and began to dry it with purposeful movements. 'No, I'm not,' he declared. 'Not one of those damned Londoners is going to set foot in this pub. Over my dead body! They'll be served outside in the yard, same as usual.'

'But we can come in, Ted?'

'You can,' said Ted, setting down the mug and taking up another. 'All my regulars will be welcome, at the *back* door, if you please. But the front door remains closed for the whole month of September and they can like it or lump it. Vandals, that's what they are. Savages. Don't know how to treat a decent pub, I'm afraid, so they'll have to be kept out. What the 'Blue Fox' will do is anybody's guess. If they let them in again they deserve all they get, that's my opinion.'

Earnest discussion followed, recalling the previous year's débâcle at the 'Blue Fox' which had rashly opened its doors to the hoppers. A fight had broken out and the fixtures and fittings had suffered – over fifty pounds' worth of damage, it was rumoured. Dozens of glasses had been smashed before the local constable managed to restore order. The main culprits had been promptly dispatched back to London and their names removed for ever from Foxearth's list of approved workers. They would never be employed in the area again, but that was small comfort to the proprietor of the 'Blue Fox'.

'Let's hope the weather holds fine,' said Andy, 'or else it'll be a poor crop and that won't improve their tempers.'

Tim Bilton shook his head. 'The weather can't save it,' he said. 'Nothing can, for it's a meagre crop this year. It'll be slow picking for the money, I'm afraid. The master's been looking none too happy these last few weeks.'

'No disrespect,' said Ted, 'but Julian Lawrence isn't half the man his father was, poor old Colonel.'

'Oh, but be fair,' said Maisie. 'The Colonel was an Army man. That makes a difference. All that fighting and danger – I reckon it makes a man.'

Tim slapped his leg delightedly. 'Oh, you fancy the brave soldier lads, do you, Maisie? You'll have to watch her, Ted!'

Ted, mopping the bar top with a cloth, was not to be roused.

'He'd have to be a brave man to take her on!' he said and even Maisie joined in the general laughter.

Jarvis leaned back and stretched his legs. 'Well,' he said, reverting to an earlier theme, 'at least the hoppers will bring down a few new songs. They're always good for a sing-song and they certainly know how to enjoy themselves.'

'They need to, the way they live down here,' said Andy. 'That old barn of yours, Tim – it's a wonder it's still standing. Leans like the devil and the roof's rotten. I wouldn't sleep under it for all the tea in China! Isn't it time it was put to rights? It must leak like a sieve.'

Tim was forced to admit that it did leak. 'Vinnie's always on to him to get it fixed, but the old man won't hear of it. Waste of money, he reckons, to spend good money on a barn that's only used in September.'

'You can see his point,' said Joan, twiddling her empty glass meaningfully. 'But I pity those poor souls who have to live in it. Andy's right – it could fall down any time. Kill someone, that barn could.' Her husband took the hint and lurched over to the bar with their empty glasses.

'Same again,' he told Maisie, and then raising his replenished glass, cried, 'Here's to this year's hops! Where would we all be without them?'

'Or without the Londoners,' said Tim, draining his glass. 'We may not like 'em, but where would we be without them?'

*

The courtyard at Westlands echoed to the blows from Allan's axe as it bit into the logs. It was nearly two o'clock in the afternoon and the temperature had crept above eighty degrees. Allan worked stripped to the waist and his face and body glistened in sweat. He heard his employer's footsteps before the man actually appeared and his heart sank. Frank Lidden was every bit as hard as his reputation would have it, and now he was crossing the cobbles with a face like thunder.

'Where the hell's Bryce?' he demanded.

Allan rested the axe and straightened up, wiping the sweat from his face with a bare forearm.

'I couldn't rightly say, sir,' he said, glancing round in feigned innocence at the empty courtyard. 'He was around earlier, but where he is now . . .' he shrugged, leaving the sentence unfinished. In fact, he knew very well that Tom Bryce was in the barn not two yards from where they stood, sleeping off the effects of a bout of drinking.

Frank Lidden eyed him suspiciously. 'If you're covering up for him . . .' he began.

Allan shook his head furiously. 'No, sir, I'm not, sir. I just didn't see the going of him and that's the truth. I've been busy with these logs for the last two hours.'

But the older man remained unconvinced. 'God help him when I find him!' he said. He glared round the courtyard, where a few chickens pecked languidly between the cobblestones and a large black cat slept in the shade of a waggon.

'Well, get on with it, man!' cried Frank irritably and Allan seized his axe and swung it with renewed vigour. He did not look up as his employer strode into the barn in search of his missing pole-puller.

It took a few seconds for Lidden's eyes to accustom themselves to the gloom of the barn's interior, but once they had he made his way along the piles of hay, sacks of meal and various farm implements with an ease born of long familiarity.

'Bryce, where the devil are you?' he shouted.

He carried on looking, but there was no sound except the startled flutter of a bird which swooped from the hay-loft above him and flew out of the door into the sunlight. There was no sign of Tom Bryce and Frank was about to retrace his steps when a sudden thought occurred to him. Crossing the barn, he climbed the ladder which led up to the hay-loft.

'Bryce!' he called again. 'You up here?'

There was a movement further over and he made his way towards it, his temper growing with every step. He found Tom Bryce sprawled face downwards on the hay, surrounded by empty bottles.

'Christ Almighty!' The words came through clenched teeth as Frank swung his foot and kicked Tom's legs.

'Get up, you lazy bastard!' he shouted. 'Do you hear me, Bryce? Get up, I say!'

Tom groaned and rolled over. He stared blearily into his employer's face, one hand shading his eyes as he squinted into the shadows.

'Up, I said! Now!'

Tom pulled himself into a sitting position and mumbled

something unintelligible. With an effort, Frank Lidden kept his hands to himself, although his fists were tightly clenched.

'You've gone too far this time,' he cried. 'Less than a month till the picking and you're nowhere near ready. Bins not repaired. Faggots not ordered. You've organized nothing, and if I hadn't checked I would have had four hundred hoppers turning up on the first of September with nothing ready for them. You're a useless, hopeless drunk, Tom Bryce, and I've reached the end of my tether. I'm a Christian man and I've made allowances for you, but no more. You've had your last chance with me, Bryce and I'm getting rid of you! Do you hear me?'

He could not tell whether his words were making any sense to the man sprawled below him. Tom's head lolled suddenly to one side and he clutched his stomach with his left hand, his right fumbling amongst the hay to reach for another bottle. Frank Lidden's patience was exhausted; he snatched up an empty bottle and thrust it in front of Tom's face.

'Is this what you're looking for?' he roared. 'More drink? Well, you're going to be unlucky. You've drunk it all, haven't you? Look!' He tilted the bottle and Tom focused with an effort on the few drips which trickled out.

'You've drunk yourself out of a job, Tom Bryce – and out of a house, too. You and your family can get out and the sooner the better!'

Frank cursed under his breath as Tom began to slip slowly sideways, apparently oblivious to his threats. He threw down the bottle, knelt down and grabbed Tom by the shoulders, shaking him violently and shouting at him as he did so.

'Do you hear me, Tom Bryce? You're finished here! Do you understand what I'm telling you?'

Tom struggled feebly to push him away, but his efforts were ineffectual.

'I want you off my land and out of my property by the end of the week, Bryce. Is that understood?'

At last Tom seemed aware of what was happening. 'No,' he said thickly. 'No, I can't—' With a great effort he rallied his senses, protesting weakly. 'You can't!' he muttered. 'I'm sorry, it won't happen—'

Frank Lidden released him with a final push and stood up, staring down at him with a look of disgust.

'but Colonel Lawrence spoke so highly of you—' He sighed heavily. 'Three weeks to hop-picking and I've no pole-puller,' he said. 'That's all the thanks I get from you, Tom Bryce. Well I've learned my lesson, don't you worry!'

He turned and began to walk away, but with a superhuman effort Tom struggled into a kneeling position and threw himself forward, clutching Frank's right leg.

'Don't say that!' he mumbled. 'Let me stay – I promise – you can't do this.'

'Let go of my leg, damn you! I tell you you're finished.'

Frank tried to pull his leg free, but Tom's grip tightened as his desperation increased. He was rapidly sobering up under the threat of eviction and the loss of his job. The dreadful hopelessness of the situation became apparent to him and he grew reckless, tugging at Frank's leg until his employer lost his balance and fell almost on top of him.

'You stupid bastard! Take your hands off me or you'll regret it.'

'No!' cried Tom. 'Don't talk like that! One more chance – I promise you – no more drink . . .'

Suddenly his face contorted and he doubled up, his folded arms clutching his stomach, his head bent. He groaned loudly and Frank Lidden saw his opportunity to scramble clear and make for the ladder. He was half-way down it when he heard Tom's stumbling footsteps above him and looked up in time to see the man falling towards him head-first. With a crash the two men landed together at the bottom of the ladder. Frank had taken the impact of Tom's full weight and was winded, which gave Tom a slight edge. To Frank's horror he found himself struggling with Tom, who was now behaving like one demented, uttering a mixture of threats, groans and pleas that was horrible to hear.

'Allan!' shouted Frank. 'Get over here quickly!'

It seemed an eternity before Allan appeared, silhouetted in the doorway, his axe still in his hand.

'Get him off me!' cried Frank. 'Help me, you fool!'

Allan dropped the axe, sprang forward and tried to pull Tom away from his employer, but somehow Tom flung him across the barn and into the wall which momentarily stunned him. He shook his head dazedly, then struggled back to his feet to see that the other two were still struggling violently together. Allan sprang on to Tom's back, locking his arms round his throat and forcing him backwards. Slowly Tom's grasp relaxed as he grunted with pain.

Frank tore himself free and staggered back against the jamb of the door, gasping for breath, blood running from the corner of his mouth.

'You animal!' he gasped. 'You bloody animal! That's all you are, Tom Bryce.'

Even as he spoke, Tom turned on Allan and swung his right fist into the side of his jaw. There was a crack as the bone fractured and Allan, with a squeal of pain, fell backwards clutching his face. Frank Lidden started to cross over to him but Tom was too quick for him, lunging forward and barring his way. In his right hand he held a pitchfork. Tom's face was ashen, his eyes staring; his cheeks were sunken and his lips trembled. One eye was half-closed and there was a long graze down the left side of his face which oozed blood.

'Now it's your turn to listen,' he said thickly, 'and you'd better listen hard, because I'm not moving out of that cottage with nowhere to go. I've got a wife, a mother and five kids and you're not going to make them homeless. Punish me if you must, but leave them out of it. They've done nothing to harm you. It's *me*, I'm the one!'

He took a few steps forward with both hands clenched round the pitchfork and Frank Lidden's mouth was dry with fear. Allan was in no fit state to come to his aid and he knew that Tom Bryce in his present mood was a very dangerous man. Yet he could not and would not retract his words, for what he had said was true. He had given Tom Bryce chance after chance, but the hop harvest was almost ready and could no longer be entrusted to him. The man had to go.

Tom was moving closer now, the pitchfork held threateningly. 'Now, you tell me that you won't harm them,' he said. 'Tell me you'll leave them out of it. At least let them stay there until I can find somewhere else.'

'No,' said Frank Lidden, his voice a harsh whisper. 'You all go – lock, stock and barrel. I want you all out of my sight by the end of the week.'

Tom lunged towards him and he dropped to his knees as the pitchfork thudded into the wall, not a foot above his head. It went in with such force that it could not be withdrawn.

'You murdering swine!' cried Frank. Searching desperately for a weapon with which to defend himself, he snatched up the axe which Allan had dropped and which now lay in the doorway. As

Tom sprang towards him he swung it and brought the flat of the blade against the side of Tom's head.

For several seconds Tom remained upright with a look of surprise on his face, then a small moan escaped his lips and he sank slowly to his knees, pitching forward on to his face and lying still.

'Dear God!' whispered Frank. 'Pray Heaven I haven't killed him!'

He dared not approach the prostrate figure to find out, but instead stepped round him and hurried to help Allan who had now struggled to his feet again, he clutching his jaw with both hands and signalling with his eyes his inability to speak. Frank Lidden put an arm round him and helped him out of the barn without a backward look at Tom Bryce, no word being spoken as the two men made their way across the yard and back to the farmhouse. Leaving Allan in the care of his wife, Frank went straight to the telephone and with trembling fingers began to dial the doctor and the police.

*

The temperature continued to rise until it touched ninety degrees and there it hovered for nearly a week. For those fortunate enough to be able to take holidays, the weather was perfect; for those who continued to work, it made life very uncomfortable.

At Foxearth all the kitchen doors stood open in an effort to create a draught, but to little effect. The kitchen was unbearably hot because the fire was never allowed out, being the sole source of heating for cooking and the provision of hot water. During the morning and early afternoon they let it go as low as they dared, but towards evening it had to be made up so that the evening meal could be cooked and water provided for baths.

The men could abandon their shirts and did so, but the women could only unbutton their high-necked uniforms and fan themselves with anything which came to hand.

Cook stood by the table pounding away at a cake mixture in a large earthenware bowl. Tim Bilton, astride a stool, watched her humorously, a mug of lemonade in his hand.

'What's that ever done to you?' he asked. 'Anyone would think it was your worst enemy, the way you're pounding it.'

Cook snorted. 'All very well for "Her Highness" to go offering a cake, but who's got to make it? Me, of course!'

'You didn't have to,' said Tim. 'She asked you if you would and you were all smiles – "course I will, ma'am; it will be a pleasure, ma'am".'

'Well, what else could I say? Bloomin' fêtes! It's the same thing every year – five dozen buns for the children's Sunday School treat; potted beef sandwiches for the old folks' party.'

'Now be fair,' said Tim. 'You can't blame her. The other Mrs Lawrence was just as bad – it's expected of them, that's all.'

'Well then, let them bloomin' well make them,' said Cook. 'I'd like just half an hour to put my feet up, that's what I'd like. As soon as I get this cake in the oven, it's going to be time to start the dinner, and there's another day gone!'

She glanced towards the door as Janet struggled in with two laden shopping baskets. She dumped them on the far end of the table and sank into the chair.

'Get me a glass of whatever you're drinking, Tim, there's a dear,' she said.

He laughed. 'It's always "dear" when you want something! Yesterday when you were trying to sweep round me, it was "move your flat feet".'

"Oh go on, Tim, I'm gasping! It must be nearly a hundred by now out there.' She felt in her apron pocket for the shopping list and spread it out on the table. 'That Jarvis Tupp,' she went on, 'will be a millionaire, I reckon. Everything's gone up since he took over from his Dad. Look at this – rolled oats, twopence-halfpenny a pound.'

'Twopence-halfpenny?' Cook tutted. 'I'm glad I don't have to pay the bills,' she said. 'What did he charge you for those oranges?'

'Sixpence a dozen.'

'He never did! I'm going to have a word with the mistress about this.'

Tim poured the last of the lemonade into a mug and handed it to Janet, while Cook thrust a wooden spoon into the cake mixture and moved round to stand beside her. Together they went through the rest of the list, exclaiming over each item.

'He was out of cheese,' Janet said. Cook snorted and, taking the list, folded it up and put it into her pocket.

'If you ask me,' she said, returning to her mixing bowl, 'young Jarvis has taken on a bit too much. He should hire someone else for that delivery van of his. Greedy, that's what he is. Can't do two jobs and do either of them properly. Well, aren't you going to unpack the stuff?'

Janet shook her head. 'Give me five minutes,' she said, 'to cool down. Then I'll do it.' She sipped her drink thankfully. 'There was a bear in the square,' she said, 'a dancing bear. Taller than a man it was. I've never seen a bear like it before.'

'Poor thing!' said Cook. 'I think it's cruel, making a dumb animal dance like that. Was it on a chain?'

'Of course it was. Husband-and-wife show, I think. He held the bear's chain and she turned the barrel-organ. Quite a crowd there.'

'Must be hot under all that fur in this heat,' said Tim. 'I'm glad I'm not a dancing bear.'

'I've got a bit more news for you,' said Janet, 'that Jarvis told me.'

'Good or bad?' asked Cook.

'Bad!' said Janet. 'Leastways, bad for them. It's about Tom Bryce.'

Cook rubbed lard round the inside of the large cake tin and then floured it. She carefully scraped the cake mixture from the edges of the bowl and eased it into the tin.

'Well, aren't you going to ask me what it is?' said Janet, disappointed by the reaction.

'I can guess what it is,' said Tim. 'Tom Bryce has finally got the sack.'

'Partly right,' said Janet, who now had their whole attention. 'They've took him off', she told them, 'to the asylum!'

'The asylum?' said Tim. 'But that's for loony people and Tom Bryce isn't mad.'

'Well, according to Jarvis Tupp, he went mad a few days ago,' said Janet. 'According to Jarvis, Tom tried to kill his gov'nor.'

'Tried to kill him? How?' asked Cook.

'With a pitchfork,' said Janet, 'and that was after he'd already half-killed another man. You needn't look at me like that – it's true, I tell you. Jarvis got it from the place where he buys his vegetables. Apparently Tom was drunk and the boss tried to sack him, but he wouldn't be sacked. Broke a man's jaw and then tried to kill Mr Lidden. Good job he didn't or else he'd have been hanged.'

Cook and Tim exchanged astonished looks. 'Tom Bryce a

murderer?' said Cook. 'I can't believe it! It seems that we were lucky, then, that he never tried to kill any of us.'

'He's no murderer,' said Tim. 'Whatever else he might be, he's not a murderer. It's the drink that's done it, I reckon.'

'How can you say that?' said Janet. 'I mean – lots of people drink too much, but they don't go round murdering people.'

She realized suddenly that Cook and Tim were staring past her and turned to find Vinnie looking at her with a strange expression on her face.

'Who's a murderer?' Vinnie asked. 'Who are you talking about, Janet?'

Janet's dismay was obvious in her face. 'Nothing, ma'am. It was only gossip. Really, it was nothing.'

'*Who* is a murderer, Janet?'

Janet looked appealingly at Cook, who gave a slight shrug. 'I'm sorry, ma'am,' said Janet, 'but probably it's only a rumour. It was Jarvis Tupp who told me . . . it's about Tom Bryce.'

Slowly Vinnie walked into the kitchen. 'Please tell me, Janet,' she said. 'Please tell me everything you heard – it's very important that I should know.'

Reluctantly, Janet recounted all that Jarvis Tupp had told her. When she had finished there was a silence in the kitchen while Vinnie digested the information. Then she said, 'And you're sure it's the asylum where they have taken him?'

'Quite sure, ma'am.'

'Thank you, Janet.'

Vinnie hesitated a moment and then looked at Cook. 'I came in to check that you'd remembered the cake,' she said.

Cook lifted up the cake tin and held it out to her. 'I have, ma'am, and here it is! It will be ready in a few hours, unless you want me to ice it.'

Vinnie shook her head. 'No, don't bother with icing, Cook. It will be splendid just as it is – and you will remember to weigh it, won't you? They have to guess the weight of it, you see.'

'I'll remember, ma'am, don't you worry.'

'Someone is going to collect it tomorrow,' said Vinnie vaguely. 'I forget who.'

'It will be ready, ma'am,' Cook assured her. 'All on a silver base like last year, and the weight written on a piece of paper inside a sealed envelope.'

'Thank you.'

As Vinnie turned away, Cook said, 'Some time, ma'am, I should like to talk to you about the groceries. Overcharging something frightful, is that Jarvis Tupp.'

'Is he? Then certainly we must talk about it, but another time if you don't mind.'

She looked distractedly around the kitchen and then without another word turned and walked away. Once she was out of earshot, Tim said, 'She must feel terrible, being so close to them and all.'

'No doubt she does,' said Cook, 'but there's nothing she can do. Tom Bryce has gone too far this time and there's no one can save him.'

*

The asylum master – a small man, with thinning grey hair – rose to his feet as Vinnie was shown into the room. He shook her outstretched hand, but regarded her without smiling.

'I believe you refused to give your name. Although I do not normally see people under such circumstances, on this occasion I have agreed. Please sit down.'

He indicated a hard upright chair and Vinnie seated herself.

'I do not refuse to give you my name,' said Vinnie. 'I was merely unwilling to state it at the door. I wish my visit to you to remain as secret as possible and I will explain why. My name is Lavinia Lawrence and my husband owns Foxearth Farm at Teesbury. You may have heard of it?'

He nodded. 'Of course. But what can I do for you, Mrs Lawrence?'

Vinnie explained as briefly as possible that she understood Tom Bryce had been admitted to the asylum; that he had once worked for her father-in-law; that she herself had been friendly with Tom's mother some years earlier and that she wished to help the family if she could.

'The family,' he said, 'is no concern of mine. Mr Bryce was committed to the asylum on the recommendation of the police. The certificate was signed by his wife and he is now in our care. As far as I am concerned, the matter starts and ends there.'

Vinnie took a deep breath and clasped her hands together to hide her shaking fingers. 'Has he been examined by a doctor?' she asked. 'Is he really mad?'

He rested his elbows on the table and pressed the fingers of one hand against those of the other while considering his answer. 'He is not insane,' he stated, 'in the sense that he is suffering from an affliction of the brain or a malfunction of the mind. His madness is sporadic and is directly linked to alcohol. You might say it is a form of alcoholism, that the mind becomes temporarily deranged. In my view Mr Bryce should be treated as a criminal; in other words, he should be locked up in a prison and not put into the care of an asylum which is already over-burdened by more deserving cases. I did not wish to admit him to this establishment, but pressure was put upon me to do so. His employer was very anxious that he should not go to prison. On arrival here, Mr Bryce became extremely disturbed and violent and we were forced to put him into a strait-jacket.'

Vinnie closed her eyes as the full horror of Tom's position dawned on her. 'Is he alone?' she asked.

'Certainly not! Accommodation is always limited; we are very overcrowded here and he does not merit a room to himself. He is in the general ward.'

'I should like to see him,' said Vinnie. 'Is that possible?'

'I am afraid not. Only authorized visitors are allowed.'

'Has anyone been to see him?' asked Vinnie. 'His wife . . . his mother?'

'No one,' he told her. 'The doctor has advised that he be left severely alone. Visits from his family might provoke further reaction and I do not choose to take that risk. I have other patients and my staff to consider.'

Vinnie covered her face with her hands for a moment to hide her despair. At last she lowered them, but did not look at the asylum master. 'I had considered making a small contribution . . .' she said. 'No doubt you have some such fund for the welfare of the patients?'

His eyes narrowed. 'We do indeed have such a fund.'

'If I made a contribution,' said Vinnie, 'would you agree that some of the money be spent on Mr Bryce?'

'I could not do that,' he answered. 'His needs are no greater than those of the other inmates. The money would have to be used in a general way for the good of everyone.'

'I am considering a donation of five pounds,' said Vinnie. 'If you felt able to change you mind and allow me to speak to Mr Bryce, I would be prepared to double it.'

His eyebrows shot up. 'You are trying to bribe me, Mrs Lawrence,' he said.

'Yes,' said Vinnie desperately. 'But the money could be divided in any way you wished. Say five pounds for the general good of the patients, perhaps, and another five pounds to be used as you thought fit.'

He still hesitated, but eventually picked up a small brass bell on his desk and rang it. A young man soon arrived, wearing a white jacket to which the smell of disinfectant clung.

'Take this young lady to see Mr Bryce,' the asylum master told him. 'Her name is known to me and I have authorized a visit of not longer than three minutes. Wait outside the ward for her.'

The young man nodded respectfully and withdrew.

Vinnie immediately opened her purse, but the master shook his head. 'Send it to me,' he said, 'in a separate envelope. You understand?' She nodded.

'Mark it "Personal".' She nodded again.

'Three minutes,' he warned her. 'No longer!' Then he opened a file which lay on his desk and began busily to rearrange the papers.

Vinnie followed her escort down a long corridor, keeping her eyes on his back as he walked purposefully ahead of her making no conversation. Finally they came to a door which was locked. He selected a key from a bunch which hung at his waist and opened it, locking it behind them after they had passed through. Then he pushed open double swing-doors and Vinnie found herself in the main ward. About twenty beds were arranged down one side, but they were all neatly made with the sheets tucked in firmly. No one sat or lay upon them, although there were no chairs to be seen – only a long wooden bench nailed to the far wall on which nine or ten men were crowded together. The rest of them sat on the floor, stood at the window staring out or moved aimlessly around in the large empty area.

Apart from the beds and the bench, the room was devoid of furniture. It was in fact devoid of anything other than its occupants – no flowers, no books, no pictures on the walls, no carpets on the floor. Vinnie supposed that this was for the patients' own good – perhaps for their own protection. In the hands of a madman, the most insignificant object could become a dangerous weapon.

As she entered, several faces turned in her direction. Another white-coated man sat at a table just inside the door and her escort spoke to him briefly.

'Far end on the left,' said the second attendant. 'He can't hurt you.'

As Vinnie began to walk down the room an elderly man shuffled towards her, holding out both hands, but the man at the desk shouted at him and he withdrew wordlessly. She tried hard to fight down the mixture of fear and distaste which threatened to overwhelm her. 'There but for the grace of God . . .' she told herself, but her heart still raced and her body felt cold as ice in spite of the heat. She tried not to look directly into any faces she passed, yet gained an impression of each one – some apathetic, some curious, others suspicious. One or two looked distinctly hostile.

At the far end of the room, Vinnie found Tom Bryce between two of the beds. He was propped against the wall with his feet bound together and, as she had been warned, his arms and the upper part of his body enveloped in a white canvas jacket. His arms were crossed in front of his chest and the long sleeves which hid his hands were fastened behind him. She knew at once that he was fully conscious, fully aware of his predicament; as she looked into his eyes, she read desolation and utter defeat. He recognized her at once and his cheeks burned with humiliation as Vinnie fell to her knees beside him.

'Tom!' she whispered. 'Oh, my poor, dear Tom!'

Almost imperceptibly he shook his head, closing his eyes and remaining silent.

'I know what has happened,' she said quickly. 'Don't worry, Tom, I'm going to look after your family. I shall take them to Foxearth with me – there's an empty cottage they can have. And Tom, I promise I will do everything in my power to get you out of here if I possibly can. Are they treating you well, Tom? Do they feed you properly? Oh, my dearest man! I swear I will take you away from here somehow – I'll find a way, I promise you. Please don't lose heart, Tom! Don't give up!'

At last he spoke in a voice which she hardly recognized. 'If I leave this place, I shall go to prison,' he said hopelessly.

Vinnie stared at him. 'Who told you that?'

He shook his head wearily. 'Don't let them come,' he said. 'Don't let them see me like this.' He glanced down at the strait-jacket. 'Rose, I mean. It would break her heart.'

'It's breaking mine,' whispered Vinnie.

For a moment her eyes held his and she saw an anguish which matched her own. 'If I could get you released,' she began again. 'If I say I will take responsibility for you, or whatever else I need to say . . .'

'It's no use, Vinnie, I'm finished,' he said. 'Let me be! Just care for Rose and the kids if you can.'

'Don't say that. You mustn't give in, Tom!'

'No, Vinnie, don't meddle. I just want to die and be forgotten.'

'Tom, no!'

A white-coated figure materialized beside Vinnie. 'That's enough,' he told her. 'You will have to leave now.'

Vinnie looked up at him. 'Oh not yet, surely?' she protested. 'That's not three minutes. I have only just arrived. Another minute or two, please!'

'I'm sorry, but you are upsetting the other patients.'

'Upsetting them?' Vinnie glanced around and saw to her dismay that a small group of inmates had gathered round to watch her. Hastily, she scrambled to her feet.

'Please,' she repeated. 'Just one more minute?'

'I am sorry. We have to abide by the rules. He is a difficult patient and we can't risk any trouble.'

Vinnie gasped. 'Trouble? How can he possibly give any trouble, trussed up like a—' For Tom's sake she bit back the angry words.

One of the other patients reached out a hand and plucked at her sleeve. 'You see,' said the white-coated man, 'you are upsetting them. You must leave at once. Please follow me.'

Vinnie glanced at Tom, then quickly knelt beside him. Awkwardly she leaned forward and kissed the top of his head. Tears shone in his eyes, but he said nothing. There was a murmur from the watching circle of men and one of them laughed – a high-pitched childish sound that made Vinnie shudder. Her escort took hold of her arm and began to urge her away. She tried to say 'Goodbye' but her voice failed her and only her lips formed the words. Then she was stumbling back along the ward.

The memory of Tom's eyes would haunt Vinnie for the rest of her days.

CHAPTER EIGHT

Wintering the bees was a task which Clive le Brun took very seriously. Normally it could be done at any time during the months of September or October, but Clive liked to complete the work before the hop-picking commenced in earnest. He therefore gave his bees their last feed of sugar syrup on the twenty-ninth day of August and now he was preparing to close the hives. Sometimes when the summer was exceptionally fine, he would take a chance and leave the wintering until after the hop-picking, but this year, the weather had broken suddenly and after several days of heavy rain, he had decided now was as good a time as any.

Clive had abandoned the traditional straw skeps in favour of the more modern wooden hives, seven of which were placed along the top edge of one of his orchards at intervals of four feet. Six of these hives contained swarms; the seventh was empty, awaiting the hopeful collection of a new swarm whenever it might occur. The hedge behind the hives protected them from the north-west wind and the entrance faced south-east so that they benefited from as much sunlight as possible. Clive le Brun was very fond of his bees. Looking after them was one of the few relaxations which he allowed himself, and since telling them of his wife's death he had gradually spent more time with them.

Now the Queen bee had finished laying her eggs and the colonies had to be protected against the hazards of winter. Their arch-enemies, the wasps, must be kept out at all costs and mice were also a problem. In order to repel these unwanted intruders, the entrance to the bottom of each hive must be partially closed, leaving only a small area covered with excluder zinc. The holes in the zinc would allow nothing larger than bees to pass through.

Most years the prospects of an hour with the bees pushed all other thoughts out of his mind, but this year Clive found himself unable to give his undivided attention to the task. Try as he would, he could not keep Vinnie Lawrence out of his thoughts and the knowledge of this failure irritated him. Her unfortunate encounter with Tom Bryce at the pigeon shoot had been disturbing. The girl's unpredictable behaviour had embarrassed him, but at the same time he felt himself partly to blame for she had attended the shoot at his invitation. If he had not left her alone, the incident would never have taken place. He sighed as he pulled on his boots and adjusted the protective netting around his hat.

He took the smoker – a small canister with a funnel and miniature bellows – and thrust into it a piece of oily rag. He should have known better, he reproached himself. The girl was still so unworldly. He thought again of the chess they had played during the weekend at Foxearth and found himself smiling – she was so eager to learn. Julian Lawrence could have helped her more than he did, Clive thought resentfully. He should never have married such a girl if he was not prepared to involve himself in her education. Left to her own devices, she would never make a suitable mistress for Foxearth.

He lit the rag and then closed the lid of the canister. Immediately the flame went out and the rag began to smoulder. Pulling on gauntlet gloves, he turned his attention to the six excluder strips which he prepared earlier in the day.

As for the Bryce fellow – it was quite preposterous that he and Vinnie could ever have formed a liaison, yet it was rumoured she had borne his child. That there was some kind of bond between them was unfortunately obvious. Christina Lawrence had acted wisely in banishing Tom Bryce from Foxearth, he thought, but it was a pity that he had remained in the immediate vicinity. Better that he had disappeared completely from the scene.

Clive pumped the bellows once or twice to ensure that the smoker was working properly, then gathered up the excluder strips and made his way through the orchard where the trees hung heavily with ripening fruit. The Bramleys were going well, but the Conference pears were small. At any other time this would have concerned him, but now his mind returned stubbornly to Vinnie and her problems. Julian Lawrence, he thought, was not the right man for her. He had married too young and lacked the maturity necessary if the relationship was to develop as it should. Had Julian been ten years older the situation would be very different, but his youth made him vulnerable. The young man had married hastily and with the best intentions, but was he now repenting at leisure?

He had also noticed the way in which Julian regarded Mary Bellweather and that, too, had dismayed him for, she was exactly the kind of well-bred young woman who would make an excellent match for his own son, William. However, Mary had obviously been attracted by Julian's undeniable good looks and charm and Clive had sensed the unspoken rivalry between the two younger men. Regretfully he knew that Vinnie also had been aware of it. Now he sighed deeply and glanced up at the sky. Heavy clouds were running in from the west and he would have to work quickly if he was to escape the rain which had been threatening all morning.

Working his way methodically along the first five hives, he treated each one in turn in the same way. First, he removed the wooden lid of the hive and puffed in some smoke to calm the bees. Then he lifted out the upper chamber and replaced the lid. The bees were still foraging but they ignored his presence, for he was careful to keep out of their flight path. Gently he tilted back each hive, slid in the excluder strip, then resettled it firmly on its base. He worked slowly, carefully and without fear. Only the sixth hive would present a problem, for their Queen was more volatile than the others and the bees were therefore easily aroused and quick-tempered. A swarm of thirty thousand angry bees constituted a formidable adversary!

At each hive a few puffs of soporific smoke were sufficient, but it would not be so easy at the last hive. He approached warily, making sure his shadow did not fall across the entrance way to signal his approach. Thirty or forty bees hovered round the entrance and, to his experienced ear, the pitch of their humming was higher than that of those in the other hives and indicated that they were already uneasy. Inside the hive, a mass of dark, furry bodies clambered over the comb. Fifty or maybe sixty bees issued suddenly from the entrance and darted up into the air enquiringly. A few more followed as Clive removed the top chamber and put it on the grass. Slowly he edged the roof back into position but the note of the bees was changing, becoming higher and definitely angry. They were leaving the hive in ever-increasing numbers, buzzing all around him, clinging to the netting which surrounded and protected his face and neck. If he delayed much longer, the whole swarm might leave the hive and then he would be in serious trouble. He decided to fit the excluder strip the following day when they had calmed down.

The air was full of small, hurtling bodies which thudded against him as he collected the smoker and straightened up, but as he moved away from the hive the bees pursued him, their hostility evident. He made for the trees and walked as close to the leafy branches as he could go, so that some of his attackers would be diverted by the foliage. By the time he reached the far end of the orchard, he was glad to see that perhaps half of them had been left behind. The rest would stay with him for a considerable time and there was nothing he could do about it but wait for them to lose interest. In a quarter or perhaps half an hour, they would return to their hive – it was merely a matter of waiting.

Clive had given strict instructions to the servants that whenever he was dealing with the bees, no one should approach him. Now he stood with feet slightly apart and lightly clenched hands resting on his hips, waiting for the bees to leave him. While he waited his thoughts returned once more to Vinnie Lawrence.

*

Bernard Cann sat on his high stool poring over a large ledger. Pale, spidery writing covered each page, for he was not averse to diluting the ink with water if by so doing he could defer making another purchase. From the age of thirteen he had planned to be a wealthy man but the pawn-broking business, inherited from his father, had not proved a very lucrative occupation. Now, at sixty, he was aware that time was running out and that if he was ever to become a wealthy man, he must make small economies wherever he could. If there were no large sums of money coming in, then he would at least do all he could to prevent small sums going out. This was the extent of his philosophy on financial dealings.

Business was not at all brisk, he reflected, and during the coming month of September would become even less so for his clients would all be in the hop-gardens earning and having no need of his services.

Bernard was a short, tubby man and his feet did not reach the bar two-thirds of the way down the legs of the stool. He ran a podgy finger down the preceding page and his lips moved in silent addition and multiplication. At the very bottom of the page, as on all the other pages, a sum was underlined in red. He nodded, satisfied that this was correct, and began to transfer the balance to the next page. He wrote the date in untidy figures – 29th August, 1901 – and tutted over the quality of the ink. Perhaps he had diluted it a little too often? But he would admit that to no one else. His wife had a sharp tongue and a way of making caustic comments; she called him a miser, which he knew was merited. He took up a pen and dipped it into the small glass inkwell which stood on the counter in front of him.

From the counter, a metal grid rose to the ceiling; there was a small aperture in it through which money could be passed. Further along, where the grid ended, the results of yesterday's transactions were piled untidily. The first hour of the morning was always a slack time and Bernard made use of it by bringing his ledger up to date and sorting the previous day's intake. He looked up as the bell jangled noisily and the cool draught blew in a few raindrops, and was surprised to see a well-dressed young woman regarding him nervously.

'Mmm?' he said, his tone uncompromising.

The young woman swallowed nervously as she cleared her throat, never taking her eyes from his face. He looked past her and through the glass window of the shop door could see a private carriage parked outside.

'Well?' he said.

She glanced round the tiny shop to reassure herself that no one could overhear their conversation.

'I need some money,' she said. 'I have plenty of things to sell – I mean to pawn.' He nodded. 'They are outside in the dog-cart.'

'Not much good out there,' he remarked.

'No. I was going to bring them in, but first I wanted to ask your terms.' She glanced round again. 'Is there somewhere more private where we could talk?'

'No,' he said, 'there isn't.'

'Oh. You see, I don't want it known—'

'No one ever does.'

Her embarrassment was plain to see, but Bernard Cann did not allow his tone to soften. It was always the same, he reflected sourly: the young women would tell a pathetic story in the hope of improving his terms. Over the years he had learnt to resist all such feminine wiles.

'And your terms?' she asked.

'Twenty-five per cent over twelve months,' he told her. 'That is the statutory rate since the last Act was passed in 1872. Anything from five pounds to fifty pounds. Above that it means a special contract. On a monthly basis, of course,' he added.

It was plain she did not fully understand and equally obvious that in her present state of mind she would not query whatever terms he offered her. However, Bernard Cann was an honest man and the terms would be fair, neither more nor less than the going rate.

'Twelve months,' she repeated. 'That means I can redeem them at any time within the next twelve months?'

He nodded and there was a slight pause. Without showing further interest in his customer, Bernard Cann dipped his pen once more into the ink and began to write.

'I'll get the things then.'

He ignored the tell-tale quiver in her voice. Tears would not earn her an extra penny! He continued to write while she hurried outside. When she stood before him again, slightly breathless, she indicated a collection of items she wanted to pawn which were now piled on the counter. Carefully he slid down from the stool and made his way along the counter, trying to hide his growing eagerness. He picked up a pair of slippers and shrugged disparagingly.

'Slippers don't fetch much,' he told her.

'There's a ring here,' she said. 'See!' She found a small leather case and snapped it open to show a large opal in gold setting. He sighed, as though with disappointment, while mentally assessing its value.

'And a silver locket,' she went on. 'There's an ivory fan, hand-painted, also a silk purse. Three books, bound in leather – that's Moroccan leather, the very best. Oh, and a muff in real mink. A brass inkwell that's almost new and this picture frame which is solid silver. It was a wedding present . . .'

'Mmm.' He pursed his lips and regarded the collection with a jaundiced expression which suggested he was tired of continually being offered goods of such poor quality. The young woman watched him with growing anxiety.

'They are all of first-class quality,' she insisted. 'The opal ring is Italian.'

He shook his head, apparently in deep despair.

'Oh, please, you must give me something for them!'

With a slight shrug, he moved back to the grille and climbed back on to his stool.

'Twenty-five per cent,' he repeated, 'over a twelve-month period. Do you understand? If you redeem after six months, you will owe only half the money.'

She nodded, glancing round the shop and out through the shop door to satisfy herself that no one was about to hear the next part of the conversation. Bernard drew a pad of forms towards him and raised his pen.

'Name?' he demanded.

The young woman's nervousness increased visibly. 'Do I have to give my name?' she asked. 'Is it really necessary? I mean, you have the security. You have all my property – and if I don't redeem them, you will sell them and recover your money. I don't want anyone to know that I am pawning these things.'

She looked at him appealingly, but Bernard Cann hardened his heart. 'You could have stolen them,' he said.

'Indeed I haven't!' she cried indignantly. 'They are my own possessions. I swear to you that they belong to me.'

'Well, now, you'd say that even if they were stolen. I'm afraid the law requires me to have a name and address.'

He held the pen poised in his right hand while the fingers of his left drummed impatiently on the counter top.

'Can you produce receipts,' he asked, 'for all these?'

'Receipts? Why, no. At least, I imagine the receipts are some-where. My husband no doubt has kept them. But since I do not wish him to know what I am doing, I can hardly ask for them.'

Bernard Cann spread the fingers of his left hand and scruti-nized each nail in turn. Then he picked at a tooth with a languid movement which somehow managed to convey his growing exasperation.

'If I had stolen the things, then surely I would give you a false name,' said Vinnie in increasing desperation.

'You might, and then again you might not.'

'I assure you they are mine to dispose of as I wish.'

'You want to pawn them?' he said.

'Yes, I do.'

'You want me to lend you money?'

'Yes, please.'

He dipped his pen once more into the ink. 'Then we'll start with your name,' he said.

The young woman sighed deeply. 'Lavinia Lawrence,' she said in a low voice.

'How are you spelling "Lavinia"?' he asked, although he knew perfectly well.

She spelled it for him and then spelled out 'Lawrence' and gave her address. Just then the bell jangled behind her and she turned in alarm as a small boy came into the shop carrying a pair of boots.

'Shall I see to this young lad?' he asked her.

'Please do.'

Bernard Cann looked at the boy. 'Same as before?' he asked. The boy nodded shyly and glanced up at the young woman who stood beside him.

'A shilling, then,' said Bernard. He wrote hurriedly on a separate form, tore it from the pad and gave it to the boy, then counted out a sixpence and six pennies and handed them across the counter. The boy scuttled from the shop and the door clanged behind him.

Slowly, the pawnbroker wrote down everything, stating a price for each item and entering that alongside. When he was finished, he totalled it. 'That's twenty-five pounds, five shillings and three pence,' he told her.

He counted out the money and pushed it through the grill where the young woman scooped it up. She looked as though she would like to protest at the smallness of the amount, but Bernard Cann knew it was fair. They always wanted more. He hoped she would not come back, in which case he would make a reasonable profit. He had in fact done a day's work in a quarter of an hour. She thanked him and turned to go, but as she reached the door she looked back. 'It *is* confidential, isn't it?' she asked.

He nodded. 'I shall be pleased to be of service at any time,' he told her.

'Thank you.'

The door closed, the bell jangled again and Bernard Cann reached for the opal ring. It was a fine example of Italian workmanship as she had suggested. He loved beautiful things; if she did not come back, he might give the ring to his wife.

*

Vinnie took the money and Tim Bilton drove her back to Teesbury where she went into Tupp's village store and ordered a box full of groceries. Joan Tupp looked at her curiously.

'Are these for the big house?' she asked.

'No,' said Vinnie. 'I want them delivered the day after tomorrow to Brook cottage.'

Joan raised her eyebrows in surprise. 'I thought that was empty?' she said.

'It won't be,' said Vinnie, as casually as she could. 'A family will be moving in, but I don't want it talked about. Do you understand?'

'You don't want it talked about?'

'No. I'll give you a regular order for them, on the condition that you don't discuss it with anyone else.'

'I see.' Joan looked as though she did not see at all but she had no wish to lose a weekly order. 'Well, I'm not one to gossip, I'm sure,' she said.

'Thank you,' said Vinnie.

'What name will it be?' asked Joan. 'Just so that I know.'

Vinnie hesitated. 'It doesn't matter about the name,' she said. 'Just "Brook Cottage" will do.'

Joan scribbled. 'And that's the day after tomorrow,' she said, 'which is Saturday. Will that be every Saturday?'

'For a while, yes.'

Vinnie settled the bill, left the shop and climbed back into the dog-cart.

'Now the blacksmith's,' she said.

'Yes, ma'am.'

Five minutes later Andy Roberts was in the dog-cart behind her, and Tim was driving them both to Brook Cottage. When they got there, Vinnie and Andy alighted.

'Wait here, please, Tim.'

Tim nodded. There was something very odd going on, he mused, but he had seen that look in Vinnie's eyes which dared him to ask questions. Still, there would be plenty to talk about in the kitchen later on.

Vinnie led Andy through the rickety gate. 'Can you do something with the gate?' she asked.

'New hinges,' he said. 'A couple of new hinges, maybe.'

'Right.' She led the way along the overgrown path. 'Latch and hinges on the front door,' she told him.

'You could say that,' he agreed, for the front door hung crookedly on one hinge.

He followed Vinnie inside, where paper peeled from the walls and most of the whitewash had descended from the ceiling to settle in flakes on the passage floor.

'Not my job,' he said determinedly. 'I can't abide painting and papering.'

'I am not asking you', said Vinnie. 'There's already plenty for you to do.'

Andy looked around him in disbelief. 'You mean someone's moving in here?' he said.

'That's right,' said Vinnie. 'I know it's in a state, but at least it will be a roof over their heads. This is the kitchen.'

She pushed open the door which creaked mournfully. Cracked and broken linoleum of an indeterminate colour covered the floor and the blue flowered paper on the walls was stained with large patches of damp. Cobwebs hung in every corner and the window was grimy. A large, rusting kitchen range stood along one side.

'The door's missing,' said Vinnie, pointing. 'It needs a new door and the flue is rusted away in places.'

'God Almighty!' he said. 'I wouldn't know where to start with that lot.'

'Well, you must do the best you can,' said Vinnie. 'I can't buy another one – I mean, they can't afford a new one. You must do the best you can with it, Andy – just make it usable. The window latches, too,' she told him. 'Most of them are missing or rusted.'

'I'm not surprised,' said Andy. 'This place must have been empty for twenty years – ever since old Mrs Jolly died. I never thought to see anyone live here again.'

'You'll remember what I said,' Vinnie reminded him, 'about not gossiping?'

'Oh, I'll remember,' he said. 'Don't worry. Your secret – whatever it is – is safe with me.'

'It's not exactly a secret,' said Vinnie, 'since it's bound to come out sooner or later. I'd just rather it was later, that's all.'

'What about the water pump we passed as we came in?' he said. 'Is that working?'

'I don't know,' said Vinnie. 'I didn't think to try it.'

'We'll have a look on the way out.'

Vinnie pulled open a door which concealed the bottom of the stairs. They too were in poor shape and one tread had rotted away almost entirely.

'I'm no carpenter,' said Andy. 'You need a carpenter for that job.'

She nodded, leading the way up the stairs to reach a large attic which had been divided into two small bedrooms. In one of these was a large water tank with a wooden cover.

'It's empty,' said Vinnie. 'It probably leaks.'

'Almost certainly,' he agreed grimly.

'So we need a new tank?' she asked.

Andy crossed the little bedroom and rubbed the side of his head against the window; then he peered out.

'Well, it's a nice view,' he said. He turned and looked at Vinnie. 'It's the Bryces, isn't it?'

She began to stammer, but Andy interrupted. 'Look,' he said, 'we all know they're in trouble and now you're trying to help them. That's nothing to be ashamed of.'

'But it's my husband,' said Vinnie. 'I haven't told him yet. I thought I would move them in and tell him later – then perhaps he will let them stay.'

Andy shook his head. 'I wouldn't be in your shoes,' he said. 'You've got pluck, I'll say that!' He leaned back against the side of the window and folded his arms. 'They letting Tom out then?'

'I don't know.'

'They say he's gone a bit—' He tapped his forehead.

'I don't know what to think,' said Vinnie. 'It's all so hopeless.'

'It's the way of the world,' he told her. 'Some problems can't be solved.'

'I can try,' said Vinnie.

Andy laughed softly and shook his head in admiration.

'Aye,' he said. 'I reckon you will.'

*

The following day Vinnie went to Harkwood to see Clive le Brun. Emily, the maid, showed her into the morning room.

'The master's closing up the last hive,' she said. 'I daren't go near. Really nasty-tempered, those bees, and I'm not allowed within a hundred yards of them. Not that I'd want to go any nearer, but the master says I'll excite them. I hate bees!'

Vinnie hardly heard a word she was saying, preoccupied as she was.

'I mean, they can be very spiteful,' continued the girl. 'They can kill a person, bees can. My Mum heard of a man once who got stung by some bees, he threw a fit and was dead within an hour. Just like that! I think they're dangerous, and all for a few pots of honey – well, I don't reckon it's worth it. You won't catch me near them, not if I can help it. You ever been stung by a bee?'

'I beg your pardon?'

'I said, have you ever been stung by a bee? I was stung twice last year. They turned real vicious and we were all scared to go out into the garden. Buzzing everywhere, they were, and stinging folks as had done them no harm at all. They stung Master William just under his eye. Came up something terrible, it did, and they stung one of the chickens to death! Poor thing, just minding its own business and pecking around. They just went for it and stung it to death. I'd get rid of the lot of them if they was mine.'

Vinnie nodded. 'How long do you think he will be?' she asked. 'Could you call him, perhaps?'

'He wouldn't like it,' said Emily, 'but he shouldn't be long now. He's been gone about ten minutes and there was only one hive left. As soon as he's back, I'll tell him you're here.'

Vinnie waited. It was almost ten minutes before Clive appeared and before he had even greeted her properly, she began to stammer out her request.

'I know you will not approve of what I'm doing, Clive,' she began, 'but I must do something and I'm sure you will grant me that much, for I can't let them starve. The Bryces, I mean. I'm moving them into a cottage on our estate tomorrow.' He tried to interrupt but she rushed on. 'I haven't spoken to Julian about this, but of course I shall tell him eventually. The pickers arrive tonight and I think he has enough on his mind. I have a little money to carry them over the first few weeks and I shall find work for Rose to do so that they won't need poor relief.'

'But Vinnie—' he protested.

'No, please, let me finish, Clive, before my courage fails me! I've come to ask you a very big favour and if you say "No" then I am quite lost.' She closed her eyes. 'It's Tom Bryce. I wondered if you could give him a job, no matter how humble. Just give him a chance, Clive, that's all. Could you bring yourself to do that? If he was allowed home and the family were together, I think they just might survive. Otherwise, I don't think they can.'

She opened her eyes and stared at him beseechingly.

'My dear Vinnie, that's *all*, you say. You are asking me to take a madman into my employ – on to my staff – and you say that's *all*?'

'Tom's not mad,' said Vinnie. 'I've been to see him. I believe he is as sane as you and me. It was only the drinking, you see, and now he's given it up.'

'How do you know that, Vinnie?' he asked. 'He cannot obtain drink while he is in the asylum, but that does not mean he has given it up.'

'But he *will* give it up,' said Vinnie. 'I know he will.'

Clive shook his head. 'I admire your spirit, Vinnie and I know you mean well, but you really should not interfere with people's lives this way. I'm afraid I cannot help you in this matter – no, let me finish, Vinnie – for I think that the doctors probably know better than you about the state of Tom Bryce's mind. People are not committed to an asylum without a very good reason and we have no guarantee that if he was allowed out he could behave normally. It would at best be an unwise and dangerous experiment. Have you thought that he might lose control of himself again? This time he might kill somebody and then he would hang. Have you considered carefully enough, Vinnie, what you are asking?'

'Yes, I have thought about it, Clive,' said Vinnie. 'I have known Tom Bryce for a long time, and for reasons which I can't explain to you I feel I owe him this one chance. Oh Clive, please help him!' She rubbed her face tiredly with her hand.

'So that you can shed your guilt,' he said. 'That's it, isn't it, Vinnie? You blame yourself for something which happened a long time ago, and what you are trying to do now is get rid of your own guilt.' Clive hoped to bring Vinnie to her senses and his tone was intentionally harsh. 'Listen to me, Vinnie. I will be quite honest with you. You have regrets about something which happened earlier in your life and you believe that because of that mistake, Tom Bryce and his family are in distress whereas you have married well and will live comfortably for the rest of your days. Now, you have survived that earlier tragedy and Tom Bryce has not. You feel that life is very unfair and you are trying to redress the balance. It's all very admirable, Vinnie, but it doesn't work like that. Things are not that simple. Life *is* unfair and you cannot make it otherwise. By trying to right one wrong, you may well provoke another even worse than the first.'

Clive saw her growing despair and wished most sincerely that he could comply with her request, but his common sense prevailed and gently he took her hands in his. 'I'm not blaming you, Vinnie and I'm not disapproving, because I know how keenly you want to help them. I think I even know why – but that's all in the past. What I do think is that you have made a mistake in arranging to move this family into property which belongs to your husband. When he finds out, he will be within his rights to evict them again and *if* you are able to arrange for Tom Bryce's release, which I very much doubt, you will be putting innocent people at risk.'

He saw that her mouth trembled and continued more gently, 'You are out of your depth, Vinnie. Please believe me.'

Vinnie sighed deeply. 'I know,' she whispered, 'but it's too late to turn back now. Oh, Clive, I beg you to help him. There is no one else I can turn to. Trust me, Clive, and give Tom a chance. If you will offer him a job of some kind, I can at least *ask* the authorities to release him?'

Briefly Clive wavered. 'You realize what you are doing?' he asked. 'You are asking me to share your responsibility. That is hardly fair.'

She smiled faintly. 'Life is not fair,' she said. 'You just told me that yourself.'

He walked to the window, thrust his hands into his pockets and stared out into the garden. The recent rain had kept the trees green but soon they would turn to orange and then to brown and would litter his lawn. *Maybe* he could use an assistant gardener. More than anything, he wanted to grant Vinnie's request. Then it was his turn to sigh, for he knew he could not be party to so dangerous a scheme.

'I'm sorry, Vinnie,' he said. 'I believe it would be a mistake and I will not do it.'

He heard her sharp intake of breath, then a flurry of footsteps. When he turned back from the window Vinnie had gone.

*

'Well!'

Janet, Cook, Edie and Young Harry all looked up in alarm as Mrs Tallant swept back into the kitchen and folded her arms. Her expression was outraged and she held herself stiffly as though preventing herself from making a violent movement of some kind.

'Now I've heard everything!' she exclaimed.

The others waited impatiently. Mrs Tallant had been summoned to Vinnie's presence and had now returned obviously deeply distressed.

'Whatever's happened?' Janet asked her. 'What did she want?'

'I have now heard everything,' Mrs Tallant repeated. 'That young madam has gone too far!'

'But what's happened?'

'Too far!'

Cook and Janet exchanged exasperated looks while Edie moved forward a few steps with a knife in her right hand, a half-peeled potato in her left.

'Have you got the sack?' she asked.

Mrs Tallant gave her a withering look and did not condescend to answer.

'Is it about tomorrow?' asked Cook, for the following morning the hop-pickers would arrive. Still they all waited.

'Well,' said Mrs Tallant again, 'Cook's not going to be very pleased with the news, I'm afraid—'

'Ooh!' gasped Edie. 'Cook's got the sack!'

'Oh, do stop it, you foolish girl!' said Mrs Tallant. 'Nobody's got the sack. It's the wretched Bryces.'

'Wretched what?'

'Bryces. It's that wretched Bryce family.'

Janet shook her head. 'I don't understand. What have the Bryces got to do with Cook?'

Mrs Tallant deigned to explain at last. 'Cook was expecting some more help in the kitchen,' she said. 'Someone to replace Janet, who is now nurse to the Colonel.'

'What do you mean?' said Cook. '*Was* to have had some help?'

'Exactly what I say,' said Mrs Tallant. 'Now it seems that Rose Bryce is to be given the work instead.'

They gathered round Mrs Tallant, all talking at once until she unfolded her arms, put a hand to her head and demanded silence, declaring that her nerves would not take any more. She then proceeded to explain the gist of her conversation with the mistress of the house.

It seemed that Rose Bryce, her children and her mother-in-law had moved into Brook Cottage, which might or might not prove to be a permanent arrangement. Tom Bryce *might* be joining them if the asylum would release him. All the Foxearth washing and ironing would in future be taken to Brook Cottage and the work would be done by Rose Bryce, who would be paid on an hourly basis. All the bread for Foxearth would be baked at Brook Cottage by Tom Bryce's mother. All mending of the laundry would also be done by Rose or her mother-in-law.

Edie set up a loud wail. 'Then what's left for me to do? It's me what's going to get the sack!'

Mrs Tallant glared at her. 'I have told you once, Edie, that no one is going to get the sack, so stop that ridiculous noise at once! I have a headache and you are making it worse. The Bryces will keep hens and all our eggs will come from them instead of from Tupp's Stores.'

The housekeeper sat down heavily at the table and told Edie to put the kettle on to make a cup of tea.

'But what a muddle!' said Janet, puzzled. 'We shan't know where we are.'

'Exactly my view,' said Mrs Tallant. 'I tried to argue, but she would not listen. She has quite made up her mind, it seems, and nothing I can say will change it. It is quite unpardonable to take the staffing of the kitchen out of my hands in this way. Not to say irresponsible.'

Young Harry frowned. 'I don't much like the thought of Tom Bryce being on the loose again,' he said. 'One minute he's a dangerous madman and they're shutting him up – the next he's being offered a job. He might go berserk again and Brook Cottage is barely a mile away. It's too near for comfort.'

'I don't understand it,' said Janet. 'What's Vinnie's up to?'

'That's the strangest part of all,' said Mrs Tallant. 'All this is to be carried out *without the master's knowledge*! It's an unforgivable deceit. The mistress says she will tell him in her own time when the hop-picking is over.'

Janet sat down opposite Mrs Tallant. 'It's Vinnie's way of helping the Bryces,' she said, 'because they have fallen on hard times. The old lady brought her up, remember?'

'But there's more to it than that,' said Young Harry. 'There was something going on between her and Tom Bryce a few years back. No one knows quite what it was, but—'

'That's just gossip,' said Cook.

'But there's no smoke without fire, you know what they say.'

'But *I* do the ironing,' said Edie. 'I've always done the ironing. What am I going to do now?'

Mrs Tallant fixed her with a beady eye. '*You*, my girl, are going to learn to wait at table.'

Edie was so shocked that she dropped the potato and the knife and put both hands to her mouth.

'Wait at table? *Me?*'

They all stared at Mrs Tallant.

'Edie could never wait at table,' Janet said. 'Has Vinnie gone off her head?'

'You may well ask. I told her Edie would be quite unsuitable, but all she said was that she must do the best she can.'

Edie began to cry, thrusting a fist into each eye. 'I don't want to wait at table,' she sobbed. 'I'm going to tell my Pa. I want to do the ironing!'

Young Harry put a comforting arm around her shoulders, but she continued to wail. At this point Mrs Tallant rose dramatically to her feet.

'I cannot stand any more,' she said. 'I have simply reached the end of my tether. I shall be in my room and if anyone asks for me, say that I am indisposed.'

And she swept out of the kitchen, leaving her demoralized colleagues to discuss this latest turn of events.

CHAPTER NINE

The ramshackle train allotted to the hop-pickers pulled into the Bricklayers Arms Goods Station seven minutes late. The platform was empty, but beyond the barrier more than two thousand Londoners waited impatiently. Many of them had been there for hours, determined to get a seat if it were possible, but a heavy downpour of rain had somewhat dampened their normal high spirits. For at least an hour they had been arguing with railway officials to be allowed on to the platform, but this had been refused. The previous year an elderly woman had been pushed on to the rails, and the railway company did not intend to risk a similar accident. But at last the train shuddered to a halt, the barrier was opened and the eager throng of people flooded on to the platform: women, children, elderly relatives, babes in arms and a few men, all crowded into the first carriages, anxious to ensure – if they could – a reasonably comfortable journey into the wilds of Kent.

Two vans had been added to the train to take any excess baggage which was too large to be wedged into the racks or under the seats, or carried on the laps of the passengers. Much of this large excess baggage took the form of small wooden wagons; these were made to a specific design which suited the hop-pickers' way of life when they reached their new environment, where there was often a fair distance to be walked between the accommodation provided and the hop-gardens. Kitchen utensils, food and babies were transported to and fro in the little carts, pulled sometimes by a weary mother or pushed by an over-enthusiastic elder brother.

Babies cried, children screamed with excitement and anxious parents scolded in a babble of noise. On the platform large numbers of railway staff and a sprinkling of police herded the hop-pickers on to the train. Normally an attempt would have been

made at this point to check that all the passengers had tickets, but
the train was already late and the mood of the pickers disconsolate, bordering on sullen; so after a brief consultation, it was
decided to abandon that part of the procedure and allow the train
to leave before any serious trouble developed. A few latecomers
were still arriving, rushing along the platform and squeezing
themselves into the already overcrowded carriages. At last the
guard raised his green flag, the whistle blew and the 'Hoppers'
Special' pulled slowly out of the station, to the relief of those left
behind on the station platform.

Mollie Pett was triumphant, for she sat in a corner seat facing
the way in which they were travelling, while her son Alex stood
nearby. She winked at him and he grinned.

'We made it, love!' she said and he nodded proudly.

Her triumph was only partly due to the fact that she had
secured a seat. The rest of it arose from her appearance, for she
sported a new red jacket and a red straw hat adorned with flowers
and ribbons. Her son wore a second-hand – but stout – pair of
boots which did *not* let in the water. She had purchased these
things with the money which Mary Bellweather had given her for
the train fare down to Wateringbury; however, she felt no guilt
about this, for she knew that among the many hoppers she might
well meet a personable young man who would take a fancy to her
and marry her. It was therefore, she argued, her 'bounden duty' to
look her best. Fortunately no one had checked the tickets before
they left the station, since the two tickets which Mollie carried in
her purse would only take them as far as Maidstone and, if this
was discovered, they would have to walk the rest of the way.

With a glow of satisfaction, she looked round at her companions and felt that none of them compared with her and her son.
None of the other children's boots compared with those that Alex
was wearing. If the worst happened, the walk from Maidstone to
Teesbury could not be more than ten miles, she told herself, and
the exercise would do them both good. Of course, if they were not
discovered, so much the better. Should they get as far as Wateringbury before the tickets were checked, she might be forced to
pay the difference out of her first week's wages, but that was a risk
she had to take.

Already, she noticed, there was a young man eyeing her from
the opposite end of the carriage, but Mollie decided he was not
quite suitable; he looked very young, only about seventeen and his

face was dreadfully pale and his cheeks sunken. His eyes looked suspiciously bright – as though he had recently recovered from a bad illness or was about to succumb to one in the very near future. Mollie grinned to herself as she thought of the fight Lena Tulson had put up to keep her working at her machine, but Mary Bellweather had argued that Alex was in need of a holiday in the country air and had persuaded Lena to keep the job open for Mollie for four weeks. Meg Wilson had sneered, referring to Mary Bellweather as a 'guardian angel', but Mollie knew that they were all jealous of the privileged position she now held in their midst. She did not know why Mary had selected *her* for special attention, but she did not care. It was enough that she had done so and Mollie was quite prepared to accept the benefits of the situation.

Her two little girls had been left in the care of an elderly aunt, whom Mary had paid well for her pains. As the 'Hoppers' Special' clattered its way out of London and into the darkness of the countryside, Mollie felt a great lightening of spirit as though she was leaving all her cares behind her. She had nothing to do now for a whole month except pick hops, earn money and enjoy herself. She patted her lap.

'Sit on my lap for a bit, love,' she told her son.

But Alex shook his head. Laps were for babies and he would soon be nine. He preferred to stand up and stare out of the window. Later, when the town had been left behind, the darkness would be broken only occasionally by the lights from remote farmhouses and cottages. He shuffled his feet, proud of his new boots, even though they were two sizes too large and had been stuffed with newspaper to make them fit. He shivered a little in his damp overcoat and self-consciously straightened his cap. Shooting a quick glance at his mother, the sight of her perky, cheerful face and the smart new hat cheered him. He had seen the young man eyeing her and fervently hoped nothing would come of it. There was no reason to suppose that the man was going to Foxearth, for there were other stops along the way. Still, if Fate was taking him to Foxearth and he did strike up a friendship with Alex's mother, there might be the odd coin here and there for himself – either to encourage Molly's affection or to bribe him to make himself scarce.

Alex felt vaguely hopeful about the coming month and the rewards it might bring. The chatter around him grew more boisterous as the hoppers settled down and eventually someone began to sing. Soon they were all either singing or dozing and finally, overcome by fatigue, he settled himself down on the floor of the carriage, closed his eyes and surrendered himself cheerfully to whatever Fate might hold in store for him.

*

Alex awoke with a jolt to hear the porter shouting 'Maidstone . . . Maidstone . . . Alight here for Lordswood, Senacre, Tovil.' He looked guiltily towards Mollie, who shook her head imperceptibly, but her luck did not hold.

A uniformed figure climbed into the carriage. 'Tickets, please! Show your tickets, please!'

Mollie made a great show of looking for her ticket. She felt in her pockets and then in her purse, shaking her head with a worried frown while the official inspected everybody else's ticket. At last Mollie and Alex were the only two left.

'Tickets, please, madam!'

She knew she would have to produce them now. If she pretended not to have any tickets or to have lost them, she would no doubt be made to pay the full fare. Slowly she drew them from her purse, feigning surprise.

'Oh, here they are!' she said. 'Can't see for looking!'

He took them from her and then drew his brows together ominously.

'Oh, I see you have reached your destination, madam,' he said. 'This is Maidstone station and these are tickets for Maidstone.'

'Are they?' said Mollie. 'Let me have a look.'

He handed them back to her and she inspected them carefully.

'Well,' she said, 'I don't understand that at all. I distinctly told the man Wateringbury and I don't know how he could have made a mistake like that.'

'Perhaps you would be good enough to leave the train,' said the official. 'Is this your son here?'

'That's Alex, yes.'

'He, too, will have to leave the train, unless you care to pay the rest of the fare.'

'I can't do that,' said Mollie, 'because I've no more money, but I'll have plenty by the end of the week.'

'That's as maybe,' he said sourly. 'The fact is that you have bought a ticket to Maidstone and this is Maidstone. This, madam, is where you get out. I do hope you are going to be sensible about this and not going to cause any trouble. I should hate to have to call a constable.'

Mollie looked at him piteously. 'But it's pouring with rain,' she protested. 'Surely you can't expect us to walk from Maidstone to Wateringbury in this weather. It's got to be ten miles or more and my boy's got a weak chest.'

'I'm sorry, madam, you should have thought about that when you bought the ticket.'

'But I tell you I *did* ask for tickets to Wateringbury,' she persisted.

He shook his head with a patient smile. 'This is where you get out, madam. You and your son.'

Mollie's expression changed abruptly as she stood up. 'Well, I hope you rot, then!' she said venomously. 'You and yours! Turning us out on a night like this – and anyway I've got luggage in the van. You'll never find it.'

'I am sure we will, madam,' he said firmly. 'You are not the only person trying to evade paying the full fare; there is quite a little crowd of you. We will restore your luggage to you, never fear.'

Mollie made a very rude remark as she climbed down from the carriage. Alex had already jumped out, and together they followed the railway official to the front of the train where a dozen or more people, looking either sheepish or rebellious in the pale gaslight, waited while their luggage was discovered and returned to them. The guard turned at last to Mollie.

'What's it like, then, this luggage of yours? Case, bag, box?'

'A box of things with a blanket round it,' said Mollie. 'It's got a label on with me name written on it.'

Eventually he found it and passed it out to her.

'And rot you, too!' said Mollie as she spat derisively. 'Come on, Alex.' They turned to go as the guard waved his flag once more.

'And I hope the wheels drop off,' she shouted bitterly.

Turning her collar up close around her neck, she took one side of the bundle and Alex took the other. Mollie would never have admitted it, but what grieved her most was the damage the rain was doing to her new red hat.

*

Amos Hearn watched the geese in the neighbouring field as they stood in the sunlight, white against the grass, like statues framed by the gap in the hedge. They were silent, busy about their early morning toilet, apparently oblivious of the world awakening around them. One goose preened, with its head under its wing. Another polished its yellow beak against its back with small quick movements. A large grey goose spread its wings, facing sideways on to the sun, the bulky body balanced on large yellow legs and broad webbed feet. Amos admired them, savouring the moment.

Behind him was the rod tent and the two caravans belonging to his immediate family. Further along, nearly a dozen other caravans rested in the shade of the hedge, protected from the wind. Beyond the field where the geese stood, he could see the barns where the Londoners slept. Amos pitied them; the faggots of wood allotted to each family for their fire would be sodden from the overnight rain and useless for fire-lighting, even if there was enough time – which there never was on the first morning. Many of the younger men were housed under simple shelters built of sheep hurdles – sufficient in fine weather, but sadly inadequate in the rain. The sun was shining now, but it would not last for long. From a lifetime on the road he had learned to understand the vagaries of the weather and more rain-clouds were being blown in from the west.

The geese began to mutter to each other and several of them turned in Amos's direction, fixing him with their small black eyes, blinking and suspicious, as though aware of his interest. The largest bird flapped its wings with a sudden violent flurry and stretched its neck forward, but it made no sound and almost immediately furled the huge wings neatly. Amos smiled. They were noble birds.

From beyond the geese came the sound of voices as the Londoners roused themselves for their first day's picking. He wondered idly how many new faces there would be. Not that it mattered much to him, for the gipsies were a proud race and did not mix easily with the other pickers; knowing this, the bin man would allot the gipsies adjoining bins. Amos stretched lazily and at once the geese were disturbed, turning towards him with necks outstretched, honking raucously in alarm. Slowly they waddled towards him, bent on intimidating him with harsh noises and the aggressive movement of their large bodies. He laughed. They came through the hedge at a rush but slowed down as they drew nearer to him, looking at each other indecisively. When he waved his arms and sprang forward, clapping his hands and shouting, they turned tail and hurried back through the hole in the hedge.

'You great bully!'

He turned at the unfamiliar voice and saw a young woman at the gate wearing a bright red jacket and hat.

'I saw you,' she shouted. 'Frightening those ducks!'

Grinning, he walked towards her. As he drew nearer, he saw that a small boy accompanied her; they both looked very weary and their clothes were sodden.

'They're not ducks, they're geese,' he said, 'and where did you spring from at this time of the morning?'

'From bloody Maidstone, that's where!' she said. 'Shanks's pony, thanks to some pig of a railway man who thinks a uniform makes him God.'

'Well,' said Amos, 'you're just in time for breakfast.'

'If we had any, we would be,' she retorted.

'You do look a bit bedraggled,' he told them.

'Rain is wet stuff,' she replied shortly. 'God knows what it's done to me hat!'

In fact the red dye from the cheap straw had run down the side of her face, giving her a bizarre appearance, but Amos did not have the heart to tell her this.

'It will dry out,' he said, 'with a bit of sunshine. Like a bite to eat?'

The boy stepped forward. 'I would,' he said, but the woman gave him a quick cuff on the side of the head.

'Mind your manners!' she said, 'and what about please and thank you.'

'I would, please,' he said.

Mollie looked at Amos. 'I wouldn't say no to a bit of something,' she said. 'I've had good times, but last night wasn't one of them.'

He grinned. 'Come on, then.'

The two late arrivals followed him back to his tent. There Amos invited them to make themselves comfortable on a pile of straw covered with a blanket, which they did under the curious gaze of the rest of his family. From a clean white cloth he produced two small carcases roasted to a crisp brown.

'Now then,' he said, 'put that inside you. It's good, that is.'

Mollie and Alex eyed the tiny carcases dubiously. 'What is it?' asked Mollie. 'Pigeon or something?'

'Taste it,' he said.

She hesitated and the boy glanced up at his mother. 'How can it be a pigeon?' he said. 'It's got four legs!'

'Oh, so it has. It's a baby rabbit, then,' said Mollie, but Amos shook his head.

'It's not a cat, is it?' she said with a grimace.

He laughed. 'Taste it!' he told her again.

They nibbled gingerly and found the flesh soft and sweet. Amos watched them for a few moments with amusement, then Lotty Hearn came down the caravan steps and joined them, obviously hoping for an introduction.

Amos looked enquiringly at Mollie. 'Ah, this is—'

'I'm Mollie Pett and this is my boy Alexander. Should have been Alexandra really, because I wanted a girl. I was going to name her after the Princess.' She turned to her son. 'Say hullo.'

'Hullo,' he said.

It was Mollie's turn then to look enquiringly at her host.

'I'm Amos Hearn,' he said. 'This is Lotty, my cousin's wife.' He jerked his head in the direction of the second caravan. 'My grandmother and grandfather live there.'

'You all one family, then?' Mollie asked.

'We Romanys stick together,' said Lotty shortly. 'We look after our own. Will you be wanting a cup of tea?'

They nodded gratefully and she moved away without further comment.

Mollie finally finished eating and wiped the grease from her mouth with the back of her hand.

'Well, I've eaten it,' she said. 'So what was it?'

'Hedgehog,' he told them.

She let out a scream and dropped the remains of the carcase. '*Hedgehog!* Oh, how horrible!'

The boy grinned, however. 'They roll them in dough,' he told his mother. 'They told us that at school.'

Amos shook his head. 'We shave them, singe off what's left of the hair, then split them down the back to open them right up. After that we wash them out and cook them on a spit over the fire. You won't find a pheasant that tastes better than a hedgehog at the right time of the year. Mind you, they're better the other side of Christmas. January or February, that's the best time to go hedgehogging.'

Mollie felt her stomach heave slightly at his graphic descrip-tion, but fortunately for her Lotty returned just then with three mugs of tea. An old couple emerged from the second caravan and were duly introduced. Sebastian, nearly eighty, studied the horizon with a practised eye. 'There'll be rain later,' he forecast.

'You mean *more* rain!' said Mollie.

He smiled. 'There'll be a fair bit of grumbling today,' he said. 'You Londoners, you don't like the rain, but to a Romany it's just a bit more weather. We're used to it, you see. Out in all weathers, we are. Brought up to it all our lives. A bit of rain won't hurt you.'

What he said was true. The gipsies would continue to pick hops whatever the conditions and were, for that reason, highly regarded by the growers. The local people would give up for the day and go home if the weather was too severe. The Londoners, eager for the money, might continue to pick in bad weather, but they would grumble and complain and ask for more money to compensate for their discomfort. If the rain persisted for long they would often grow quarrelsome and disgruntled pickers were the bane of a hop-grower's life.

Soon it would be time to join the rest of the pickers for the first morning's 'briefing', when the various families would be allotted the bins into which they would pick and the rules and regulations governing the field would be read out to them. The hours and conditions of work would be spelled out for the benefit of newcomers and then the day's work would begin in earnest.

'Right then,' said Amos five minutes later. 'If you two are ready, we'd best go.'

*

Julian Lawrence stood on an upturned apple crate and waited for the chattering to cease. Hundreds of pairs of eyes watched him as he cleared his throat nervously. Most of the faces he vaguely recognized – they were the regulars who came year after year. But there were a few unfamiliar ones and it was to these people he mainly addressed himself. Raising his voice, he began loudly.

'Now, I'm Julian Lawrence. I'm the man who employs you and I expect the whole month's picking to be conducted in an orderly fashion.'

He turned and nodded towards a tall, rather bulky figure on his right. 'This is Ned Berry, chief pole-puller, and what he says, goes. I want that clearly understood. I know that for most of you this month at Foxearth is partly a holiday, but it is also a working holiday. We have acres of hops to be gathered in and that means a lot of hard work on your part. My part is to pay you for doing it. If you have any problems, take them to Ned; if he can't deal with them, he will bring them to me. Is that understood?'

There was a murmur of assent but someone cried out, 'D'you know your barn roof leaks?'

A few more voices joined in, backing him up. Julian hastily raised a placating hand.

'All those problems will be dealt with,' he told them, 'but we can't do everything at once. The main thing is to get the picking under way, then I can sort out the other matters. The weather doesn't look too promising, and we don't want to waste this fine spell having useless arguments about leaking roofs. Now, Adam Forrest is known to most of you already . . .' Here Julian indicated another man on his left and a slight cheer went up. Adam grinned self-consciously and made a thumbs-up sign. 'When I have finished,' continued Julian, 'Adam will read out the bin numbers and you will go at once to whichever bin has been allotted to you. Anyone who wants to change bins can see him about it later. We will do our best to please everybody, but once again I don't want to waste time on sorting it out now. Tallyman is Lou Stark – he was here last year, so most of you will remember him too. He'll be along later. The only other people I have to introduce are the Brothers in Jesus, who come every year and are known already to most of you.'

He turned and smiled at the group standing a little way behind him. 'Mary Bellweather, Roland Fry and Gareth Brooks,' he said. They all smiled cheerfully and someone in the crowd called out, 'Keep the tea and buns coming, love!' and Mary called back, 'We will!'

'Now,' said Julian, 'I know you are tired. You haven't had much sleep and no doubt you had a rough journey.' More assenting shouts from the crowd. 'But if the sun comes out you will all feel a lot better. The Brothers in Jesus have pitched their tent further over this year, towards the gipsy encampment, so if anyone hurts themselves or has any personal problems, that's the place to go for help. We very much appreciate their giving up their own time to be here with us. Now I'll hand you over to Ned Berry, who will read the regulations, then it's down to work as quickly as possible. It only remains for me to wish you all a happy and lucrative stay at Foxearth.'

There were cheers and some applause as Julian stepped down

and Ned took his place. He was obviously nervous and the pickers eyed him speculatively, weighing him up, deciding how far they could go with him.

Ned read from a well-worn sheet of paper, gabbling the familiar words: 'You will start work at eight o'clock and no one will leave the hop-gardens without obtaining permission. No loose hops to be left on the ground. All hops to be picked clean, with no leaves and twigs. Punishment for breach of the regulations will be one bushel of hops forfeit. The signal to start and finish will be a bell. There will be no picking during the dinner break. No one is allowed into the adjoining orchard. No lucifer matches to be brought into the gardens. Any pilfering of fruit or anything else will be prosecuted. No fighting allowed. No litter to be strewn in the gardens. No immoral language or behaviour will be tolerated. Camp fires to be put out by ten o'clock each night. Is there anyone who has any questions?'

There never were any questions. Adam Forrest took Ned's place and began to read out the list of pickers and bins and finally the preliminaries were satisfactorily concluded. Ned took up a small gong and struck it twice – the first day's hopping had officially started.

*

Colonel Lawrence opened his eyes and looked at Vinnie, who sat on the end of the bed reading from J. M. Barrie's *Sentimental Tommy*. She was a good reader with a clear voice and a reasonable command of vocabulary.

' ". . . I suppose",' she read, ' "you want me to give you some idea of his character, Thomas, and I could tell you what it is at any particular moment; but it changes, sir, I do assure you, almost as quickly as a circus rider flings off his layers of waistcoats. As though a puff of wind blows him from one character to another, and he may be noble and vicious, and a tyrant and a slave, and hard as granite and melting as butter in the sun, all in one forenoon . . ." '

There was a sudden spatter of rain against the long windows and Vinnie glanced anxiously towards the forbidding clouds which rolled overhead.

'This wretched rain!' she exclaimed. 'Why can't it be fine for them?'

'The pickers, you mean?'

Vinnie nodded.

'It's no worse than other years,' he said. 'They take their chance. Sometimes it's fine and sometimes it's not. One year, I remember, we didn't have a drop of rain the whole month. Glorious, it was. They all went back to London brown as berries, glowing with health. Eighty-nine, I think that was. Or was it eighty-eight? I forget, but anyway it was a wonderful month.'

Vinnie sighed. 'Well, if this dreadful rain keeps up they will all go down with pneumonia instead. That roof leaks badly. I have spoken to Julian about it so many times and he promised to do something about it before this year's picking. It's so miserable for them.'

The Colonel smiled gently. 'Vinnie, you mustn't take on other people's problems,' he said. 'The accommodation of the pickers is something for Julian to worry about, not you. Your job is to run the household.'

'It runs itself,' said Vinnie. 'The household would still run even if I wasn't here.'

'And the pickers will survive, rain or shine, with or without a leaky roof. So do stop agitating about it. You will make yourself ill if you try to take too much on those young shoulders.' He peered at her shortsightedly. 'You do look a little pale,' he said. 'Are you quite well, Vinnie?'

She nodded impatiently as the wind increased and doubled the sound of the rain on the windows until it rattled like hailstones. Then she jumped up from the bed, crossed to the window and stared out at the darkening landscape.

'I must speak to Julian,' she said. 'He must do something about that roof!'

The Colonel sighed. 'Have you finished reading to me then, Vinnie?' he asked and she turned back to him.

'I'm sorry. Please forgive me! I've so much on my mind. Of course I will read longer if you wish.'

'I do wish it, Vinnie. It seems so long since you were able to spend a little time with me. Are you enjoying the story? What do you think of Barrie as a writer?'

She shrugged lightly. 'You know I have no opinion on style,' she said. 'All I know is that I enjoy reading it. Does that make it a good novel?'

'I suppose it does,' said the Colonel. 'I think our Mr Barrie is a most promising writer. We shall hear more of him, no doubt.'

'I expect so,' said Vinnie. 'Shall I go on?'

He nodded and she picked up the book. 'You should read more, Vinnie,' the Colonel told her. 'You could improve yourself. You have the time, you know and my library is full of books.'

'I don't know where to start,' said Vinnie, frowning slightly. 'There are so many books.'

'Julian ought to help you,' he insisted. 'You told me once, Vinnie, that you wanted to be a good wife to Julian – a *suitable* wife, you said. Do you remember?'

She shook her head, although in fact she remembered very well.

'Julian used to read to me,' the Colonel went on, 'when he was still very young – and Eva too, although she was never his equal – too idle by half, that little miss. Is there any news of Eva? Have we had a letter from her this month?'

Vinnie shook her head. 'Probably any day now,' she told him.

Just then there was a knock on the door and Edie came into the room, wearing one of Janet's old uniforms and looking extremely nervous in her new role as parlourmaid.

'Please, miss – I mean ma'am – there's a letter for you.'

'Thank you, Edie.'

Vinnie took it from her with trembling fingers, while Edie looked at the Colonel with ill-disguised curiosity.

'Well, what are you staring at girl?' he cried. 'Never seen an invalid before? Well, take a good look. An invalid is just an old man sitting up in bed. Now, when you've finished gawping, get along downstairs.'

'Yes, sir.' Edie glanced at Vinnie, who nodded briefly, the letter still unopened in her hand. Vinnie could see from the official style of the envelope that it came from the asylum and she had no wish to open it in front of the Colonel.

'From Eva, is it?' the old man demanded.

'No,' stammered Vinnie. 'From . . . it's from a friend of mine, but I'll read it later on. I'll finish reading that chapter now.'

But the Colonel waved her away irritably. 'Oh, go and read your letter, child,' he said. 'All these interruptions! That's not the way to enjoy a book. Send Janet up to me. Tell her I'm thirsty and tell her to leave her thermometer behind. Wretched girl's the most enthusiastic nurse I've ever come across. She's gone quite mad since Nurse Ramsey left. Thinks she's Florence Nightingale. It's "Must take your temperature, sir", and "Must take your pulse".

If she ever learns to do amputations, I shan't have a limb left—'

Meanwhile Vinnie fled to the bedroom where she opened the letter, tearing the envelope in her haste. It was brief but to the point:

Dear Mrs Lawrence,

With regard to your communication dated August 28th, we have given this matter our earnest consideration, but regret we cannot see fit to grant your main request. Thomas Bryce is not in our opinion fit to return to normal life.

However, we have decided to grant your second request and the patient will be released from his strait-jacket for a period of one week, under close supervision. If his behaviour is satisfactory, we shall consider extending this period.

We appreciate your concern for the patient's welfare and assure you that we, too, have his best interests at heart.

I trust this letter will afford you some satisfaction.

I also thank you, on behalf of my colleagues, for your donation which will of course be put to good use for the benefit of all our inmates.

    I remain,
        Your Obedient Servant,
        James H. Collyer

Vinnie closed her eyes and then covered her face with her hands, willing back the tears. All her efforts had been to no purpose. She crumpled the letter in her hand and threw it to the floor, then sank into a chair, abandoning herself to an overwhelming sense of defeat and desolation.

Later that afternoon, red-eyed, she made her way to Brook Cottage to break the news to Rose that she had been only partly successful in her appeal. She promised, however, to go on trying.

By a quarter past six she had collected Young Harry from the stable and, armed with a long ladder, had marched him over to the large barn which housed most of the pickers. The interior was a depressing sight. Water dripped from at least a dozen places in the roof and buckets and pails had been placed underneath them. Outside, Vinnie stared upwards.

'What can you do about that roof?' she demanded.

Young Harry also looked up, shaking his head. 'Not a lot, I should say. Too far gone, that old thatch. No amount of patching will put that right – you need a new roof on this barn.'

'I know that,' said Vinnie crossly. 'But since it hasn't got a new roof, there must be something we can do with it. Just look at the mess here. The water is splashing out of the pails as fast as it goes in and everything on the floor will be soaked. Even the horses are better cared for than these people; at least their stable roof is sound and their bedding is dry. Why can't you stuff up the holes with rag or something?'

He shook his head again. 'Start meddling with that roof and you'll only make it worse,' he said.

'Go up and look anyway,' said Vinnie. 'Perhaps we could lay tarpaulin sheets over the top of the roof.'

'We've none left,' he told her. 'They have all been used.'

'But there must be *something* we can do,' she urged.

'I don't reckon so,' he said, but nevertheless he propped up the ladder against the wall and climbed up to inspect the ageing thatch.

His verdict was disappointing. 'It's terrible!' he called down. 'Even worse than I thought. Look at this—' He scrabbled with his fingers and threw down a handful of wet, decayed reed. 'Rotten, it is,' he shouted. 'Falling apart and full of holes. I reckon the birds have had a field day up here. It should have been netted years ago to keep them out.'

'And you can't stuff up the holes?'

'Not a chance! Lord knows what the roof timbers are like – if they're as rotten as the thatch, I should think the whole roof could come down.' Vinnie muttered furiously under her breath and her expression was grim.

'You'd best come down, then,' she told him and steadied the ladder while he did so. 'And keep what you've seen to yourself,' she said. 'I shall have another word with Julian about it, but meanwhile we don't want it put around that the roof's dangerous and likely to fall or we are likely to have a panic on our hands.'

'Rebellion, more likely,' he said. 'Oh Lord, here it comes again!' A few heavy splashes of rain heralded another heavy shower and they sheltered just inside the door of the barn. Vinnie had picked in the rain often enough when she was younger and understood the misery of the pickers out in the gardens. There was nowhere they could shelter, yet they would be loth to give up. For an hour sheltering in the barn meant an hour's money lost and every penny counted if they were to survive the coming winter.

Suddenly Vinnie saw Julian approaching. 'You can go now,

thank you,' she told Young Harry and he was glad enough to hurry back to the comparative comfort of the stable.

Julian hurried into the shelter of the barn, shaking the rain from his head and hands.

'What are you doing here, Vinnie?' he asked. 'Shouldn't you be supervising the laundry or discussing the evening meal with Cook?'

His tone was sarcastic and his mood matched Vinnie's own. He had spent most of the afternoon in the hop-gardens, assailed on all sides by irate Londoners who did not mince their words. They were dissatisfied with their accommodation and said so plainly. The young men who had slept under the makeshift hurdles were refusing to do so again unless the weather improved and Julian had promised to try to hire a tent. However, they all knew this was unlikely, for tents had become an increasingly common way to implement accommodation for the hoppers and every available tent in the area would no doubt be spoken for already. Roland Fry had offered to sleep eight of them in the small Mission tent as a temporary measure, but that was little comfort to the rest of them.

The first day's picking was meagre and the quality of hops, as everyone had predicted, was poor. At the oast-house Julian had watched Steven Pitt, the head dryer, empty out the first of the hop pokes on to the horsehair mat of the drying room. He watched as the damp hops were raked into an even layer four inches thick and then together the two men had stood back, eyeing them critically. Stephen Pitt had taken up a handful and spread them in his palm; then he shook them through his fingers.

'We'll not win any prizes this year,' had been his only comment, and Julian had good reason to be despondent.

Now Vinnie and Julian stood in the doorway of the barn looking out across the hop-gardens. She sensed his depression and knew that a few encouraging words from her would make a great difference to him. While she sensed that he needed her support, yet her own mood made it impossible for her to give it. Her disappointment over Tom Bryce and her concern for the hoppers' miserable plight seemed to outweigh her duty as a wife. Behind them the rain fell into the metal receptacles in a loud syncopated rhythm, demanding attention. Meanwhile the silence lengthened until neither of them wanted to be the first to break it.

'This roof,' said Vinnie suddenly. 'I sent Young Harry up to have a look at it. He says it's beyond repair – that there's nothing we can do to stop these dreadful leaks.' She turned and waved a hand towards the silver ribbons of water which fell relentlessly from ceiling to floor.

Julian's eyes narrowed.

'*You* sent Young Harry up on to the roof,' he said. 'Since when has it been your job to inspect the properties?'

'Since last night,' said Vinnie firmly, 'when all those poor people had to sleep in these awful conditions. Julian, why haven't you done anything about it? You promised me you would have the roof seen to and I think it's your duty to do so.'

'*You* think it my duty,' cried Julian angrily. 'I hardly think it is your place to tell me my duty!'

'You were telling me mine,' answered Vinnie. 'You told me that I should be discussing the menu or checking the laundry.'

'Those duties are part of your responsibility,' said Julian.

'And your responsibility is to care for the pickers,' she retorted.

'I do care for them.'

'You obviously don't care for them enough.'

'I care for them as well as any other grower in this area and I very much resent your interference, Vinnie. It's about time you learnt your place.'

She faced him, hard-eyed. 'What you mean, Julian, is that you want me to ignore your neglect.'

'Are you suggesting that I neglect my pickers?'

She hesitated, then said rashly, 'Yes, I am. You promised last year and the year before that you would do something about this beastly barn and yet you have done nothing. If you admitted that it needed doing, yet you haven't done it, then isn't that neglect?'

The argument was interrupted suddenly by the appearance of Tim Bilton, who was propelling a small boy along by the scruff of the neck.

'Caught him pinching, sir!' he called out as he approached. 'In the hen house, he was, pinching the eggs. See?' He held out three eggs.

'Two in one pocket and one in the other,' said Tim, 'and barely been here twenty-four hours.'

Vinnie groaned inwardly as Julian seized this opportunity. 'There!' he said. 'These are the people that you concern yourself with. Stealing at his age! How old are you, boy?'

'Eight.'

'Eight, *sir*,' Julian corrected.

'Eight, sir,' repeated the boy sullenly.

'We shall have to make an example of him,' said Tim, 'or else they will all be at it. We always lose a few apples, but eggs are something else. There's no knowing where it will end – it could be the chickens next!'

He shook the boy roughly. Vinnie was staring at the child and said nothing.

'What's your name?' Julian demanded, his eyes bright with anger.

It was strange, Vinnie thought, how the same features on a man could look handsome in some circumstances and yet be ugly in others. Now she found Julian's soft blond hair and finely chiselled features unattractive in the extreme.

The boy remained silent.

'Shake it out of him,' said Julian and Tim gave the boy another shake. 'Your name, boy?' he said.

'Alexander.'

'Alexander what?'

'Pett.'

'Well, Alexander Pett, does your mother know you are a thief?'

'It was her that told me to.'

Vinnie's dismay increased. 'Do you hear that, Vinnie,' said Julian. 'His mother sent him to steal our eggs. Delightful people!' He turned to Tim. 'Do you know the mother?'

'She came last year,' said Tim. 'Arrived this morning, having walked from Maidstone.'

'Because they had no money?' Vinnie intervened.

'I suppose so,' said Tim.

Vinnie understood that people without money often stole just to stay alive. Not so many years ago she had done the same thing, but she had not been caught; she was one of the lucky ones. Suddenly she reached out and took hold of the boy's hand.

'You're to come with me. I will give you a sixpence,' she said, 'and you are *never* to steal again.'

Tim's mouth dropped open in surprise and Julian began to remonstrate, but Vinnie had no intention of waiting to hear what either of them had to say.

'Hurry!' she whispered to the boy and gathering up her skirts she half-ran along the track towards the house. Before they even reached it, she had almost repented her rash action – it would lead to further trouble between her and Julian, of that she was certain.

Yet she found something in the boy very appealing, although she could not say why. Julian's voice rang in her ears – 'Does your mother know you're a thief?' Had he no compassion? No understanding? Was he really as cold as he seemed, she wondered, or was it his upbringing which made him so different? She found sixpence for the boy and extracted his promise not to get into any further trouble. As she led him back to the front door, Mary Bellweather came running up.

'What has he done?' she gasped. 'One of the women told me. Alex, what have you done?'

The boy hung his head and Vinnie was surprised by Mary's concern.

'I know the mother,' Mary explained. 'She's basically a good woman – at least, I believe so.'

'It's no matter,' said Vinnie. 'He stole some eggs, but he's promised not to do it again. I've given him sixpence. I think they're probably without money and that will feed them for a day or two. Go on, Alex. Off you go before I change my mind – and keep out of Mr Lawrence's way.' He ran off without a backward glance.

'The Petts are one of the families we are helping,' said Mary. 'We take a particular interest in them. The mother's a feckless creature and the boy has stolen before, I'm afraid. I meant to keep an eye on him; I blame myself.'

They watched the retreating figure. 'There is something about him . . .' Vinnie began. 'He reminds me of someone.'

'Pett,' said Mary. 'Alexander Pett. Do you know the name?'

Vinnie shook her head and sighed. 'I think,' she said to Mary, 'it's going to be a difficult month.'

Mary glanced up at the sky. 'If the weather doesn't improve, it most certainly will be,' she said. 'We shall have to pray harder than usual and then perhaps God will send us sunshine. The world always seems a better place when the sun shines.'

Vinnie sighed once more. Her own small world was disintegrating around her and all her problems seemed insuperable. She thought rather bleakly that it would take more than sunshine to put *her* world right.

CHAPTER TEN

Mrs Bryce straightened up, a hand to her aching back. Returning one flat-iron to the ledge in front of the fire, she took up the other and spat on its flat surface. It sizzled properly so she continued her ironing, covering the sheet with long, even strokes.

'Reckon the old Colonel must be incontinent,' she said, 'the number of sheets we've had this week.'

Rose bit off a thread. 'Probably,' she agreed without looking up. She reached for the reel of white cotton and rethreaded her needle.

'Nice pillow-slips, these,' she said. 'Must have cost a pretty penny. Real Irish linen, by the look of them. They're a pleasure to mend, they really are.'

'That's eleven sheets so far. Six double and five singles.'

'It's a big household,' said Rose.

There was a scuffling from upstairs, where all the children slept on a large mattress. Rose listened for a moment with needle poised and heard angry voices. She put the needle through the material and carried the pillow-slip with her to the door, shouting up the stairs:

'What did I tell you five minutes ago? Stop that noise or I shall bring my slipper to the lot of you! Not another sound, do you hear me? Not one more sound!'

The effort exhausted her and she carried the pillow-slip back to the chair and sat down thoughtfully.

'Give yourself a bit of a break, Rose love,' said Mrs Bryce. 'Make a pot of tea.'

Rose shook her head. 'I'm all right,' she said. 'Let's save it for a bit later.' She sighed. 'I keep thinking about poor Tom. If only they'd let him come home – he'd be all right then, I know he would.'

Her mother-in-law shrugged. 'Vinnie did her best,' she said.

'That girl's really come up trumps, if you ask me. It can't have been easy.'

Rose nodded. 'At least he's out of that dreadful jacket,' she said, 'and Vinnie seems very hopeful – didn't you think so, Ma?'

The old lady set the iron on end and turned the sheet with a deft movement so that the last quarter rested across the table.

'She did seem very hopeful,' she agreed. 'Said it was a step in the right direction.'

'Well, it is,' said Rose. 'I mean, if he's all right out of his jacket and behaves himself, then they might consider letting him come home after all. If only Tommy would stop asking for him.'

'He misses his Pa, that boy,' said Mrs Bryce.

'Bertha never mentions him at all,' sighed Rose. 'It's as if she knows what's happening.'

'Bless them, they're all missing him,' said Tom's mother. 'It's only natural the children should miss their father. Poor Vinnie, she was so disappointed!'

'She's done her best for us,' Rose agreed. 'It's just the uncertainty of it all. Every time I hear a footstep outside, I think it's Julian Lawrence come to turn us out.'

'He wouldn't do that,' Mrs Bryce assured her with more conviction than she felt.

'I don't know so much,' said Rose. 'I used to think the world of him when he was a boy but now – he seems to have changed completely.'

The old lady replaced the iron in front of the fire and began to fold the sheet. The noise upstairs had died away. 'They're off, bless them,' she said. 'You've got five lovely children, Rose, and you must be thankful for that.'

She took a white damask tablecloth from the pile and shook it free of creases. 'It's funny Vinnie not having any children,' she remarked, 'when you think . . .'

'I expect she will have,' said Rose. 'All in good time. An heir for the Lawrences – what a to-do there'll be then!' She rubbed her eyes tiredly. 'I shall have to think about a pair of spectacles soon. My eyes are getting that bad I can hardly see what I'm doing, squinting away here.'

'Try mine, dear. They're on the mantelpiece behind you.'

Rose tried them, shook her head and put them back beside the small clock. 'Makes it worse,' she said and sighed. 'If only Tom could have got that gardener's job . . .'

'Now don't keep torturing yourself,' said Mrs Bryce firmly. 'What will be, will be, you know what they say. Think yourself lucky that we're not in the workhouse, because that's where we'd be if it wasn't for Vinnie, and that's a place you never get out of, so I'm told.'

Rose folded the pillow-slip and put it on one side, then took up another one and examined it for signs of wear.

'She's not happy, you know, for all her money,' Mrs Bryce went on. 'Vinnie, I mean – it's written all over her face. Should have married someone of her own sort. She was a lovely little girl. I remember when young Jarvis Tupp used to hang around the house; he used to tap on the window for her, but she wouldn't go out to him. He's not a bad lad, Jarvis Tupp. Would have been right for Vinnie and made her a good husband. Julian is not the right man for her.'

Rose was not listening. 'I'm sure there is something wrong with his stomach,' she said. 'The way he used to double up, as though he had a pain or something, but when I asked him he'd always say "No" and insist he was as right as ninepence.'

'Who? Julian Lawrence?'

'No, Tom! I wonder if that's why he started drinking, to kill the pain.'

'Surely he'd have said?' said Mrs Bryce.

'No, he wouldn't. You know Tom, Ma – very scared of doctors and hospitals, like most men. Cowards when they come to it, for all their brave talk. That could have been the start of it, but I suppose we shall never know.'

'If he comes home,' stated Mrs Bryce, 'I'm going to give him a real talking to, Rose. No, I mean it! I know and you know that he's got a lot of good in him and if he gets another chance, there's going to be no more drink put inside him.'

'*If* he gets another chance,' said Rose.

There was the sound of scuffling above their heads and then footsteps on the stairs. The door at the bottom was pushed open and Tommy's curly dark head appeared.

'Bertha keeps kicking me,' he wailed. 'I can't get to sleep.' There was another rush of footsteps and then Bertha appeared.

'He's taking up too much room,' she protested, her usual cheerful face sulky.

'Right!' said Rose, rising to her feet. 'Where's that slipper?' Tommy retreated a few steps.

'I've warned you,' said Rose. 'When your father comes home, I shall tell him you've played me up and we'll see what he has to say about that.'

Bertha fled back to bed, but Tommy stood his ground. 'Pa's not coming back,' he said. 'Not ever.'

'Who said that?' Rose demanded.

'The boys at school.'

'Well, you don't go to that school now, do you?' said Rose. 'Vinnie's going to try to get you into the Teesbury school. You'll like it there. That's where I went to school and that's where Vinnie went too. And your Grandma as well.'

'I don't want to go to school,' said Tommy. 'I want to go hopping – I don't like school.'

'And I don't like to keep hearing what you do and don't like,' snapped Rose. 'Now get upstairs this minute and back into bed, or I'll lay this across your bottom, I really will. And Tommy . . .' she added as he moved back up the stairs, 'you take no notice when the boys say things like that to you. They're just ignorant and they don't know any better.'

'But is he coming back, Ma?'

'Of course he is.'

'Isn't he mad, then?'

'Of course he's not mad! He's just as sane as you and me. Now, I don't want to hear any more talk like that from you, Tommy Bryce. Upstairs and not another peep out of you!'

With loud sighs he departed, moving as slowly as he dared. Rose pushed the door to, but the latch was still missing and it hung open.

'I'll have to get down to the blacksmith tomorrow,' she said, 'and hurry him up. The children's window won't stay shut either and the end of the bed was all wet this morning where the rain had got in.'

She sat down, making no effort to continue her mending. Vinnie's first appeal for Tom's release had been turned down, but she had promised to try again and again.

'He will come back, won't he, Ma?' she said.

'Of course he will,' said the old lady firmly. 'Everything is going to turn out right, you'll see, and Tom will be his old cheerful self again.' But her tears, unseen by Rose, fell silently on to the tablecloth and sizzled under the hot iron.

*

Outside the Mission's tent Gareth Brooks tended a fire with twigs
and small pieces of coal. The first week's hop-picking was nearly
over and today, Saturday, the pickers would be paid. The weather
had been unkind, with rain falling for a large part of each day, but
this morning it was dry. It was nearly eleven o'clock and the early
morning mist which had lingered had finally cleared. Now there
were breaks in the cloud and very occasionally the weary hop-
pickers caught a glimpse of the sun.

Above the fire was a large tea urn supported on two rows of
bricks and behind Gareth was a small wheeled trolley, its second
tier stacked with tin mugs. A spoon was tied to the trolley handle
and there was also a big bowl of sugar and two large biscuit tins
full of sliced cake. The words 'halfpenny plain, penny seedy' had
become imprinted on Gareth's brain. For a penny the pickers
could buy a mug of tea and a slice of plain cake. The seed cake
cost a halfpenny more and was consequently less in demand.

It was Gareth's turn to push the trolley through the hop-
gardens, a task he quite enjoyed for most of the pickers were
cheerful enough and he was always welcome wherever he went.
Roland Fry, meanwhile, was also making the rounds of the
hop-fields, but for a different purpose. He tried to encourage the
hop-pickers to tell him their problems, and whenever he could he
helped them. The most frequent problem was shortage of money,
but on this point he was quite adamant: the Brothers in Jesus did
not lend money. Most of the pickers knew this quite well, but a
few were not averse to trying and Roland had learned to refuse
without giving offence. This year had been particularly difficult,
for the majority of complaints concerned the disgraceful living
conditions and he was almost helpless to solve that particular
problem.

Mary Bellweather remained in the Mission tent where a
first-aid post had been set up to deal with minor emergencies. She
was not a trained nurse, but had learned a great deal from Lydia
Grant who was so trained, and who spent two weeks with them
whenever she could arrange it. This year they had managed to buy
half a dozen folding beds, which was just as well for already three
contained patients: an elderly man who had collapsed with
fatigue; a small girl with an unpleasant rash who was isolated by a
screen at one end of the tent; and a middle-aged woman with a
touch of dysentery. Mary came out of the tent wearing a long
white apron over her blue dress. Her dark hair was tucked up

under a straw boater and she looked calm and efficient, strength of purpose apparent in every movement.

'How's the tea going, Gareth?' she asked.

'Ready any moment now,' he told her.

'Good! I'd like four mugs before you set off. Three for the patients and one for me. Do you think the sun's going to come out?'

'I certainly hope so,' said Gareth. 'Will you cut some more cake for me while I'm gone? I shall only get half-way round with this. Oh, and help me set the second urn over the fire.'

She agreed readily. 'Keep an eye open for young Alex, will you?' she asked him. 'He promises not to get into mischief, but he's so unreliable.'

Gareth smiled. 'He's a bit of a favourite with you, isn't he?'

'I must confess I like the boy,' admitted Mary, 'but the whole family needs constant support. The mother is utterly irresponsible, I'm afraid. She needs a husband, but the fathers of her children seem unwilling to go as far as marriage! I saw her last evening and on Thursday night with one of the gipsies.'

Gareth nodded. 'Amos Hearn,' he said. 'I wonder whether *his* intentions are honourable?'

Mary sighed. 'We can only hope so,' she said, 'but he's a true Romany and they don't often marry outside their own race do they? Ah, thank you!' She took two mugs of tea and hurried back into the tent, then returned for the other two.

'Wish me well!' grinned Gareth.

The trolley wheels had sunk into the wet ground and their combined efforts were needed to get it moving. The mugs clattered together and the urn swayed precariously.

'Rather you than me,' said Mary. 'I'll cut the rest of the cake while you're gone.'

He moved across the field and down towards the gate which led into the first of the hop-gardens.

'Remember to look out for Alex!' Mary called after him and he acknowledged with a wave of his hand. As he went through the gate, she heard the familiar cry, 'Halfpenny plain, penny seedy!' and stood for a moment sipping her tea.

While Mary cut the cake into generous slices, she tried to compose a little speech for the evening's entertainment. The first Saturday of each year's hop-picking was always a difficult time, for the men and women had money in their pockets and would congregate in large crowds outside the 'Horse and Cart' or the 'Blue Fox'. Frequently, a small proportion of the men would drink away most of their earnings and end up drunk and disorderly. Sometimes there were fights. Sometimes they would wander through the village when all respectable people had gone to bed, screaming and shouting and banging on their doors, safe in the knowledge that their considerable superiority of numbers rendered them safe from retaliation.

In an attempt to keep as many as possible away from the public houses, the Brothers in Jesus had planned a magic lantern show, which would of necessity be shown out of doors, with the picture thrown on to a makeshift screen hung between two trees. When Mary's cake-cutting was over she could continue her job of stitching together two of her mother's best sheets to make the screen. She smiled faintly, imagining Mrs Bellweather's look of horror if she could see the use to which her linen was being put. Having cut the cake and neatly stacked the slices, she covered it with a large white cloth edged with beads. Then, checking once more that her patients did not need her, she carried a chair outside into the sunshine, collected the sheet and began to sew.

Mary made an attractive picture, but was quite unaware of this. Her mind was occupied with more weighty problems. She thought of the four women in the sweat-shop where Mollie worked and wondered how and when legislation would be brought in to eradicate such places, or at least to improve them to the point where they were fit for women such as Mollie to earn a living. She considered unemployment and the vast numbers of poverty-stricken people who filled the East End of London – Whitechapel, Shoreditch, Stepney and many other similar areas. She pondered the fate of such boys as Alex Pett, who received so little education that he would inevitably join the ranks of the unemployed or drift into crime when he grew to manhood. Such children had no hope at all, she reflected. The small amount of good which voluntary workers like herself could do was no more than a drop in the ocean.

Uneasily, she considered her own wealth, for on her mother's death she had inherited much more than she had expected. The question was how best to use it in order to alleviate some of the suffering she saw around her every day. She could turn her own home into a small hostel, but that would require permanent staff and permanent funds and her own resources would be quickly exhausted without a source of regular additional income. So far her personal contribution had been to offer support to Mollie Pett and her children, but already she was debating the moral implications of such action. Mollie should not be encouraged to rely on Mary's money indefinitely; how then could Mollie earn more money of her own and thus be helped to independence? If she married, should Mary then withdraw her help? If not, she might find herself supporting Mollie's husband as well. Should Mollie's liaison with Amos Hearn follow its natural course, there might well be another mouth to feed before the following year's hop-picking! Mollie was not bright but she would work hard when necessary. But if Mary rendered this unnecessary, what then?

If only the Government would take some action, Mary thought. It was not enough merely to blame people for being poorly educated, ignorant and unemployable. It was false to claim that the poor knew no better and were happy with their lot. The problem was too vast and individual groups, no matter how well-meaning, were powerless to put it right. The basic difficulties of poor housing, poverty and unemployment were the responsibility of the Government, yet neither political party seemed prepared to tackle the situation. Often they seemed to deny that there *was* a problem at all.

She sighed and her thoughts turned to Emily Hobhouse. Mary had contributed to the fund which had sent her out to Africa to inspect the concentration camps set up by Kitchener for the women and children made homeless by his scorched-earth policy. Kitchener, in his efforts to finally rout the Boers, was transporting thousands of Boer women and children from their native villages to special camps. The villages were then razed to the ground, thus providing no more shelter for the guerrillas who were so successfully harassing British troops. Emily Hobhouse had sent back reports of women and children dying of enteric fever and dysentery and all right-minded people in Britain were appalled by them, yet there were many who still defended Kitchener's actions if they should contribute to bringing about an early end to the war.

There was so much misery in the world, Mary reflected sadly. The enormity of the problem depressed her if she allowed herself to dwell too long on the subject. Where, she wondered, were her energies and her money most needed? How could she, in her small way, do the maximum good? She wondered if perhaps she should start a fund to help the Boer women, but the task of administering and organizing such a venture was daunting, especially as her practical experience in campaigning amounted to no more than a few letters of encouragement written to the Suffragists. Her upbringing had not prepared her for such a path, but she was fast approaching the stage where she could not sit back and do nothing with an easy conscience.

Her thoughts were interrupted by the arrival of three women, two of them supporting a third who was obviously experiencing severe breathing difficulties. The latter was a woman of indeterminate age, somewhere between thirty and fifty, with a small wizened face and dark eyes which watered with the violence of her coughing. They stopped several times on their journey from the gate to Mary, who ran down to meet them. A grey-haired woman spoke up. 'It's her asthma, Miss, catching her something chronic,' she said. 'Can't hardly get her breath and then when she coughs, it half shakes her to pieces. Been a martyr to asthma ever since she was a little girl . . .'

'She's your daughter, is she?' asked Mary. 'Here, let me take her, I'm stronger than you.'

She took the grey-haired woman's place and they carried her in to the Mission tent. The sufferer's face was scarlet with exertion and her breathing was so erratic that all her efforts to talk were drowned by either a burst of coughing or a long-drawn-out struggle for breath.

'How long has she been in this state,' Mary asked, her heart sinking. 'Was she like this when you left London, because if so, she should have stayed at home.'

'She wasn't nowhere near so bad,' said her mother. 'It's all this wet straw and damp blankets – enough to kill a body off.'

Mary could not argue on that point. She knew that Roland had approached Julian on the subject without success.

'She can't get no sleep,' the grey-haired woman continued. 'Can't lie down, you see; has to be propped up all the time. As soon as she goes flat it's cough and gasp and everyone round her starts moaning because *they* can't get any rest.'

'We've got a spare bed,' said Mary. 'She can sleep here, but I think we shall have to call out the doctor. What's her name?'

'Vicky Simmons. She married Herbert Simmons, but he couldn't get down this weekend because he's working nights.'

The sick woman tried to protest that she had no money to pay doctors or the like, but another burst of frantic coughing effectively silenced her. Her mother translated for Mary's benefit.

'She won't have to pay,' Mary explained. 'The Brothers in Jesus have funds for such emergencies. I think we must first get her into bed and then I will discuss the matter with Mr Fry when he comes back. You two return to your work – she will be quite safe with me.'

Only too eager – for they were losing valuable picking time – the two women made their way back to the hop-gardens.

'Do you have a nightgown?' Mary asked Vicky Simmons.

The woman, sucking in painful breaths, shook her head, so Mary produced one from a trunk in the corner, one of half-a-dozen made by the sewing circle. She busied herself with the second tea urn while the woman undressed and got into bed, then gave her an extra pillow so that she could sit up and fetched her a cup of tea. Once the woman was as comfortable as Mary could make her, Mary went back outside where – to her surprise – she found Julian waiting.

'I saw that you were busy,' he said, 'and thought it best to wait for you here.'

Mary smiled warmly at him.

'I have been trying to catch you alone,' he said, 'ever since you arrived, but you are always fully involved with someone else who needs you more than I do.'

The last four words surprised Mary, but she did not allow this to show in her face.

'I am only doing my job,' she said. 'That's what I am here for.'

Julian laughed. 'I suppose if I want your attention I must break a leg or throw a fit?'

'Don't!' said Mary. 'I feel very conscious of the fact that I am not a trained nurse and I shall be thankful when Lydia joins us next Wednesday.'

'You seem to be managing very well,' said Julian.

'I thought I was, but I've just admitted a woman suffering from a severe asthma attack.' She glanced back towards the tent where another paroxysm of coughing bore out her words. 'I am waiting to discuss the case with Roland when he gets back from his rounds. But enough about me and my problems. What about yours? How's the picking progressing?'

'Not at all well,' he said. 'The yield is as poor as we feared it might be. The pickers are having a hard job and their earnings are well down on last year and the year before. They are not at all happy about that, I'm afraid. This damned weather doesn't help either!'

His manner was disconsolate and Mary decided that this was not the moment to broach the subject of the leaking barn. It was very obvious to everyone that no matter how bad the weather, nothing could usefully be done within the next three weeks which would improve the pickers' lot to any appreciable degree. She felt sorry for Julian; he looked very young and vulnerable and she knew that the responsibility he bore was a heavy one.

'What was it you wanted to talk to me about?' she asked him.

'Nothing specific,' he confessed. 'The truth is that I just wanted a few moments of your company. Perhaps I feel in need of a sympathetic ear – I don't know.'

'I am all attention,' said Mary, 'if I can be of any help.'

'You've been here a week now,' said Julian, 'and every evening I have asked you to join us for dinner but you never accept. Have we offended you in some way?'

'Of course not!' Her denial was genuine. 'I merely feel that since the two men have volunteered to live in the Mission tent, I am already privileged to have a room of my own at Foxearth. I think the least I can do is to keep the men company in the evening and help to prepare their meals. Of course I would prefer to dine with you, but it seems a betrayal really. Does that sound very foolish?'

'Not foolish at all,' said Julian. 'Very much in character, Mary. I suppose I should have expected no other answer, but my offer still holds. I shall be very hurt indeed if you don't accept at least once or twice before you return to London.'

His words were spoken lightly but there was a wistful look in his eyes. Mary hesitated. 'Perhaps tomorrow evening?' she suggested.

'I look forward to that enormously,' Julian said. 'Now I suppose I ought to get back about my business and leave you to your patients.'

He looked at her, a long yearning look which rendered Mary speechless because she read there all that he had not spoken aloud. She was disconcerted and longed to say 'Stay a while longer,' but dared not, knowing that once the words were uttered there would be something exclusive between them, a bond of some kind which should not exist. So she lowered her eyes and made no answer.

Julian laughed a little awkwardly. 'I thought you might beg me to stay,' he said, 'but you are right. Neither of us has time for idle chit-chat. If I don't see you before, then I shall look forward to seeing you at dinner tomorrow evening. That is a promise, isn't it, Mary?'

She looked up. 'It is, Julian,' she said.

*

In the 'Horse and Cart' that night, Andy Roberts and Jarvis Tupp leaned back against the bar and drank deeply from the first pints of the evening. As they drank they watched the growing throng of hop-pickers in the courtyard outside the front of the inn.

'They don't look at all happy,' said Andy. 'If you ask me, there's trouble brewing.'

Maisie bridled. 'Well, we've done all we can for them,' she said, 'short of letting them in. It's not our fault if the weather's not nice, but it's not actually raining – just drizzle in the air, and we've given them all the spare chairs and a couple of trestle tables. We have done what we can.'

'I'm not saying you haven't, Maisie, love,' said Andy. 'No need to get on your high horse about it.'

Jarvis emptied his glass in three quick gulps. 'What do you mean, Andy, trouble?'

'Why, for them up at Foxearth,' Andy replied. 'See those women? Heads together – mutter, mutter. They're up to something . . . they're plotting. You can always tell.'

'Plotting what?' said Maisie.

Andy shrugged. 'Don't ask me, love,' he said. 'I'm not a bloomin' mind reader. All I'm saying is that they don't look at all happy and there is a sight of whispering going on, not to mention a few black looks.'

'Well, don't stare at them like that,' said Maisie. 'If they are already in a funny mood and then they see you staring . . .'

'Calm down,' said Jarvis. 'They're not going to do another "Blue Fox". Andy means trouble for the guv'nor. The money's down, you see and they're up in arms about their accommodation. You can't blame them, either, poor devils! I wouldn't like to be sleeping up in that barn in this rain. They took one woman to hospital this afternoon. Coughing and gasping, so they say, with damp in her lungs. Asthmatic, she was and real bad with it. That sort of thing upsets the others.'

All the local customers of the 'Horse and Cart' were enjoying the comfort of the newly decorated saloon bar. The public bar was empty except for Ted Hunter, who served the never-ending queue of hoppers waiting patiently at the window in the failing light.

'Look at them!' said Jarvis. 'Most of them can't even sit down, the ground's so wet. Just standing around, dreaming up mischief.'

'Well, I hope you're wrong,' said Maisie.

John Burrows got up from his corner seat and joined them, staring out of the window at the discontented crowd outside. He worked in the oast-house as one of the driers – a job he had done for the past nine years.

'The kids keep coming round the oast-house,' he said, 'trying to get warm. Mr Pitt gets that mad with them, you know what he's like.'

Maisie poured herself a port and lemon. 'Not much fun for the kids this year, is it?' she said. 'Poor little mites!'

John Burrows took off his cap, scratched his head and put the cap on again. 'I suppose you know the Bryces are back in Teesbury?' he said. 'The womenfolk and kids, anyway.'

The others nodded. 'But it's all a bit hush-hush,' said Jarvis. 'I reckon there's something funny going on there, but I can't put my finger on it.'

Maisie sipped daintily at her drink and smacked her lips appreciatively. 'Well, I heard a rumour,' she said, 'that they were letting Tom Bryce out.'

'I hope that's not true,' said Ted. 'The man's a menace to himself and everyone else. No matter how sorry you feel for his family, the fact remains that I certainly don't fancy the idea of him prowling around the place, free to do as he likes. None of us would feel safe in our beds. If he was mad enough to be put into the asylum, they can't have cured him already.'

Jarvis sniffed. 'You can't cure madness,' he said. 'Anyone knows that. I reckon he'll end his days there.'

At that moment one of the women pickers happened to glance up and see the concerted stares from the three men. Immediately taking umbrage, she marched over to the window, stuck her thumb on the end of her nose and waggled her fingers at them in a gesture of defiance. For a moment the men were taken aback.

Jarvis said, 'Well I'm damned! Cheeky little hussy!' and took a step forward.

'Jarvis!' cried Maisie. 'If you start something, out you go. I won't tell you twice – I'm having no trouble in this pub.'

Andy and John had hastily turned away and were now staring pointedly across the bar. Jarvis hesitated, stuck up two fingers in a rude gesture and then turned his back on the young woman at the window.

'Cheeky trollop!' he grumbled. 'Who does she think she is? I'd like to tan her hide for her.'

Andy grinned. 'Yes, I reckon you'd enjoy that, Jarvis,' he said.

'That's quite enough of that smutty talk,' said Maisie, watching out of the corner of her eye until the woman at the window gave up and moved back to rejoin her friends.

'I don't know what the world's coming to,' said Maisie. 'I really don't.'

*

On Saturdays the fires were allowed to stay alight until eleven, but since no one could be bothered to supervise this operation it was nearly half-past the hour before the last flames were dowsed and darkness fell over the hoppers' camp. Inside the large barn most of the pickers had apparently settled down for the night and the hurricane lamps – suspended from the rafters or hung from the wall – had been extinguished. Outside, Amos Hearn and Mollie Pett stood together on the barn's sheltered side, huddled close.

'I shall have to go soon,' Mollie whispered.

'Not yet!'

'Amos, I must!'

'You could come back with me,' he suggested. 'Plenty of room in my tent and it's dry. You said you would.'

'I did not,' she protested. 'I only said I might and tonight I can't, so there!'

'Why not? What's special about tonight?'

'I mustn't tell you,' she said, 'but I can't, that's all.'

'You've got something on, haven't you?' said Amos.

'We might have or we might not.'

'You be careful,' he warned. 'You could get into a lot of trouble.'

'Well, that would be nothing new,' Mollie told him. 'I've been in and out of trouble all me bloomin' life, so a bit more won't make much difference.'

'I mean real trouble,' he persisted. 'What are you going to do?'

'Nothing too terrible,' said Mollie. 'We're just going to spoil their night's sleep – see how *they* like it!'

'You do any damage,' he warned her, 'and you'll have the police after you. Julian Lawrence is a lot harder than he looks, and if you think he will take it as a bit of a joke, you'll be wrong. Whose idea is this, anyway, whatever it is?'

'We're not allowed to say,' said Mollie. 'It's a secret.'

'Come back with me,' urged Amos, pulling her closer and kissing the tip of her nose. 'I can show you a better way to spend the night and one that won't mean you getting into trouble.'

'Oh no? I know what you've got in mind, Amos Hearn and it might very well land me in trouble – the sort of trouble I've already had three times.'

'I'll be careful. Nothing will happen.'

'I've heard that before and the answer's no.'

'But suppose I was to ask you to marry me?' he suggested.

Mollie drew back a little so that she could see his face better. 'Marry me?' she repeated.

'Why not?' said Amos. 'Just for September – a hoppers' wedding. It's been done before, you know.'

'Hoppers' wedding? What do you mean?' she said. 'Married just while we're down here?'

'That's right. Never heard of a hoppers' wedding? All you do is jump over a hop-pole in front of all the others, then you're man and wife until the hopping ends.'

'Oh, that's very nice!' said Mollie sarcastically. 'And what happens then?'

'Well, you go your way and I go mine.'

'I bet it was a man dreamed up that idea! Hoppers' wedding, my foot!'

'But it would mean you could sleep in a nice dry tent every night. All private like, just you and me. We could have some good times, Mollie. You do like me a bit, don't you?'

'Suppose I do?'

'Well, why not take a chance then?' he coaxed. 'Life's too short to hang around, that's what I say. Might as well enjoy yourself while you've got the chance.'

He pulled her back towards him and slid his left hand around her waist and then down over her thighs. With his right hand he caressed the back of her neck and her earlobes.

'Mind my hat!' she said unromantically.

'Better take it off, then?' he suggested.

'Oh yes? And the next thing it'll be "mind my shawl" and you'll have that off me as well. I'll be stark naked before I finish.'

'That's a lovely thought,' he said. 'Now why didn't I think of that? It warms me up all over just thinking about it. I bet you've got a lovely body, Mollie Pett. Young pink flesh and soft curvy bits!'

'Ooh, listen to him,' she scoffed. 'I suppose you say that to all the girls you lure into your tent.'

'There's been no one but me in my bed this whole week,' he declared, his tone full of righteous indignation. 'I've been saving it for you, seeing as how you're the only one I fancy.'

'Oh, you fancy me then?' she said.

'I fancied you from the first moment I saw you looking over that gate in that red hat of yours,' he told her. 'We could make each other very happy, I said to myself, but now it seems you're going to turn me down.'

Mollie was thoughtful for a moment while his hands moved freely over the upper part of her body until they crept up beneath her shawl.

'Leave off!' she protested.

'You know you like it, Mollie,' he whispered. 'You don't have to pretend with me. I can make a girl feel like a princess, I can. Don't you want to try me?'

Mollie had to admit she was finding it increasingly difficult to pretend she was not enjoying herself.

'Come on,' he whispered. 'Come back with me.'

She wavered. 'But what about Alex?'

'He'll be asleep by now and he won't know you're not there. You can slip back in the morning. He'll be none the wiser and you'll have done yourself a favour.'

'Oh, you *have* got a good opinion of yourself,' said Mollie.

Now his hands slid down and experience told him she was almost his. His own growing excitement matched hers.

'See what you've done to me,' he whispered. 'Can you feel it? That's all yours, Mollie, if you just say the word. I'll have you screaming with delight and begging me not to stop. Cross my heart, I will. If you sleep with me tonight, Mollie Pett, you'll never want to sleep in that old barn again, I can tell you. You'll be begging for it every night.'

Mollie had no doubt of that as the familiar sensations swept through her.

'It's only for you, Mollie love,' he whispered. 'I swear to it. If you won't sleep with me, I'll sleep on my own for the rest of the hopping. There's no one else I'll take into my bed, for there's not another woman here who could hold a candle to you. I think we're well matched and I think you know it in your heart of hearts. Tell me you don't want it, Mollie. Go on. Try and tell me!'

Her legs felt weak under her and she was half swooning with pleasure. 'I can't, Amos,' she murmured, 'because I do want it.'

Suddenly they were startled by the sound of footsteps as a group of people appeared round the corner of the barn.

'Is that you, Mollie?' cried a woman's voice in a hoarse whisper. 'We've been looking for you. Come on!'

'Oh Christ!' said Amos. 'What do they want?'

Very reluctantly, Mollie withdrew herself from his persuasive hands. 'I told you,' she hissed. 'We've planned something.'

'I thought you were coming to bed with me?'

'I was – that is, I would have done, but I forgot.'

'Tell them to go without you. Say you're not going, that you're coming with me.'

'I can't do that. I promised.'

Dimly, in the darkness, he made out a crowd of twenty or more women. 'Come on, Mollie,' they called.

'She's not coming,' said Amos loudly, holding her firmly round the waist.

'Oh yes she is,' said Mollie, struggling with him.

One of the women laughed. 'What he's got will keep till tomorrow night, love.'

'You silly cow!' cried Amos. 'What the hell are you up to, anyway?'

'None of your business!' the woman answered. 'You coming, Mollie, or aren't you?'

'Of course I'm coming!' She wrenched herself free and ran to join them, while Amos cursed furiously under his breath.

'You'll be sorry, Mollie Pett,' he called after her, but she had vanished with the others into the darkness. Curiosity got the better of him and he followed in the direction that they had taken, intrigued to know what it was all about.

'Strewth!' said Mollie to one of her companions. 'I forgot my saucepan.'

'Here, take one of these lids and find yourself a bit of a stick or a stone.'

The woman carried an assortment of tin plates, saucepans, saucepan lids and cutlery. Giggling nervously, they crept up towards the house and finally tiptoed on to the lawn where they ranged themselves in a semi-circle facing the front of the house. They wore scarves wound round their faces, hiding everything except their eyes, so that if they should be spotted by anyone they would not be recognized. Only Mollie's face was uncovered.

'Where's your scarf?' whispered one of the women. 'They'll see your face.'

Mollie's scarf was tucked under her pillow in the leaking barn and she cursed under her breath.

The women knelt down on the damp grass, heads bent so that anyone glancing from the house would not immediately identify the shapes were kneeling women. When they were all in position, the leader began to tap on her saucepan with a spoon, very softly at first. Then one by one, in a pre-arranged order which had been carefully rehearsed, the others joined in. There was something exhilarating about the situation which suited Mollie's already excited state of mind. At first the tapping was no more than a murmur but it gradually grew, louder and louder, until the women forgot to bow their heads and looked up eagerly to see the first lights go on in the house. There was not long to wait – a rectangle of light shone suddenly above and to the left of the front door.

'I wonder who that is?' whispered Mollie.

'Mr Lawrence himself, I hope,' came the answer.

The banging and rattling grew to a crescendo and another light appeared. Further along they saw the flicker of a candle flame and heard the sound of a window being pushed up.

'What the devil!' came a furious voice which they recognized gleefully as that of Julian Lawrence.

Regardless of the rain, the women then stood up, holding their saucepans and thundering a tattoo on them. More lights appeared as the noise continued to shatter the night with its discordant symphony. Then they began to chant, shrieking to make themselves heard above the noise.

'We can't sleep. Why should you? We can't sleep. Why should you?' A lone voice broke the pattern and called out, 'What about that sodding roof?'

Others took this up with cries of, 'Mend the roof!'

This last chant was seized upon by the others: 'Mend the roof! Mend the roof!'

Suddenly the front door opened and one or two of the women faltered for a moment. Julian stood there in his dressing gown, outlined in the doorway.

'That's enough!' he shouted. 'Have you taken leave of your senses?'

'Mend the roof! Mend the roof!'

From an upstairs window Vinnie called out, 'Wait, Julian, I'm coming down.'

He cupped his hands to his mouth and tried to shout above the din. 'If you don't stop this at once, I shall telephone for the police.'

This had some effect and one or two of the women took fright. The noise temporarily subsided.

'He's bluffing,' shouted Mollie. 'He wouldn't dare. Treating us like animals!'

'Worse than animals.'

They took up the chant again. 'Mend the roof! Mend the roof!'

Those who remained edged forward a little and stepped up the volume of their metallic protest. Vinnie appeared beside Julian and they all saw that she was tugging at his arm and speaking urgently. Roughly, he shook her away and took a few steps forward.

'Stop it!' he screamed. 'Stop it, I tell you, or I'll sack the lot of you!'

This further threat also had its effect and a few more women defected and vanished into the darkness. Mollie Pett, incensed by their betrayal, redoubled her own effort.

'Mend our bloody roof!' she screamed and impulsively hurled the saucepan lid towards the house.

It was purely a gesture of defiance and the lid was not intended as a missile, but a freak gust of wind snatched at it and curved it upwards straight into one of the first-floor windows. There was the unmistakable sound of breaking glass, followed by a woman's scream.

'Christ, Mollie!' cried one of the women. 'Now you've done it.'

Mollie stood transfixed with fright, staring at the upstairs window, while behind her the remaining women melted away, urging her to do likewise. Panic-stricken, she remained on the lawn and saw Julian turn to run up the stairs. After a moment's hesitation, Vinnie herself came down the steps on to the lawn.

'Who are you?' she shouted.

Mollie shook her head dumbly. She wanted to run but her legs refused to carry her. As Vinnie drew nearer she finally found her tongue. 'I didn't mean it!' she gasped. 'I didn't!'

For a moment she and Vinnie stood only yards apart, staring at each other. 'You'd better go,' Vinnie hissed. 'Quickly!'

Too late Mollie realized that her face was uncovered. Dimly she could make out Vinnie's features, so presumably Vinnie could make out hers. The warnings about the police rang in her ears and with a gasp of terror she turned and ran.

Upstairs, Mary Bellweather stood in her nightgown, her hands covering her face. She was barefooted and dared not move for broken glass littered the floor around her. There was a hasty knock at the door, then it opened and Julian rushed in.

'Mind the glass!' she cried, but then realized that he wore slippers.

'Mary!' he cried and lifting her into his arms, carried her away from the window and set her down on the bed.

'Are you all right?' he asked. 'Those crazy women! I'll make them pay for all this. Are you hurt?'

'No,' said Mary. 'A bit shaky, I must confess, but by some miracle not hurt at all. I was standing only inches from the glass when it broke.'

'You could have been blinded! My God, I'll make them pay for this.'

'Oh no!' cried Mary. 'Please don't, not on my account, Julian. There's no real harm done ... except for the broken window.'

'If they had harmed one hair of your head—'

His earlier anger had turned to passionate rage and he struck the wall several times with his clenched fist. 'How dare they? How dare they do this?' he raged. 'And to you of all people.'

'It was an accident, Julian, I'm sure. They're misguided, yes, but they're not vicious.'

'How can you try to defend them?' he cried.

He crossed to the window and looked out. The light from the front door illuminated Vinnie's figure as she stood staring into the darkness and he turned back. Mary now stood between him and the candle, with the soft light haloing her head, her long dark hair tumbling about her bare shoulders in delicate disarray. Her eyes were large and dark in her oval face and her bare arms shone palely in the darkness.

'Mary!' His anger vanished suddenly at the sight of her and her softness made him want to weep.

'Mary,' he whispered again. 'My dearest Mary—'

'Oh Julian,' she begged, 'please don't say anything you will regret.' She put up a warning hand to keep him at a distance, but he took hold of it and kissed the fingers and she could not take it away. Instead she raised her other hand and gently touched his hair. Then suddenly Janet was in the room, staring at them, fully aware of what was happening.

She gasped in dismay. 'Sir! I'm sorry, sir, I never meant to . . . that is, I heard glass breaking and I thought—'

Mary drew back as Julian rounded on Janet. 'How dare you come bursting in here like this?' he cried.

'I'm sorry, sir, but the door was open and I thought someone was hurt.'

'No one is hurt. When I want you, I will send for you.'

She backed hastily into the passage and he slammed the door and leaned against it.

'I'm sorry,' he said to Mary, 'about Janet and about everything. No, that's a lie! I am not sorry, but this is neither the time nor the place . . .'

They could hear Vinnie's voice calling to Janet, asking if anyone was hurt. 'No, ma'am,' cried Janet.

Julian said quickly, 'Get back into bed!' As she did so, he took the candle, set it on the floor by the window and began to pick up pieces of broken glass. Mary meanwhile pulled the coverlet up to hide her shoulders, then there was a tap on the door.

'Mary, are you all right?' It was Vinnie's voice. 'May I come in?' Julian glanced at Mary and she nodded.

'Come in!' cried Julian, busying himself once more with the pieces of broken glass. Vinnie hurried into the room while Janet hovered outside, fearful of incurring Julian's wrath by coming in again unless she was called.

'Oh Mary! It was your window,' Vinnie said. 'Are you hurt?'

'No,' said Mary. 'I was very lucky. Fortunately I was still in bed.' As soon as she had told the small white lie, she realized how it would sound to the maid who was still outside and who had seen her out of bed and standing with Julian.

'However can we apologize?' said Vinnie. 'Oh, what a dreadful thing to happen!'

'Whoever is responsible will be punished,' said Julian, keeping his face half-averted. 'Make no mistake about that!'

Hastily, Vinnie turned back towards Janet. 'Heat some milk, Janet, please, and put a spoonful of honey in it. It will help Miss Bellweather to sleep.'

'Yes, ma'am,' said Janet as she hurried off.

'Don't cut yourself with that glass, Julian,' Vinnie warned. 'Perhaps you should leave it and Young Harry can see to it in the morning.'

'It's nearly done now, Vinnie,' he replied. 'You go back to bed and I will be along in a moment when I am sure there are no more splinters left lying around.'

Vinnie looked at Mary. 'Goodnight then, Mary,' she said.

'Goodnight, Vinnie.'

Mary did not meet Vinnie's eyes and Vinnie left the room with the uneasy feeling that everything was not as it should be.

*

Vinnie returned to the bedroom and stood beside the bed – their bed, hers and Julian's – but could not get back into it. She was shivering slightly, partly with shock and partly with fear. However, it was not the shock of the pickers' demonstration, much though that had alarmed and dismayed her. It was the looks on the three faces she had just seen: Janet had been embarrassed and confused; Mary was ashamed; Julian . . .

Slowly Vinnie sat down on the edge of the bed and covered her mouth with trembling fingers. How exactly *had* Julian looked at her? His expression had been utterly new to her, the look in his eyes unfamiliar, so how could she read it with any certainty?

'Julian!' she whispered, drawing his recent image into sharper focus so that she could study it. There was coldness there, but she had seen that before; it was nothing new. Disapproval? No, not disapproval. There was a certain amount of anger in his eyes, but that was understandable. He was angry with the pickers; angry about the broken window; angry that Mary might have been injured. But Janet had hardly been able to meet her eyes – why should that be, Vinnie wondered. What had Janet seen that had made her reluctant to face her mistress? Naturally she would have been shocked and upset by the incident. She might even have found it exciting – the servants loved melodrama. But Janet had looked embarrassed . . .

Restlessly Vinnie stood up again and crossed to the window, looking down on the silent and deserted garden. She could go down and ask Janet point-blank what she had seen, but the idea was unthinkable.

'Julian,' she whispered again. 'I don't understand what's happening, and I don't think I want to know. I don't think I dare.'

Julian's face, insubstantial as a ghost, refused to leave her mind and she saw again the cold eyes, tight jaw and slightly bent head. Hate? No, that was too strong. Indifference? She sighed. That was not it either. But if it had been, could she bear his indifference? She decided that she could not.

Just at that moment she heard his footsteps approaching along the passage and the knowledge that she must face him made her stomach churn in desperation. He came into the room and stared at her with exaggerated surprise.

'Are you going to stand there all night?' he asked. 'Won't you get rather cold?'

His voice, she thought, was as cold as his eyes had been. She hesitated, trying to hold back the words which sprang to her lips. Once said, there would be no retracting them.

'Vinnie?' He moved towards her, a forced smile on his lips. 'Aren't you coming to bed?'

'I don't want to come to bed,' she said, her voice sounding to her own ears unnaturally loud. 'I don't want to lie beside you.'

She saw the wariness in his eyes as he shrugged, 'Please yourself.'

'Aren't you going to ask me why? Don't you care?'

'If you want to stand around getting cold, that's up to you,' he said. 'I have already lost half an hour's sleep, thanks to your friends, and I don't intend to lose any more.'

'They're not my friends,' said Vinnie. 'They are *our* pickers. Why are they suddenly *my* friends?'

'You always take their side against me. Doesn't that make them your friends?'

'No.' She swallowed hard, fighting down her sudden rage, trying to remain calm.

'Oh,' said Julian. 'My mistake.' He turned away, threw off his dressing gown and climbed into bed.

Vinnie's fragile self-control snapped. 'Julian!' she shouted.

'Don't you dare turn over and go to sleep! Don't you dare do that to me! I'm not stupid or blind. I *know*!'

He froze in the act of sliding down into bed as Vinnie's words echoed in her head. 'Don't blow out the candle,' she cried. 'I want to see your face.'

She crossed the room and stood looking down at him. The alien expression was still there, but still Vinnie could not define it. His small mouth looked smaller than ever and a muscle throbbed in his neck.

'Know what?' he asked. 'I don't know what you're talking about. Why are you behaving this way? Has this stupid incident —'

'Please, Julian!' she begged, sinking to her knees on the floor beside him and looking imploringly into his face. 'Please don't pretend with me, Julian. You look so strange . . . no, strangely. You look at me strangely and I know something is wrong. I know—'

He interrupted her. 'You know nothing of the kind, Vinnie! There is nothing wrong and you are being ridiculous. How on earth do you expect me to look after the events of the last half-hour? Happy? Those ignorant, ungrateful wretches put on that pathetic display of bad manners and one of them breaks a window and terrifies one of my guests – of course there's something wrong. I should think you could work that out for yourself. What's wrong is those hooligans you are always so quick to defend.'

'Someone has to defend them,' cried Vinnie. 'And they are *not* hooligans. Those "hooligans", as you call them, are just ordinary women like my mother. She was no hooligan, just an honest, hardworking woman trying to earn a few pounds to see the family through the winter. Any one of them could have been my mother, Julian, or don't you care to remember that? Is that something shameful you would rather forget? Or it could be *me*, Julian! But for the grace of God I might be out there with them – I might be trying to sleep on wet bedding – *I* might have thrown that lid through Mary's window!'

'You might indeed.' Julian's tone was icy, and Vinnie wanted to hit him, to knock the smugness from his voice. She almost groaned aloud in her frustration.

'Please!' she said. 'I am not trying to fight. I do not want to quarrel with you, but you must understand why I feel for them.

They need someone to care, they're so helpless.'

'Helpless!' cried Julian. 'That's the last thing I would call them. You must be out of your mind if you call that rabble helpless!'

'They are not rabble!' cried Vinnie. 'Just poor people who do a good day's work for not much money and you know it. You need them as much as they need you. All they ask is decent lodgings and that leaking sieve you call a roof is a disgrace. You promised me ages ago that you would attend to it. Now you know how they feel, maybe you will do something about it!'

'Yes, perhaps I will do something. Perhaps I will sack them all!'

'You can't do that!' said Vinnie, aghast.

'We shall see about that!'

In the flickering candlelight they glared defiance at each other, oblivious of their raised voices and aware only of their anger. Vinnie's heart banged painfully against her ribs. She did not want him to carry out his threat, but he might do so just to punish her for interfering. With a tremendous effort she fought down her rising hysteria.

'Please don't, Julian,' she begged. 'I'm sorry, I'm truly sorry, but please don't sack them, Julian. Promise you won't!'

He was silent for a moment, savouring the small victory. Then he shrugged. 'I'll talk to Mary about it,' he said.

The words were like a slap in the face to Vinnie and she gasped.

'Mary!' she whispered. 'Why to Mary? Why do you have to talk to her about it instead of to me?'

'Because she is the one who was frightened,' he told her triumphantly. 'She is the one who might easily have been seriously injured. You can't have forgotten already. Moreover, she is a member of the Brothers of Jesus, who are down here for the sole purpose of seeing to the pickers' welfare. It is her job, rather than yours, to discuss the matter with me.'

'What about Roland Fry?' Vinnie asked rashly. 'I thought he was in charge. Or do you prefer to discuss things with Mary? Were you in fact discussing something with her when I found you in her room just now?'

'I don't care for your choice of words, Vinnie,' said Julian steadily. 'You did not "find me in her room". You came to her room to see if she was hurt – to find out what had happened – and found that I was already there on the same errand.'

Abruptly Vinnie scrambled to her feet and stared down at her husband. 'So why did you look at me as though I was intruding,' she demanded, her voice dropping suddenly to a whisper. 'Whatever you may say, Julian, I know you *did* look at me like that. Oh God, I wish I knew what to say – how to tell you how frightened I am!'

She covered her face with her hands, waiting vainly for a reassuring word; for Julian to tell her that she had imagined it after all; that Mary was nothing to him; that he loved only her.

The silence lengthened until at last he broke it. 'Vinnie, I'm tired and I want to go to sleep. This is not the time to discuss anything—'

She snatched her hands from her face to stare at him in wild-eyed apprehension. 'So there *is* something to discuss!' she said. 'About you and Mary!'

'I did not say that, Vinnie,' Julian protested. 'Please don't put words into my mouth. I simply said that I am tired and I would like to go to sleep.'

'Julian!'

'Don't look at me like that, Vinnie!' he said irritably. 'Why do you have to be so damned dramatic? I will spell it out for you: I am woken up in the middle of the night to find a minor rebellion on my front lawn, which doesn't much please me. Someone breaks a window and one of our guests could have been hurt. Now you come up with this nonsense about Mary Bellweather and complain about the expression on my face. I have tried to explain it all, but more than that I am not prepared to do. There is no reason at all why you should be behaving like an outraged wife and I find this whole conversation unworthy of you. You are behaving like a hysterical child. In the morning I shall decide what to do about the pickers. If it makes you feel any better, I will agree not to sack all of them, but I may not be so lenient with the person who actually broke the window.'

He waited and she said dutifully, 'Thank you, Julian.'

A terrible cold despair had settled over her and she felt drained and defeated.

'Now I insist that you get back into bed, Vinnie. I suggest we forget this whole conversation and both try to get some sleep.'

She nodded dumbly and Julian slid down under the bedclothes. Then he leaned forward again to blow out the candle, leaving Vinnie to climb into bed in the dark. She lay straight and still, anxious not to touch the still form beside her. Suddenly she felt an overwhelming surge of despair as she identified the expression she had seen on Julian's face in Mary's room – it was guilt.

CHAPTER ELEVEN

Rose hesitated outside the forge, gathering enough courage to go inside. It was many years since she had last done so and a great deal had happened in that time. Andy Roberts would know it all – rumour and gossip were rife, she knew. Once she had been the wife of the Colonel's chief pole-puller and that had been something to be proud of. Now she was wife to a man in the asylum – a man with no job and no prospects, described by the authorities as dangerous and unbalanced. But no! She would not think that way, she told herself fiercely. Whatever Tom's change in fortune, she was still proud to be his wife. She straightened her back and lifted her head. 'I'm Tom's wife and proud of it,' she whispered, then pushed open the door and went into the forge.

All was exactly as she had remembered and the sight of it brought back an immediate memory of herself at the age of fifteen, hanging about outside hoping that Tom Bryce would call in on business – a new fire basket for Foxearth, perhaps, or hopping tools to be repaired or replaced. Once he had brought in a cart-wheel to be fitted with a new metal tyre. She saw him in her mind's eye as though it were yesterday, his large hands bowling the wheel as though it was a child's hoop. Was that the day she had decided to marry him? Andy had teased her about what he called her 'fancy' for Mrs Bryce's only son, but then Andy had fancied her too. Momentarily a slight smile brushed her face, then her expression changed again. It was all such a long time ago. She sighed. The young Rose Tully was a different person, not Rose Bryce at all.

Inside, the forge was a vast L-shaped shell of whitewashed brick, turned grey now with years of soot. There were large windows, their frames hung with various tools, and smaller windows in the sloping roof. On her left were two large tables piled with templates, curls of copper and a number of half-finished wrought-iron brackets. Shelves covered the walls behind the table and on these were laid various lengths of iron of different thicknesses. Beneath the tables huge copper cooking pots jostled a badly dented kettle, and an ancient coal-scuttle without a handle lay on its side. Beyond the tables she saw the fuel store, its wooden door ajar, coal spilling out onto the bricked floor. In the centre at the far end was the heart of the forge – a glowing waist-high hearth on a brick base under an iron hood. Its tall brick chimney reached up and out through the roof.

A man stood beside the hearth with his back to her, pumping the bellows. Rose recognized Andy Roberts at once, although perhaps he carried a little more weight than she remembered. He had not heard her, for the place was as ever full of noise – the roar of the hearth and the clang of metal on metal. Someone was working at an anvil round the corner, out of sight. Overhead two beams hung with rusting horseshoes supported the roof and a large clock ticked high on the right-hand wall. It was ten to three already. Rose coughed to attract attention to her presence and Andy turned towards her. He held a pair of long tongs in his hand and his face gleamed with sweat.

'Rose! Come right in. No one's going to eat you,' he cried. 'You're a sight for sore eyes!'

It was a kindly lie, she knew, but it was comforting to feel so welcome. Willingly she crossed the room to stand beside him.

'It's a long time, Andy,' she said. 'You're looking well.'

'Looking well? I'm looking magnificent,' he laughed. 'In the prime of life, let me tell you.'

'And modest too,' said Rose.

'Modest too! The man's too good to be true,' he laughed, 'but it's good to see you back in Teesbury after all these years.'

Rose hesitated. 'You know we're at Brook Cottage?'

Andy nodded. 'Mrs Lawrence said as how you were staying there on the "QT" like.'

He tapped the side of his nose with a grimy finger and then, with a sudden oath, turned to snatch a length of iron from the glowing coal with the tongs. He examined it briefly and nodded. 'Just in time,' he told her. 'It's one of your latches, so don't you go distracting my attention with those wicked eyes of yours.'

'They're not wicked,' Rose began, but her words were drowned as Andy laid the bright glowing metal across the anvil and began to pound it with a round-ended hammer. She watched, fascinated, as he slowly flattened the end of the inch-wide metal and shaped it until it was the size of a penny but spear-shaped. He worked quickly but within a minute the metal was cooling, the colour fading from a bright orange to a dull red. Andy's lips moved as he worked, but Rose could not hear what he said. When he had finished he held out his handiwork for her approval.

'How's that suit you?' he asked. 'I'm doing thumb latches with Norman ends.' He thrust it back into the fire, treadled the bellows and then picked up a sheet of yellowing paper on which Rose could just make out several pencilled sketches.

'The latches, see?' he explained. 'Different designs. There's the penny end – that's just a circle. A bit plain, but some folks like it. The Norman end – like yours. Mrs Lawrence left it to me to decide. And this one's called a fish-tail, with a flared end, cut off straight like—?'

'Like a fish's tail.'

'Clever girl!'

He turned back to repeat his earlier work on a second strip of metal, explaining that it saved time to do two at once, but once again the clang of the hammer drowned his words. While Rose waited, she peered curiously round the corner to see whose banging was rivalling Andy's. A slim young man with straight dark hair glanced up, saw her and smiled briefly. Then he resumed his work.

'You're not alone now, then?' Rose asked when she could hear herself speak.

'Had to take on a lad,' said Andy. 'I'm so busy here, I was turning away work. His name's Martin. He's good though – been with me nearly two years now. Picks it up fast. I shall have to take on another lad soon.' He grinned. 'Turn away work and you turn away money. That hurts here, that does.' He patted his pocket.

Rose took a deep breath. 'I suppose you've heard about Tom?'

'Yes. I was very sorry to hear it too. But don't you worry, Tom's a tough nut. He'll come through, you'll see, and be his old self again one of these days. We're all very sorry, but the way I see it is that if he needs a doctor's help to put him on the right road again, then he's in the best place. You just keep your chin up and it'll turn out fine, I'm telling you.'

This time when he pulled out the hot metal, he brushed it with a wire brush and dark flakes of iron flew in all directions, making Rose jump back. From a respectful distance she watched as he tucked the handle of the long tongs between his legs and rested the glowing latch-to-be on the anvil. Then he took up a punch and placed it on the metal. With swift, sure strokes he drove the punch half-way through the metal, reheated the latch and then drove the punch through the other side to make a slot.

'I heard your wife had died,' said Rose. 'I'm so sorry.'

Andy shrugged. 'She was in such pain,' he said, 'it was the best thing. She never would have got well again. I hated to see her like that, with her face screwed up and trying not to cry out for fear of worrying me. Poor lass!' He wiped the sweat from his forehead with the back of his hand.

'She's in a better place,' said Rose and he nodded, then raised his voice and shouted, 'Martin, brew up, will you? And make it three mugs – we've a visitor!'

He smiled at Rose. 'Cup of tea? The cup will be chipped and there will be tea leaves floating on the top, but it's drinkable.'

Rose smiled and glanced down at the end of the hearth where a rack held an assortment of iron tools. 'Do you use *all* these?' she asked.

Andy laughed. 'Some I use a lot, some hardly ever. They're all tongs: flat tongs, round tongs and duck-billed tongs – from its shape, you see. Looks like a duck's head and when I open it – quack!' She nodded. 'And,' he said 'it's for—?'

'Picking things up,' suggested Rose.

He nodded. 'Picking up small things like rivets. You're learning fast. You wouldn't like a job here, I suppose? I told you we shall need another pair of hands soon.'

'I'll think it over,' she said, smiling.

'You do that,' he said. 'And your mother-in-law – is she well?'

Rose shrugged. 'Not really. She worries so much about Tom that it's making her ill. She can't sleep and hardly eats a thing.'

'What about the children? I don't suppose I'd recognize any of them now.'

'They're well enough,' said Rose. 'They miss their father but they eat and sleep, thank goodness.'

Andy finished the two latches and began on the 'tongues' which would fit on to the other side of the door and be used to raise and lower each latch. At one end he curled the narrow metal into a decorative scroll. The other end was beaten into a flat spoon shape, large enough to take a man's thumb.

'Aren't you going to plunge it into the water trough?' Rose

asked. 'The farrier always did that – I used to watch him when I was a child.'

'That's because he wanted to harden his metal. I want to keep mine soft and workable—'

They both looked up as the door opened and a police constable entered the forge. They stared at him, but Andy's look was puzzled, Rose's apprehensive.

'I'm looking for Brook Cottage,' the constable began.

Rose put a hand to her mouth. 'Brook Cottage? That's me!' she cried. 'Oh, it's not one of the children, is it? Something's happened to one of the children!'

'No, no, it's not the children,' he said. 'Are you Mrs Bryce?'

'Yes—'

'Mrs Tom Bryce?'

She cast an agonized look towards Andy. 'Oh, it's Tom, then! It must be! What's happened to him?'

The constable, a very young man, looked uncomfortable. He glanced towards Andy for support and the blacksmith put a protective arm round Rose's shoulder.

'Tell her quickly,' he said, 'whatever it is.'

'I'm afraid it's your husband, Mrs Bryce. He's escaped from the asylum. No one quite knows how, except that they had freed him from the straitjacket and somehow he—'

'But he is all right?' insisted Rose. 'He's not hurt or anything?'

'No, he's not hurt.' He hesitated.

'What is it then?' cried Rose fearfully. 'There is something else, isn't there? I know there is. Tell me, for pity's sake. I must know the worst.'

'It's just that – well, ma'am, it seems very probable that he's stolen something. A man was seen running off who fitted his description.'

Rose's face was very pale and when she spoke, her words were barely audible.

'What has he stolen?' she asked.

'I'm sorry, ma'am, but your husband is on the run and he's stolen a loaded shotgun.'

*

Next morning the hop-gardens were still empty of life at half-past eight. Thin sunshine filtered through the dense green foliage, lighting the pale yellow cones which were the hops. The rows of

bins stood empty and the bines remained uncut. Here and there a
bird pecked at yesterday's crumbs, or foraged below the dying
leaves in search of wood lice or the occasional worm. Somewhere
among the green depths a thrush beat a snail upon a stone with
hurried taps, until the shell disintegrated and he could pull out the
soft juicy morsel within. A black cat stalked along the rows, tail
erect, green eyes glinting purposefully, in search of an unwary
bird or mouse.

Two mongrel dogs chased playfully in and out of the hop-poles
until one of them discovered a lost rag doll which lay, bedraggled
and wet from the night's rain, beside one of the bins. One of the
dogs snatched it up and as the other seized hold of a leg, a tug of
war developed. The owner, a little girl from Islington, was not
there to rescue it. With her two brothers, she was waiting outside
the big barn with her mother and the rest of the pickers. The gong
had not sounded for picking to begin and something was obviously very wrong. The hop-pickers knew well enough what this was
and waited uneasily for the inevitable retribution. Meanwhile they
were losing valuable picking time but this, they realized also, was
part of their punishment for the previous night's rebellion.

At last Ned Berry appeared, closely followed by Julian Lawrence. There was a murmur among the pickers as they exchanged
worried looks. To one side of the group, the gipsies also waited,
innocent of any misdemeanour but involved nevertheless in the
general breakdown of routine. Ned Berry stepped on to an
upturned tub and addressed them all briefly.

'You all know,' he said, 'that something happened last night
which never should have occurred. Mr Lawrence is very angry
indeed and has plenty to say on the matter. The gipsies, however,
are not involved and are free to start picking. When I step down
from here I shall go and cut a few bines for them. Whether you
Londoners pick today will be entirely up to you, as you will hear.'

He stepped down and strode off while the crowd muttered
uneasily. Black looks were cast towards the gipsies who began to
move off in the direction Ned Berry had taken. From the middle
of the crowd a voice was raised.

'It's all right for the likes of you, with roofs over your head and
dry beds.'

One or two of the gipsies shrugged and several hesitated, but
then they all moved off. It was not their quarrel and they needed
money as urgently as anyone else.

When Julian took Ned Berry's place on the upturned tub, his expression was thunderous and his hands were clenched by his sides.

'Last night,' he said, 'some among you saw fit to trespass on my lawn and to disturb my household. I understand this was meant as some kind of protest – a childish and pathetic attempt in my opinion, but no doubt you view it differently. You are no doubt aware that many farmers in my position would sack the lot of you. Oh yes, they would,' he repeated as murmurs arose. 'They would pack you off back to London at the drop of a hat, for there are plenty of others willing to take your places. My first instinct was to do just that, but my wife has persuaded me to overlook your behaviour – that is, on this *one* occasion. If anything of the sort happens again, you will *all* be sent home immediately. Is that understood?'

No one answered him. They stared at him with hostile eyes and for a moment he was disconcerted. Then he went on, 'However, someone threw a saucepan lid through one of my windows and terrified one of my guests. Miss Bellweather, whom we all know, was badly shaken by the episode. She came down here out of the kindness of her heart to help you in whatever way she can, and this is how she has been rewarded. Now, my last word on the subject is this. There will be no more picking for any of you until the person who threw that lid comes forward. Probably many of you know who it is, but don't bother to tell me. I want the person concerned – he or she – to come forward voluntarily. The cost of repairing the window will be deducted from their wages. That is all I have to say.'

He stepped down and strode away, leaving the crowd of pickers grumbling openly. Several spat. Others shouted insults from the safety of the crowd, but Julian did not turn back. Mollie stood white-faced as a clamour broke out around her, the pickers divided into those who felt that her identity should be kept a secret and those who did not.

'She only done what any of us would have done—'

'Mollie never meant to do it, anyway. She never meant to break the window.'

'It was an accident.'

'We was all in it together and we should sink or swim together.'

'But we've got mouths to feed. We never meant to do no damage or to break no windows. She never should have thrown it.'

'She got us into this mess, she ought to get us out!'

Alexander stood beside his mother, his small peaky face pale with fright. He looked up into his mother's face, but she had no thought for him and in fact was hardly aware of his presence. Panic-stricken, she wondered what to do – where to go – or who to turn to? All around them the arguments increased. The sun was shining and picking hops would be pleasurable compared with the past days of rain they had suffered. Most of them wanted to get on with the day's work, but a minority wished to continue the battle with the Lawrences on principle.

'If we give in now, we'll get nowhere.'

'We've got to show them we mean business and can't be pushed around.'

'A dry bed is not much to ask, is it?'

One of the women turned to Mollie. 'You go and tell him,' she said. 'Say it was an accident.'

'Suppose we all club together to pay for the window. How'd that be, Mollie?'

She shook her head despairingly. 'I don't know,' she stammered. 'I don't want to tell him; he'll send me back to London.'

'He never will. You'll just have to pay for the window, that's all.'

'But I can't afford it. Maybe he'll send for the police!'

'You should have thought of that last night.'

'Well, I say she goes,' said a large, belligerent woman on Mollie's left. 'I say we make her go so that we can all get on with our work.' Without further ado she seized Mollie's arm and Mollie screamed in panic.

'Let me go!' she shrilled. 'You're hurting my arm!'

As she struggled to extricate herself, Alex hurled himself immediately to her defence, snatching at the woman's arm and biting her wrist fiercely. With a howl of pain and rage, she released Mollie and turned on her attacker.

'Bite me, would you, you little runt!' she shouted. 'I'll teach you to go biting people.' She made a grab at his hair and began to shake him. 'Bloody little animal, that's what you are and your mother's no better.'

Mollie, hearing Alex cry out, began to pummel the woman's broad back. Someone tried to pull her away, but she lashed out with her foot and landed a blow on the unfortunate woman's shin.

'Proper little savages, the pair of 'em!'

'I reckon we're better off without 'em.'

'You wouldn't like it if someone was laying about your kid!'

Tempers grew, voices became shriller and language more abusive. One by one the onlookers took sides in the affray until at last a full-scale fight was under way, and those not actually taking part were giving vociferous encouragement to those who were. Somehow in the general mêlée Mollie Pett slipped away, leaving her son to his fate.

Adam Forrest, the bin man, heard the commotion and hurried to the scene. He shouted as loudly as he could but his voice was drowned by the noise and eventually he muttered, 'Oh, let them damn well get on with it!' and carried on towards the oast-house with a message for Steven Pitt.

'Bedlam, it was,' he told the head dryer. 'People screaming and arms and legs going in all directions. Never seen such a fight.' He shook his head. 'What a month!' he said. 'I had a feeling in my bones there was going to be trouble. Thank God for the gipsies, or there'd be nothing picked at all today. You might as well take a nap, Steven, for they'll not be bringing you any hops to roast yet awhile.'

Steven shook his head despondently. 'What are they like this year – the hops, I mean?' Adam asked him.

'Not good at all, I'm afraid.' He wrinkled his nose in disgust. 'Poor little things,' he went on. 'The flavour's there right enough, but they're so small. Still, it's the same story everywhere, I hear. It's not just us. The weather's been against us and that's all there is to it.'

'Has Mr le Brun been over?'

'Expecting him any day,' Steven told him. 'In fact, if he comes soon he can take a sample from that lot.' He jerked his head towards the rows of well-stuffed hop pockets that leaned against the far end of the barn, awaiting collection. Each long sack contained a hundred and twelve pounds of hops which had been dried the previous day. A sample taken from one of the sacks would be carefully examined, and a price would then be negotiated with the brewer's merchant. This price varied slightly from week to week, sometimes even from day to day, depending on the condition of each day's pickings.

Adam Forrest nodded towards the bulging hop pockets. 'How long did you have to give them?' he asked.

'Best part of twelve hours,' said Steven, shaking his head.

'They were very wet. I couldn't even turn them for nine hours, and then they needed another three to dry out properly.'

Adam Forrest whistled. 'Twelve hours! I've known you to finish in nine.'

The dryer shrugged his shoulders. 'There's just no way to hurry hops,' he said. 'I know some who will raise the temperature to hurry them up, but it doesn't do. It doesn't do at all. Slow, steady heat, that's what hops need and while I'm head dryer that's what they'll get – even if it does take twelve hours.'

They chatted a while longer, until Adam Forrest decided he ought to go and see if the fighting had run its course. Steven Pitt watched him walk off, tutting quietly to himself and wondering what the world was coming to. Then he went through the arched passage-way to inspect the fires through the small openings in the whitewashed walls. The fires were never allowed out, except possibly for a few hours on a Sunday, since once the correct temperature had been reached it was easier to maintain it for the entire month. The charcoal glowed yellow-white and the familiar smell of brimstone tickled his nostrils. If the trouble with the hoppers was resolved shortly, the hop gardens would soon be in full production again and within a very few hours the hops would start to arrive and he would be busy once more. Now was a good time to take a nap, he decided. Round the corner from the furnace an old alley bodge – a deep-sided wagon – had been turned into a makeshift bed and without bothering to unlace his boots, Steven climbed into it, pulled a few sacks over himself and settled down to sleep.

When he awoke, he pulled out his watch and studied it in disbelief. 'Nearly four o'clock!' he muttered, struggling into a sitting position. 'John,' he shouted, 'are you there?'

John Burrows, who had been his assistant for several years, peered round a corner of the door as Steven was struggling out of the alley bodge.

'I reckoned to let you sleep on,' said John. 'Courage's came out and picked up their hops an hour since. They were all for waking you, but I said to let you be.'

Steven stretched his cramped limbs and rubbed his face, returning only slowly to full wakefulness. 'Are they picking again now?' he asked.

John Burrows shook his head. 'It's a right old do,' he said. 'Only the gipsies are picking and they're not likely to pick tomorrow if the Londoners don't get back to work. It's caused a lot of bad feeling and you can't really wonder at it.'

'Damnation!' said Steven. 'A whole day's work lost! I'd best get up there and see the master himself. He'll maybe want the fires let out if this is likely to go on.'

John shrugged. 'Me, I'm keeping well out of it,' he said. 'Mr Lawrence is in a fine old temper and I've no wish to exchange words with him while he's in that mood.'

'Well, someone's got to exchange words with him,' said Steven irritably. 'I suppose it will have to be me.' He ran his fingers through his hair to tidy himself up and hitched the belt of his sagging trousers on to the next hole.

'Right,' he said, 'I'm on my way. You hold the fort here, John. If the hops start to come in from the gipsies, you begin spreading them. I'll be back before too long, but you can be making a start.'

He took a short cut to the hop-fields and discovered Julian Lawrence in earnest consultation with Roland Fry. Seeing them there, he hesitated, but Julian called to him and he made his way forward, taking off his cap and waiting respectfully while the two men continued to argue. Roland was putting the pickers' case, supporting them in their grievance though not approving the demonstration which had taken place during the night. According to him the standard of the hoppers' accommodation was well below the recommendation made in 1866 by the Society for the Employment and Improved Lodgings of Hop Pickers. He had facts and figures at his fingertips, most of which were new to Steven Pitt but apparently not to Julian Lawrence.

'The Society can go to hell!' Julian exclaimed angrily. 'I've read their report and I know their recommendations off by heart. Every grower does. Talk to any of them and they'll all tell the same story. *Give them proper ventilation – a window eighteen by fourteen.* I'll tell you what happens then. They stuff old rags into them so that no air gets in. *Fit the doors with bolts and locks* – no one will ever use them. In fact by the end of September, someone will have stolen them! At the end of last September most of my lanterns disappeared with the hop pickers when they went back to London. *Supply them with shelves and cupboards?* They'll break them up for firewood and cook a meal over it. We dressed the small barn with tar and cod oil last year to make it weatherproof, and what happened? They complained about the smell! I could follow those recommendations to the letter and I still wouldn't get a thank-you for it. So don't come preaching to me, Mr Fry, for your hoppers are far from angels and the sooner you realize that the better. You may encourage them in their foolishness, but I don't have to put up with it. Oh, don't look at me as though I am some kind of ogre. Ask any of the other farmers. Look at Merryon, for example. Poor old Meddows went to the cost of hiring two large tents, one for the single men and one for the single women. By the end of the first week there were men and women in both of them – so don't talk to me about the morals of the pickers, because I don't think they have any.' He glanced at Steven. 'What is it?' he snapped.

'It's the fires, Mr Lawrence. I'm wondering if I should let them out.'

'Let them out? Why, in God's name?'

'Well, am I drying hops or aren't I? We're wasting fuel at the moment and I just thought—'

'Well, don't! Leave me to do the thinking, Mr Pitt. If I want the fires out, you will be the first to know.'

Steven Pitt felt his face colour with the undeserved rebuff. He glanced at Roland Fry, who shrugged helplessly.

'Thank you, sir,' Steven muttered. He replaced his cap and turned away and for a while both men watched his retreating figure without comment.

At that moment an elderly woman appeared from the direction of the barn. She moved nervously towards them, glancing occasionally over her shoulder as though afraid of being followed or seen. When she reached them she looked appealingly at Roland Fry.

'What is it, Annie?' he asked kindly.

'I've something to say that's private for Mr Lawrence's ears,' she said.

Julian glared at her. 'If you've anything to say, you can say it in front of Mr Fry,' he said sharply.

She hesitated, twisting her fingers together and glancing once more behind her.

'Well, get on with it,' said Julian. 'We haven't time to stand here listening to tittle-tattle.'

'It's not tittle-tattle, sir,' she said, stung into a reply, 'it's the truth. About last night – some of them don't want to tell, but I say we should. We have all got families to look after and we all need the money.'

She glanced at Roland who nodded encouragingly, and she took a deep breath.

'It's about the window. It was Mollie Pett what done it, but now she's scarpered. She was scared to come and tell you, so she hopped it and good riddance to her, I say!'

Julian met Roland's eye. 'Loyal, aren't they?' Julian said sarcastically.

'They're ignorant,' said Roland. 'The innocent, ignorant victims of their own environment. You should not condemn them for that. Born into their circumstances, no doubt you and I would be exactly the same.'

The woman looked at Julian anxiously. 'So can we get back to work now, sir?'

Julian raised his eyes. 'Mollie Pett has not come forward,' he reminded her. 'That was one of the conditions on which picking would re-start.'

'But how can she come forward?' Roland intervened. 'She's obviously very frightened and has run away. Supposing she doesn't return at all? Will picking never begin?'

'I'll horsewhip her if I ever find her,' said Julian. 'She's nothing but a damned trouble-maker. So,' he turned to the woman, 'you're all eager to go back to work now, are you?'

'Not all of us,' she admitted. 'Some say they won't work unless they get dry beds.'

Julian raised his eyebrows again and looked at Roland. 'It would seem there's no honour among thieves,' he commented.

'I resent that,' said Roland hotly, but Julian's eyes hardened.

'Don't become too resentful,' he suggested. 'Remember that you and your followers are on my land at my invitation and at my discretion. If I should feel that your influence here is not altogether helpful, I might be forced to ask you to leave.'

He turned to Annie again. 'You get back to your friends,' he said. 'I shall think over what you have said and you will hear from me in due course. Now, get out of my sight before I lose my temper and do or say something I shall regret.'

She needed no second bidding, but hurried away looking more ill-at-ease than when she had arrived. Roland Fry began to speak, but bit back the angry words.

'Do we understand each other?' asked Julian.

'I think we do,' said Roland, his voice flat.

'Good!'

Julian turned on his heels and strode away, his head firmly erect, the sun glinting on his blond hair. With a heavy heart, Roland Fry watched him go, then he turned and made his way back to the Mission tent. He was disappointed; he had done his best, but his defence of the pickers had served only to increase Julian's anger. It looked as though their stay at Foxearth might be a great deal shorter than they had anticipated.

*

At seven o'clock that evening Julian addressed a subdued but still disgruntled group of pickers. He told them he had learned that Mollie Pett was responsible for the previous night's outrage and he was aware that she had now disappeared. The local police had been informed and would be on the lookout for her. If she was found, proceedings would be taken against her for the full cost of repairing the damaged window. The weather forecast was good and picking would resume in the morning at the usual time for all those who wished to work. Any who did not would be paid off for the work they had already done and should prepare to return to London on the five o'clock train. Their names would then be removed from the list and they would not be offered employment at Foxearth again. As a concession to the bad weather, fresh dry straw would be made available to all for bedding and hop-pokes also provided; stuffed with straw, these would make reasonable mattresses. Extra faggots would be provided for the fires so that damp clothing could be dried out. Any further complaints about any aspect of the hopping season must be made directly to him by the individuals concerned.

'Does anyone have a question to ask me?' Julian concluded.

There was no answer.

'Then one more thing. You probably know that a man is on the run from the asylum. We now know that he is armed. If anyone sees a man behaving suspiciously in the area, the police must be told. Now I will bid you goodnight.'

*

The scene in the large barn later that evening was chaotic. The barn itself was divided into family areas, each divided from the next by a screen six foot by four foot – some partitions made of wattle, others of plaited laths. To give themselves a little more privacy, many people hung towels or sacking above this partition, so that the hurricane lamps produced shadows instead of giving light. The Londoners had made pathetic efforts to make each small area homely – a picture of a loved one would be nailed to the wooden wall or a few wild flowers thrust into a jam jar and wedged into a convenient niche. Garlands of hops were draped over the wooden beams and some of the pickers had painted their names on the wall in a decorative border.

The floor of each area had previously been covered with six inches of straw litter, but this had now been scraped out with large rakes or anything else which could be utilized for the purpose and the damp and often stinking straw had been carried outside and dumped into an old cart provided for that purpose. The promised pile of green hop-pokes was eagerly seized upon and the pokes carried to a large cart where Adam Forrest and John Burrows (both borrowed from the oast-house for the occasion) filled each poke with dry straw while exchanging a few cheery words with each picker. It was important, they knew, to re-establish friendly relations. A large number of hostile pickers could prove a very real threat to the safety and security of the farm and no one in his right mind pretended otherwise. The promised faggots were also much in evidence and large bonfires blazed in and around the court-yard, the smell of drying clothes mingling with the various cooking aromas. Here a pan of bloaters sizzled, there a dumpling stew bubbled invitingly. No fire was left unattended, for those with little to eat were likely to steal from their more fortunate fellows.

Alexander Pett went about the task of clearing his straw with a stern expression which convincingly disguised his true feelings. His mother had disappeared and he was well aware that she was not the most popular person in the camp. He felt himself abandoned and longed for her return, yet common sense told him that matters might well be much worse if and when she did come back. The police were looking for her – he had heard Mr Lawrence tell the pickers. They said she had broken the window and he saw no reason to doubt it. His mother had an excitable nature, her behaviour was frequently unpredictable and her wild ways had landed them in trouble many times before.

Now he took a hop-poke from the rapidly dwindling pile and stood by the cart. Adam Forrest smiled at him.

'Come for a clean bed, have you lad?' he asked.

Alexander scowled, not entirely trusting this friendly overture.

'Don't worry, lad,' said Adam kindly. 'Your Ma will be back before long. Try not to worry your head about it.'

The boy and his mother had shared a bin with four other pickers and Adam wrongly assumed that the whole party had travelled from London together, and that Alexander was now being cared for by one or all of them. In fact he was being cared for by no one. There was no supper waiting for him and he despaired silently. He watched Adam working quickly, stuffing the straw into the empty sack with swift regular movements of his brawny arms.

'There you are, then, tie up the corners and you're well away. Don't I get a thank-you?

But Alexander hoisted his new bed on to his skinny shoulders and staggered away with it without a word. Mary Bellweather found him half an hour later, sitting in splendid isolation in a small corner of the barn allotted to himself and his mother.

'All alone?' Mary asked briskly.

Alexander stared at her as she looked round. He was determined to be uncommunicative, for he had a built-in distrust of 'them' and was not at all sure that Mary was the sort of person in whom one should confide.

Mary hesitated. 'Alex, who is giving you your supper? Amos Hearn?'

He shook his head. 'They've all gone too,' he said.

Mary was startled. 'You mean your mother has gone with the Hearns?'

'I don't know,' said Alexander, 'but I'm not hungry. My Ma will make something when she gets back.' He looked at her defiantly, daring her to suggest that Mollie might not return.

'Of course she will,' said Mary hurriedly. 'But she may be back rather late. In fact she may not come until tomorrow. Meanwhile, you must have some supper.'

'I don't want nothing,' he insisted. 'I'll wait till me Ma gets back.'

Mary sighed. 'You work hard all day and you must eat in the evening. I shall ask Mr Fry if you can eat with us in the Mission tent. How would that do?'

He hesitated, torn between insisting on his independence and satisfying his growing hunger. Before he could make up his mind, she said quickly, 'That's settled, then! Come to the Mission tent in half an hour and we'll give you something to eat. Don't be afraid, I shall go and talk to Mr Fry now.'

And without giving him an opportunity to refuse her offer, Mary turned away and retraced her footsteps. Roland agreed that until Alexander's mother returned he should eat with the Mission. He was of the firm opinion that – left unsupervised – the boy would get into mischief, and Mary was forced to agree with him, for it seemed unlikely that he would do anything else. They also decided that the boy should sleep in the Mission tent until such time as his mother returned.

Roland suggested that the Lawrences should be notified of their decisions and Mary offered to go to tell Julian. She therefore made her way up to the house to discuss the matter, but Julian was not to be found and Vinnie, Janet told her, had gone to the church. Undaunted, Mary set off on foot to find her.

*

Vinnie knelt in the second pew, the one reserved from time immemorial for the Lawrence family. Her knees rested on a hassock made of rough tweed and her elbows on the back of the front pew, while her hands covered her face. There was no one else in the church, although freshly arranged flowers in the various vases showed that someone had been busy much earlier. The brass on the lectern in front of her shone dully in the weak September sunshine coming through a side window, slanting its beams through the dusty air of the little church. The wooden pews had recently received their monthly polish, filling the church with the familiar smell of beeswax and lavender. The narrow red carpet ascending the altar steps had been carefully brushed until it was spotless, and even the organ had been lovingly dusted although Vinnie could not see this from where she knelt. It was very quiet in the church and the air was still, but Vinnie's thoughts were anguished. She pressed her face into her hands with an almost painful intensity, as though the uncomfortable pressure might add weight to her prayer. Finally, she raised her head and stared up at the large crucifix above the altar.

'Dearest Jesus,' she whispered. 'Please speak to God on my behalf. Ask him to pay special heed to what I say, for it is very important – more important, at least to me, than anything else in the world. It's about Tom Bryce. You'll know him of course, as well as I do – probably better. He has run away from that place and I am fearful for him. They say he's taken a shotgun, but I don't know why; nobody does. I can't think of anyone he might want to shoot, unless it's the farmer who had him put away there. But it's not like Tom to want to shoot anybody, so I think maybe he's taken it to defend himself. I'm sure he wouldn't mean to hurt anyone, but he just might and then he will be in even greater trouble. They could send him to prison or even hang him, that's why I ask you to look after him.'

Vinnie took a deep breath and once more hid her face in her hands. Then she looked up at the crucifix again.

'If he does hurt somebody, then it ought to be me because it's my fault all this trouble has come about. But for me, he would be safely at home with Rose and the children and everything would be different. Oh, dear Jesus, I have done all I can to try to make amends, but somehow everything I do turns out wrong and makes things worse. I think it might be best if he could give himself up and go back to the asylum until he's quite better.'

Two large tears rolled down her cheeks. 'You see, even this is my fault, because I asked them to let him out of that dreadful jacket and that made it possible for him to escape. I didn't mean it to happen.'

Hearing a sound behind her, she turned to see Mary Bell-weather tiptoeing down the aisle. Vinnie jumped to her feet, greatly confused and for a moment the two women regarded each other without speaking.

'What do you want?' stammered Vinnie. 'It's a private place. You shouldn't spy on people—'

Startled, Mary took a small step backwards. 'Forgive me,' she said. 'I didn't mean to intrude. They told me you were here, and I have something to tell you, but if it's not convenient I can talk to you at some other time.'

Vinnie shook her head. 'Tell me now,' she said, 'and then leave me alone.'

Mary explained about Alexander and Vinnie nodded from time to time. 'Do whatever you think best,' she said. 'I expect his mother will show up tomorrow. She can't go far – apparently she has very little money.'

'Oh, but she hasn't gone alone,' said Mary. 'It seems the whole Hearn family have gone with her.'

'You mean the gipsies?'

'Yes. She and Amos Hearn have been seen around together.'

'Well, it's comforting to know she isn't alone and destitute.'

'Of course it is.'

Vinnie sighed again. She looked the picture of misery. 'It's all been very unfortunate,' she said, 'and so difficult for me. My heart is with the pickers, of course, but Julian is my husband and it is my duty to support him. I thought the best thing I could do would be to keep well out of this matter. Sometimes when I try to help I only make things worse. I argued with Julian about the barn and it merely made him more determined than ever not to mend the roof. If I had said nothing . . .' she shrugged helplessly.

'Don't blame yourself,' said Mary. 'I am quite sure you meant well and that's what matters.'

'Is it?' said Vinnie doubtfully. 'Is it enough to mean well? I don't feel sure about that any more. In fact I don't feel sure about anything any more.' There was a long silence.

'Well,' said Mary, 'the worst is over now. Tomorrow morning they will all be back at work and it will be as though nothing had happened.'

'Oh, the pickers?' said Vinnie. 'Yes, I hope everything is going to be all right. I have so much on my mind at the moment that my head spins with the worry of it all.'

'I heard about Tom Bryce,' said Mary gently. 'I'm very sorry, Vinnie.'

Vinnie shook her head. 'I have been praying for him,' she said. 'I hope someone is listening.'

Mary was shocked. 'Of course someone listens to your prayers,' she said. 'There is great strength in the power of prayer. A greater strength than many people dream of.'

'Is there?' said Vinnie. 'It never seems that way to me. I pray and pray, but nothing ever happens. I prayed so hard that Bertie would come back—' She swallowed hard and could not go on.

'I'm sure he will,' said Mary.

'I don't think so,' said Vinnie. 'And I prayed for my sister, Em, and yet she died. I don't see that praying is much good at all.'

'God cannot grant all our prayers,' said Mary quietly.

'But why not?' Vinnie burst out passionately. 'Why can't He? If He's all powerful, He can do anything. And if He has to pick and choose which prayers He answers, why does He never answer mine? Why did He let Em die?'

'Perhaps it was the kindest way for her,' said Mary.

'What's kind about dying?' Vinnie persisted. 'Would it be the kindest way for you to die? If God lets me die, I shan't think that's very kind.'

'You don't really understand,' began Mary.

'Oh, but I *do*,' replied Vinnie. 'I ask Him for His help and He never gives it. That's simple to understand.' She sank down on to the pew suddenly and put a trembling hand to her mouth.

'Perhaps I should go,' said Mary.

Vinnie made no answer and she began to walk away, but suddenly Vinnie called after her.

'You will pray for him, won't you? All of you? You will pray for Tom Bryce?'

'Of course we will,' Mary promised.

Vinnie gave a slight nod. She watched Mary until she had left the church, then turned round to face the altar once more. Feeling for the hassock, she knelt on it and closed her eyes.

'I have said all there is to say,' she whispered. 'Please help Tom before it's too late. Let Mary be right about the strength of prayer.'

She searched her mind for anything else which might add weight to her plea, but nothing presented itself to her weary mind. Slowly she stood up, then she followed Mary out of the church into the sunshine.

*

It was still dark at five o'clock in the morning when Tim Bilton made his way across the cobbles and into the stables. The bread and cheese, left for him as usual on the kitchen table at Foxearth, would last him until six-thirty when he could return for a proper breakfast. In his right hand he carried a lantern and after letting himself into the stables, he hung this on a hook on the wall. Always the first riser on the farm, he considered himself very superior to the rest of the staff and enjoyed his solitary hour alone with the horses before anyone else was about. Tim loved his animals as a mother loves her children: Lancer, the Colonel's old hunter, rarely ridden today; Brownie, a black miniature pony that Eva had ridden as a child; Duff and Dorrie, the two Clydesdales used for the heavy work around the farm; and last but not least, Arrowmint, the new brood mare which was Tim's pride and joy.

After many years he had persuaded his master that breeding their own foals was the only way to guarantee good horse stock. The mare had been purchased a month ago, giving her time to settle down in her new home. Today the travelling stud horse was due. Booked several months ago, the stallion would be presented by his groom at the appointed time. He would be immaculately turned out and Tim Bilton was determined that Arrowmint would outshine him. If the foal was perfect, it might be shown at the next horse fair and sold to the highest bidder. Or it might remain on the farm to replace Duff or Dorrie at some later date.

Whistling cheerfully, Tim prepared the horses' *bait* – a meal of oats, chaff, ground-up roots and stover. Having measured and mixed the ingredients, he tipped them into a baiting-sieve, then shook this gently so that all the dust fell through the fine cane bottom. If he did not do this, the horses breathed in the dust, which irritated them and disturbed their feeding. The chaff was chopped hay, the stover chopped straw. The root content was a mixture of mangel-wurzel and carrots which had been dried and ground up and stored in a large bin. Many horse men in the area added beans to this mixture, but Tim Bilton would not hear of it.

Quietly he went from stall to stall giving each horse its allotted portion, ending with Arrowmint. Here he paused to take a small leather bag from the pocket of his breeches, from which he took a large pinch of powder and sprinkled it into the mixture.

'What are you doing?' Tim turned and saw a small boy watching him from the doorway.

'What's that stuff?' Tim grinned. 'It's tansy,' he said.

The boy looked puzzled. 'What's tansy?' he asked.

'Dried tansy leaves. You pick the leaves, dry them until they are all brown, then you rub them up small and store them in here.' He held up the small leather bag. 'It will make her coat shine. Sometimes I give them sweet saffron leaves, but that's funny stuff. Too much of that and it could bring out a sweat. What are you doing here, anyway, at this hour?'

'I don't like it here now,' said Alexander. 'No one will let me pick with them, 'cos me Ma lost them a day's money.'

Tim narrowed his eyes. 'You Mollie Pett's boy?'

Alex nodded.

'Hmm. Well, you can watch me for a bit, but then you will have to get back where you belong. They'll have a search party out for you, else.'

Alex shrugged. Everywhere he went he felt unwanted and he was becoming philosophical about his rejection. He sidled a little nearer to the chestnut mare as Tim Bilton took down curry comb and dandy brush and began to groom her.

'Like horses, do you?' asked Tim.

The boy shrugged.

'Perhaps you don't know much about them?' Tim suggested. 'They're beautiful beasts, make no mistake about that – the finest creatures that ever worked for man. They've all got names, you know, just like us. This one's Arrowmint and today I'm prettying her up. Today is special.' He glanced at the boy's impassive face. 'Don't you want to know why?'

Alex nodded.

'Well, she's got a gentleman caller coming today.' He grinned. 'She wants a husband, you see, and we haven't got one for her here so we are borrowing one. A stud horse, that's what he's called; his master will bring him along by and by. Major, his name is and he's every bit of eighteen hands.'

He put down brush and comb and with his outstretched hands, one above the other, measured Arrowmint so that Alex would understand what he was saying.

'See that? She's only fourteen hands, going on fifteen. Now you've learnt something, haven't you?'

The horse, well aware that she was the subject of their discussion, fidgeted slightly and turned her head enquiringly towards the boy.

'She knows you're here, you see,' said Tim, 'and she knows you're a stranger. See the way she flicks her ears? They're clever animals, horses. They're intelligent – not like sheep and cows.'

'Or pigs?' said the boy.

'Or pigs,' Tim agreed.

'Or chickens?' Alex persisted.

'Or chickens! They've got a bit of a brain, but they're nowhere near as intelligent as a good horse.'

Tim's arms moved smoothly over the horse's body with firm, downward strokes. 'They are all different, though,' he went on. 'Like we are. Some are lazy, some scare easily, others are as cunning as the devil. There are greedy horses, and spiteful horses and horses that like a bit of fun – and if a horse doesn't like you, watch out! They'll tread on your toes, butt you with their head and kick you as soon as look at you. So never take liberties with a horse. D'you hear me?'

Alex nodded.

'So if you come down next year,' said Tim, 'as like as not we shall have a foal for you to see. Would you like that?'

'Maybe.'

'Only maybe?' Tim raised his eyebrows. He worked steadily, chatting to the boy in a friendly way, trying to encourage him to talk more freely, for Alex communicated mainly with nods and shakes of the head or an indifferent shrug of the shoulders. As the sun rose it grew lighter and Tim put out the lamp.

'Your Ma will be back, never you fret!' said Tim suddenly. 'And perhaps your Pa will come down at the weekend.'

'He *won't*.'

'No?'

'He's gone to another country. He's a soldier, my Pa.'

Tim whistled. 'A soldier, eh? Well, that's a grand thing to be! Perhaps you'll be a soldier like your Pa. Is that the idea, then?'

'Don't know.'

'Where's he gone to then, your Pa?'

'He's gone to India. It's a long way away, hundreds of miles. Ma told me.'

'Did she? Then it must be right. India, eh? It's hot in India, you know.'

'I know,' said Alex. 'One day Pa will come home. I've never seen him.'

Tim grinned. 'Ah, like that, is it? Well, never you mind! He'll be back one day and he'll find a great big son all grown up and ready to be a soldier like him.'

Alex smiled at this appealing prospect, then asked suddenly, 'Have you seen the mad man?'

'What mad man?'

'They're all saying there's a mad man around with a gun.'

'Oh, *that* mad man! He won't come here, don't you worry.'

'But is he mad? Has he got a gun?'

'So they say,' said Tim, 'but the police will soon catch him. You worrying about that, are you?'

Alex shrugged. 'He might meet my Ma,' he confided.

'Ah, so that's what you're bothered about. Well, just put those thoughts out of your head, young-'un, 'cos your Ma's run off in *that* direction,' he jerked his thumb, 'and the mad man has gone off in the other direction. So there's no way they can meet each other, is there?'

Alex considered this for a moment. 'Who said?' he asked suspiciously.

'Who said? Well, I said it. Everybody says it. Cross me heart and hope to die, it's the truth.'

The scowl finally gave way to a smile which lit up the small peaky face, making Alex almost attractive.

At that moment, from the far end of the stable yard, there came a steady clip-clop. Arrowmint's 'gentleman-caller' had arrived and together they went out to greet him. He was a massive animal, towering above his groom who was a small middle-aged man with bow-legs and a badly pocked face. Major was magnificent. He weighed more than a ton and was jet-black except for his forelegs which were feathered in white. He was a Shire, inheriting his colour from the English Black Horse and his huge feet and massive shoulders from his Flemish ancestors. The groom displayed him proudly, as well he might, for the stallion was immaculate. His leather halter had been polished until it shone. Apart from that he wore nothing except a back band on which were two leather pouches containing his curry comb and dandy brush. His mane had been plaited and his tail arranged in an intricate knot; his hooves shone with oil above the heavy metal shoes; his coat gleamed and when he moved his muscles rippled like undulating satin.

Tim and Alex walked all round him, expressing their admiration and making the requisite sounds of delight and satisfaction.

'A very fine animal!' Tim told the groom. 'He does you great credit.' The little man nodded.

'I'll fetch Mr Lawrence to have a word with you,' Tim added. Then he turned to Alex.

'You've seen all there is to see now, lad,' he said, 'and you'd best get back to the hop-gardens before you're missed. If you're a good boy, I might let you come back later this evening before you have your supper. Might even let you have a ride on one of the other horses. Like that, would you?'

Alex shrugged, then thought better of it and said, 'I reckon so.'

'Then off you go!'

The two men watched the small boy walk away and Tim, noting the dejected set of his shoulders, shouted after him, 'And don't worry about that mad man. He'll be miles away from here by now – you remember that!'

If Alex heard, he gave no sign and with a little sigh, Tim turned back. It was an important date in his calendar and he was eager for the day's business to begin.

CHAPTER TWELVE

Adam Turner came out of the 'Harrow', pushed his cap back on his head and squinted up into the sunshine. It was warm to his face, for the weather had taken a dramatic turn for the better and for the past two days the temperature had reached eighty degrees. While he stared up into the bright blue sky he became aware of a certain uneasiness in the region of his stomach, attributable no doubt to the recent consumption of two large veal pasties and three pints of Kenward and Court's light dinner ale, a Tonbridge brew of some potency. His companion, a wizened elderly waggoner, followed him out, wiping the froth from his lips, and stood beside him in the sunshine.

'Nice drop of stuff, that Kenwards,' said Adam. 'You can't beat a local brew, that's what I always say.'

'You can't, no,' the old man agreed. 'My son works for them. He's got a nice job there – he's a cooper. They do a good stout, too.' He unhitched the reins and climbed nimbly into the seat of the waggon, while Adam walked round the back and climbed in the other side.

'Simmons do a nice stout, too,' the old man told him, 'but I reckon Kenwards have the edge on them. My old woman loves a drop of stout.' He flicked the reins across the horse's back and they moved smoothly forward, the waggon groaning under its load of twelve sacks of oats on the way to the mill. Adam closed his eyes as the old man rambled on and the small village of Hadlow was left behind, drowsing in the late September sun. They made slow progress, as the horse was well past its prime and though it leaned well forward into the collar, its hooves slipped now and then on the rough road; it seemed that only the encouraging noises of the driver persuaded it to keep going. They came through Wateringbury and continued along the Tonbridge Road towards Barming and Maidstone.

'It's Teesbury, you want, is it?' he asked Adam.

'Aye, Teesbury.'

'And who is it you're looking for?'

'Vinnie Harris.'

The old man shook his head. 'Never heard of him,' he said.

Adam grinned. He was a pleasant looking man of twenty-six with an untidy thatch of mid-brown hair. His features were large in a square face and his broad shoulders disguised his height. His eyes were light brown and his short curly beard almost ginger in colour; his smile was expansive and his manner lazy and relaxed. Adam Turner took life very much as it came, accepting the good with the bad and affording each the fleeting importance they deserved. As each day passed, he let it slip from his mind and waited cheerfully to see what the next would bring. He made friends quickly and lost them with the same speed, for he was not a man to form deep and lasting relationships. Life, he considered, was too short for that and his philosophy had served him well for twenty-six years, so he saw no reason to change it.

'Whoa up!' called the old man and the waggon creaked to a halt. He stabbed a bony finger towards the dense green hop-gardens on his right.

'That's your best bet,' he told Adam. 'You see the valley down there? Well, you can't rightly make it out now because of the hops, but down there is the river and up the other side is Teesbury. Over that gate, then keep to the right-hand side of the field. Make your way down the valley and past that cottage there – they might be able to help you. It's a mile or two at the most.'

'My thanks to you,' said Adam as he jumped lightly down on to the road.

'You're welcome,' said the old man, 'and thanks for the bite of dinner. It went down a treat!'

Adam wished he could say the same for his own meal, but the uncomfortable feeling in his stomach persisted. He stood at the side of the road and watched horse, man and waggon until they had turned a bend out of sight, then he crossed the road and vaulted over the gate. For a moment he leaned back against it, resting his elbows on the top bar and surveying the scene around him. In whichever direction he looked, hops grew in long green rows, patterning the countryside with their diagonal lines. Since coming to Kent, he had seen very little else, he marvelled, and he had worked his way across country from Southampton thumbing

a ride whenever he could. Now he had nearly reached his
destination and hopefully would soon meet Bert's sister, about
whom he had heard so much. He pushed himself away from the
gate and began to walk down the side of the field which sloped
steeply towards the river. Somewhere above him a lark sang and
he raised an imaginary gun, searched the sky for it, took aim and
pulled an imaginary trigger.

'Got you, you little perisher!' he muttered, grinning to himself.

On the far side of the hop-garden through which he walked, he
could hear voices and occasionally caught glimpses of the pickers
at work there, but he kept his eyes open, not wishing to bump into
anyone in authority and unsure whether or not he could trust
them. As he walked with the hedge on his right-hand side, the
hops beside him towered over him, the rich green foliage stirring
gently with the very light breeze that blew from the south east.

'Hops, God bless 'em,' he muttered. 'Nothing but ruddy hops!
I wager that's where I shall find young Vinnie. She'll be picking
the dratted things, no doubt.'

Adam wondered if he might do a little picking himself. His
Army pay was almost spent and he had another fourteen days of
leave left. A little extra money would not come amiss. Suddenly,
ahead of him, he heard voices and peered through the dense
greenery, but without success. His military training had taught
him that discretion was often the better part of valour and quickly
he pushed a way through the hedge and continued on the other
side. To his right he saw a small copse of trees and made towards
them; the midday sun on the back of his neck was doing his
stomach no good and an hour's nap in the shade had much to
recommend it. He jumped the small ditch at the bottom of the
field and clambered through the straggly bramble hedge which
circled the trees. He had now lost sight of the cottage which the
old waggoner had pointed out to him, but he knew he was moving
generally in the right direction. He was in no hurry to find Vinnie
Harris, he reminded himself. He had come so far that another
hour or two would make very little difference.

As he cast around him for a suitable tree against which to prop
his weary body, he nearly stepped on the prostrate figure of a man
who was half-hidden in the undergrowth. He sprang back in
alarm, for held firmly in the man's arms was a shotgun. Adam
cursed inwardly. Just his luck to stumble across a poacher! Or was
it the gamekeeper? He prayed that the man would sleep on but

luck temporarily deserted him for the man on the ground opened his eyes, the animal instinct in him warning of danger. In one swift movement he was on his knees, shotgun in hand, two barrels pointed at Adam's heart. Adam swallowed and reflected somewhat bitterly that never in his years as a soldier had he faced an enemy unarmed.

The two men stared at each other, separated by no more than three yards. Afraid to move a hand in case his action was misinterpreted, Adam smiled nervously.

'I'm sorry if I woke you,' he said, his tone unconcerned. 'I was looking for a place to nap, but it looks as though you beat me to it.'

The man's appearance was not reassuring. His clothes were unkempt, his hair tousled and the hand that held the shotgun trembled visibly. The face was haggard, dark stubble covered the jaw and the dark eyes shone with an emotion which might have been fear but could have been anger. Adam hoped he would not discover which of the two it was. He smiled again, but the other man still said nothing and made no movement; he remained frozen, his shotgun at the ready. Only his rapid breathing revealed his agitation.

Slowly, Adam began to raise his hands, gradually bringing them up until they were level with his shoulders in a gesture of surrender.

'I'm looking for a friend,' he told him. 'I don't want any trouble.'

'That makes two of us,' the man growled.

While Adam continued to smile and show as little concern as possible, his mind was racing as he examined the possibility of escape if this man proved to be as dangerous as he looked. All he could hope for was to reach the safety of the tree and hide behind it, but the man would doubtless come after him, dodging from tree to tree. Even with his military training, this offered very little chance of escape. And those trembling hands! Adam prayed that the finger curling unsteadily round the trigger would not tighten involuntarily. A blast from one barrel would blow him in half at such a short range, as Adam well knew. No, he was not a gamekeeper, Adam decided; the furtive manner was proof of that.

His mind worked quickly. 'I'm not poaching,' he said. 'Honest to God! You can search me if you like.'

By pretending that he thought the man was a gamekeeper, Adam was giving him something to hide behind. But the wretch seemed too stupid to take the opportunity being offered to him, and Adam felt his hair prickling with fear as he took an unsteady step towards him.

'You haven't seen me,' he said thickly. 'I'm not here, you understand? If you *have* seen me, then it's all over – for you as well as for me. Because if you tell anyone you've seen me, I'll come looking for you. And as God is my witness, I'll find you before they find me. My God, I will! Do you hear me?'

'I hear you,' said Adam, 'and I give you my word.' He crossed himself. 'I never set eyes on the man in the wood,' he repeated.

'If I thought—' the man began.

'I tell you, I give you my word,' cried Adam. 'What is it to me, anyway? I don't even belong here. Just passing through and looking for a friend on the way. I won't tell a soul that I've seen you. I swear it, on my mother's life.'

'I don't know . . .' the man hesitated.

Adam was growing increasingly alarmed. Even if this man allowed him to back away, what guarantee was there that once he turned his back he would not be shot? The armed fugitive had a lot to lose – that was obvious. Would he allow Adam to walk away unscathed and risk a betrayal? It seemed unlikely, so he decided on a change of tactic.

'Look,' he said, 'I could help you. Bring you a bit of food and something to drink? You look done in.'

The man's eyes narrowed. 'You must think me a fool,' he growled. 'You'd bring someone with you, wouldn't you?'

'I wouldn't, I swear it.'

To Adam's horror, the man leaned forward slightly and raised the gun, sighting along the barrel. A faint sweat broke out on his forehead and his throat was suddenly dry. He tried to speak but fear closed his throat; he could only stand and wait, shaking his head helplessly. Fleetingly he wondered if he dared jump the man. In an equal fight he reckoned he could beat him, but this was no equal fight for even in the hands of the weakest opponent, a shotgun weighted the scales heavily.

Adam closed his eyes and waited. At least it would be merciful-ly quick, he told himself. He thought fleetingly of Vinnie Harris, unsuspecting, destined never to receive her brother's message.

'Get out of here!' He opened his eyes in disbelief. The man had lowered the shotgun and although he still held his finger over the trigger, the barrel now pointed towards the ground.

'Get out!' he said again, with a jerk of his head. 'And remember, one word about me and by Christ, you're a dead man!'

Adam wanted to say 'thank you', but the words seemed ridiculously inadequate. What did one man say to another who had spared his life? Instead he began to back away, keeping his eyes firmly on the other man's face. After going a short distance, he paused and said, 'Are you sure there's nothing you want? I meant it, I can bring you some food?'

A shake of the head was his only answer and at last he saw the fellow drop to a crouching position with the shotgun resting across his knees. Only then did Adam turn and run, stumbling and panting, out of the wood and into the sunshine. He was shaking and his flesh was clammy. His stomach churned suddenly and he leaned forward, supporting himself with one hand against a nearby tree until he had vomited the contents of his stomach. Immediately he began to recover.

*

In the morning room, Vinnie sat at the table with a pad of paper and a pencil in front of her. She had just rung the bell and was waiting for Janet to appear. Her hair was parted in the middle and swept up at each side of her face to cover her head with soft curls and she wore a gown of cinnamon silk, cuffed and collared with heavy cream lace. It was one of her favourites, but today the wearing of it gave her no satisfaction. Her eyes were haunted and her manner preoccupied.

The door opened and Janet entered. 'Yes, ma'am?'

Vinnie turned to face her. 'Please tell Cook that I am ready to do the menus now.'

'Yes, ma'am.' Janet hesitated. 'Are you all right, ma'am?'

'Why do you ask that?' Vinnie's tone was sharp.

'I'm sorry, ma'am, but you do look so pale.'

Vinnie put a hand up to her face. 'I do feel unwell,' she admitted. 'I think the duck last night at supper must have disagreed with me. I thought the sauce was over rich, but no matter, we enjoyed it. Perhaps I ate too well! How is the Colonel today, Janet?'

'Middling, ma'am, really. He sleeps a lot, but the doctor said last time he came that this was nothing to worry about. Apparently it lets the body repair the tissues, whatever that means.'

Vinnie smiled. 'I don't know either, Janet, but if the doctor says there is nothing to worry about, then I'm sure we should take his advice. I will go up to see the Colonel as soon as I finish talking to Cook.'

She dismissed Janet with a small nod and the maid was half-way to the door before she turned back.

'Tim said Arrowmint is doing very nicely, ma'am. You didn't see the stallion, did you?'

Vinnie looked guilty. 'I'm afraid I didn't,' she confessed with a sigh. 'I have so many things on my mind at the moment that I quite forgot he was coming. Julian was not at all pleased with me, but unfortunately it's too late now.'

She did not add that she had spent the day partly with the Bryces and partly on horseback scouring the country for any sign or word of Tom.

'But everything went well, I believe?' she said.

'Oh yes, ma'am!' Janet giggled. 'Tom said it went very well and that Arrowmint enjoyed herself.'

Vinnie smiled faintly. 'I'm pleased to hear it,' she said. 'I shall look forward to seeing the foal when it's born.'

'Will it be black like its father, ma'am?'

Vinnie shrugged. 'I don't know,' she said. 'You will have to ask Tim – he knows more about these matters than I do.'

She glanced at the small carriage clock which stood on the mantelshelf. 'Look at the time! Nearly two o'clock. Ask Cook to come up directly, please Janet, then I can spend an hour with the Colonel.'

She waited impatiently until Cook arrived and then they sat together, one each side of the table, planning the menus for the coming week. But Vinnie found it hard to concentrate on such mundane matters and her thoughts wandered frequently, much to Cook's ill-concealed annoyance. In spite of the open window the room was stuffy, for there was no breeze. Vinnie felt a great tiredness. The events of the last few weeks had taken a severe toll of her strength and her anxiety was spoiling her appetite and ruining her sleep. She knew that her looks suffered, but could not find it in her heart to care. Cook, noting her changed appearance, began to wonder . . .

'Thursday lunch,' said Vinnie. 'We could use up the rest of the cold tongue and perhaps start one of the hams . . .'

'That'll be the last one, ma'am,' said Cook. 'Should I ask the butcher to slaughter another pig? He will need a week or so's notice, he's that busy.'

'Yes, do that, please, Cook,' said Vinnie. 'Perhaps Young Harry can help him. I think Bilton has more than enough to do in the stables. I wonder whether we need another pair of hands around the place. I must speak to Mr Lawrence about it.'

Cook saw her opportunity and took a deep breath.

'Talking about pairs of hands, ma'am,' she began, 'you did say you would replace Janet. No offence to Edie, but she's not a great deal of use and never will be, and I do prefer to make my own bread, ma'am, if you'll forgive me saying so. Helping folks is fine, but I've got my reputation to think of and sometimes the bread that comes up from Brook Cottage just isn't up to standard and I'm ashamed to serve it up. Last Wednesday it was *burnt* and I had to scrape it. In all my days I've never sent burnt bread to the table, ma'am, and I don't care to start doing it now.'

'I know, Cook, and I am very grateful for your patience so far,' said Vinnie. 'It isn't an ideal arrangement and I certainly don't intend it to continue much longer. I needed time to think, that's all. As a temporary measure I had hoped you would bear with it.'

'It's my reputation, you see, ma'am. I've always taken pride in a good table and bread may be humble, but I like it to be good and wholesome.' Her tone was at once righteous and aggrieved as she went on, 'I mean, I'm as sorry as the next person for the Bryces. It must be terrible for them waiting to hear the worst like that. But we've all got our own lives to lead and—'

Hastily Vinnie interrupted her.

'I do understand, Cook,' she said, 'and it won't be for ever, I promise you. As soon as I can make other arrangements, I will do so. Now, where did I get to?'

They were half-way through Friday's evening meal when there was an excited knock on the door and without waiting for a 'Come in', Janet rushed into the room.

'Vinnie – I mean, ma'am – there's someone to see you and, oh ma'am, it's a friend of your brother, come all the way from India.'

Vinnie sprang to her feet. 'A friend of Bertie's?' she cried. 'Where is he? Who is he?'

'He's in the hall, ma'am. His name's—'

But Vinnie had thrown down pencil and paper and without waiting to hear more, ran out of the room and along the passage.

As she turned the corner she collided with her visitor, who was strolling in the direction taken by the maid.

'Steady!' he laughed. 'Are you trying to knock me over?'

Vinnie gasped, the breath knocked out of her, while Adam held her at arm's length, astonished by what he saw. Bertie had not told him to expect a beauty. Vinnie, for her part, stared up into the cheerful face and felt that here was someone she could trust, someone of her 'own kind'. Abandoning any pretence at decorum, she flung herself into his arms and hugged him.

'I don't believe it!' he laughed when at last she released him. 'You are a grand lady – it was the last thing I had expected. Bert said—'

'You've seen him? You've been with him?' cried Vinnie. 'And you look cheerful, so the news must be good. Bertie's alive, isn't he? Please tell me he's alive.'

'Very much alive,' said Adam. 'Alive and kicking, as they say. Mind you, he can't afford to wink any more, but he won't let that worry him.'

Vinnie's face had clouded. 'So it was him, he did lose his eye. Poor Bertie!'

'Oh, don't waste your pity on him,' said Adam. 'He would be most put out if he heard you speak of him that way.'

Janet and Cook had followed Vinnie along the passage and she rounded on them excitedly.

'Cook! Janet! This is Bertie's friend. Oh,' she turned back, 'I don't even know your name. I'm so sorry.'

'I'm Adam Turner,' he said. 'We docked at Southampton and I'm on my way to my parents' home at Margate. Bert asked me to find you, so I did.'

'From Southampton?' cried Cook. 'But that's miles away.'

'It's taken me a week or two to get here,' said Adam.

'But you must be starving!' said Cook. 'Shall I get him something to eat, ma'am?'

'Oh yes, Cook, please do!' said Vinnie. 'And Janet, see if you can find the master. Oh, and tell the Colonel that we have a visitor and we'll be up shortly.'

Cook and Janet hurried off on their respective errands and Vinnie took hold of Adam's arm.

'Come into the morning room,' she said, 'and tell me everything about Bertie. You can't imagine how much it means to me to know for certain that he's alive. All these years I have wondered and worried.' She pushed him unceremoniously into an armchair and sat down opposite him, leaning forward eagerly with her hands clasped round her knees.

'Start at the beginning,' she said. 'I want to hear everything. Oh, my dearest Bertie is safe. That sounds so good!' She clasped her hands and then covered her face, quite ashamed of the intensity of her emotions. Adam watched her, enjoying her excitement.

'It's almost like having Bertie himself here,' Vinnie told him, 'but no, I won't say another word. You talk, Adam, and I shall listen.'

Adam was a good talker. He had a way with words and his humour was infectious. For the first time for months Vinnie found herself laughing aloud as the tale unfolded. In Vinnie's mind Bertie was still the young boy who had run away from Merryon Farm so many years ago. It was hard to imagine him as a grown-up man.

Cook brought in a tray of refreshments and Adam, finding his appetite returned, ate hungrily, talking with his mouth full and scattering crumbs around him. His gestures were expansive and from time to time he threw back his head and laughed as he recounted some of their more harebrained escapades. He told Vinnie how they had worked together at the Grand Hotel in Margate where Bertie was training to be a waiter and Adam was the lift boy. Together they had decided to chance their fortune in the Army where, according to all the recruitment posters, adventure beckoned round every corner and life was never dull.

'And was it?' Vinnie asked him.

'Dull as dishwater some of the time,' he told her, 'but we managed to liven it up a bit. The Sergeant-Major hated us.'

He sat upright in his chair, adopting the stern manner and mien of a Sergeant-Major. 'You 'orrible pair!' he bellowed. 'I've got my beady little eye on you.'

The two of them had joined the Artillery and after their training, had been sent to India. There was a minor local uprising and that was when Bertie had been wounded.

'But even on a stretcher he was as chirpy as a cricket,' Adam told Vinnie. '"Tell me straight," he said to the doctor, "I've lost my eye, haven't I?" Just like that.'

Vinnie shuddered.

'But he'll be fine,' said Adam. 'They were going to send him straight back to England, but he got a bit of a fever just as the boat was sailing so they took him back to the hospital. That's the last time I saw him. "Adam", he said, "you'll get back home before I will. Pop down to Teesbury and find that little sister of mine. Tell her I'll soon be home and give her this." '

He fumbled in the pocket of his trousers and drew out a small square of linen carefully folded into a package, which he handed to Vinnie with a mock bow.

'For me?' cried Vinnie. 'A present. Oh, Bertie!'

She unwrapped it with trembling fingers and a small white object fell into her lap. It was a tiny elephant, carved out of ivory, which could be threaded on to a chain and worn as a necklace.

'Oh, it's beautiful!' Vinnie exclaimed, fingering it lovingly. 'And you've brought it all this way, just for me. How very kind you are.' Adam shrugged modestly but Vinnie impulsively sprang to her feet and kissed him lightly on the cheek.

'You'll never know what it means to me,' she said, 'to have news of Bertie after all these years. To know that he's safe and that he remembered me and sent me a present.'

'He thought about you a lot,' Adam assured her. 'He was always talking about "young Vinnie".'

'I'm not so young now,' she said. 'I'm a grown woman, with a husband and a home,' – her face clouded suddenly – 'and so much responsibility, I hardly know which way to turn.'

He was surprised by her changed manner and seeing this, Vinnie smiled brilliantly. 'But they don't matter any more,' she said. 'Having you here and hearing all your news has made everything brighter. I can't let you go away just yet. You realize that, I suppose?'

He grinned, an appealing, boyish grin.

'I was rather hoping you would ask me to stay,' he admitted.

'But of course I shall,' she said. 'You must meet Julian and tell him all the news about Bertie and you must stay here as long as you like as our guest. We can show you the house and the farm.'

She glanced at the tray. 'Good heavens, it's all gone!' she said. 'You must have an appetite like a horse. Would you like some more? Dinner isn't until eight.'

'I wouldn't say no,' responded Adam and Vinnie jumped up and rang the bell.

Adam grinned again.

'What are you laughing at?' she asked him.

'It's you,' laughed Adam, 'and all this.' He waved a hand round the elegant morning room. 'Bert's going to be knocked all of a heap when he knows that his young Vinnie is mistress of Foxearth.'

'It will be fun,' said Vinnie wistfully. 'I do hope they send him home very soon.'

*

A few days later Janet was preparing for the Colonel's morning blanket bath. First she carried in a small table and set it beside the bed while the Colonel, reading his newspaper, pretended not to notice. Then she carried over the large washing bowl into which she poured cold water, and brought over soap, flannel and two towels, one large and one small. She not only wore a rubber apron over her white nurse's uniform, to protect herself from any splashes, but also what the old man called her 'nurse's face'. This was what Janet hopefully imagined was an air of stern professionalism, for the Colonel did not take kindly to being washed by 'a slip of a maid' and there were frequent tussles before the operation could be successfully completed. Now the Colonel rustled his paper irritably and frowned.

'Don't know what's happening to the stock market these days,' he grumbled. 'Up, down, up, down, like a damned yo-yo. How the devil do you know if you're a rich man or a pauper?'

'I'm sure I don't know, sir,' said Janet obligingly.

'Of course you don't, girl! And neither do I. Neither does anyone.'

He glanced surreptitiously towards the small table to see if preparations were complete and seeing that they were, said, 'Don't bother me yet, girl; I have half a page to get through before I'm ready.'

Ignoring him, Janet poured a jug of hot water into the bowl and stirred it with her fingers to test the temperature.

'There we are, sir!' she said, as though he had not spoken. 'Just right.'

He rustled the paper angrily, but while both his hands were concerned with it Janet took hold of the bedclothes and with one quick movement pulled them half-way down the bed.

'Now, sir,' she said briskly, 'if you'll just take off your night-shirt?'

He let go of the paper with one hand and struggled to pull the bedclothes back over his body, but Janet attempted a firm bedside manner.

'Now, sir, we're not going to be silly this morning, are we?' she said. 'I have plenty of other things to do with my time.'

'Plenty of other things to do with my time,' he mimicked, so that Janet found it hard to keep her face straight. 'You can't fool me, girl, you've got nothing to do with your time except to look after me.'

'Oh, very well, sir,' said Janet. 'If you want to be washed with cold water, I shall just sit here and wait for you to finish reading the paper.'

'Hm!' The Colonel glared at her and then turned his attention once more to *The Times*.

Janet sat down on the chair a few feet away from the table and inspected her nails carefully, then tucked a wisp of hair under her cap and flicked an imaginary speck of dust from her apron. Stubbornly the Colonel read on, so after a few more moments she crossed to the bowl of water, dabbled her fingers in it and 'tutted' crossly. The old man crumpled the paper in an angry movement.

'No, no!' Janet protested. 'You carry on reading, sir. Of course, the newspaper will wait but the water won't . . .'

With a deep sigh he threw the newspaper on to the floor and made signs to her to help him remove his nightshirt.

'First the towel, sir,' she said as she pulled the blankets down the bottom half of the bed. Then she rolled him on to his left side and arranged the towel over the right half. With part of the towel neatly rolled, she then moved round to the other side of the bed, turned him on to his right side and unrolled the rest of the towel.

'There we are, sir,' she said. 'Now I'll help you to sit up and we can take that nightshirt off.'

She covered him up to the waist with the bedclothes, but as soon as his nightshirt had been removed the Colonel shivered.

'There's a window open, Janet,' he protested. 'I'm freezing to death here.'

'Of course you're not, sir, and there's no window open.'

She dipped the flannel into the hot water, soaped it vigorously, squeezed out the surplus water and handed it to him.

There you are, sir. Face and neck.'

He rolled his eyes despairingly, but proceeded to wash his face and neck as instructed. Even this small activity tired him, however, and he relinquished the flannel gratefully. When Janet had rinsed the soap out of it and handed it back, the Colonel wiped the lather from his face and neck and Janet handed him another towel.

'It *was* nice and warm from the airing cupboard,' she said pointedly. 'I expect it's got cold by now.'

'Well, you're wrong,' he said. 'It hasn't.'

'That's good then, sir.'

She lathered the flannel again and washed his arms, chest and stomach. While she worked, she chatted to him about the goings-on in the household and the farm and passed on any scrap of village gossip that had come her way.

'They haven't found Bryce yet, then?' he asked and Janet shook her head.

'I just hope they find him soon, before he kills somebody,' she said. 'That asylum may not be a nice place, but at least there he would be cared for and not a threat to honest folks like he is now.'

She lathered the flannel again. 'Here you are, sir,' she said and then hurried to the window saying, 'Haven't had a chance to look at the garden today,' for there was a certain part of the old gentleman's anatomy which he would not allow her to wash.

Looking down into the garden, Janet saw Vinnie and Adam playing croquet. They were laughing together as Vinnie tried to instruct him in the mysteries of the game, which she herself had only recently mastered. Janet smiled, for it seemed the ball was going anywhere but where it was intended. Adam stood with his feet slightly apart, gripping the mallet with one hand above the other. He swung it gently so that the mallet head swung backwards and forwards between his feet; then, with a powerful thrust, he struck at the ball which bounced across the lawn to go right over the top of a hoop and end up in the shrubbery on the far side.

Vinnie, her hands on her hips, laughed delightedly while Adam ran after the ball.

'There's the mistress outside,' Janet told the Colonel, 'with that Mr Turner. He's a nice young man, isn't he, sir? Full of fun and never too busy to talk to folk.'

'He seems nice enough,' said the Colonel. 'Here you are, girl.'

She turned to take the flannel from him, rinse it out and return it, then went back to the window. Now Vinnie had joined Adam in his search for the ball.

'Croquet must be a very difficult game,' said Janet. 'Poor Mr

Turner's just hit the ball into the bushes and they're both looking for it now.'

'Croquet calls for self-control,' said the Colonel. 'Any fool can whack at a ball, but that's not control.'

Janet shook her head, marvelling. 'Miss Vinnie's a different person,' she said, 'since she heard that her brother was safe. I've never seen anyone change so fast. I'm that glad for her; we all are, sir. She's been so worried and upset lately over poor Mr Bryce.'

'Don't mention that name to me,' said the Colonel irritably. 'Tom Bryce, Tom Bryce. That's all I've heard for the past few weeks. Talk about something else, can't you, Janet?'

With an effort, he sat up and leaned forward while she washed his back and then together they pulled on his clean nightshirt. Only when his top half was decently covered would he allow Janet to wash the rest of his body and his legs. He was ashamed of his withered frame and Janet, aware of this fact, always made an effort to say something complimentary to him.

Today she said, 'You've got a nicely shaped foot there. What do they call it, sir – bone structure? I reckon it's neater than mine. Not that my poor old feet are anything to boast about. "Plates of meat" is about right for mine.'

'Plates of meat?' he echoed. 'Where did you hear such an outlandish phrase?'

Janet grinned. 'It's the Londoners,' she told him. 'It's the way they speak, sir. Plates of meat – feet. Apples and pears – stairs.'

'Rubbish!' said the Colonel. 'Why can't they speak the Queen's English like the rest of us?'

'King's English, sir,' she corrected him. 'We've got a King now, remember.'

'Oh, so we have. I do forget, I must confess. The old lady was with us so long that it's hard to remember that she's gone.'

'But you're still here, sir,' Janet reminded him. 'You wanted to outlive her and you have.'

She knew the remark would please him and grinned as a satisfied smile lit up his face and crinkled the corners of his faded blue eyes.

'*And* you'll live a long time yet,' said Janet.

'I don't know about that.'

'Oh yes you will, sir. I'm not having you dying on me,' she said, 'and everyone saying it was my fault. I'm not working my fingers to the bone so that you can die on me, so don't let such an idea enter your head. If you don't live to be a hundred, sir, I shall want to know why.'

'Nag, nag,' he grumbled. 'You've become a proper nagger, Janet. God help your husband if you ever get one.'

'Well, I shan't get one sir, 'cos I shan't go looking. I've got my hands full with you, sir. You're a full-time job, you are.'

He laughed, becoming more cheerful as she replaced soap and flannel and emptied the dirty water into the slop bucket.

'I suppose they haven't found that wretched woman yet?' he said. 'Mollie whatever-her-name-is?'

'No, sir, not yet.'

'Good riddance to her, then,' he said. 'Breaking windows! Whatever next?'

Janet repeated the earlier process to withdraw the towels he had been lying on, then tucked in the bedclothes and tidied everything to her satisfaction.

'There you are, sir, all smart and clean,' she said. 'Here's the brush for your hair; you like to do that for yourself, don't you? Is there anything else?'

The old man sighed and looked round the sunlit room, but could find nothing to grumble about.

'No, thank you, Janet,' he said. 'You can get along now and take that,' – he indicated the crumpled paper on the floor – 'take that to Cook with my compliments and say I should like to read her *Daily Mail*.'

Janet picked it up, smoothed the pages and refolded it. 'I'll take it, sir, but I don't think she ever reads it.'

'That's her loss,' said the Colonel. 'She could improve her mind if she wanted to. Tell her that from me. Tell her she'll find the City page very exciting.' He began to laugh. 'Yes, tell her that, Janet!'

Janet grinned. 'You're a wicked man, sir – but I'll tell her.' And she left him, still laughing wheezily, and hurried downstairs with the slop bucket.

CHAPTER THIRTEEN

Young Tommy Bryce was nearly ten years old, his sister Bertha half-way to eleven – or, as she insisted on telling people, ten and three-quarters. Normally, with Jim and Grace and Sam, they would have spent the month of September hop-picking, but this year it had been forbidden in case Julian should see and recognize them and discover their whereabouts. Teesbury School was closed, but in any case they had not yet begun to attend for the same reason. Rose therefore had sent the older two blackberrying while Jim, Grace and Sam remained in the garden, picking stones out of the soil which Rose had turned over the previous day. In an optimistic mood, she had decided to grow some vegetables and had taken time off from the baking and washing to prepare a small area of ground at the far end of the garden.

Tommy and Bertha each carried a basin and a large basket stood on the ground between them. It was already half-full of blackberries and both children had smears of bramble juice round their mouths and purple fingertips. Inevitably they were arguing, as this was proving one of the few sources of amusement to help to pass the time.

'You've eaten more than me,' said Bertha, 'and I'm telling.'

'Have not!'

'You have that. I've been counting.'

'You have not,' said Tommy. 'You're not even looking at me. How can you count if you're not even looking?'

'I'm looking sideways out of the corner of my eye.'

'Liar!'

'You're not to call me that,' said Bertha triumphantly, 'so I'm telling about that, too.'

'You would,' said Tommy, 'because you're a sneak.'

'I'm not a sneak!'

'You are.'

'I'm not.'

'Yes, you are!'

Tommy turned his head away and popped another blackberry into his mouth.

'I saw that!' cried Bertha. 'You said I wasn't looking, but I am.' Her brother's scowl deepened. 'Ma didn't say we weren't to eat *any*. She said we weren't to eat too many. I haven't eaten too many.'

'Yes, you have,' said Bertha, 'and you'll be sick.'

'I will not.'

'You will.'

'I will *not* be sick!'

'Ouch!' Bertha had pricked herself on a bramble. She sucked the offending puncture while Tommy crowed over her misfortune.

'Serves you right,' he said. 'You should look what you're doing instead of spying on me.'

'You're glad,' she accused him. 'You're glad I've hurt myself and I'm telling.'

'Tell, then. Don't care if you do.'

From the wood on their right came a staccato drilling sound and they both paused to listen.

'It's a woodpecker,' said Tommy.

'So what if it is.'

He took no notice but continued to listen, a rapt expression on his face. The young Tom Bryce was fascinated by all wild creatures and wanted very much to be a gamekeeper when he grew up. Books and learning held no interest for him, but he knew the names of all the trees and could distinguish them at all seasons of the year. He was familiar with every flower that grew and knew which stone walls to search for snails. He could find a toad whenever he wished and he knew where the birds were nesting long before they were discovered by other children. His interest stemmed from his earlier years when his father had passed on his own love of nature, but in recent years he had relied entirely on his own observation and patience, discovering the secret tracks of the rabbits and hares and learning to imitate the cry of the fox.

'We could go and look for it,' he suggested.

'*You* can,' said Bertha. 'I don't want to see a stupid old woodpecker.'

The drilling sound was repeated and young Tommy waited, his

head on one side and his eyes closed. Taking advantage of this last fact, Bertha snatched the basin from his hand and emptied his blackberries into her own. Tommy opened his eyes and, with a cry of rage, snatched back the empty basin and threw it to the ground in temper.

'Now *I'm* telling!' he shouted. 'That's stealing and I'm telling.'

'I haven't stolen them,' she said, growing nervous in the face of his rage. 'I've only borrowed them, I'm going to give them back.'

'All right then, give them back.' He controlled his anger with an effort and reluctantly she began to tip blackberries from her basin into his as slowly as she dared.

Tommy tilted the basin suddenly, hastening the transfer. 'Oh thank you, Bertha,' he mocked, but now it was her turn to throw down the basin. This freed her hands to pummel his back and shoulders with fierce fists, while, unobserved, the basin rolled into the densest part of the brambles and disappeared. As the two children struggled wildly, the other basin of blackberries was spilled and trampled into the long grass. Suddenly Tommy noticed that his sister's basin had gone and her anger evaporated immediately, to be replaced by anxiety.

'It must be somewhere here,' Bertha told him. 'It's rolled, it must have done.' She began to search around, but there was no sign of the basin. 'Help me look for it, then, can't you?'

'Why should I?' he said, although in fact he was gazing all around.

'Because I say so,' said Bertha, 'and I'm older than you and if you don't I shall tell.'

Tommy watched her, his own basin clasped firmly to his chest. As the minutes passed, she became more agitated. Basins cost money and money was something of which they had very little. She stopped searching and looked at her brother, hating him but needing his help.

'Tell you what,' she said, 'you help me find the basin and I'll come with you to look for the woodpecker.'

This was a stroke of genius and she knew it as the expression on Tommy's face changed.

'It was somewhere around here,' he said. 'Just about here. It must be under the brambles. Fetch a stick and we'll poke around a bit. A thick stick.'

She scampered off and returned with a small dead branch.

Tommy knelt down and thrust the branch under the lowest clump of bramble.

'You take the stick,' he told her, 'and lift the brambles up as high as you can while I crawl underneath – and *don't* let go of it while I'm under there.' Bertha did as she was told, clasping the branch firmly in her hand and easing the bramble up and away from the grass. Tommy threw himself on to his stomach, ducked his head and began to wriggle underneath the prickly mass.

'Can you see it? Is it there?' she asked anxiously. The basin had rolled into the entrance of a large burrow and Tommy saw it at once.

'I've found it!' he called, and retrieving it from its earthy resting place, he wriggled out backwards. When at last his head was clear, Bertha relaxed her hold on the brambles.

'That was heavy,' she complained.

He handed her the basin and stood up to brush grass and leaves from his hair and clothes. Then both children looked at the half-filled basket and the two empty basins.

'We'd better pick a few more,' said Bertha. 'Mum said not to come back until the basket was full.'

'We can pick them later,' said Tommy. 'We'll go to the wood now and look for that woodpecker.'

For a moment she hesitated, her lips already forming a protest, but something in the steely glint in his eye warned her not to do so and she gave in with bad grace. Tommy took the basket while Bertha carried the basins and they set off in the direction of the wood. Outside the sun shone, but within the circle of trees it was cooler and full of shadows. Tommy wandered from tree to tree, staring upwards, his ears tuned for the sound of the woodpecker.

'It must have gone,' said Bertha. 'I don't like it in here – let's go back now.'

'Shh!' He put a finger to his lips. 'It can't be far,' he whispered. 'Ah, there it goes again!'

He stood still with one hand raised for silence, but Bertha had wandered on and it was she who found the headless corpse. For a moment she stared down, puzzled by what remained of the body, then she screamed and within seconds her brother stood beside her. Fearfully, their eyes moved to the shotgun propped in the crook of a tree and the string still tied to the trigger. Although the head had gone, the body was intact. It wore a grey flannel shirt and a pair of shapeless corduroy breeches fastened by a leather belt. There was a waistcoat fastened by its top button and over that a worn jacket with patched elbows.

Where the neck ended a mass of dried blood and splinters of bone was congealing into a brown mass over which flies and insects hurried, gorging on the putrefying flesh. Tommy felt the bile rise in his throat and he made a small choking sound. He tried to think clearly about what he saw while Bertha's gaze travelled slowly over the clothes. There was a terrible familiarity about them. They could not look at each other, nor could they tear their eyes away from the hideous sight.

'It's a dead man,' Bertha said at last, her tone flat.

Tommy found his voice. 'Don't look at it,' he whispered urgently. 'It's not nice.' He tugged her away from the dreadful neck towards the other end of the body.

'Those breeches—' Bertha began.

Tommy knelt down and ran his fingers over the buckle at the dead man's waist. He knew that he recognized it, yet he also knew that it was preposterous. His father was alive and well and his father had a head between his shoulders. Suddenly he drew back his hand as though the metal of the buckle had burned his fingers. Then he took several steps backwards, dragging Bertha with him and his lips began to tremble.

'It's not nice,' he repeated. 'Not nice.'

At last he turned to meet his sister's gaze and their faces reflected a mutual horror. Sudden large tears burst from Tommy's eyes and he began to tremble all over. Bertha put her arms round him briefly in a helpless attempt to comfort him.

'We'd better tell,' she whispered, but Tommy could only sob uncontrollably – an ugly, tearing sound. Carefully averting her eyes from her father's body, she picked up the basket of blackberries and laid the two basins on top of it. She transferred the basket into her left hand and put her right arm round Tommy's thin shoulders. Murmuring soothingly, she led her brother out of the wood, while overhead the sound of the woodpecker went unheeded.

*

Vinnie and Adam Turner wandered through the hop-garden. The sun was dropping low in the sky and those poles which were already bare of hops, cast long shadows across them as they passed. Further over in the field, the hop-picking continued, but the day's work was nearly ended. Soon Ned Berry would call 'Pull no more bines!' and the pickers would gather up their belongings and make their way back to the barn, with nothing more on their minds than to cook their eagerly awaited suppers.

Vinnie glanced up at Adam mischievously.

'For someone who drinks so much ale,' she teased, 'you know very little about hops.'

'You grow them, I drink them,' he answered. 'But since you are determined to educate me, tell away, Mrs Lawrence.'

He had taken to calling her that in a gently mocking tone which Vinnie found rather endearing. She slapped the nearest hop-pole, saying, 'Pole without hops', then pointed to the nearest hop-bine which climbed its way upward, 'and pole with hops!'

He laughed. 'I think I'm getting the hang of it,' he said. 'It's not too difficult.'

'Oh, but it is,' said Vinnie. 'This is just the beginning.'

They cut across the sloping field between the empty hop-poles. 'Bin,' said Vinnie, pointing to the canvas hammock-like container slung between crossed poles.

Four women were picking into the bin, their fingers snatching deftly at the greeny-yellow cones, their experienced eyes searching among the leaves so that none of the hops should escape their vigilance and incur the wrath of Ned Berry or Adam Forrest.

'We pick into the bins,' Vinnie told him, 'then four times a day the measurer comes round and empties them with a bushel basket. They count up the bushels in each bin and note down the number, then at the end of the week they add them up and pay the picker whose name belongs to that particular bin. It's up to him or her, then, to divide up the money.'

The four women glanced shyly towards Vinnie and her companion. 'Another ten days of this sunshine will do us a treat,' one of them volunteered. 'Perhaps you could arrange it with Him up there?' She jerked her thumb skyward and Vinnie smiled.

'I'll do my best,' she said and they moved on.

'So,' said Adam, 'they load all the hops into a waggon and take them to the brewery.'

Vinnie wagged a finger at him reprovingly. 'Oh, no,' she said. 'We're not nearly there yet. They measure out from the bins into the hop-pokes – a poke is a kind of sack and it holds ten bushels.'

He nodded solemnly, secretly amused by her earnestness.

'Don't laugh at me, Adam,' she told him. 'I'm doing my best.'

Laughing, he put an arm round her shoulder and squeezed it gently. 'Couldn't ask for a better teacher,' he said.

For a moment Vinnie felt flustered, then she recovered her poise.

'Where was I? Oh yes – the pokes are stacked by the bins until the waggon comes along the rows to collect them. They are loaded on and then they're taken to the oast-house.'

Adam raised his eyebrows in pretended amazement. 'And am I going to see the oast-house, too?' he asked.

'You are, sir,' said Vinnie, 'but we've a little way to walk yet. You see those cowls?' She pointed to the conical roofs of the oast-house and he nodded. 'That's the oast-house,' she told him. 'Steven Pitt is our head dryer and what he doesn't know about drying hops could fit on a postage stamp. He's not very happy at the moment, because the beginning of the month was so wet and the hops are of such poor quality. He takes a great pride in his work.' She tried to copy Steven Pitt's accent: 'I can't abide these puny little hops. They give a man no heart.'

Adam laughed, striding along on his long legs unaware that Vinnie was struggling to keep up with him. As they passed the top end of the field various pickers glanced up and waved or exchanged a friendly greeting. The unpleasantness of the first week had been forgotten now and the timely change of weather had brought about the usual holiday atmosphere. Everyone worked willingly and cheerfully and Mollie Pett's disappearance had ceased to be a topic of conversation. Children old enough to do so picked with their mothers and the youngsters huddled or crawled among the fallen leaves, enjoying the fresh air and freedom from the squalor of their London homes. From the next field came the ringing of a bell and Adam looked at Vinnie enquiringly.

'That's the lollipop man,' she told him. 'He comes round each day with his donkey-cart full of sweets for the children to buy. He has aniseed balls and sherbert dabs, mint humbugs and liquorice sticks—'

'And lollipops?'

'Oh yes, and lollipops!'

'Any gob-stoppers?' asked Adam.

She nodded. 'Gob-stoppers and humbugs and barley-sugar sticks.' She screwed up her eyes, thinking hard. 'And if you're rich enough, there's coconut ice or peardrops in little paper cones.'

'Peardrops,' said Adam. 'What, pink and yellow?'

She nodded.

'Come on, I'll buy you some,' he said, and taking her hand began to run. The two of them raced across the field, through the gate and into the next field where a line of children was already forming beside the little cart. To the children's amusement, Adam and Vinnie joined the end of the queue. When they finally reached the cart, Adam dipped his hand into his pocket.

'A pennorth of peardrops,' he told the surprised vendor and as soon as they were in his possession, he popped a pink one into Vinnie's mouth.

'That will keep you quiet for a little while,' he said, putting a yellow one into his own mouth. 'Maybe it will last you until we reach the oast-house. Now, not another word!'

When at last they reached the oast-house Vinnie introduced Adam Turner to Steven Pitt and asked if they could have a look round.

'Unless you have a few minutes to spare,' Vinnie said, 'and could show us round. You know so much more about it than I do.'

Flattered, Steven was glad to oblige. He showed them the fires, two on each side of the brick archway, then he took them upstairs where the thick layer of hops was part-way through the drying process.

'Two hours, they've had,' he told them, 'and they'll want another three at least before turning. This here is what we turn them with.' He took up the long-handled canvas shovel and handed it to Adam, who inspected it curiously.

'That's a scuppet,' Vinnie told him. '*Never* call it a shovel. It scoops up the hops, you see, when they have to be turned over.'

'It's very light,' Adam remarked, returning it to the head dryer.

'It's not so light when it's full of hops,' he assured them.

Adam nodded. 'What happens to them when they're done?' he asked.

'Why, they're pressed into a pocket,' said Steven.

He showed them the press, of which he was very proud for it had been installed only two months earlier and was the most modern of its kind. It was set above a hole in the drying-room floor and an empty hop-pocket was suspended through it into the room below.

'The hops are tipped into the pocket,' he told them, 'and then that plunger goes down into the pocket and presses them flat. That one pocket will hold nigh on a hundred weight of hops,' he explained, 'and it'll be taller than most men. You'd not move that on your own, I can tell you. We have a little trolley to move them around.'

From downstairs there suddenly came a familiar voice. 'Mr Pitt? Are you about?'

'It's Clive le Brun!' cried Vinnie. 'We expected him yesterday.' She turned to Adam as Stephen went down to greet him.

'Clive le Brun is a factor,' Vinnie explained. 'What Julian calls a middle-man. He buys the hops from us and then sells them where he can when the price is right. Clive is a good friend of ours. Come down and I'll introduce you.'

They followed Stephen downstairs and Vinnie made the introductions, including the fact that Adam had brought news about her brother.

'I can imagine how welcome that news was,' Clive said, taking Adam's hand in a firm grip. He was pleasantly surprised to see the change in Vinnie's appearance and manner.

'Are you staying long?' he asked Adam.

The young man shrugged. 'Possibly another day,' he said. 'I'm on extended leave from the Army and was making my way to Margate to see my parents. Then I must report back to my barracks in Greenwich, where I shall have to decide whether or not to sign on again.'

Clive le Brun had come to take hop samples for the London market and after extracting a promise that he would join them later for a glass of wine, Adam and Vinnie left him discussing business with Stephen Pitt. Slowly they made their way back to the house. It seemed to Vinnie that she had always known the young man who walked beside her, which was a strange sensation. She thought perhaps it was his closeness to Bertie which made him seem so familiar to her.

'So the tour's at an end,' she said. 'I hope you've learnt a lot—'

'At an end?' said Adam. 'But what happens when it leaves the oast house?'

Vinnie looked rather sheepish. 'I'm not quite sure,' she confessed. 'It goes into store and then Clive will sell it either to one of the local breweries or in London. After that it's mixed with malt and yeast, but I'm afraid I'm rather vague about the process. I was hoping you wouldn't ask!'

'Then forget I did so,' he said gallantly. 'It was a most useful and instructive tour and I thank you for it.'

'You're mocking me again,' said Vinnie, 'but I'll forgive you. I think I could forgive you anything.'

'Anything?' He raised his eyebrows quizzically and Vinnie laughed.

'Almost anything,' she amended.

'Are you still eating that peardrop?' he asked her.

'No, it's gone,' she said.

'You crunched it up,' Adam accused her.

Vinnie nodded and he tutted as he offered her another.

'Never crunch them, my Ma used to say, or you'll break your teeth. I always did crunch them, but I never did break a single tooth. I realized that one day when I was about fifteen, but somehow I didn't like to tell her.'

'Why not?'

'She would have boxed my ears for my trouble.'

'I like the sound of your mother,' said Vinnie. 'I wish I could remember mine.'

He smiled. 'Perhaps you'll meet mine one day. I could share her with you.'

Having reached the house, they went up the steps and in at the front door, which stood wide open to let in the sunshine. Almost immediately Janet appeared. Her face was very pale and Vinnie noticed with surprise that her eyes were reddened as though from crying.

'Oh, Vinnie – I mean, ma'am—'

'What is it, Janet?' Vinnie asked quickly.

Janet's eyes filled again with ready tears. 'I don't know how to tell you, ma'am. It's so terrible. The constable called—'

'Oh no!' said Vinnie. All the laughter fled from her face and the haunted look returned to her eyes. With it came the beginning of fear.

'Not Tom, Janet! Please not Tom?' But Janet was nodding. 'Oh dear God!' cried Vinnie 'What has he done? What's happened? He's killed somebody, hasn't he?'

Janet shook her head. 'He hasn't killed anyone. Or at least, I suppose he has – that is, he's killed himself, ma'am.'

Tears ran down her face as Vinnie stared at her in horror. Adam touched Vinnie's arm and found that she was trembling. Then she stared at Janet. 'Killed himself . . .' Vinnie whispered. 'No!' She shook her head disbelievingly.

'I'm sorry, ma'am, but he has. Rigged up a shotgun and blew off his head.'

Vinnie uttered a sound that was a half moan, half protest and put up a hand to hide her eyes.

'Who is it?' Adam asked. 'A friend of yours, Vinnie?' But she did not answer.

Janet put out a hand and clasped Vinnie's wrist. 'I'm so sorry, ma'am,' she sobbed. 'Poor Mr Bryce!'

'And Rose,' said Vinnie, 'and those poor little children. Oh God! How could he have let it happen?' Her lips began to tremble, but she made an effort to control her feelings.

'Don't cry, Janet,' she said. 'Please don't cry like that.' Janet's grief was rapidly undermining her own fragile control.

'Cook said at least it was quick,' Janet mumbled. 'And at least he didn't suffer. Cook said we should be grateful for that.'

Slowly Vinnie turned and looked despairingly into Adam's face. 'He was a good man,' she said. 'Why should such a thing happen? And to Tom of all people.'

'Cook says that maybe it's for the best—' Janet went on, but Vinnie turned on her fiercely.

'Well, Cook's wrong!' she cried. 'It's not for the best. How could it be? When a man shoots himself? Oh God!'

'Those poor little mites,' said Janet, wiping her eyes. 'It was them that found him – Tommy and Bertha.'

'*What?*' cried Vinnie.

'So the constable said. Found his poor body with no head—'

Vinnie screamed and, springing forward, pushed Janet out of her way and ran to the stairs. Janet staggered backwards, tripped over a chair-leg and fell sprawling. Adam started to follow Vinnie, but when she was half-way up the stairs she stopped and turned.

'Janet . . .' she whispered. 'I'm sorry, Janet. I just . . .'

Her eyes closed and she swayed suddenly. Adam dashed forward and was just in time to catch her as she collapsed in a dead faint.

*

The doctor fastened his bag with a snap and straightened up. He smiled at Vinnie.

'Think yourself very fortunate,' he said, 'that someone was there to catch you when you fell. Otherwise it could have been a very nasty accident. Of course, most accidents do happen at home. People choke on bones, or cut themselves with knives that are too sharp, or slip on—'

'I have to go down to Brook Cottage,' Vinnie interrupted him, 'to see Rose and poor Mrs Bryce.'

'Not today,' said the doctor, with a firm shake of the head. 'You'll be going nowhere today, Mrs Lawrence.'

Vinnie was struggling to sit up but he put a hand on her shoulder and gently but firmly pressed her down on to the bed.

'Not today,' he repeated. 'Doctor's orders! Their grief will be no more and no less for you being there. Give them today to be alone with their sorrow and come to terms with their loss. The Bryces have enough on their plates,' he continued, 'without a fainting woman descending on them. Send a note if you must – a letter of condolence is always welcome – and tell them you will visit tomorrow when you are recovered. Would you like me to call in on them and see if I can help in any way?'

'Oh, please do!' said Vinnie. 'I cannot bear to think of them alone and helpless when there is so much to think about and so much to be done – the funeral arranged and everyone to be told. Perhaps the Reverend Parsloe could also call on them?'

'I'm sure he will,' said the doctor. 'He may have been already, but if not I shall certainly ask him to do so.'

Vinnie struggled up on to one elbow. 'And Mary Bellweather,' she cried. 'Perhaps Mary would call in on them later this evening. I'm sure she would be a great comfort at a time like this.'

'There you are, then,' said the doctor, smiling. 'There is no lack of volunteers and the Bryces can manage without you for one day. You can get up tomorrow and do whatever you wish, but try not to over-tire yourself, for the baby's sake.'

Vinnie frowned. 'Oh yes, the baby,' she said. 'I had forgotten . . . Isn't that terrible?'

'Oh, very terrible,' the doctor smiled. 'It's not every day a woman learns she's pregnant!'

'I think I already knew,' said Vinnie.

'Some women do,' he agreed. 'Some can tell the morning after conception; it's amazing. Others can go six or seven months and still not know. Occasionally, a woman is surprised when she finds herself giving birth. Well now, you will have some good news for your husband when he comes in tonight.'

'I may not tell him just yet,' said Vinnie. 'He is very busy at the moment and distracted by other problems. Somehow it doesn't seem quite the right time to tell him.'

The doctor shrugged. 'You must make up your own mind about that,' he said, 'but whenever you decide to tell him, I am sure he will be quite delighted. And the Colonel, too – another grandchild for him!'

He hesitated before he spoke again. 'I hope you won't mind my mentioning this, Mrs Lawrence, but you know – and of course your husband does too – that you have already lost one child. No doubt your environment and lack of proper nourishment had a great deal to do with the child's failure to survive. But it is also possible that you have some kind of weakness which makes it difficult for you to bear a live child, in which case we must take every precaution. I don't want to alarm you, but we must take no chances. I will draw up a diet sheet for you and you must take a little exercise each day and rest in the afternoons. I shall not ask you to alter your life-style drastically, but merely to bear in mind that you have a responsibility for another life as well as your own and that you should behave accordingly. Try not to get upset emotionally. Perhaps it would be better if—'

Vinnie's eyes blazed suddenly. 'Don't tell me to stay away from Tom's funeral,' she said. 'That is what you were going to say, isn't it?'

'It had crossed my mind,' he admitted.

'No, doctor, I cannot agree to that,' she said. 'If Rose will allow me to attend, I shall do so.'

'Your husband may not allow it, Mrs Lawrence.'

'If you think there is any likelihood of that, then I shall not tell him about the child until the funeral is over. I may not do so in any case. I hope, doctor, that you will not consider it your duty to tell him before I do?'

'I shall respect your wishes in the matter, of course,' he said, 'unless you delay so long that I think your health may suffer as a result. Your husband should be told that you are in a delicate state of health. And of course, it is his child as much as yours, you know. I should think it very unfair if you kept the news from him too long.'

She sighed. 'Yes, you are right. I promise you I shall plan to tell him within the week. At the very latest I shall tell him when the hopping ends. He is a little unapproachable at present, I'm afraid. The hops have been so poor this year and it is a great disappointment and worry to him.'

'It has been a very bad year,' he agreed. 'The situation is the same wherever I go. All of Kent has suffered, but there . . . we must not dwell on the gloomy side of life.'

Vinnie smiled wanly. 'The gloomy side is the only one we see these days,' she remarked.

'Now, Mrs Lawrence, that's not true, is it?' he said. 'What about this splendid news concerning your brother, and this friend of his who has come all this way to bring it?'

Vinnie's expression changed and a smile softened her face.

'My lovely Bertie!' she whispered. 'Yes, of course, you're quite right. How could I forget such marvellous news? I'm an ungrateful wretch.'

'You're not a wretch at all,' said the doctor. 'You're a very charming young woman. The last few weeks have been very difficult for you, but now you have something to look forward to – two things, in fact. Your brother's return and the birth of your child. Give thanks for your blessings, Mrs Lawrence, and please do as I say. Rest for the remainder of the day and get up tomorrow morning if you feel able. Now I can let myself out.'

He paused on his way to the door. 'And if you do go to the funeral,' he advised, 'let that be an end to the matter, Mrs Lawrence. Try to put all unhappy thoughts out of your mind for the baby's sake.'

Vinnie nodded.

'Good girl! I shall send Janet up to you with a glass of warm milk and a spoonful of honey. I will call in on Friday to see how you are and can take a look at the Colonel at the same time.'

With a cheery wave the doctor was gone and Vinnie was left alone, at the mercy of her thoughts.

*

There were very few people in church on the occasion of Tom Bryce's funeral. A group of perhaps a dozen people sat at the front while Vinnie, her head covered with a heavy veil, stayed at the back. Julian had forbidden her to attend the service, but she had slipped away from the house in defiance of his wishes. She possessed no mourning clothes, but had thrown a length of black lace over her head – partly as a token of her respect and partly as a means of disguise. Rose had asked her to be present and this was Vinnie's compromise. She was one of the congregation, yet sat apart from it. She sang when they sang and prayed when they prayed, yet she was not with them.

She had not yet told Julian she was expecting his baby. That must wait for a more fitting occasion. She was not even sure that she wanted the child, for of late her relationship with Julian had been deteriorating and she felt lonely and insecure. She could not rid her mind of the suspicion that Julian was attracted to Mary Bellweather. It seemed to Vinnie that his interest in her increased daily, for her name was never far from his lips and he made no attempt to hide his admiration for her. She had seen them together in the bedroom that night and had sensed the spark between them, but dared not ask Julian outright for fear he confessed it to be true. Even if he denied it, she would not wholly believe him because her intuition was too strong. No, she decided – the time was not right to speak of the coming child.

Tom Bryce's death had not troubled her husband at all. He had said merely that the best part of Tom's life was obviously over and his death should be considered a merciful relief by all those who loved him. Vinnie found this detached coldness frightening. She had not dared to approach him on the subject of Tom's funeral expenses, for the Bryces had no money. Instead, she spent what money she had left from the pawnbroker and the rest, surprisingly, was offered by the Colonel. More charitable than his son, he had called Tom 'a good man gone to the bad', and had sent a short note of condolence to Rose and her family.

Vinnie stood up, suddenly aware that the coffin was once more being raised on to the shoulders of the bearers. It was not a pauper's funeral, but it was an extremely simple one and briefer than most. Very few flowers lay on top of the coffin: a large bunch of dahlias from Tom's family and a small circle of dark red roses. The latter were from Vinnie, although she had not put her name on the card, consoling herself with the thought that Tom would know and no one else mattered. At least he was at peace with himself and the world, she thought sadly. Nothing and no one could hurt him now.

Rose walked immediately behind the coffin wearing her Sunday best, as did the rest of the family. They all wore black armbands. Vinnie's heart contracted painfully as she saw their faces: the children awed and silent; Rose and Tom's mother haggard from lack of sleep, their faces distorted by grief. Grace and Bertha walked with their mother, one on either side. Jim and little Sam were with Mrs Bryce. For some reason Tommy stalked behind them, alone, his head held high and his face grim and set.

Vinnie lowered her head hastily, unable to meet their eyes. She had visited them twice since Tom's death and knew the exact depth of their despair.

With a deep sigh she followed them out of the church, along the gravel path and across the grass to the newly dug grave. Tom had been a large, strong man, yet the coffin looked small and insignificant. The Reverend Parsloe cleared his throat, but his voice did not impinge on Vinnie's consciousness. The family stood grouped around the open grave, but Vinnie hung back out of their sight. One or two of the villagers also stood at a respectful distance, their heads bowed – a few elderly men and an old woman with a young baby in her arms. Most of the village and all the pickers were busy at work, for Julian had not considered it necessary to allow them time off to attend. He had argued reasonably enough that Tom Bryce was no longer chief pole-puller at Foxearth and there was money to be earned in the gardens.

Bertha began to cry and Rose bent to comfort her. At last the Reverend Parsloe began his concluding sermon:

'Look down on us, we beseech you, oh God, gathered here to mourn the passing of Tom Bryce, taken from us suddenly in the prime of manhood. While we grieve for his passing, let us not forget that he was among us for many years, beloved son of Mary Bryce, beloved husband of Rose Bryce and beloved father of his five children. For many years he was of this Parish, a loved and respected member of this community. His life was a full one and not without faults and failures, but we are all human and none of us is perfect. We will remember him only for his kindness—'

But his words had touched a chord in Bertha's mind. 'My Pa was a good man,' she cried suddenly. 'It's not true what they said. He didn't do those things.'

Rose and Mrs Bryce tried to comfort her but she began to cry. 'He's not a bad man,' she sobbed loudly. 'He didn't want to die. It's not fair. I don't *want* him to be dead. I *don't*!'

The child broke away from their restraining hands and ran blindly in Vinnie's direction. Ashen-faced, Vinnie watched her approaching and then, throwing back the dark veil, she knelt and held out her arms.

'Bertha, Bertha!' she cried. 'It's Vinnie – it's me!'

The little girl flung herself into Vinnie's arms and Vinnie sank down on to the grass hugging her.

'Don't let him be dead! Please don't,' wept Bertha and Vinnie cried with her, her tears falling on to the tousled dark curls. Bertha, with her father's colouring, had been the apple of his eye. Gently Vinnie rocked her, murmuring soothingly until the frantic child grew calmer. Seeing that she was in good hands, the vicar hastily concluded his oration and Tom's coffin was lowered into the grave. The family stood for a while staring down in disbelief. Vinnie saw the vicar say a few words to Rose, then he hurried back into the church.

Rose, her mother-in-law and the other children walked across the grass towards Vinnie and, as they approached, she stood up wearily with Bertha clinging to her skirt. Rose met Vinnie's eyes and gave a little nod of thanks and Vinnie looked at her wordlessly. Mrs Bryce, wiping her eyes with a handkerchief, gave no sign of recognition. She had lost her only son and the future looked very bleak. Rose held out a hand towards Bertha and gently Vinnie disentangled the little fingers from her own.

'Go to your Ma,' she whispered. 'Be a good girl now.'

The child looked up at her beseechingly and Vinnie swallowed, steadying her voice. 'Go on, Bertha,' she repeated. 'Your Pa would have wished it.'

These words had the desired effect and Bertha moved slowly to rejoin her family. Vinnie watched them walk back on to the path, through the churchyard and out of the gate to where Tim Bilton waited with a cart to take them home to Brook Cottage. It was very quiet in the little churchyard. Vinnie pressed her fingers to her mouth, her heart full of misery. She stood there for a long time until at last the Reverend Parsloe reappeared, wearing his day clothes. He hurried past with a brief nod of his head.

'Vinnie?' She turned and saw Clive le Brun.

'I thought you might be here,' he said. 'I have just come from the house. They are looking for you. I think Julian suspects you are here, so I said I thought I had passed you in the village and asked if I might spirit you away for an hour or two.' Vinnie stared at him, uncomprehending. 'I thought you might care to come home with me,' he said. 'Your second lesson in chess is long overdue.'

He did not smile, but there was a quality in his expression which Vinnie could not fathom. Dazed with grief and shock, her mind seemed to move very slowly. A game of chess? Anything, she thought, to take her mind from the dark reality of the past hour.

She thought of Clive's home and remembered its well-ordered tranquillity. He has integrity, she thought. He makes no demands on my emotions, asks nothing from me except my company over a game of chess. He asks nothing because he needs nothing. He is a complete person.

'Vinnie?' He was still waiting for an answer.

Vinnie wondered if she would ever be a complete person – it seemed very unlikely. She imagined she would continue to butt her way through life, torn by conflicting loyalties, at the mercy of her emotions, vulnerable and afraid.

'Will you play chess with me, Vinnie? Just for an hour.'

She made no answer, but he took her arm and led her quickly across the grass, along the gravelled path and into the waiting brougham.

*

In the Mission tent the evening meal was about to begin. The small trestle table was laid with knives and forks and there was a bowl of pears in the centre. A makeshift screen of wattle hurdles supported with posts divided the area into two halves. At the far end, three patients lay on camp beds in the process of being nursed back to health. At the dining end of the tent, up-ended apple boxes served as chairs and on one of these Alexander sat with a sullen look on his face. His expression to some extent disguised the extent of his anxiety, for although he found the members of the Mission kindly and well-intentioned, their continued interest in himself and his activities was beginning to prove unwelcome. Being singled out for their attention effectively separated him from the other children and he had to endure their various taunts and teasing. Someone had dubbed him 'Mary's little lamb' and the nursery rhyme was frequently chanted when he appeared. At first he had seized on this as an excuse for a fight or at least an exhilarating scuffle, but Mary Bellweather frequently appeared to put an end to the excitement. Her championing of his cause was making his life very difficult.

Alexander did not relish, either, the fact that he now shared an evening meal with the Brothers in Jesus. Before, he had eaten his meagre supper with the day's dirt still upon him, since his mother was no great believer in soap and rarely bothered to fetch water from the stream. In the Mission tent, however, it was quite different for everyone was expected to wash hands and face thoroughly before presenting themselves at the table. Mary even inspected his fingernails and his independent spirit rebelled at these humiliations. However, it seemed that if he did not share the Mission meal he would go hungry; he was therefore forced, much against his will, to be initiated into the mysteries of hygiene.

He had even been allotted a task, he reflected gloomily.

'When there is work to be done, we all share in it,' Mary had told him. 'While Gareth and I do the cooking, you shall lay the table. Knives on the right and forks on the left and don't forget the cruet. Good gracious, child, have you never heard of a cruet? It's a salt cellar and pepper pot and you will find them in that small box in the corner. And put out a glass for each person and a jug of water.'

Alexander swung his legs irritably, drumming his heels against the side of the apple box and staring out through the open tent flap. From where he sat he could see Mary standing beside the fire, stirring the large pot of nourishing rabbit stew. He knew it was 'nourishing' because he had heard it described as such to the patients at the other end of the tent. He felt uneasy, for during the day there had been various whisperings amongst the adults and certain interested glances in his direction had added to his misgivings. Something was afoot, although he had no idea of what it could be except that he was almost certainly involved. He worried in case his mother had been discovered in dire circumstances of some kind and 'they' had thought it best not to tell him.

He was deeply upset because his mother, when she ran away, had not taken him also. He liked Amos Hearn and envied his mother her life with the gipsy family. With very little effort he saw himself sitting up in front of one of the gipsy caravans, a whip in his hand, urging the horses to a greater speed than they had ever achieved before. He pictured himself poaching rabbits or pheasants or slitting open a couple of hedgehogs. Life on the open road, whatever its disadvantages might be, held great charm for Alexander and his spirit writhed under the imposed yoke of his present respectability.

Mary bustled into the tent, tucking up a stray wisp of hair and smoothing her apron.

'Nearly ready!' she said. 'I expect you're hungry.'

He nodded. 'Lost your tongue, have you?' said Mary. He shook his head.

'Then I wish you would answer me when I speak to you,

Alexander. It is very rude not to do so. You're eight years old now and it's time you began to learn these things. There are acceptable ways to behave and others which are unacceptable.'

'Why can't I get down until it's ready?' he grumbled.

'Because you are clean now and if you get down you will get dirty again,' explained Mary. 'Then you would have to wash again. I explained all that to you yesterday.'

'I wouldn't get dirty,' he protested. 'It's boring sitting here.'

'Well, there's no need to get bored,' said Mary. 'Whenever you have nothing to do with your hands, use your head. Think – think about something useful!'

He swung up his feet suddenly and kicked the underneath of the trestle table so that the knives and forks rattled and the pepper pot fell over and rolled perilously close to the edge. He hoped it would fall off but it did not do so. Next time, he thought, he would kick a little harder. He sighed noisily.

'Rabbit stew for supper,' said Mary, ignoring his unspoken protest. 'Do you like rabbit stew?'

Obstinately the boy shook his head. In fact he liked it very much, but he saw no reason to admit to this.

'Now what did I say about shaking your head?' said Mary. 'The polite thing to do is to answer the question.' She put her hands on her hips and regarded him quizzically for a moment, then an expression which he did not recognize crossed her face.

'Never mind,' she said, 'there's plenty of time for you to learn these things. It doesn't do to expect too much too early.' She smiled at him and he realized for the first time that among women she would be judged very attractive. Perhaps 'pretty' was the word for her.

'Plenty of time,' she repeated, nodding her head slightly. She seemed pleased with herself, Alex decided, which bothered him.

From the far end of the room came the sound of coughing and Mary hurried away to attend to one of her patients. Carefully Alexander changed all the knives and forks so that they were in the wrong positions, then sprinkled some pepper and salt into all the glasses. After that he took a pear and began to eat it hungrily. When Mary passed through again on her way back to see to the stew, he hid the half-finished pear under the table and finished eating it when she had gone. Having eaten it right down to the core, he hurled it towards the box in the corner of the tent where the knives, forks and cruet were kept. It pleased him to see that his

aim was true and the successful execution of this slight misdemeanour cheered him. When Gareth came in with a large bowl of
stew, he was feeling much happier. A moment or two later Roland
arrived and they all stood while he said grace:

'Dear God, look down on Thy brethren here below and give
your blessing on this humble meal, for which we give most hearty
thanks. Amen.'

Alexander's lips remained firmly closed, but if anyone noticed
they made no comment.

They all sat down except Gareth, who waited to take the first
three portions of stew into the sick room. Finally he settled
himself opposite Alexander and smiled at the boy encouragingly.

'Well,' he said, 'and what do you think of the news, eh?'

'I haven't told him yet,' said Mary hastily. 'He doesn't know
anything about it.'

'About what?' Alexander demanded, suspicion and anxiety
crystallizing immediately into a fearful anticipation.

'I mean to tell him later,' Mary protested.

'Tell him now,' said Roland. 'You know what they say, no time
like the present.'

'They also say, more haste less speed,' retorted Mary, 'but I will
tell him.'

She finished ladling out the stew and then sat down and took a
deep breath. Alex was aware that all eyes were on him and he
wriggled uncomfortably.

'It has been decided,' said Mary, 'that until such time as we
trace your mother, you will live with me.'

There was a long silence while Alex stared at her in horror.

'Isn't that splendid news?' Gareth prompted. 'You really are a
very lucky boy!'

'You certainly are,' said Roland encouragingly. 'Miss Bellweather's offer is really most generous. What do you say to her,
eh?'

For a moment the boy sat stunned and silent, staring at her with
huge eyes. 'I dunno,' he stammered at last.

'"Don't know",' said Mary, 'not "dunno". You have a lot to
learn, Alex, but you are an intelligent boy and I'm sure you will
learn new ways.'

The last two words had a fearful ring to them, Alex thought,
and he summoned up all his courage. 'I want to go home to Ma,'
he said.

Mary's fork hovered half-way between the plate and her lips. 'Alex,' she said gently, 'your mother isn't at your home. We don't know where she is at the moment and we can't let you go back to an empty house.'

'My Ma will be there,' he insisted.

'She's *not* there, Alex,' said Roland. 'We have been to the house and there is nobody there.'

'Who's been to the house?' Alex demanded. 'You haven't – you haven't been anywhere!'

'The police, Alex,' said Mary. 'We asked them to make enquiries to see if your mother was at home, but she's not there.'

Gareth leaned across the table. 'Look, Alex, your mother has disappeared. We don't think any harm has come to her and she's probably with the Hearns, but we can't find them, either. So what are we to do with you, if there's nobody to care for you?'

'She'll be back,' he said, a note of rising desperation in his voice.

'Of course she will,' said Mary, 'and when she does come back, then you will go home to her.'

'Miss Bellweather,' said Roland, emptying the salt and pepper out of his glass, 'is only trying to help you by offering you a home until your mother returns. The hop-picking will be over at the end of next week and then what will you do? Have you got the fare back to London? Have you got money to buy food when you get there? Have you got a key?'

Alexander fought down rising panic. He had none of these things. They were right – if his mother did not reappear, he had nowhere to go. He stared fixedly at the plate, his food untouched. Without glancing up, he knew the others were exchanging disappointed looks, but he would not – could not – go to live in a strange house with a strange woman, especially one who made him wash frequently and insisted on 'don't know' instead of 'dunno'.

'You can go to a new school,' said Mary, 'and the first thing we will do when we get back to London is buy you some new clothes. How would you like that? A pair of boots, socks, trousers, maybe a Norfolk jacket?'

He shook his head dumbly.

'You think it over, young man,' said Gareth, 'and you will realize how lucky you are. It's a marvellous opportunity for you. Most boys would give anything to be in your shoes.'

Alex stared at him. The phrase 'Mary's little lamb' rang in his ears.

'I wanna go home,' he said, 'to me Ma.'

'You *will* go home,' said Mary, 'as soon as your mother comes back. It is not our fault that she has gone away and we are doing the best we can for you.'

The knowledge that she spoke the truth did not help him.

'Now, eat up,' she said. 'We've got to put some flesh on those bones of yours – fatten you up a bit, like a pig for the market!' She laughed to show that this was meant as a joke, but his scowl deepened.

Listlessly, he plunged his fork into a piece of meat, then put it into his mouth and sucked the juice from it noisily. He looked up at Mary daring her to correct him, and Gareth winked at him.

'Miss Bellweather's a very good cook,' he said in a loud stage whisper from behind his hand. 'You like food, don't you?'

Alex nodded. 'Ma can cook,' he said.

'Of course she can,' said Roland. 'I'm sure she is a very good cook and when she comes home you will go back to her and she will cook your dinner, but in the meantime you will be in good hands and well cared for.'

Alex swallowed the meat in one gulp and stabbed a piece of potato so violently that the gravy splashed over the side of the plate and on to the table. With an effort, Mary said nothing.

'Have you got a dog?' he asked.

'No, I haven't,' said Mary.

'A cat?'

'No, nor a cat either, I'm afraid.'

He raised his eyebrows in what he hoped was a look of great disgust.

'But I have a pony,' she told him. 'Do you like horses?'

The first gleam of interest showed in Alex's eyes as he nodded.

'There you are, then!' said Gareth. 'I'm sure Miss Bellweather would let you help to look after the pony – have a ride on it, maybe?'

Alex glanced at her and she nodded. 'I should think so,' she said. 'If you like riding, you might also take riding lessons.'

His mouth fell open at this glittering prospect and Mary, seeing his expression change, continued eagerly. 'There is a riding school not far from my home. We might arrange for you to have regular lessons. Then we would have to buy you some riding gear . . .'

Alex swallowed the potato and followed this up with a piece of carrot and some more meat. He did not splash gravy over the plate, nor suck noisily at his food. His mind was racing.

'And a whip?' he asked.

They laughed.

'A riding crop,' Mary told him. 'Yes, I suppose a riding crop would suit you very well.'

He wavered visibly.

'I think you are beginning to see reason,' said Roland. 'That's splendid. So you'll go back to London on Saturday with—'

'Saturday? The hopping won't be over by Saturday,' interrupted Alex.

'No,' said Mary, 'but I'm not staying down here for the whole month. A friend is coming down to take my place and we shall go back on Saturday. You're not enjoying it very much anyway, are you?'

He was silent, recognizing the truth of what she said.

'So that's settled,' said Roland, exchanging a triumphant glance with Mary over the top of the boy's bent head.

They waited, but Alexander did not demur.

'What do you say, then?' prompted Roland. 'What do you say to Miss Bellweather?'

'I dunno,' he said.

It occurred to Alex that perhaps he had given in too readily – had made it all too easy for them. Yet somehow it had happened and he had been swept away by a small tide of enthusiasm without quite realizing what was going on. He was out of his depth and very confused, but it would only be until his mother came back and of course she would come back. She *must* come back – but in the meantime there would be horses to ride and he would carry a riding crop. They had promised. Well, almost. He looked around him warily, but no one had commented on the knives and forks or the salt and pepper. Perhaps it would be all right after all. He could try it and if it was unbearable, then he would run away. His face brightened at the thought.

'So what do you say to Miss Bellweather?' Roland repeated.

Alex looked from one face to the next, ending with Mary. He opened his mouth and suddenly a new thought struck him.

'My Pa!' he cried. 'What if my Pa comes home?'

'Oh, I don't think . . .' Mary stopped suddenly. 'If your father comes, then of course you will go home to be with him.'

She laughed and that made her look prettier. 'I am not kidnapping you, Alex,' she said. 'I'm just offering you a home until your mother or father come back, then *they* will look after you again. Please try to understand, it is for your own good and there is nothing to be afraid of.'

They all looked at him and waited. Deliberately he continued to eat his dinner. When only the gravy remained, he lifted the dish to his lips and drank it with a loud slurping sound. No one said a word. He put down the bowl and stared fixedly at it.

'Thank you,' he growled and with that Mary had to be content.

CHAPTER FOURTEEN

The four women looked up from their machining as the door opened and Mollie Pett walked in. They stared at her in astonishment, then Meg Wilson spoke.

'Crikey! Look what the cat's brought in! We never thought to see you again, Mollie Pett.'

Mollie had taken great pains with her appearance. She had patted colour into her cheeks with the tips of her fingers and arranged her bright red hair under the red straw hat as attractively as possible. Her gown was the old blue calico which they all knew well, but she wore a single rosebud pinned to one shoulder. There was a broad grin on her freckled face, but this was to hide her nervousness as she stood with her hands on her hips, surveying the room.

'Hasn't changed much, has it?' she said. 'I was hoping it would have.' The women laughed and Mollie realized with a sinking heart that there was a fourth woman in the room: a dark-haired stranger, noticeably pregnant, occupied the chair where she herself had sat for so long. Snotty introduced them.

'This is Jessie Brannigan,' she said, 'and that's Mollie Pett.'

'It's not the end of September yet,' said Dulcie. 'We thought you'd be away for the whole month.'

Mollie gave a slight toss of her head. 'So did I,' she said, 'but things change, don't they? Something turned up, so off I went.'

'Off you went where?'

'Off I went with my new fella.'

'Go on!' cried Snotty. 'You've never got *another* fella, Mollie?'

'Well I have, so there!'

All work had stopped as the four women regarded her with growing interest. Mollie perched herself on one of the side tables and swung her leg, showing a provocatively slim ankle.

'Tell us about him, then, Mollie. You know you're dying to,' said Snotty.

'All in good time,' said Mollie. 'First tell me how things are with you lot.'

Dulcie shrugged. 'Same as ever they was – rotten,' she said. 'Sammy's always up the pub and Lena never stops nagging us. Jessie here's got your job.'

'So I see,' said Mollie. 'What made the old cow decide I wasn't coming back, then?'

'Gawd knows,' said Snotty. 'You know our Lena. She got it into her head that three of us wasn't producing enough work.'

Jessie looked embarrassed. 'I'm ever so sorry,' she said. 'I mean, I never knew it was your job. I never knew you wanted it back.'

'Never said I did want it back,' said Mollie with another toss of her head. 'Just called in to see how you are and say goodbye. I shall be joining my chap soon, you see. Amos his name is and he's a real good-looker. You'd love him, Meg, just your type!'

'How do you know what my type is?' Meg demanded.

'Well, if you like good-looking men that's generous with their money and a bit of all right in bed . . .' – the women giggled delightedly – 'well, then you'd like him,' Mollie finished.

'What colour hair's he got?' Meg asked.

'Very dark.'

'I like fair hair,' she said.

'Come off it!' said Mollie. 'You'd like anything you could get your hands on – dark, fair or bald.'

Jessie, a shy young woman, found this banter embarrassing and for a moment she resumed her machining. However, seeing three faces turned towards her in disbelief, she stopped hastily and said, 'I was just finishing that seam.'

'You still don't get it,' Dulcie told her. 'You only work when there's nothing else to do or when Lena's around.' She turned to Mollie. 'Jessie's due in a month's time.'

'Oh, lovely,' said Mollie.

The girl coloured slightly. 'But I still want the job, I'm afraid. It's my first baby, you see, and my Ma's going to look after it. We need the money, see.'

'She's got a husband,' Dulcie explained, 'but he's off work, sick with his lungs.'

'It's bronichal,' Jessie said earnestly. 'It's making him very weak and he keeps coughing up blood. The doctor says he's got to rest for a while.'

Her companions turned back towards Mollie.

'Go on then, Mollie, tell us what's been happening.'

'Getting married, are you, to this Amos?'

Mollie settled herself more comfortably on the table, wrapping her hands around her knees. 'We will, if he can. He'd marry me tomorrow if he could, but it's his family.'

'Ooer!' said Meg. 'Don't they like you or something?'

'They like me well enough, but I'm not one of them, you see.'

Snotty let out an excited shriek. 'He's Jewish!' she cried.

Mollie shook her head. 'He's a Romany,' she said, 'and they're—'

'Romany? What, like a gipsy?'

Mollie gave her a withering look. 'Not like a gipsy,' she said, 'he *is* a gipsy. Romanies are gipsies.'

'What?' said Dulcie. 'Does he live in one of them caravans pulled by a horse?'

'He will,' said Mollie, 'but at the moment he hasn't got a van of his own and he lives in a rod tent.'

They regarded her blankly and she laughed. 'Don't you lot know anything about gipsies?' she said. 'A rod tent is made of rods, with blankets and things over it – and very cosy it is too.'

Meg's face was a study in disbelief. 'You never mean you live in a tent, Mollie Pett?' she asked.

'And why not? Hundreds of Romanies live in tents until they can afford their own caravan. Those vans are very expensive. All that fancy painting and flowers and patterns and things. Not to mention the horse. Amos had a van once. He had a wife too, but she died in childbirth – oh, sorry, Jessie, I never meant to scare you.'

'I'm not scared,' said Jessie with an unconvincing shrug.

'Anyway,' said Mollie, 'he got into a lot of debt at the hospital trying to save his wife. So he had to sell the van and the horse, but he's a hard worker, my Amos, and before long he'll have enough money to buy another one. Then we should be able to get married, provided his family comes round – they're not too keen on Romanies marrying ordinary folk.'

There was a silence while they considered this dramatic turn-about in Mollie's life.

'So you haven't come to get your job back, then?' said Jessie.

' 'Course not! I don't need a job, do I? I mean, I've got Amos. I just came up to London to get me things, except the old cow's got rid of them all. Said I owed some rent.'

'What, all your furniture and everything?'

'The lot! Not that I had much, but the bed's gone and all the pots and pans. Wicked old whatsit! I could cheerfully strangle that old woman with my bare hands.'

'Where's Alex?' said Dulcie. 'Have you left him down the hop-fields?'

Mollie bit her lip, undecided as to how to present the next part of her story. 'He's being looked after down there,' she said. 'Me and Amos hopped it.'

'What, left, you mean?'

Mollie nodded. 'I was in a bit of bother,' she said. 'Well, a lot of us were in this bother, but I was the sort of ring-leader so I got all the blame. They turned a bit nasty, so Amos and me scarpered.'

'Tell us it properly, then,' said Meg. She glanced at the clock. 'And make it quick, or we'll have Lena back breathing down our necks and we've hardly done anything.'

Briefly Mollie told them what had happened, making the adventure as glamorous as possible. They listened in awed silence, impressed by her part in the pickers' protest.

'So I left Alex down there,' she concluded, 'with this friend of mine. He was having such a good time, bless him. I said to Amos, "I'll go back to London and get me things sorted out and pick up the two little-uns".'

'But are the police after you?' asked Dulcie.

' 'Course they're not. That was just to scare me. If they was after me, they'd have found me by now.'

'Here,' said Meg, 'you say you'll marry this Amos if his family agrees, but what about that soldier? And the other one?'

Mollie shrugged. 'I can't hang about waiting for them when I've had a better offer.'

'Well, I don't know,' said Dulcie, glancing round. 'I reckon you've fallen on your feet, Mollie Pett. Lucky you! There's the rest of us sweating our guts out for Sammy-bloody-Tulson while you go hopping and find yourself a nice husband.'

Mollie shrugged again. 'You've got to win sometimes,' she said.

Just then they heard the street door open and close.

'Lena!' cried Snotty and the four women took up the respective garments on which they were working while Mollie slid off the table and smoothed down her skirt.

'Well,' she said. 'I must be off. Love you and leave you! I'll give the lovely Lena a hallo-goodbye as we pass on the stairs.'

The others made their farewells and wished her luck. Then she

left the room and went downstairs, meeting Lena Tulson half-
way as she had expected.

'Well,' Lena began, 'didn't expect to—'

'Can't stop, I'm afraid,' said Mollie. 'Just popped by to see the
girls,' and she pushed past and made her way downstairs, humming cheerfully.

Once outside in the street however, her jauntiness deserted
her. Things were not quite as she had described and she was
vexed at the loss of her job, for Lena had promised not to replace
her. Amos was indeed hoping to marry her, but they were very
short of money and neither of them was able to work at present for
fear of discovery by the authorities. Mollie had come to London to
pawn her belongings, but now that Mrs Wallbridge had appropri-
ated them there was nothing to pawn. She had no money for her
return train fare and if she collected the two youngest children,
how would she feed and care for them with no roof over her head?
The regular sum of money which Mary had given her was no
longer forthcoming, as Mary did not know where she was.

Mollie paced the streets while her mind wrestled with the
problem. She had lived on her wits all her life and her present
position did not alarm her unduly. Eventually she knew she would
think of something and when at last the idea came to her, she gave
a satisfied grin of self-congratulation. Ten minutes later she was
knocking on the door of Mary Bellweather's house.

The housekeeper opened the door. 'Good gracious,' she said,
'it's Mollie what's-her-name, isn't it? Come in, dear.'

Mollie followed her into the hall, her story well-rehearsed.

'I've had the most dreadful bit of luck,' she began. 'Miss Mary
sent me up to London to make sure that my two little-uns were
quite well and happy . . .'

Mrs Markham smiled. 'Miss Mary is so thoughtful,' she said.
'That's just the sort of thing she would do. If she only took as
much care of herself as she does of other people. She does too
much, you know; she wears herself out.'

Mollie nodded. 'Yes, I know,' she agreed. 'She's a very good
person.'

'Oh she is, dear,' said Mrs Markham. 'A very good person –
and so was her dear mother. The Bellweathers are a sweet family.'

'The thing is,' said Mollie, 'that she bought me a return ticket
and the first thing that happened to me when I stepped off the
train was that some blighter stole my purse!'

The housekeeper's expression changed to one of horror. 'My dear!' she said. 'What a dreadful thing to happen. Mind you, I'm not surprised – London is not the place it used to be. There's a very rough element creeping in – I've said so for a long time. A criminal element, I mean dear. You would think that with all these new policemen they're giving us, things would be getting better, not worse.'

'You would,' Mollie agreed, 'but the trouble is that now I can't get back. I've seen that my little-uns are well, but I've no ticket for the train. I felt sure that if I came to you and explained the situation, you would be able to help me in some way.'

Mrs Markham's kindly face softened at once. 'Help you? Why of course I'll help you, dear,' she said. 'I expect you want to stay the night? I'll phone Miss Mary at once and—'

'No!' cried Mollie. 'Don't do that. I mean . . . she won't be at the house, you see, she'll be at the Mission tent. I thought perhaps if you could lend me the train fare home, I could catch the next train and be back before it gets dark. I don't want Miss Mary to worry about me.'

'Oh no, dear,' said Mrs Markham, 'we don't want to worry her, do we? I suppose that would be best. Now, let me think.'

Mollie did not want her to think for too long, so she glanced at the grandfather clock and said, 'Goodness, is that the time? Oh dear, I believe I shall miss the train.'

'Miss the train? Oh you mustn't do that, dear,' said the housekeeper. 'Perhaps I should lend you the money. Tell me how much you need, and then later on I'll ring Miss Mary and tell her you're on your way. How would that be?'

'That's very kind,' said Mollie. 'I knew you'd help me.'

'Well, of course I will, dear. I'll just fetch my purse.'

She returned a few moments later, still talking.

'I mean, what are we put on this earth for if not to help one another? Now, I think the train fare will be about two shillings, but I'm not really sure – I don't know about such things.' She laughed. 'I've not actually been on a train, you see. I don't care to travel very much. I have all I need within walking distance and if I want to visit my sister, I take the horse tram – it's only a threepenny ride and she's always so pleased to see me, but it is rather a strain – it's her hearing, you see.'

Mollie smiled brightly as she held out her hand.

'There's three shillings, dear,' said Mrs Markham, 'and don't you worry about it, because Miss Mary will repay me. I've given you a bit extra so that you can buy yourself something in the dining car if you're hungry. I think that's what Miss Mary would do if she were here.'

'I'm sure she would,' said Mollie, 'and thank you very much. I hope you won't think I'm rude if I hurry off, but I don't want to miss the train.'

'Oh no, dear, you mustn't do that whatever happens. Off you go then, and God bless you. Give my regards to Miss Mary when you see her.'

An hour later, Mollie was indeed on the train, but not heading for Wateringbury station. She had a ticket for Canterbury in her pocket and, together with the children, was on her way to rejoin Amos Hearn.

*

About a week later, Vinnie tapped on the door of the study and went in when Julian called. He was seated at the large mahogany desk which the Colonel had always used and glanced up irritably when Vinnie approached.

'Are you very busy?' she asked.

'Very! Did you want something?'

'No – at least, yes, I did want something. I wondered if we might walk in the garden together. We see so little of each other at the moment.'

'It's September,' he said. 'That is to be expected.'

'I suppose so,' she agreed.

She glanced down at the papers which covered his desk and Julian gave a gesture of helplessness.

'We won't be able to survive if things go on as they are,' he said. 'These damned foreign hops will ruin us. Something must be done about it. There is a meeting being held in London tomorrow and I think I shall go up for it. Several of the others are going from this area. Ned Berry will manage without me for one day, I'm quite sure.'

'Shall I come with you?' Vinnie suggested. 'I would enjoy a day in London and—'

But Julian was already shaking his head. 'That really wouldn't be suitable, Vinnie. Wives are not going. It is purely business – a private function being held in one of the Clubs and then lunch will be provided. Bilton can meet me from the train. I'll telephone and let you know what time I'll be arriving home.'

He fussed with the papers again and Vinnie crossed the room to stare out of the window for a few moments, then came back to sit down in an armchair near the desk.

'I would like to be a fly on the wall at Mary Bellweather's house,' she said. 'I think that young Alex will liven things up for her.'

'I'm sure she doesn't need livening up,' responded her husband. 'She is a well educated woman, intelligent, with a very comfortable income. Her life is obviously very full already.'

Vinnie bit back an angry retort. Julian frequently referred to the fact that Mary was both intelligent and well educated and she thought, justifiably, that this was meant as a slight to *her* – who presumably had none of these attributes. But she had not come to the study to quarrel. She had decided to tell her husband about the child she was carrying and had been awaiting a suitable opportunity. Mary had travelled home the previous day and, today being Sunday, now seemed as good a time as any. However, Julian's manner was not conducive to the imparting of such news; he appeared harassed, distracted by her presence and distinctly unfriendly. Vinnie wondered if he was missing Mary Bellweather, but it seemed an unworthy thought and she pushed it to the back of her mind.

'How long will you be with these papers?' she asked, keeping her voice calm with an effort. 'There is still an hour until dinner. Perhaps we could walk together for half an hour?'

He shook his head slightly. 'Now if you were suggesting a ride—' he said.

'Julian, don't!' said Vinnie. 'You know I'm nervous of horses – they are so big and they frighten me, you know they do. It's not that I don't want to come riding with you—'

He interrupted her. 'That reminds me,' he said, 'that I must have a word with Bilton about Arrowmint later on and make sure everything is satisfactory.' He scribbled a note on the pad in front of him and Vinnie thought that perhaps she should leave him to get on with his work. Or was that giving in too easily?

'Could we walk after dinner, then?' she asked.

'If you are so keen on a walk, why don't you go out and walk on your own,' he said. 'You have an hour before dinner, as you said.'

'It's not just the walking,' Vinnie protested. 'I wanted us to be together, that's all.'

'But why, for heaven's sake?'

'No particular reason. We just seem to see so little of each other and it's not only the hop-picking – you are always so busy.'

'I have work to do,' he reminded her. 'I have a farm to run, so of course I am always busy.'

'Too busy to spend any time with me?' cried Vinnie. In spite of her efforts, her voice rose slightly and Julian's irritation increased.

'Look, Vinnie,' he said, 'I have a farm to manage and you have a household to run, so we are both busy people. We see each other from time to time, we eat together, we sleep together. You can't expect me to live in your pocket.'

'But we're man and wife,' Vinnie protested, 'and I don't—'

'Yes, we are man and wife,' he said and the tone of his voice indicated to Vinnie that he did not relish the thought much. She felt a terrible coldness – it was fear, and she found herself wishing for the hundredth time that she was not pregnant.

'Julian, please don't let—'

'Vinnie, I am busy – you can see that for yourself. This is the busiest month of the whole year. Now, will you please let me attend to these papers?'

She rose to her feet. 'Will you walk with me tomorrow evening, then?' she suggested. She had, it seemed, gone too far and would have to postpone telling him about the coming baby.

'Oh, for heaven's sake!' he exploded. 'How do I know how much time I shall have tomorrow evening? Do be reasonable. Surely you can amuse yourself without needing me by your side? I told you, I am a busy man with other things to think about.'

'I only wanted to walk in the garden with you for a while,' said Vinnie. 'Why are you getting so angry? I just wanted us to be together.'

Julian sighed heavily. 'Why can't you leave well alone, Vinnie, before anything is said that either of us might regret? You come in and interrupt me when you see I have work to do. That is not considerate. For the last time, I have *no* time to walk in the garden today. And I shall not have time to walk in the garden tomorrow, because I shall probably be on my way back from London.'

'Oh yes,' said Vinnie. 'I had forgotten the meeting.'

'Now please, Vinnie,' he said, waving a hand towards the papers on his desk, 'I would like to finish these calculations in time to change and read *The Times* before dinner. Is that too much to ask?'

'No, of course not.'

He made her a small mocking bow and she felt her face flush. For a moment she hesitated, then half-ran out of the room without another word. Closing the door, she leaned back against it with her heart thumping. 'Oh God,' she thought, 'I am expecting his child. What *am* I to do?'

*

The following evening Vinnie closed the door to the Colonel's room and hurried down the stairs. She wore a warm travelling cloak over her gown, for it was past nine o'clock and the night was very cool with a clear sky that hinted at an early frost. Once out of the front door and down the steps, she made her way round the side of the house towards the stables. She was glad of something to do, for Julian had neither returned from London nor tele-phoned as promised and the feeling of misery within her grew hour by hour.

She went straight to Lancer's stall, where Tim Bilton awaited her return. He was deepening the layer of straw on which the horse stood. The animal was obviously in deep distress; his upper lip curled and from time to time he jerked his head upwards. Sensing her approach, Lancer turned towards her and she saw that his eyes rolled wildly, showing the whites.

'What did the Colonel have to say?' Tim asked.

'He agrees with you,' said Vinnie, 'that it's probably colic. He asked about the pulse and I told him what you said, then he wanted to know whether or not Lancer sweated.'

Tim broke open a new bale of straw, shook it free and tossed it into place. 'There's no cold sweat,' he said. 'It's colic all right, but at least we've caught it early. I've given him a drench – he wasn't too keen on taking it at first, but I got most of it down him. Then he rolled.'

'Poor old Lancer!' said Vinnie.

'Don't get too near him,' Tim advised. 'He'd not hurt you normally, but he's all over the place when the pain gets to him.'

Lancer's head jerked up and he raised one of his hind legs, making frantic efforts to strike his own belly.

'The Colonel said to try putting a warm cloth to his stomach,' said Vinnie.

'I've got a brew heating,' said Tim.

'A brew of what?'

'Hop tops.' For a moment his grim expression relaxed and he smiled at her. 'Hops aren't only good for beer, you know,' he said. 'They're good for all manner of things.'

At that moment the pain in the horse's stomach intensified and to Vinnie's horror the animal collapsed suddenly on to the straw and rolled over, kicking out wildly with his legs. She gave a gasp of concern.

'He's not dying, is he, Tim?'

'No, he's not dying,' he assured her.

'But Tim, what's happening to him?'

Tim shrugged. 'The drench is not relieving the pain,' he said. 'I might give him the rest of it with some powdered ginger. I kept a third of it back.'

Vinnie turned away, unable to bear the horse's suffering any longer. 'Isn't there something I can do to help?' she asked. 'We mustn't let anything happen to Lancer, I don't think the Colonel would get over the shock. He's so attached to this old horse.'

'I don't think so,' said Tim. 'I don't want you to get too near him while he's in this frantic state. If you were injured, the Colonel would never forgive me. Ah, Lancer's getting back on his feet again – the worst of that attack is over, thank the Lord. I'll have a go with the warm cloth now. You can stay if you want to, but please keep well clear.'

Vinnie moved well back and watched as Tim fetched a bucket of the warm water in which the hop tops had been boiled. He then soaked a large cloth in the brew, wrung it out and, murmuring soothingly, moved gradually closer to the horse until he was able to place the warm cloth against its belly. Lancer at first shied away, but Tim continued to coax and wheedle until at last he stood still and Tim was able to apply the comforting warmth. Vinnie was impressed by his patience with the fretful animal and secretly thankful that she had not been required to give assistance. Lancer's movements were still erratic and when he did move, he did so with surprising speed. More than once Tim had to leap out of the way to avoid being crushed against the side of the stall, but never once did his calm manner desert him.

As Vinnie leaned back against the stall door, her thoughts returned to Julian and Mary. Intuition told her that her husband would not be home until the following day. When she allowed herself to think about this, her emotions swung from fear to anger and back again to fear. How was she expected to react if he did not come home? If she made a scene, she would be dubbed hysterical. If she treated the matter as if it were of no concern, Julian would think her indifferent and might be encouraged to repeat the performance at some later date. With an effort, she forced her thoughts back to Lancer.

'The Colonel wants to know what brought on the attack,' she said.

Tim groaned. 'Oh Lord, I was afraid of that! The Colonel may be old but he's all there – begging your pardon.'

Finally he stepped back, taking the bucket with him.

'It's nearly cold,' he said. 'I'll have to heat it up again. I think it's eased him a bit; he's not jerking his head quite so much.'

'He's not rolling his eyes, either,' said Vinnie. They watched him for a moment, pleased to see that the horse did seem a little calmer.

'How *did* it happen?' Vinnie repeated.

'Well, it's my fault really,' Tim told her. 'I let Young Harry exercise him earlier today while I dealt with Arrowmint. I told him half an hour, but it was more like an hour and a quarter. It's not his fault – he thought he was doing the horse a favour. "Lancer was enjoying it so much", he told me. Next thing I know, he's watered him before Lancer had a chance to cool down and the poor beast got a bellyful of stone-cold water.' He shrugged. 'No good blaming Young Harry,' he said, 'because the horses are my responsibility. I should have warned him. Perhaps when you go back into the house you would ask the Colonel if he wants to see me. I'll explain and make my apologies, but right now I'd rather stay with Lancer.'

They stood in silence, watching the old horse for hopeful signs.

'He hasn't rolled over again yet,' said Vinnie.

'No, and he's got a nice deep layer of straw now so if he does roll he can't do himself any harm. He certainly does seem a little easier.' He smiled at Vinnie. 'You really shouldn't stay out here too long,' he said. 'You'll catch a chill. I don't want to have you on my conscience as well as the horse!'

She pushed herself away from the door and put a hand on the latch, hesitating. 'What exactly did my husband say to you,' she said, 'about meeting the train tonight?'

'That he would telephone you and tell you what train I was to meet.'

'When is the last train?' Vinnie asked, wishing she need not make her concern quite so obvious.

'I'm not sure – I don't think anyone's ever travelled on the last train. There is a train that leaves London about nine o'clock and gets here about ten-fifteen.'

'He can't have caught that,' said Vinnie, 'unless he didn't bother to telephone. Anyway, I can't ask you to meet the train with Lancer in this condition. The horse really shouldn't be left alone.'

'No, he shouldn't, but Young Harry could meet the train for you. I think he's still in the kitchen – you could ask him to stay on, maybe sleep the night. There's plenty of room in the hayloft and he could bed down with a few blankets.'

'That's a good idea, Tim,' she said. 'I'll go and have a word with him now.'

She was half-way up the front steps when the telephone rang and she reached it before Janet came hurrying along the passage from the kitchen.

'I'll take it, Janet,' she called and, willing herself to remain calm and dignified, she slowly lifted the receiver and gave her name.

'Vinnie, is that you?' There was a crackle somewhere on the line. 'It's Julian!'

She wanted to say, 'Hullo Julian,' but the words stuck in her throat.

'Vinnie, can you hear me?'

'Yes, Julian, I can hear you. I was worried about you.'

'There's no need,' his voice sounded unnaturally bright. 'I'm at Mary's, Mary Bellweather's.'

'Oh!' Her intuition had proved correct, yet the knowledge still came as a shock and she could think of nothing to say.

'Do you hear me, Vinnie? I said there is no need to worry. I'm at Mary Bellweather's.'

'Yes, I heard you. Why are you there, Julian?'

'We happened to meet in the square at St Martin's. She was taking young Alexander to fit him out with new togs. When you think of the size of London, it was quite a coincidence.' The little speech had been rehearsed, Vinnie knew.

'Young Alexander wanted to see the pigeons in Trafalgar Square,' Julian continued. Vinnie imagined the three of them laughing together, holding out their hands with food for the birds.

'He's a lively young lad,' Julian said heartily.

Vinnie's thoughts were chaotic. She knew she was expected to say something – anything to stop Julian's flow of excited, unlikely chatter.

'You wouldn't recognize him now in his new clothes,' Julian went on. 'He looks quite the little gentleman. Mary's so proud of him.'

He waited for her comments and the pause lengthened.

'Is she?' Vinnie said at last.

'Is she what?'

'Is she proud of him?'

'Yes, of course she is. She's been most generous to him.'

Vinnie swallowed, her mouth was dry. 'Which train will you be on?' she asked him and could almost feel his anxiety. She could visualize him standing in Mary's hallway, for she had visited the house several times herself in the past.

'I'm afraid I shall not be able to get back tonight,' he said, 'but Mary has kindly offered me a room.'

Vinnie closed her eyes. 'Stay calm,' she told herself. 'There is nothing you can do about what is happening except make a fool of yourself.'

'Alexander's here and Mrs Markham of course, so we won't be unchaperoned!' He laughed lightly. 'You don't mind, do you, Vinnie?' he said.

'Of course I mind.' Immediately she regretted her words, but it was too late.

'Oh Vinnie, do be reasonable,' he said. 'I should have to catch the late train and that would mean dragging Bilton all the way to Wateringbury in the middle of the night.'

'But I want you to come home, Julian,' she said desperately.

'I have just explained that it's not possible. I've missed the nine o'clock train. Suddenly I realized it was too late, the day just flew. After the pigeons it was Eros, and then Alex must look at the Thames. We were quite walked off our feet.'

Slowly Vinnie sat down on the small chair beside the table, staring at the receiver as though it was responsible for her confusion.

'I want you to come back, Julian. It's very important.'

'Vinnie! You're being unreasonable.'

'Am I?'

'Well, of course you are. I shall catch an early train home tomorrow and be there by eleven. Twelve at the latest. I'm sorry if it upsets you, but it's just one of those things. As I say, the day just flew by.'

Vinnie's mind was clearing a little. 'How was the meeting?' she asked suddenly.

'Meeting?'

'The meeting you went up to London to attend at the private Club. The meeting about the foreign hops.'

There was a deathly silence at the other end and Vinnie knew with a sickening certainty that he had not attended it. Maybe he had never intended to be there and the meeting had been merely an excuse to meet Mary in London. She felt a terrible cold sickness in her stomach.

'Oh, I nearly forgot,' he went on quickly. 'Guess who turned up here a few days ago? Mollie Pett! She had the audacity to borrow money from Mrs Markham with some cock-and-bull story about Mary buying her a train ticket which had been stolen.'

Vinnie did not register a word he said. 'Julian, please come home,' she said. 'I have something to tell you. Please come home tonight. It doesn't matter how late the train is; I have already spoken to Tim about it and Young Harry will meet you. At least he will if I catch him in time. I was just going to ask him—'·

'Something to tell me. What do you mean?'

'I can't tell you on the telephone, but it is important. Very important.'

'Don't be so mysterious, Vinnie. Just tell me what it is.'

'No, I won't.'

'Vinnie!' He sounded exasperated, as though dealing with an unruly child. 'Whatever has got into you this evening?'

'Julian, I want you to be here, because I want to tell you something and I want to see your face when I tell you.'

'Is it bad news, Vinnie?' he asked anxiously.

'No, it's good news.'

'Well, I'm sure it will keep until tomorrow morning. I will be home as early as I can and—'

'Stop it, Julian!' Vinnie cried. 'Stop pretending that it doesn't matter if you don't come home.' In her agitation, she had risen to her feet and her voice rose also.

'For God's sake, Vinnie!' She heard his tone sharpen. 'Keep your voice down unless you want the servants to hear you. There is no need to get so upset.'

Vinnie's fragile self-control deserted her suddenly. 'I won't keep my voice down,' she cried, 'and there is every need for me to get upset. You may be able to fool yourself, Julian, but you are not fooling me – not for one minute. You have done all this deliberately, I know you have and nothing you say will make me believe otherwise.'

'Stop this, Vinnie!' he snapped. 'Your imagination is running away with you.'

'Is it?' she cried. 'Then tell me all about the meeting. I want to know everything that happened. Who the speakers were, what they said, whether you spoke?'

'I didn't go to the damned meeting!'

Vinnie wondered miserably whether Mary was listening to Julian's side of the conversation and if so, how she was reacting.

'I know you didn't,' she told him. 'It was all lies. All of it, except that you *are* at Mary Bellweather's and you plan to spend the night there. I'm not blind, Julian, I know what's going on. I may be ignorant – oh, I know you think I am—'

'Vinnie, for heaven's sake. If you can't calm yourself, then there is no point in continuing this conversation. I don't know how poor Mary must be feeling—'

'Damn "poor Mary"!' Vinnie screamed. 'And damn you! I can be upset, I suppose, but we mustn't upset Mary. You're supposed to be married to *me*, Julian, not to Mary Bellweather.'

'Oh, for God's sake!' he said furiously. 'I've put up with enough of this nonsense.'

'Don't you dare put the telephone down on me,' cried Vinnie wildly. 'If you're so determined, then stay there with your precious Mary who is *so* generous and *so* beautiful and *so* intelligent. To hell with the pair of you and to hell with this child of yours that I'm carrying!'

Vinnie banged down the receiver and replaced the instrument on the table with hands that trembled. She stood staring at the telephone, refusing to allow a single tear to fall. Within seconds it rang again, but she made no move to answer it, letting it ring until Janet came running down the passage once more. When she saw Vinnie she stopped, puzzled.

'No one is to answer the phone,' Vinnie told her. 'Do you understand? No one.'

'But ma'am . . .'

'I mean it, Janet. It may ring all night for all I care but it is not to be answered.'

'No, ma'am.'

The telephone continued to ring and at last Mrs Tallant appeared at the end of the passage. 'Answer it then, Janet!' she called, not seeing Vinnie.

Janet looked appealingly at her mistress.

'I told her it is not to be answered,' Vinnie called. 'Not at all. Not by anyone.'

Mrs Tallant came along the passage towards them. 'But it might be something important, ma'am,' she ventured rashly.

'It is of no importance,' said Vinnie coldly. 'It is my husband.'

'Well!' said Mrs Tallant, affronted by Vinnie's attitude. 'If it rings like that all night, then none of us will get any sleep.'

'That's quite true,' said Vinnie, her face impassive.

She folded her arms, staring at the two women and willing them not to make an issue of the matter. Already she felt that she was behaving in a ridiculous way and that the present conversation would be repeated in the kitchen, and later in the village. Servants, no matter how good they were, were rarely discreet; it was a failing of human nature.

The noise stopped abruptly and the silence grew deafening. Janet looked at Mrs Tallant, who looked at Vinnie.

'What are you waiting for?' asked Vinnie.

'Nothing, ma'am,' said Janet and made herself scarce in the direction of the kitchen.

Mrs Tallant, however, stood her ground for a few moments longer, eyeing her mistress warily. Vinnie's gaze did not waver, however, and at last the housekeeper mumbled something and followed Janet down the passage. Vinnie drew a long shuddering breath and cursed. Mrs Tallant had almost reached the kitchen door when the phone began to ring again and she stopped and turned.

'No one is to answer it!' screamed Vinnie and with an indignant toss of her head, Mrs Tallant followed Janet into the kitchen.

Vinnie remained as though turned to stone, her arms still folded, her small chin jutting aggressively, her heart thumping. For what seemed an eternity, the phone trilled, but Vinnie made no move towards it and at last it stopped.

*

Mary waited in the drawing room, her heart like lead. Every word of Julian's had reached her through the door he had so carefully closed and she knew that Vinnie had seen through the pretence. A woman's intuition was not a thing to be overlooked, but Mary had hoped against hope that Julian would stay the night in an atmosphere of good will. That way her own conscience would have been clear. Obviously that was not now to be the case, although it might have been worse – Julian might have been persuaded to go back to

Teesbury. At least now she would have his company for a few hours longer.

For the first time Mary admitted to herself that she was much too fond of Vinnie's husband and that she had knowingly allowed this to happen. She had always admired him, but during the weekend house party at Foxearth her admiration had developed into a physical attraction which she should have suppressed. Her mother's strict moral values had not prepared her for such an eventuality – indeed, she had never believed it possible that she would ever find herself in such a predicament. Once it happened, however, she should have taken steps to see that she and Julian were not 'thrown together', but she had not done this. She had even fostered the relationship, finding ways to justify her actions, arguing that Julian had been attracted to her and had made no effort to disguise his feelings. Today they had shared a few brief hours of joy and Mary had been foolish enough to hope it was the first of many such meetings, but Vinnie had been too shrewd and had foreseen the danger and reacted promptly. Mary could not blame her for that, but she could – and did – wish she had not acted so quickly. Now the happy atmosphere was spoilt, the supposed innocence of the relationship tarnished and the heady excitement reduced to a more sober level.

She sighed heavily as she stood by the window, looking out into the street but seeing nothing. And what, she wondered, was the news Vinnie had spoken of? Was that just a lure to persuade him to return? Was that why he was so angry?

When Julian came back into the room she forced herself to turn towards him, hoping her bright smile had lost none of its sincerity.

'Did you get through?' she asked. 'I sometimes wonder how we managed before the telephone was invented.'

Julian looked into her eyes and read the distress. He swallowed, his throat suddenly dry.

'Oh – yes I did, thank you.' He stared at her and neither spoke. Then, frowning, he turned away and ran his fingers through his hair.

'I'm sorry about that,' he said, 'if you heard, that is. I shouldn't have lost my temper and I apologize.'

'There is no need,' said Mary. She wanted to say something casual, to behave naturally, but a suitable phrase eluded her. 'Are you able to stay overnight?' she asked at last, unable to bear the suspense of not knowing.

'I beg your pardon?'

He hadn't been listening, she realized, as she calmly repeated her question.

'Oh yes, of course. I told Vinnie I would be home in the morning.'

'Julian, did she mind very much?' She was trying to make it easier for him, but he seemed strangely preoccupied.

'She did rather,' he said. 'Vinnie seems in a strange mood, very jumpy and nervous. She hung up on me, actually. It's all very silly.'

He looked so wretched – yet there was also another emotion. Mary was at once puzzled and apprehensive.

'Well,' she said, keeping her voice level with an effort, 'we have a few more hours then. I'm so pleased. Are you, Julian?'

'Pleased?'

'That we have the rest of the evening together. That you don't have to rush away in a hansom to catch the last train. Now you can relax. It will do you good. You work too hard – oh, Julian!' she cried.

'I know, Mary. I'm so terribly sorry.'

'Sorry about what? My dear Julian, tell me what's happening. I'm lost!'

Startled, they faced each other as the unfamiliar endearment hung in the air between them, accusing them.

'No,' she whispered, 'I shouldn't have said that but . . . No, maybe it was right. I don't mind confessing that I think I love you, Julian. Oh I know it's hopeless – quite hopeless.'

'Mary, my poor dear girl! What have I done to you? Come here.' With a cry, Mary threw herself into his outstretched arms and he felt her tremble with the force of unshed tears.

'Mary, don't cry!' he begged. 'Oh, what a fool I've been – what a cruel stupid fool.'

'Don't say that! You are not any of those things,' she cried, looking up at him with anguished eyes. 'You are just a very nice person and I have been foolish enough to let myself love you. I am the stupid one – I know it can't ever be – nothing can come of it – but if I can just tell you then it is said and understood between us. Allow me that much, Julian! Will you, please, let me tell you just once that I love you? Oh dear God! I didn't mean to even tell you. I was going to be so noble, so very noble! Now I'm making a fool of myself, but does it matter, Julian?'

'Of course not. Nothing matters between . . .' he hesitated, 'between two people who are fond of each other.' He stroked her hair, confused by the conflicting emotions surging through him. To be holding Mary in his arms and hearing that she loved him, and at the same moment to know that Vinnie was expecting his child! He shook his head in amazement at the capriciousness of fate and Mary, sensing the movement, looked up at him enquiringly.

'What is it?' she asked. 'Why did you shake your head?'

Julian struggled between a desire to tell someone the wonderful news and a desire not to inflict further pain.

'It's nothing,' he told her, but his tone was unconvincing. He knew she would not accept his answer and moreover he wanted her to discover the truth. The realization that he could be so insensitive disappointed him. He did not want to dwell on self-knowledge and tried to ignore the prickings of his conscience, but as he looked down into the tear-stained face he experienced a pang of real remorse. It might have been, he told himself. They had drawn so close, he and Mary, that very probably – maybe even tonight – they would have become lovers. He had wanted this to happen, they had both wanted it, but now Vinnie's news had put an end to the matter. There was no doubt now in his mind: Mary might have given him her body and her love, but Vinnie was giving him his heart's desire.

'It's Vinnie,' he blurted out. 'She's going to have a child!' Now that the words were spoken and he had heard them, his delight seemed to surface even as he felt Mary tense in his arms. She kept her face hidden against his chest while Julian's delight grew into a warm glow of triumph. He had given Vinnie a child and she in turn would give him an heir. It would be a boy – they were going to have a son!

Gently he tilted Mary's face so that he could see her expression.

'Please wish us well,' he said. 'I couldn't bear it if you did not.'

'I wish you well. Yes, of course I do.' She spoke with an effort. 'I envy her, Julian, with all my heart, but she is your wife.'

'And you are not . . .' he shrugged, '. . . hurt?'

She lowered her eyes hastily. 'Oh yes, Julian, I am! I will not pretend I am not hurt because it will be written all over my face for anyone to see. But if it makes you happy and it's what you want . . .'

'Every man wants a son, Mary.'

'I know. I understand. And since I cannot be the one to give him to you, I should be glad that someone can. But I'm only human, Julian, and I'm so terribly jealous. Oh, I shall get over it,' she reassured him, 'and I'll come to the christening if I'm invited and I'll say and do all the right things.'

'You are so dear to me, Mary, I hate to hurt you. Will you forgive me for leading you into this unhappiness? I feel so terribly guilty.'

Mary walked away from him and sat down heavily in one of the armchairs. She gave a shaky laugh and sighed deeply. 'What an unexpected ending to our day,' she said. 'I think we are both rather overwhelmed. I know I am. I have surprised myself by my lack of discretion, but I am not sorry for that – at least, I don't think so. We have shocked each other, I suspect. I with my declaration and you with your news, but let us not waste the rest of our time together in regrets. It was such a wonderful day, you and me and Alexander together. Nothing can take today away. And I don't want to spoil your pleasure in the news about your child.' She swallowed. 'I am pleased for you, Julian and I congratulate you both. I shall write a cheerful note to Vinnie tomorrow. Now, how am I doing, Julian? Am I recovered, do you think? Am I good, kind Mary Bellweather again?'

If Julian detected the bitterness in the last few words, he made no comment. 'I hope,' he said, 'that you will always be one of my closest friends. I should hate to lose you from my life.'

'Oh, I shall be around, don't you worry.' She held out her hands and when he took them, pulled him down gently towards her and kissed the tip of his nose. 'That was a chaste kiss,' she said lightly, 'to thank you for being you. Now, shall we ask Mrs Markham to bring us some supper? These emotions are very exhausting and I think we should replenish our energies!'

He nodded and sat down opposite her on the other side of the fireplace.

'One day you will make someone a beautiful wife,' he said, 'and then it will be my turn to be envious.'

Very slowly Mary shook her head. 'No,' she whispered, 'I never shall marry. I am sure of that now, but in a strange way I think I have always known it.'

CHAPTER FIFTEEN

Edie came into the kitchen next morning, rubbing her eyes blearily. She had overslept and rather than be late for the fires, she had dressed hurriedly without washing and hoped that Mrs Tallant would not notice. Now she filled the kettle and stood it on top of the range, then opened up the doors and began to rake the embers with a piece of bent wire kept specifically for that purpose. Slowly her mind revolved around the events of the previous evening, but she was still unable to grasp exactly what had happened. She remembered that the telephone had rung for a very long time and that Mrs Tallant had said some sharp words about the mistress.

She carried the ashes out into the back-yard and emptied them into the dustbin, then collected some kindling wood which Young Harry had chopped the day before. It was also one of his jobs to bring in a scuttle full of coal ready for the fire lighting in the morning, but he had not done so and Edie muttered balefully under her breath. She took the previous day's *Daily Mail* and began to screw it into twists which she pushed into the grate. When the whole paper had been utilized she added the kindling wood, snapping some of it into smaller pieces across her knee. Then she took up the scuttle and shovel and went outside to the coal store to refill it.

It was not yet six o'clock and a heavy mist hung in the air. Edie shivered. There was something wrong with one of the horses too, she thought vaguely, and her father had said he would stay up all night if necessary. So much went on around her of which she was only dimly aware, and she was constantly trying to understand the behaviour of the rest of the household.

The master had not come home the previous evening and that, she knew, was something to do with the telephone being un-answered, but quite why that should be she was not sure. She struggled back inside with the coal and arranged a dozen pieces on top of the kindling wood. It was always a dozen when Edie laid the fire, no matter what size the lumps were. If they were small they would barely cover the wood. If they were large lumps, she would have to force in the eleventh and twelfth and then it would be awkward to close the front of the range. But somewhere in the long-distant past the number twelve had fixed itself in her mind as being required to light a fire successfully. Today she was lucky, for there were some small and some large. She hunted along the mantelpiece for the matches, secure in the knowledge that today the door of the range would close. Kneeling down in front of the fire, she set the paper alight and then gently closed the front. She remained in front of the range, staring at its flames, enjoying the crackle and curls of smoke. When at last she straightened up, there were two dirty patches on her apron where her knees had touched the floor.

'Oh, fish!' she muttered, rubbing ineffectually at the marks.

Tim Bilton had brought his daughter up to avoid bad language.

Edie stared round the kitchen, her mind suddenly vacant, waiting to remember what it was that she had to do next. The fire was lit, the kettle was on, but there was more to be done – other tasks to be completed before breakfast. Was it Tuesday or Wednesday, she wondered, and did it matter which? As she frowned in concentration her plain face became positively un-attractive with the effort. Hoping for a clue, she looked slowly round the kitchen. Pots and pans had been scoured clean the night before and were waiting to be used again. The kitchen table had been scrubbed. The row of bells over the door hung still and silent. Trays were stacked on the large dresser.

'The breakfast trays,' she muttered. 'That's it!'

It was Edie's job to prepare the trays with an early morning pot of tea for Mrs Tallant and Cook and breakfast trays for the Colonel and the master and mistress. She laid the four trays on the table and began to set each one with the necessary crockery and cutlery. She did them one at a time, despite the efforts of Cook who had pointed out many times that it was more efficient to do them together. Edie simply could not understand why this should be and since she was always unobserved at this particular task, was able to continue in her own sweet way. She always did the Colonel's first, chanting to herself as she ran backwards and forwards: 'Butter knife, other knife. Cup, saucer, sugar bowl, milk jug, teapot, butter dish.'

She counted the items on her fingers. Something was missing. She stared at the tray, then hopefully round the kitchen, waiting for inspiration.

'Marmalade!' came triumphantly.

She counted again and a look of panic crossed her face, for still something was missing.

She counted once more. 'Bread plate!'

At last Edie was satisfied and proudly she moved the first completed tray to the opposite end of the table, then went back to lay the three remaining trays. 'Mrs Tallant's,' she said to herself and began to collect what was necessary . . .

A little later she tapped on the door of Mrs Tallant's bedroom and when the housekeeper called 'Come in!' she opened the door, knelt to retrieve the tray and carried it into the room. Mrs Tallant was already sitting up in bed, her hands folded in her lap. Her hair was tied up in curling rags and her nightdress was of sprigged wincyette with a high neck and long sleeves.

'Good morning, Mrs Tallant,' Edie said dutifully.

'Good morning, Edie.'

The housekeeper stared at her as she set the tray down on the bedside table and her eyes narrowed. 'Have you washed your face this morning?'

'Yes, ma'am.'

'Well, it doesn't look like it to me.'

'I have, ma'am,' said Edie with exaggerated innocence.

'Smile,' said Mrs Tallant.

'What?'

'Don't say "What?", say "Pardon",' said Mrs Tallant. 'I said smile. Show me your teeth. I thought so, you haven't cleaned them and you haven't washed your face. Show me your hands. Look at those fingernails! How many times do I have to tell you, Edie Bilton? There's coal dust all over your fingers. I've told you over and over again. You wash properly when you get up and then you wash your hands again when you've laid the fire. You really are a lazy girl, there's no other word for it! I shall be downstairs myself in ten minutes and I shall expect to find you a lot cleaner. Is the fire alight?'

'Yes, ma'am.'

'The water heating?'

'Yes, ma'am.'

'And the trays?'

'They're ready, ma'am.'

'Good. You'd better take another jug of tea out to your father. If he's been in the stable all night with that dratted horse, no doubt he'll be ready for a hot drink. Do that as soon as you've taken up Cook's tray. Off you go and remember what I said. And Edie—'

'Yes, ma'am?'

'Have the eggs been washed?'

'Eggs, ma'am?'

'There's a basket of eggs inside the back door which Young Harry brought in. They'll need to be washed.'

'Yes, ma'am.'

Edie went downstairs to fetch Cook's tray, repeating the word 'eggs' so that hopefully she would not forget.

*

Half an hour later Edie was stirring porridge, Cook was boiling an egg and buttering bread for the Colonel's tray and Mrs Tallant was preparing a shopping list for the day's meals which Edie would then take down to Tupp's Store. Edie had washed and now wore a clean apron. The eggs had been washed, dried and put into two large basins which stood on the floor of the larder.

The back door opened and Tim Bilton came in with his empty jug.

'Very welcome that was,' he began, but was interrupted by Mrs Tallant.

'Wipe those boots before you come in, Tim, or else take them off and leave them outside.'

Janet, coming in to the kitchen from the hall door, wrinkled her nose in distaste.

'Don't tell him to take his boots off,' she protested. 'I've smelt his socks before. Worse than the stables, they are. Put me off my porridge, that will. You should change your socks more often!'

'Can't,' said Tim, wiping his boots laboriously on the mat. 'Only got one pair without holes. I need a good woman to darn the others for me.'

'Well, don't look at me,' said Janet. 'You want to find yourself another wife!'

She had already roused and washed the Colonel and now

waited beside the breakfast tray for the last of the bread and butter.

'No brown bread?' she asked.

'No,' said Cook, 'I shall have to make some more later on today. I know the Colonel doesn't like white bread so much, but it can't be helped.'

Tim set the empty jug by the sink and sat down at the table, resting his elbows on it and lowering his head on to his hands.

'Is Lancer going to be all right?' Janet asked.

'Yes, he'll live. He's a wonderful animal; he's got the stamina of a lion.' He grinned at her. 'So don't you fancy darning my socks, then?'

'No, I don't. I've got enough darning of my own to do, thanks very much.'

'Not volunteering to be my wife, then?'

'Not bloomin' likely.'

Cook caught Tim's eye and winked. 'Be a different story if Mr Turner asked her, wouldn't it?'

Janet blushed and was lost for words. She had thought her adoration of Adam Turner had gone unnoticed and Cook's remark took her by surprise.

'Oh, I've seen the way you look at him,' said Cook, 'running to the window every time he goes past. It's Mr Turner this and Mr Turner that. You've got a soft spot for him, Janet, haven't you?'

'Of course she hasn't,' said Tim, coming to her rescue. 'She's always had a soft spot for me, though she won't admit it!'

'I have *not*,' said Janet, 'and what if I do like him? He's a good-looking man and he makes me laugh. Always larking about he is and never too busy to stop and chat. I'll be glad when he gets back from Margate or wherever he went.'

She picked up the tray, then set it down again. 'Edie, there's no teaspoon,' she called. 'Do you think the Colonel's going to stir the tea with his finger?'

Edie giggled and rushed to the cutlery drawer.

Tim grinned. 'How'd you like it, Edie, if Janet was to be my wife? She'd be your Ma then!'

'My Ma?'

'Well, your stepmother.'

Edie's face fell. 'I don't want no stepmother,' she began.

'Don't worry,' Janet told her, 'because if it's up to me, you won't be getting one. And if your father doesn't change his socks more often, he'll never find himself a new wife anyway.'

Before Tim could answer back she hurried out of the room, anxious that the Colonel's breakfast should reach him before it got cold.

As soon as the first rush of activity was over, they all settled at the table. Cook dished out large helpings of creamy porridge and they helped themselves to milk and sugar. There was a loaf of bread on the table, a dish of butter and a large pot of home-made marmalade. The huge teapot had been refilled. Inevitably the topic turned to the previous night's excitement.

'Well, what are we supposed to do if it rings this morning?' said Janet, blowing on her porridge. 'I don't know what all the fuss was about. I mean, if Master Julian had missed the last train—'

'Ah, but had he?' said Mrs Tallant. 'Or was he just pretending? There's something funny going on there.'

'Where?' said Edie. 'Something funny going on where?'

Nobody bothered to answer.

'It's the green-eyed monster,' said Cook thoughtfully. 'You mark my words!'

'This porridge is bloomin' hot!' said Tim.

'It's come from a hot place,' Cook snapped. 'You don't have to eat it so fast.'

'Well,' said Janet, 'I told you, didn't I, that night when I saw the master in Miss Bellweather's room. Real close together they were and he was that mad that I'd seen. Snapped my head right off.'

'The master and Mary Bellweather?' mused Mrs Tallant. 'Could be.'

'Well, I should hope not,' said Cook. 'They've only been married a few years. What is the world coming to? He's got a nice little wife, what more does he want?'

Janet shrugged. 'The King's got a nice little wife,' she said, 'but he's also got all his lady friends. He always has had – I've lost count of them all. There's Mrs Keppel and that millionaire's daughter—'

'Sarah Bernhardt,' put in Mrs Tallant.

'And the other one,' said Tim, 'Lady Mordaunt.'

Cook snorted again. 'Lady Mordaunt – but that was years ago,' she said, 'and nobody ever proved anything against him there.'

'That doesn't mean nothing happened,' Tim pointed out.

'Steady on with that sugar, Tim!' said Cook, 'if you put any more on, you'll have more sugar than porridge.'

'Well, I like it sweet,' said Tim.

'We can see that all right. Just leave some for someone else, that's all.'

Tim seized the sugar bowl and held it out. 'Any more sugar for anyone?' he mocked. 'Take it now while you've got the chance!'

'Mrs Kettle,' said Edie, trying to catch up with the conversation. 'Who's Mrs Kettle?'

'Not Kettle,' said Janet. 'Keppel – with a "p". Two "p"s, to be precise.'

Edie looked more confused than ever. 'It doesn't matter, love,' said Tim. 'Take no notice of them and eat up your porridge.'

At that moment the telephone began to ring.

'Who's going to answer it?' said Cook. 'Somebody must.'

'Don't look at me,' said Janet. 'I got a telling-off last night and I'm not going to risk another one. The mistress said it wasn't to be answered.'

'That was last night,' said Cook. 'She didn't say it wasn't to be answered this morning.'

Nobody knew what to do.

'I'm not going to answer it,' cried Edie. 'I won't answer it. You can't make me!'

'Oh, stop snivelling,' said Mrs Tallant. 'Nobody's asking you to answer it. You've never answered a telephone in your life and I'm sure you're not going to start now.'

'Well, who *is*?' cried Edie as the noise continued.

Mrs Tallant hesitated. 'If we do answer, it will be wrong, but if we don't, that will probably be wrong, too.'

'I'm not going,' said Janet. 'I had my orders straight from the mistress. "That phone is not to be answered", she told me.'

'Oh, this is ridiculous!' said Mrs Tallant. She pushed back her chair and hurried out of the kitchen and they all listened breathlessly to see what would happen, crowding together at the kitchen door. Just as the housekeeper reached the telephone, Vinnie appeared at the top of the stairs and Mrs Tallant drew back her hand.

'Should I answer it, madam, or not?' she asked.

'Yes, please.'

Vinnie wore a warm blue dressing-gown over her nightdress and as she came down the stairs she tied the belt securely.

'Good morning, sir . . . Yes sir . . . She's right here beside me, sir.'

Mrs Tallant handed the telephone to Vinnie in a way that conveyed her disapproval of the whole affair, then turned on her heel and stalked back to the kitchen.

Vinnie had slept very little. She had tossed and turned all night, beset by fears about Julian's relationship with Mary and regrets for her rash behaviour the night before. The sound of Julian's voice brought tears to her eyes and for a moment she could not answer.

'Vinnie? Is that you?'

She nodded.

'Vinnie, please speak to me,' he begged. 'I'm so terribly sorry about last night and so thrilled by your news. Vinnie, I want you to believe me. It was such marvellous news and I wanted to tell you how pleased I was – but of course you wouldn't answer the telephone and I really cannot blame you. Vinnie, please say something!'

'I'm here, Julian.'

'Vinnie, say you're not angry any more. I am so truly sorry. I want you to know that I love you, Vinnie, love you very much and the news about the baby has made me the happiest man in the world. You must believe that. Nothing else matters now – just you and me and our little son.'

'Or daughter?' said Vinnie.

'Son or daughter – it doesn't matter, Vinnie. I didn't sleep all night, I was so excited.'

'Where are you?' she asked cautiously.

'I'm at Mary's, but she's not here, Vinnie. She's serving breakfast to the poor. I don't know quite where, but she has just left the house and I couldn't wait to talk to you.'

'And are you coming home, Julian?'

'Of course I am! I've been an utter fool and I admit it. I'm coming home and I shall never leave you like this again. I want you to be happy, Vinnie. I shall make you happy and our child will make everything perfect.'

'Oh Julian, do you mean that?' Vinnie could hardly believe her good fortune.

'I mean it, Vinnie, with all my heart. Say that you love me and that you forgive me for last night.'

'I do forgive you, Julian.'

'I still can't believe it,' he said. 'I had given up hoping.'

'Julian? Did you tell Mary?'

He hesitated. 'Will you be angry if I say yes?' he asked. 'I didn't mean to tell her but I was so overjoyed and she could tell something had happened. In the end I just blurted it out.'

'What did she say?'

'She was pleased.' He hesitated between the second and third word.

'She wasn't!' said Vinnie. 'She was jealous! Mary Bellweather was jealous of me – she was, wasn't she Julian?'

'I think she was a little, but Vinnie, it doesn't matter now. Nothing matters but you and me and the baby. I'm going to the station in about ten minutes. I'm longing to see you. And Vinnie, I love you.'

'I love you, Julian,' said Vinnie joyously.

*

Julian arrived home soon after two o'clock and Vinnie flew down the steps to meet him, hardly able to believe the transformation that her news had wrought in him. As she ran into his arms she had the feeling that their marriage, apparently so near to disaster, was suddenly stronger than it had ever been.

'My dearest Vinnie! Oh, you clever girl!'

Vinnie gasped as his arms closed round her in a fierce embrace and he released her abruptly, a note of concern on his face.

'I'm sorry! Have I hurt you?' he cried. 'I'm so thoughtless.'

'I'm not hurt, Julian,' laughed Vinnie. 'It's no use looking at me like that – there will be nothing to see for ages yet.'

He looked at her with eyes that shone and Vinnie, remembering her temper the night before, was ashamed of what she had said.

'I didn't mean it, Julian,' she said. 'About the baby. When I said to hell with everything.'

'I know you didn't.' He held her at arm's length and studied her carefully.

'You haven't looked at me like that for a long time, Julian,' said Vinnie, 'as though you really love me. You looked at me that way when we went to the hopping supper, before we were married. Do you remember?' She sighed. 'Everything was like a wonderful dream to me that night. I've never forgotten it.'

Gently he drew her close and kissed her. 'Today is like a

wonderful dream to me,' he said. 'And tomorrow will be the same. And the next day!'

She laughed. 'It's really so important to you, isn't it? I didn't realize.'

'Every man wants a son,' he said. 'And it will be a son, I feel certain of it. I know it will be a boy. Oh Vinnie, I want to keep hugging you!'

With an arm round her waist, he led Vinnie into the house. They ordered some refreshment for him as he said he had been too excited to eat breakfast.

'Have you told my father?' he asked Vinnie. 'Do the servants know? And when will the baby be born?'

Vinnie sat beside him on the morning-room sofa and answered all his questions. No one else knew yet except the two of them and the doctor, she told him. The baby was due at the end of May, some time after the twentieth – the doctor could not be certain.

Julian did not take his eyes off Vinnie's face while she was speaking and she saw in them all the love she had craved for so long. A deep contentment filled her and the despair of the past months faded away, leaving only the bright future. For a moment she thought of poor Tom Bryce and his family and her own pleasure dimmed a little. It seemed unfair that they had lost everything and Vinnie had gained a child and a loving husband. But Clive had said that life was unfair and she had certainly had her share of trouble. There was no point in grieving over past mistakes; she must seize this new opportunity with both hands.

'We must prepare the nursery,' said Julian. He had wanted to do so ever since their marriage but Vinnie had objected, believing it to be unlucky. 'And we must write to Eva. A cousin for her little ones! She will be delighted for us.'

His enthusiasm was infectious and gradually all Vinnie's doubts were swept away and she began to experience some of his excitement. Janet brought tea and a plate of small beef sandwiches.

'You eat some, Vinnie,' Julian said. 'You must keep up your strength.'

'I'm not hungry,' she laughed.

'And I'm sure you should rest every day. Did the doctor not advise it?'

'Yes. For an hour or so in the afternoons.'

Julian frowned. 'I wonder if you should have a maid of your own now? Janet is too fully occupied with the Colonel to be much help and Edie would be no use. I think we must find someone else for you. A woman usually has her mother to lean on at such times, but you have neither mother nor mother-in-law. Or should we wait until the child is born and find a suitable nanny?'

Vinnie put a finger to his lips. 'So many decisions to be made! I'm quite overcome by it all. Some of them can wait a while, Julian, can't they?'

'Of course they can.' He relapsed into thought and then his eyes lit up again. 'The hopping supper!' he cried. 'We'll announce it at the hopping supper!'

The hopping supper was traditionally held on the last Saturday of the season after the pay-out. There would be free food and drink for the pickers and dancing until well into the night.

At Foxearth, however, this event was now followed by the Sunday Hopping Fair which Christina Lawrence had introduced several years earlier. For many of the hoppers, the month's hop-picking provided their only holiday and they were often reluctant to go back to London, delaying their departure in order to enjoy one more day of fresh air and relaxation in green and pleasant surroundings. The Hopping Fair thus provided harmless entertainment on the last day.

Vinnie looked at Julian in horror. 'Announce it? Oh no, Julian. Please don't.'

'But why not? I want the whole world to know. Don't you?'

'Not just yet,' she pleaded. 'Can't it be a secret between the two of us? Just for a little longer. Oh Julian, please don't announce it.'

To her relief he agreed, albeit reluctantly. It seemed that in his present mood he could refuse her nothing. She listened to him in amazement, amused by his earnestness yet touched by his concern. He was like a child with a new kitten, she thought – at once fascinated, gentle and over-protective. Suddenly he clapped his hand to the pocket of his jacket.

'Your present!' he exclaimed. 'I almost forgot.'

He pulled out a long slim box covered in dark blue leather and handed it to her. 'With all my love,' he said softly, 'and to thank you for my little son.'

Vinnie took the box and opened it. Inside, on a blue velvet setting, was a gold locket, finely engraved with a design of leaves and flowers.

'Oh Julian!' she gasped. 'It's beautiful. It's quite perfect. What can I say except "thank you" and that doesn't seem nearly enough.'

'You like it, then?' She nodded. 'Open it up, Vinnie.'

The locket was delicately hinged and sprang open at a touch. One side was empty, awaiting a photograph or a lock of hair. On the other side, the engraving read: 'For Lavinia; September 1901'. Vinnie stared at it for a long time, shocked without knowing why. Finally it came to her: it was the use of her full name. No one called her Lavinia, not even Julian. Yet that was what he wanted – a wife worthy of his name. Vinnie Harris should at last give way to Lavinia Lawrence. It would not be easy, but she would try as hard as she could to fulfil the role she was now called upon to play. Wife to Julian Lawrence and mother to his child.

'Lavinia,' she said, looking up into Julian's eager, handsome face. 'It sounds good. I've never been a Lavinia, have I? I'll make a special effort, I promise I will.'

'I love you the way you are,' he protested. 'Here, let me fasten it round your neck.'

He led her to the mirror and they stood together, Vinnie admiring the locket, Julian admiring his wife's shining eyes. Vinnie turned to him.

'I mean it, Julian; you will be astonished,' she said. 'I'll be everything you want me to be. I *will*! Don't smile that way, Julian! *Lavinia.* Yes, I like it. I will be a Lavinia from now on.'

*

The weather stayed fine for the fourth week and the picking continued without hindrance. The temperature rose to the seventies and the sunshine made everyone feel healthier and happier. The faggots dried out, the fires burnt well and the evening meals round the camp-fires were cheerful occasions, often ending in a sing-song. The roofs no longer leaked and the pickers slept well, many stuffing their pillows with handfuls of soporific hops. The prospects of the 'pay-out' provided a great incentive and, as the last day drew nearer, the pickers renewed their efforts to earn the last possible penny before it was too late. The money earned during September would have to provide fuel for their winter fires and warm clothes for the children.

'Pull no more bines!'

Ned Berry's voice echoed across the hop-gardens for the last time and the weary pickers straightened their backs and sighed with a mixture of relief and disappointment. It was all over for another year. The bins were measured out for the last time, tokens were given to the hoppers and the tally entered in the booker's ledger.

At seven o'clock sharp, the pay-out began and the hoppers queued patiently to collect their money. The value of each picker's accumulated tokens was checked against the ledger and the money owing was duly paid. Some families had earned three pounds or more and felt well satisfied with the fruits of their labours. The earlier complaints and ill-feeling had been forgotten and all were inspired with a spirit of comradeship in the satisfaction of a job well done.

The hopping supper was a great success and Vinnie watched proudly as Julian, standing on an upturned basket, made a brief farewell speech.

'It's been a difficult season,' he told them, 'but you have all worked hard under trying conditions and it has turned out better than we thought. Remember, we need you as much as you need us! I know some of you are going back on the late train tonight and some are staying another day. But one and all, we thank you sincerely for your help. Enjoy yourselves tonight and, God willing, we shall see you all again next year.'

Next day, soon after dawn, the small meadow began to fill with an assortment of booths and stands in readiness for the afternoon's fair. The hoppers' children watched fascinated as the Punch-and-Judy man erected his gaily striped 'theatre', and looked on from a respectful distance as the dancing bear was taken from his cage and tethered by a chain to a stake in the ground. While the children were thus engaged, their parents packed up their belongings – blankets, mattresses, cooking pots, crockery and cutlery. The former were rolled up and tied with string. Some would be stored at Foxearth in the barn until the following September, but these belonged to the families fortunate enough to own a spare set. The majority of families would load their belongings on to the waggons and accompany them to Wateringbury station to catch the late train back to London.

There was an air of melancholy about the proceedings, for the return to London meant an end to freedom and friendships and a resumption of the drab existence which was theirs for eleven months of the year. The fair made the day of departure a little brighter for all concerned. It began at three o'clock and by

half-past three the field echoed to the excited screams of the
children and the more sedate chatter of the adults. Julian was
organizing the night's transport, which as always threatened to be
insufficient. Every farm in the Weald of Kent needed extra
waggons and those with a cart or waggon for hire found themselves in great demand – so much so that they often promised to
be in two places at once, which led to a certain amount of
confusion. Vinnie therefore went down to the fair on her own at
three-thirty and, with Julian's approval, met the five Bryce children at the gate. She hugged them all and together they set off to
sample the heady delights of the fair.

The jangling of a barrel organ provided a raucous musical
background and its persistent cheerfulness soon brought a gleam
to the children's dull eyes. They went first to the Punch-and-Judy
show where Punch's boisterous humour quickly had them
laughing.

'Where's the baby? Mr Punch has stolen the baby!' squawked
Judy and the children roared a warning as the wicked crocodile
reared its ugly head behind her.

When the performance came to an end, Vinnie took them in
search of the 'spud man' who sold potatoes cooked in their jackets.

'Lovely 'ot spuds! Six for a penny! Warms your 'ands a treat!'

They all walked on, each tossing a hot potato from one hand to
the other, waiting for them to cool. Everywhere they went, the
hoppers smiled respectfully at Vinnie and many stopped to thank
her for their 'lovely holiday' and asked for reassurance that they
would be on the list the following September. It was a festive
atmosphere, tinged only with regret that their long-awaited
month in the country had finally ended. Only the good times
would be remembered when they went home. Vinnie was amazed
at their resilience and impressed by their generosity of spirit.
They came across Steven Pitt bargaining with the cane man,
and watched the proceedings with interest until he finally bought
a smart-looking cane with a handle carved in the shape of a duck's
head.

Vinnie steered the children past the stall where men crowded to
buy a pennyworth of gin and on past the pawnbroker's booth
where a few unthrifty souls were exchanging a saucepan or a
bundle of knives and forks.

'Roll up! Roll up, ladies and gentlemen! Let me make you an
offer you'd be foolish to refuse!'

They stopped before a large red-faced man who stood on an upturned soap box, bellowing through a home-made cardboard megaphone. His clothes were sober grey with the exception of a brightly checked waistcoat in red and green. 'An offer you won't hear anywhere else the length and breadth of the country,' he bellowed. 'I'm offering you – that's right, ladies and gents, come a little closer – I'm offering you not one, not two, but *three* bottles of my grandfather's famous elixir for the absurd price of tuppence. Tuppence only, ladies and gentlemen, for the most enervating effervescent tonic money can buy. My grandfather's recipe has been handed down from generation to generation and that's the gospel truth, may God strike me dead if I tell a lie! A concoction of herbs and roots, honey and the bark of certain trees. It gives you energy and it makes you sleep sweeter than a dormouse in a haystack. If you lack appetite, it will make you ravenous. If your stomach is delicate, it will settle it as calm as a millpond . . .'

Bertha looked up at Vinnie. 'Should we buy some for Ma? She can't sleep and she doesn't eat her dinner.'

Vinnie smiled. 'I think not,' she said. 'Your Ma is unhappy and a bottle of medicine won't cure her. She'll sleep and eat again by and by, so don't you fret yourself.'

A sweep passed them, his face and hands blackened, a bundle of brushes over his shoulders. Vinnie gave the children a halfpenny each so that they could shake hands with him for luck and he winked at each of them and raised his curly-brimmed bowler. A scissor man was at work in a corner of the field, turning the wheel with his foot and whistling tunelessly as he sharpened a carving knife and put a new edge on a pair of rusting scissors. A large cluster of balloons was apparently strolling around on two legs, much to the children's amusement, but as soon as Tommy held out a coin the balloons were raised to reveal the weaselly face of a young man. He wore a morose expression which did not alter throughout the prolonged transaction, during which time the children changed their minds several times about which colour balloon they wanted.

Finally they sat down on the grass and ate the potatoes which were leathery outside and fluffy inside, exactly as they ought to be. While they ate, they watched an elderly woman buy a pair of cardboard shoes from the 'totter'.

'You'll not find a better shoe for the money,' he assured her. Nor a worse one, thought Vinnie ruefully. Then a lavender lady approached them with a tray suspended from a strap round her neck. The boys were not interested and began to wrestle on the grass, but Vinnie and the girls jumped up to inspect the selection of lavender bags.

'Made them all myself, lovey,' the woman assured them. 'A full ounce of lavender in each of the big ones – nice for a drawer, they are – or there's a half-size bag to go under your pillow.' She smiled at Grace. 'You'll wake up smelling sweeter than a princess with one of these. I sleep with one under *my* pillow and see what it's done for me!'

There were several designs. Some were of gingham with lace edges and some were velvet, others were satin with a few small beads sewn on in a heart shape. Vinnie bought two large ones – one for Bertha to give to Rose and one for Grace to give to her grandmother – and the girls were well satisfied.

In the middle of the large crowd they found the dancing bear. The children loved it but Vinnie pitied the huge, lumbering creature. It stood up on its hind legs and held out its paws, as though dancing with an invisible partner. Small beady eyes glittered within the dense shaggy brown fur and neat teeth showed within the half-open jaws. As it swayed to and fro to the strains of a small fiddle, it reminded Vinnie of a drunken man in a long fur coat and she was glad when the children's interest waned and she could shepherd them away towards the pie stand. A long queue discouraged them from buying pies, despite the entreaties of 'Sweeney Todd' to change their minds with his gruesome promise that 'only the best people go into my pies!'

At last, after a long afternoon, Vinnie stumbled upon the fortune-teller's tent. She sent the children off to watch the men bowl for a live pig and waited until there was no one nearby. Then she slipped into the tent and smiled nervously at the small dark woman who sat at a card-table.

'Welcome, dearie. Don't be afraid.'

Vinnie began to say, 'Good afternoon' but changed her mind and, unable to think of a suitable response, sat down on the vacant chair and put down a penny on the green baize.

'What's it to be, dearie? The tarot, the crystal ball or your palm?'

Vinnie hesitated. 'The ball, please,' she whispered.

'The ball, dearie? A wise choice.' The woman removed a pack of cards from the table and drew the large glass ball towards her.

She was a small plump person of indeterminate age and looked to be of gipsy stock, with tangled dark hair which hung untidily to her shoulders. She wore a weird and wonderful garment of black satin decorated with a confusion of coloured ribbons and braids. Her podgy fingers glittered with rings of all shapes and sizes as she began to stroke the smooth surface of the glass with almost sinister movements. Vinnie found herself fingering her new locket, but hastily dropped her hands into her lap.

'There's something coming,' said the gipsy, 'a picture of a house. A very large house . . .' She looked at Vinnie for confirmation and she nodded. 'I see you in this house and I see an old man . . .' She has recognized me, thought Vinnie, disappointed. She knows who I am.

'An old, old man. You are with the old man. You are telling him something and he smiles . . .'

Vinnie was startled. No one could have told her about the child for no one knew. She was impressed. The woman peered intently into the glass sphere and her eyes narrowed suddenly. 'He's fading, the old man, but so slowly. He is waiting for something . . . something is happening – I can't quite see it. Ah, it's going, fading. No! It's changing. The picture's changing but you are still there. I see you quite clearly, with three children. You will have three lovely children . . . there is someone standing beside you. A tall dark man. A shadowy figure . . .'

Vinnie frowned, but made no comment. She wondered if Bertie had grown tall. Bertie's hair was darker than her own, she thought, although her memory of her brother was not at all clear.

'There is a bond between you,' the fortune teller continued. 'Ah, I'm losing it again. It's going. I can't keep the picture clear . . . But wait, dearie. I'll try again for you – give me time. Give me plenty of time . . . Yes, I see a journey over water. Does that mean anything, dearie?'

Vinnie shook her head.

'You have no friends in a far country? No relatives? It may be their journey to you, not yours to them.'

'My sister-in-law is in India,' said Vinnie, disappointed by the change of direction.

'Perhaps you will visit her.'

Vinnie said nothing, thinking it most unlikely but not wanting to contradict. The gipsy woman frowned suddenly.

'What is it?' Vinnie asked.

'Nothing at all. It's nothing of consequence.'

Vinnie fancied that the woman's tone was evasive. 'There *is* something!' she said. 'There's another penny in it for you if you tell me truly!'

A look of hesitation crossed the swarthy face. 'It's a parting,' she told Vinnie. 'A parting from someone you love.'

Vinnie stared at her. 'Someone I love? But who that I love? Can't you see? Is it a woman or a man?'

'A man.'

'Oh.' Vinnie wished she had not asked – unless the man was Adam Turner, who had parted from her recently. But she did not love Adam Turner. 'I don't think I understand,' she said.

'There is a child in your life. A boy. The son of a relative, perhaps. I see a quarrel. Much trouble.'

'Not my own child?'

'No, no, but close to you. I see the two of you as one. You blend into one. You are of the same flesh, yet different. I see the letter "L" – and an "N" – but nothing more. Do you understand?'

'That's his name? Do you mean his name begins with "L"?'

The woman shook her head. 'That I can't say. I only see those letters . . . Ah, now it's all fading. The power is going. It's going darker, darker into blackness. I'm sorry, dear, it's over now. Did you understand? Good. Good.'

Vinnie had not nodded her head, but the gipsy appeared to have lost interest in her. Reluctantly, she gave her the second penny, got to her feet and pushed back the rickety chair.

'Send in the next one,' said the gipsy and without raising her head, reached for the tarot cards and put them back on the baize-topped table.

Vinnie thanked her and went outside. There was no one else waiting, so she set off to find the children. Very little of the gipsy's prophecies made any sense to her and within minutes of finding the children their excitement had driven most of them out of her mind.

'I'm hungry,' said Jim. 'Can we have a Sweeney Todd pie, Vinnie?'

Vinnie adopted an expression of pretended horror which encouraged the other four children to echo Jim's request.

'They're made from the very best people,' Bertha reminded her with a sly grin. 'Oh, I *should* like to try one. Do say we can have a pie, Vinnie!'

Laughing, Vinnie looked down into the five little faces up-turned to hers and thought wretchedly of all the heartaches she had unwittingly caused them. But the past was over now and must be forgotten. The future was what mattered now, for everyone.

'A Sweeney Todd pie?' she said slowly. 'I don't see why not!' And she followed them as they ran shrieking and laughing across the grass.

CHAPTER SIXTEEN

In 1904 the hopping season at Foxearth was an exceptionally good one. There were plenty of good quality hops to pick and plenty of money to be made by the pickers. The weather was almost perfect and the whole month passed with a minimum of friction between farmer and pickers.

As usual, when the last of the pickers had returned to London the gardens took on a lifeless, depressed air. The local community, while professing to be relieved at their departure, missed the colourful crowd with their cheerful songs and good-natured ribaldry. It always took a week or two for the village to settle back into its quiet routine and for many more weeks the people continued to talk avidly about their visitors, eagerly reminiscing about any excitements which the 'invasion' had provoked. For the shop-keepers, their busiest and most profitable month of the year was over; now they could count their gains and set about redeeming from Foxearth the hundreds of brass hop tokens which had been used as currency throughout the past month.

The work in the hop-gardens did not end, however. If the hops were to produce another harvest in a year's time, there was a great deal to be done and a lot of the labour was provided by women. First, the hop-gardens were tidied up. The bins were folded and taken away in carts to be stacked in the large barn. The trampled and decaying hop bines which littered the ground where the bins had stood were cleared and uprooted hop-poles were stacked in pyramids around the edge of the gardens. Later they would be 'replanted' but that was men's work. Any poles that had rotted would be broken up for next September's firewood; to replace them, new chestnut poles would be prepared, each one stripped of its bark and shaped to a point.

The hop plants themselves would lie dormant until the mild weather of early spring encouraged the new shoots, but they also put out underground runners and these had to be firmly discouraged when the hops were 'dressed'. Sometimes the men did the job, but this year it fell to the lot of the women. They found it heavy work, but it paid reasonably well. Ned Berry showed them how to find each root stock and draw back the earth with a special three-pronged hoe to reveal the plant below. Then they must cut round each plant with a knife to sever the runners. Without this drastic form of pruning, the main plant would be weakened and subsidiary hops would spring up everywhere in hopeless confusion.

The ground between the rows was ploughed up by a horse-pulled plough and then the alley-bodge made the rounds, filled with ox dung purchased from Merryon Farm or with old decayed woollens bought from London, both of which enriched the soil.

The job the women hated most was burying cut potatoes to distract the dread wireworms from the vulnerable hop plants. Kneeling on the frosty ground was painful to their knees and the hard, cold earth tore their fingers. Other pests were controlled by spraying, which was also men's work, and various solutions were used including soft soap and even tobacco juice. Hop-tying was done when the young plants finally appeared above the ground and the women took bundles of rushes and tied the plants into a clock-wise spiral around the pole. Later, as the hops grew higher, they would tie them again.

Julian Lawrence, normally so engrossed with the management of the hop-garden, had another problem on his mind this year. Vinnie's third pregnancy was not going as smoothly as the others had done and he was beset with fears for her health and an unreasoning dread that the child would be affected. Her early nausea persisted and her appetite dwindled. She lost weight rapidly in spite of Cook's beef tea and barley gruel, and developed anaemia. In her weakened state her resistance was lowered and she fell prey to any infection that visited the household. Her continued ill-health alarmed her husband and nothing the doctor could say reassured him that Vinnie's child would be both healthy and normal. His apprehension affected Vinnie and consequently she found it hard to hide her own depression.

Julian's devotion to her was at once a joy and a burden for his constant attention – to the neglect of his other duties – worried her. Fortunately for their relationship, at the seventh month the nausea disappeared and Vinnie's condition took a dramatic, if belated, turn for the better. When, on December 6th, Vinnie's brief but severe labour ended, their second son was perfect, with a downy head of fine gold hair and strong lungs which he used immediately to such good effect that the entire household knew within sixty seconds that Edward John had taken his place among the Lawrences of Foxearth.

*

'Dear Bertie', wrote Vinnie, 'you will be pleased to know that we have another son, Edward John, who is a perfect pet and weighs seven pounds twelve ounces and has golden hair. A perfect Christmas present! Little Louise is no longer the baby of the family and smiles and tries to talk to him, but big brother James is not so sure and glares ferociously. I have told Doll (our nanny who is very sweet), that she must be especially kind to him, for jealousy can be quite terrible. I remember how I hated poor Em when you used to hold her in your arms all those years ago.

Julian is well and happy, but very busy, and I have my hands full as you can imagine. I think I told you when I last wrote that Adam is back with us again, having grown weary of Army life. He is proving very useful, for we now have two brood mares and Young Harry helps Bilton in the stable while Adam has taken over the gardening.

Poor Rose Bryce is recovering from Tom's death and I suppose their lives are getting back to normal – if life can ever be that when a husband and father is gone from it. It hardly seems possible that Tom has been gone for three years.

I'm sorry this is a short letter, but I know you will forgive me. Doll will be in soon to hand me my new little lad, who is always greedy for his milk. I am longing for you to see my three darlings. Do come home, please, and then we can meet Beatrice. I have promised the children an aunt and uncle and they are growing impatient.

In haste, but I love you none the less for that. Do take care, Bertie, and come home soon. I sometimes wonder if I will recognize you – or you me!

 Love to you both from all at Foxearth,

  Your loving sister,

   Vinnie'

With a sigh, she replaced the pen in the ink-well which stood on the bedside table and blew on the page to dry the writing. As she slipped it into an envelope, the bedroom door opened and Doll came in.

'I have written to my brother, Doll,' Vinnie told her. 'I couldn't wait to tell him about my lovely little Edward.'

She laid the letter on the table and held out her arms.

Doll plumped up Vinnie's pillows. She was a cheerful girl with mousy brown hair which she parted in the middle and pulled back into a bun. Her round homely face was usually creased into a smile and her pale brown eyes twinkled. She lifted the baby from his crib and carried him over to the bed.

'He's a good little mite,' said Vinnie. 'Not a peep out of him all morning. Just lies there with his eyes wide open. Not a bit like his sister!'

Doll smiled down at the baby in her arms, reluctant to relinquish him to his mother. 'You're a bonny little lad,' she told him. 'You don't bawl your head off, do you, like that sister of yours did. Oh, she was a one, she was!' She leaned forward and deposited the child in Vinnie's arms. 'Lovely skin, he's got,' she said. 'Better than the other two. Just like silk, his skin. Got a lovely gloss to it.' She watched as the baby's mouth closed over the nipple Vinnie offered. 'Just look at him suck! He must have been hungry and yet he didn't make even a peep. He's a grand lad, our little Teddy!'

Vinnie said, 'We're not to shorten his name, Doll, remember? Julian is most particular that he must be called Edward.'

'Yes, ma'am. Edward it shall be.'

She watched the child feed for a while longer, then busied herself with the crib, shaking all the bedding and restoring it to order. Vinnie wished that she would leave the room, for she enjoyed the quiet times alone with her little boy. However, she would not hurt Doll's feelings by suggesting it, for she valued the devoted nanny and would share the child when necessary. She smiled to herself at the girl's insistence that this last child was the paragon, for she recalled the same enthusiasm for each of the others. The girl completed the bed-making to her complete satisfaction, then looked around for some reason to delay her departure further. Standing in front of the full-length swing-mirror, she turned sideways and smoothed her skirts critically.

'I'm blowing up like a pig,' she said. 'You feed me too well, ma'am! Tight as a tick, this uniform. Look at that!' She patted her waistline. 'It's Cook's fault,' she went on. 'Every supper time it's buns – bath buns, currant buns, Victoria buns or some other sort of bun. I never got that at my last place and I'm not used to the temptation. Give in every time, I do!'

She laughed cheerfully and it was obvious that the prospect did not dismay her in the least. 'Mind you, ma'am, the Colonel approves. Bigger the better, he says. He can't abide skinny women. He's a cheeky man. Marvellous for his age.' She came over to the bed and her face softened. 'Takes it like a little gentleman,' she said. 'No grabbing with his hands. Do you remember Master James? Always had to be pummelling with his fists as though that way he'd get his milk faster. He was lovely, though. Oh, they're all lovely, bless them!' She straightened up. 'Well, this won't butter no parsnips, as they say. I'm going to take the other two out in their pram, now, down to the village, to take Cook's order into Tupp's. We'll be about an hour and a half. Anything you want from the store, ma'am?'

'No thank you, Doll. And you can bring the children up when you get back. I'll read them a story before they have their tea and they can see the baby again.'

'Very good, ma'am.'

When Doll had gone Vinnie breathed a sigh of relief and settled down to enjoy her new son. Looking down at his face she saw that his eyes were closed, either in ecstasy or the beginning of sleep. The latter would not do, she thought, and clucked to him to make him open his eyes. They remained closed, however, the lids meeting in a soft pink line, pencil thin; the short lashes gold and fine against his downy cheeks. The tiny ears were well shaped and lay flat to his head and the neat skull was covered in short upright hairs which framed his head in a yellow haze.

'Edward John,' she whispered, 'you are so beautiful.'

She eased him away from her breast and he made no protest, except a slight turn of the head towards the source of his nourishment. Laying him against her shoulder, she patted and rubbed his back.

There was a knock at the door and Edie hurried in with a letter in her hand.

'Oh ma'am, it's from India, ma'am, and Mrs Tallant said to run it up to you—'

'From India? Let me see. Oh, it's Eva's writing! Lay it on the table, Edie, and I'll read it as soon as I have finished with this young man.'

Edie hesitated, hoping to be the bearer of exciting news when she returned to the kitchen.

'Is it good news, ma'am?'

Vinnie smiled. 'I haven't read it yet, so I don't know, but no doubt if it is you will all hear of it later. Close the door quietly, please, when you go out.'

Still Edie hovered shyly, half-way to the door.

'What is it?' Vinnie asked.

'The baby, ma'am.'

'Oh, I see! Come and have a peep at him, and then you will have something to tell them in the kitchen.'

Eagerly Edie returned to the bedside and stood looking at the baby.

'It's a nice baby, ma'am.'

'Yes, I think so. I'm glad you like him.'

'I can have a baby when I'm wed, ma'am. Cook said I can.'

Vinnie was slightly taken aback.

'Er . . . yes. Of course you can.'

'But not until I'm wed. You're wed, ma'am, so you can have one. Good girls can't have them, Cook says, leastways not until they're wed.'

'No, that's quite right. Well, off you go then, Edie.'

As the girl left the room, Vinnie watched her with a pang of remorse. It had never occurred to her that poor simple Edie might yearn as other women do for the normal joys of life. Did she, as mistress of Foxearth, know or understand *any* of her staff? Did anyone really know or understand another human being? Vinnie hoped she was not more selfish than most.

*

The letter, when she finally read it, sent her into a state of almost delirious excitement. They were coming home! Eva, her husband Gerald and their three children were coming back to England and would arrive at Southampton at the end of April.

'. . . We shall miss all our good friends in India,' Eva had written, 'but look forward to seeing you and Julian and the children. We will rent a house somewhere between Teesbury and London, so that Gerald will be within reach of his London office and you and I can meet often and be of comfort to each other. The children are greatly excited at the prospect of meeting their two young cousins – or maybe by the time this letter reaches you, the cousins will be three in number! Gerald's promotion was long overdue (or so I tell him!) but none the less welcome for that and of course his salary is open for review. I am in hopes that we may live very comfortably on our return to England. My only grief is that I must leave our dear old ayah behind. The children adore her but she is adamant that she will not leave India, even while tears stream down her cheeks!

'Dearest Vinnie, you will scarcely recognize me. I am grown so careworn and the climate is not good for the skin. Gerald insists that I am still recognizable as Julian's sister, however. How will I find you and Julian I wonder? Please tell Papa how I long to see him again and to show him his grandsons. They must both start school as soon as we can place them somewhere suitable . . .'

Vinnie finished the letter and then rang the bell. Edie appeared and was gratified to be told the news. Doll, she informed Vinnie, was still out with the children and Janet was in the kitchen giving Cook a hand while the Colonel took a nap.

'Then give Janet the letter and she can read it to him when he wakens. Is the master back from Tonbridge yet?'

'No, ma'am.'

'Then I shall sleep for a while.'

In the kitchen Janet was making beef tea, constantly referring to the recipe for reassurance.

' "Lean meat free from gristle and bone",' she read. ' "Chop meat finely and put into basin with water." Done that. "Put basin in saucepan with water half-way up the side of basin." Right—' She did this with an air of great efficiency, ignoring Cook's amused expression. ' "Cover with a lid." ' She found a matching lid and settled it firmly on the pan. ' "Simmer for three hours and then strain through a sieve. When cold, remove fat from surface and reheat as required." ' She looked up from the book. 'Sounds all right. That's something I've never had, beef tea.'

'You've never been ill, that's why,' said Cook. 'But it's nourishing stuff. It will do the Colonel good.'

'I hope so,' said Janet. 'He worries me, looking so pale and—'

Janet suddenly became aware of Edie standing in the middle of the kitchen with a smug expression on her face.

'What's up with you?' Janet asked.

'Got a letter,' said Edie, producing it from behind her back like a magician. 'Hey! Give it back here!'

Janet had seized it from her fingers and was inspecting the postmark.

'It's from India!' she cried.

'You give that back,' Edie protested. 'I'm to show it to the Colonel.'

'Oh no you're not!' cried Janet. 'I'm the only one as gets to show things to the Colonel. You know that very well. What's it about?'

'Shan't tell you.' Edie's face assumed a sullen expression.

Ignoring her, Janet took out the folded sheets and began to read the letter aloud to the accompaniment of loud cheers.

'Miss Eva home at last!' cried Cook. 'Oh, that'll do the Colonel a power of good! Like a tonic, that'll be.'

Mrs Tallant was pleased too. 'Can you imagine Miss Eva with children of her own? And they won't be too far from Foxearth. Just a run on the train. Oh, the little boys will be able to come down and see the foals. Edie, run out to the stables and tell the menfolk the news . . .' She rounded on Janet suddenly. 'And keep an eye on that beef tea. It said simmer, not boil. You'll have the beef full of water. Move the pan off the heat a bit, girl. Good job you're not cook here, that's all I can say!'

Janet pulled a face, but she moved the pan as the housekeeper had directed. When Doll came back from the village store, they repeated the news for her benefit, although she had never known Eva and the news did not excite her as they had hoped. Then Janet decided the Colonel had probably woken from his sleep and took the letter upstairs to read to him.

'Well,' said Cook, 'that only leaves the master to tell. Soon we shall have the whole house in an uproar! A new baby and now Miss Eva's coming home. I hope nothing else happens. I don't think my poor old nerves could stand it!'

*

Mary Bellweather sat opposite the prison governor, a stern-faced woman of about forty-five. The weighty record book was open on the desk and Mary was looking at the black and white likeness. Above it was printed the words: 'Photograph of Prisoner'.

'Yes,' she said, 'that's definitely the same woman.'

She read the rest of the page – 'Particulars of Person convicted of an offence in the First Schedule of Habitual Criminals Act, 1869 . . . Name – Mollie Pett. Aliases – None. 27 years. Single.

Trade or Occupation – Machinist. Any distinguishing marks – Scar below right ear.'

Mollie Pett had been convicted of prostitution, housebreaking and theft and sentenced to six months' imprisonment.

'And you want to see her? You have authority?'

Mary handed a letter across the desk. The governor read it and returned it without further comment, then reached out and pressed a small dome-shaped bell on the window-sill beside the desk.

'This is her second stretch,' she said, 'and no doubt she'll be back for a third. You people mean well, I know, but there's not much you can do for women like her. They will always take the easy way out. What's the alternative? The workhouse isn't much better. The only difference is that at the workhouse they're free to leave and here they're not. Some of them in here come regularly every winter, to be sure of food and a roof over their heads. The more brazen of them admit it quite openly. It's a scandalous waste of public funds, but what's to be done? I certainly don't know the answer.'

A wardress arrived, keys jangling from her leather belt.

'Fetch number 7102 and tell her she has a visitor. Only allow them five minutes. Take Miss Bellweather to the visitors' room.'

'Yes, madam.'

She led Mary along the passage which smelled of polish and disinfectant and unlocked a door into a small room which smelled similar. A small table and chairs stood in the middle of the room and there was one small barred window high up in the wall.

'Wait here,' she said and disappeared, her footsteps echoing in the corridors until she turned the corner.

Mary sat down in one of the chairs and then stood up again. She was very nervous and kept clasping her hands together. When the door opened once more she stared in disbelief at the bedraggled woman who stood before her, a defiant scowl on her pretty face. Mollie wore a prison dress of rough grey cloth and a grey bonnet was tied over her hair. Her face was pinched and grey and her jaw tightly clenched. Ill-fitting shoes showed below her skirts.

'Mollie!' Mary gasped and then was angry with herself for her lack of control. 'It's me, Mary Bellweather,' she said.

'I know who you are. I'm not blind!'

The wardress said sharply, 'Speak with respect, 7102,' and Mollie's eyes hardened.

Hastily Mary said, 'I had a job to find you.'

'You needn't have bothered. I don't need to be found by the likes of you.'

The wardress made to protest again, but Mary caught her eye and shook her head.

'I'm sorry to find you in this sad state,' said Mary. 'Is there anything I can do for you?'

'Who are you? Bleeding fairy god-mother or something?' Mollie made no effort to hide her dislike. 'The only thing you can do for me is get me out or piss off.'

'That's enough, 7102! I won't warn you again. You'll go straight back to work.'

Mollie's eyes blazed with resentment. 'They call it work – I call it torture. Ever picked oakum, *Miss* Bellweather? This is what it does to your hands!' She held hers up and Mary could not repress a shudder as she saw the calloused palms and raw fingers. 'Or you might prefer the laundry. You'll sweat in there until the flesh drops off you and your lungs is wrecked by the steam.'

'I came about your son,' Mary began. 'Alexander. I—'

'I *do* know his *name*!'

'Of course you do. I'm sorry. I have been looking after him for you.'

'How very Christian of you!'

In spite of her good intentions, Mary felt her patience dwindling in the face of Mollie's hostility.

'You abandoned him, you recall?' she said icily. 'Three years is a long time. You didn't even bother to find out if he was in good hands.'

Mollie shrugged. 'I knew he'd be all right. He's a tough little brat.'

'And your two little girls. You left them, too, Mollie. Are they tough, too?'

'Oh, go to hell!'

Mary realized that she was allowing her personal feelings to show and made an effort to control herself.

'I wanted you to know that they are being cared for. I am providing for the little ones – that is, I make the Hearns an allowance. Alexander is well and I have not told him you are in this awful place. Oh, Mollie!' she burst out. 'How did you get yourself into this state? How can you bear it? You look so frightfully ill. How did it all happen?'

'I didn't have to try very hard,' Mollie snapped. 'Anyone can do it. You just hawk yourself on the streets for money and if you get no takers you smash a window, climb in and take whatever you can find. You could do it if you put your mind to it. Once you get in here they feed you slops twice a day and work you to bloody death. In no time at all you'd look just like me—' She mimicked Mary's voice: ' "Frightfully ill!" '

Mary swallowed. 'I just thought I would tell you your children are—' she began.

Mollie spat suddenly. 'Don't give me that!' she said. 'I know why you came. To see how low I'd fallen. That's it, isn't it? I can see by your face. To see how disgusting I am, so that you can tell yourself Alex is better off without his own mother. Well, maybe you're right! I can't look after him – can't even look after meself. Oh yes, if a good Christian lady like yourself is looking after him, why should I worry? You want him, you have him! Satisfied, now, are you? Have them all, for all I care—'

'Mollie, please don't! I only wanted—'

'You make me sick! You and all the others like you. Bloody do-gooders, so smug and pleased with yourselves. Now don't you come here again, d'you hear me?'

'But I want you to—'

'And don't get any fancy ideas about me, 'cos when I get out of here I shall go straight back on the streets. I've got something men'll pay me for and—'

The wardress intervened at last. 'That's enough! I warned you. You will go without your supper for that!'

'Supper?' Mollie shouted. 'It's not fit for pigs!' The wardress stepped forward and slapped her across the face.

Mary was horrified. 'Please!' she begged.

But the wardress had opened the door and now called for assistance. Another uniformed woman appeared and together they dragged Mollie, still shouting obscenities, from the room. Trembling desperately, Mary sat down and buried her head in her hands. Oh God, she prayed, don't let it be true! I came in good faith. I *did*! Dear God, let her be lying!

The wardress returned after a short interval. 'Don't distress yourself,' she told Mary. 'They all act up when they get visitors. They play on your sympathies. She's no good, that one, and there's plenty more like her. No moral fibre, women like that. Abandoned her kids, has she? It doesn't surprise me.'

Mary rose miserably to her feet. Her instinct was to escape from the dreadful place – to run from the atmosphere of harsh discipline and suffocating despair.

'You can't help her sort,' said the wardress. 'So don't let her upset you. They don't want to be helped – it's too much of an effort for them to change their ways. She won't live much beyond forty. They never do. She'll be riddled with disease in a few years, the way she's going on. Honestly, you're wasting your pity on a woman like that.'

Mary nodded dumbly as she followed her along the passage. At the end of it a door was unlocked to allow her through, then relocked behind her. The same process was repeated at the street-door. When at last she stepped out into the May sunshine, she felt her stomach heave with fear and misery. Running to the grass verge, she dropped to her knees and vomited, shaking and trembling. When she stood up at last, she was still shocked with a profound feeling of guilt and dismay. 'She won't live much beyond forty!' The words rang in her ears. How old was Mollie Pett now, she wondered. Twenty-five? Maybe more?

Oblivious of the anxious stares of passers-by, she smoothed her skirt and re-pinned her hat. Alexander would never be returned to that despicable creature, she vowed. 'Riddled with disease!' The wardress had not needed to name it – it was the scourge of London. She had a brief image of Mollie as she had first appeared at the hop-gardens at Foxearth, with the red straw hat perched jauntily on her ginger hair above the impudent freckled face. Three short years had brought about her downfall and the hoppers' midnight protest had been the beginning of it. Mary sighed, but there was no turning back the clock. Mollie's life had turned sour, but Alexander's would not go the same way. She, Mary Bellweather, would see to that.

She straightened her back and lifted her head. Thinking of Alexander made her hopeful again. He had been with her for three years and was a different boy. No longer sullen and aggressive, he had blossomed into an attractive lad with more intelligence than she had dared to hope. He attended a private school where he received extra coaching and on Saturdays they rode together on horses hired from a nearby stables, where he also had riding lessons. Mary had taken him to a concert at the

Albert Hall and to several art galleries. She read to him every evening and they went to church together on Sundays.

Mollie had said she did not want the boy back – could not look after him. 'If you want him, take him.' Mary made a sudden decision. She would not try to 'save' the unwilling Mollie – she would save her son instead. She began to stride purposefully across the grass. Without realizing it, Mary Bellweather had been looking for a 'cause'. In Alexander, she had found one.

*

While Vinnie and the new baby thrived, the preparations for Christmas went ahead as usual. Adam was sent into the wood in search of greenery and returned with armfuls of holly and ivy with which to decorate the house. Young Harry made a holly wreath for the front door and Janet added a cluster of red ribbons to it. A large Christmas tree was purchased and Janet, Edie and Doll set about decorating it with candles, paper flowers and silver balls. Cook, in the kitchen, had already begun to grumble about the enormity of her task, but nobody took her seriously for the major part of her work has been finished weeks earlier and the fruits of her labours – jars of mincemeat, potted bloaters, an enormous Christmas pudding and a huge iced cake – filled the larder. A turkey weighing seventeen pounds had been ordered from Tolsen's Fish and Game Market in the Pantiles in Tunbridge Wells and chestnuts, gathered in the autumn, would later be made into what Cook considered the only suitable sauce to be served with so handsome a bird.

Doll, with the help of young James, made coloured paper chains and these were draped in the children's nursery which she shared with them. Even the Colonel was drawn into the fun by Janet, who presented him with paper and pastels and insisted that he design a Christmas card for each of the Lawrence children. After his initial protests had fallen on deaf ears, he applied himself reluctantly to the task and finding to his surprise that he could draw tolerably well, he went on to make cards for the Bryce children also.

Only Julian remained slightly aloof from the preparations and seemed impervious to the growing excitement, excusing himself on the grounds that he still had an estate to manage and maintaining that since someone ought to remain sane, it might as well be him!

Of the three children, only James was really old enough to share in the festivities, but Edie enjoyed it in her childish way, asking repeatedly 'But what *are* charades? What do they do to you?', anticipating the favourite game with a mixture of dread and delight, for charades were the highlight of the Christmas Day activities and earnest and secret plans were being made for the event.

When at last Christmas Eve arrived, everyone breathed a sigh of relief. 'Anything that's been overlooked can jolly well stay that way!' declared Cook, 'for I've not an ounce of energy left. Lord only knows how I'm going to get through tomorrow without dropping in my tracks! Now, Edie, have you called Young Harry? I want him to fetch in a bit more coal – and Janet, what did you say the Colonel's asked for?'

'Milk jelly,' said Janet.

Cook puffed up with indignation. 'Milk jelly! On Christmas Eve? What does he take me for, eh? Milk jelly indeed! If he thinks I've got time to fiddle-faddle with milk jelly, he's got another think coming. You'd best tell him we're clean out of gelatine. Say it's all spoken for, for tomorrow's salmon mousse. He loves his salmon mousse, the Colonel does. First thing he asked me to make for him when I first came here, that was . . . Edie, have you called Young Harry yet? If you don't stir your stumps I'll—' She shook a fist at Edie, who hastily backed out of the kitchen and set off on her errand.

Then she returned to the problem of the Colonel's milk jelly. 'Just see if you can talk him out of it, there's a dear,' she said to Janet. 'Remind him that the carol singers will be here soon and he'll want them up to his room to sing – he won't want to be in the middle of a milk jelly.'

'I'll try,' said Janet.

'And remind him that "Fight the Good Fight" might be his favourite, but it is *not* a carol!'

Janet grinned. 'I shall never forget last year,' she giggled. 'The vicar's face! He thought the Colonel was pulling his leg!'

As she went out of the door, Cook called after her, 'There's a bit of junket left over from lunch. See if that'll suit.'

Adam and Young Harry came in, the former carrying an armful of logs, the latter a scuttle full of best coal.

'Into the dining room with that lot,' said Mrs Tallant, 'and then a bit of kindling for the kitchen so that we can make an early start in the morning.'

Ten minutes later they were bringing in the kindling when Julian came into the kitchen.

'They're here!' he told them. 'The carol singers, I mean. You are all invited up to the Colonel's room to hear them – and Cook, will you please bring up mulled wine for all of us to have when they're finished.'

'I will, sir. It's all ready. How many will it be for, then?'

He made a quick calculation, including all the staff, and said, 'Twenty two – no, twenty one, for Bilton won't leave the stables.'

They were soon assembled in the Colonel's bedroom where the members of the church choir, sweltering in their warm clothing, were waiting nervously to begin. Foxearth was the last house on their route and was well known for its hospitality. The vicar was at home with a sore throat, but the organist had taken his place and raised his baton for silence. The family gathered round the bed, the servants stood self-consciously at one end of the room while the choir, red-nosed from the cold wind, stood in rows at the other end with the tallest at the back. Doll had brought in James and Louise; and Vinnie sat on the foot of the Colonel's bed, well wrapped in furs and blankets. Julian stood beside her with tiny Edward in his arms, but as soon as the singing began the baby began to cry and Doll took him back to the nursery, secretly overjoyed to have him all to herself for half an hour.

The choir sang lustily, safe in the knowledge that they would need their voices no more that evening. 'Away in a Manger' followed 'The Holly and the Ivy' and then, at Vinnie's request, 'We Three Kings of Orient Are'. Then came a solo from the organist – a French carol – and they ended with 'Good King Wenceslas' to a great roar of appreciation and thunderous applause. Edie helped Cook bring up the mulled wine, mince pies and spice biscuits and the room soon echoed to the sound of chinking glasses and munching of food.

Adam Turner found himself next to Vinnie, while Julian was some distance away in conversation with the organist. He leaned down to her and raised his glass.

'To a beautiful hostess,' he whispered.

Vinnie looked up into his eyes, which were full of an admiration he was making no effort to disguise.

'Thank you,' she said.

'Bert really is a lucky blighter to have such a sister,' he went on.

'I envy him with all my heart and I shall tell him so when I see him.'

'And I'm lucky to have Bertie for a brother,' said Vinnie, a little flustered and hoping to divert the conversation to a less personal topic.

'There's no comparison,' laughed Adam. 'You are much prettier than Bert!' He lowered his voice a fraction. 'When he comes home and takes you in his arms, I shall be green with envy!'

'Oh!' Vinnie was so taken aback that she could think of nothing more positive to say. Adam was flirting with her in full view of her family and staff! The sheer effrontery of his behaviour took her breath away but roused her unwilling admiration. He leaned towards her, keeping a wary eye on Julian who still had his back to them.

'If you were unattached, I should throw myself at your feet,' he whispered, 'and declare my passion. "Marry me, Bert's sister," I'd say, "and I will be your slave for life".'

Seeing the slight alarm in Vinnie's eyes, he had modified his tone so that it was slightly self-mocking and as such could not be considered offensive or even presumptuous.

'I shall tell Bert,' he continued, 'that I lay the blame entirely at his door.'

'Blame?'

'For allowing you to marry Julian instead of me!'

Vinnie laughed. 'Oh Adam! Stop this nonsense.'

'Am I making you blush? Tut, tut! I'm a dreadful man, Bert's sister.'

'You certainly are!' she cried, but now that her initial nervousness had passed she was beginning to enjoy the harmless exchange – for that, she assured herself, was what it was. A little extravagant Christmas fun, nothing more. 'And stop calling me "Bert's sister". It sounds quite ridiculous.'

'Ah, but you haven't given me your answer, have you?'

'An answer to what? Have you asked me a question?'

Instantly his eyes were serious again. 'The question is, would you accept my proposal if you were free to do so?'

'Oh Adam, please!'

He raised his eyebrows. 'Please?' he repeated. 'What sort of answer is that, "Bert's sister"?'

His continual change of manner, first humorous and then intense, threw Vinnie into a state of confusion just as it was meant to do. She did not want to offend him, if he was joking; but neither did she wish to encourage him if he were not. Adam knew exactly what he was doing and was delighted to see the helpless expression in her eyes.

'Be my bride, "Bert's sister"!' he begged in a voice that oozed melodrama, 'and I will carry you away on a white charger to my castle at the top of the mountain—'

She relaxed into laughter as he broke off and she saw that Julian was coming towards them. He looked from Vinnie to Adam and was slightly disconcerted by his wife's animated expression and the hint of colour in her cheeks.

Vinnie, seeing this, laughed and said quickly, 'Rescue me, Julian, from this dreadful man! He is flattering me quite absurdly and I can only assume the mulled wine has rushed to his head!'

Julian smiled. 'All women should be flattered from time to time,' he said. 'Flatter away, Adam! It will do Vinnie good, I'm sure. I must confess I am rather neglectful of my duties in that respect.' He put an arm round Vinnie's shoulders with an air of studied possessiveness and, leaning forward, kissed her on the top of her head. 'Remind me, darling,' he said, 'to flatter you at least once a day. It seems to suit you very well.'

As Julian spoke his expression was disarming, but Adam was too wise to risk an open reprimand and with a light shrug made an excuse and crossed the room to talk to Janet. Vinnie and Julian watched them for a moment without speaking.

'He's a funny chap,' said Julian at last. 'Quite a charmer, I should imagine and yet he's never married. What did he have to say to you?'

'Just that he envied Bertie for having such a charming sister,' Vinnie told him. 'I expect he's spinning Janet the self-same story.'

'And Doll!'

'And Mrs Tallant,' said Vinnie.

Julian grinned. 'Steady on!' he said. 'I don't think he'd manage to charm Mrs Tallant. No man could do that.'

They saw Janet laugh as she looked up into Adam's face and Vinnie felt a pang of irritation that Julian had interrupted her own conversation with him. Then she suppressed the feeling. Adam probably was flattering Janet and no doubt the other women were treated to the same attentions. It was all harmless enough as long as no one took him seriously. She did not take him seriously for a moment, she assured herself, but if his attentions had roused even a spark of jealousy in Julian (and he *was* sitting beside her with his arm around her shoulders) then the incident had served a useful purpose and she would think no worse of Adam for it.

*

Christmas morning began with a light breakfast so that justice could be done later to the enormous lunch. At seven o'clock Doll helped James and Louise to investigate their stockings, which had been hung at the end of their beds the night before. Streamers, paper hats, mottoes, raisins and an orange were pulled out with squeals of delight from James and puzzled looks from Louise. In each stocking there was also a penny whistle, a carved wooden horse three inches high and a lollipop. The two children were then washed and dressed and ate their breakfast with Doll in the nursery. It was a Christmas without snow, so Doll would take them out for a walk later while the rest of the household – with the exception of Vinnie, the Colonel and Janet – would attend morning service at the church.

The household returned home, flushed and eager from their outing to find Doll and the children already ensconced beside the Christmas tree, eyeing the huge pile of presents which lay beneath it. Traditionally, the staff received their gifts first so that they could then retire to resume their various tasks. This ritual was duly carried out and Julian handed all the women a large and small present – a length of dress material and a small hand mirror in a wooden frame – while the men received a half-sovereign. The rest of the presents were then distributed and examined amid great excitement and to everyone's satisfaction, by which time the morning had flown and lunch was announced. It was the usual feast of turkey with chestnut sauce, sprouts, roast potatoes, carrots and parsnips, followed by Christmas pudding, brandy butter and cream. The mince pies were not touched because everyone was already full. The family then dispersed, some to doze in quiet corners of the house, others to go for a walk; this led through the hop-fields, down to the river, along to the bridge and back as far as the oast-house. While the family was thus employed, the household staff ate their lunch.

After the tea at six o'clock, the party proper began. The household staff joined the family in the drawing room and various games were played. Hunt the Slipper, Poor Puss and General

Post were firm favourites, but when they were over the real entertainment started with charades. These had been prepared beforehand with elaborate care and each word was acted out with great enthusiasm. Janet and Edie, dressed as society ladies with extravagant hats and old lace curtains for trains, 'minced' to and fro while Cook made a 'pie'. The Colonel, who had been brought downstairs, guessed it at once and then it was the turn of Young Harry, Adam and Doll. The former knelt before Doll, kissed her hand and was apparently asking for her hand in marriage.

'Propose!' cried Vinnie. 'Proposal.'

'Declare or Declaration,' suggested the Colonel.

The three actors shook their heads.

'Marriage?'

'No.'

'Adoration?'

'No.'

Poor Edie listened to these attempts with growing bewilderment. 'Will you marry me?' she suggested at last, eager to contribute, but was rewarded by peals of laughter.

'Only one word, Edie,' Vinnie explained. 'It's one word that will be part of a longer word.'

Edie studied the little tableau and said 'Knee.' There was more laughter. She began to enjoy the effect she was having and racked her brain for further words. 'Foot! Arm! Elbow!'

Adam cried, 'This isn't an anatomy class, Edie! It's a charade!'

'Charade!' cried Edie, ever hopeful. Finally Julian guessed 'Love' and half of the word was known. Adam then began to stagger about, clutching his stomach.

'Drunk?'

'Dying?'

'Poison?'

He shook his head and looked at Vinnie. 'Sick,' she said. 'Love-sick!'

He nodded and a great cheer went up for her success.

'Mrs Lavinia Lawrence!' cried Adam. 'You have won the prize.'

'Prize?' echoed Vinnie. 'Is there a prize, then?'

'But of course.' With a grin, Adam sprang forward, took a sprig of mistletoe from his pocket and held it over Vinnie's head. Before anyone could protest he had kissed her and once more her cheeks flamed. Afraid that his colleague had gone too far, Young Harry hastily began to laugh and applaud and the awkward moment was saved.

'Did I win a prize?' cried Edie. 'I said "Knee", Adam. Did I win?'

'Of course you did!' cried Vinnie. 'Give Edie her prize, Adam!' and to Edie's immense delight, she received for the first time in her life a loud kiss from a young man. Unfortunately the excitement proved too much for her and she burst into tears and was hustled away to the kitchen by Mrs Tallant to help prepare the supper.

So Christmas Day, 1904, drew slowly and happily to a close and around midnight Foxearth settled itself wearily for sleep.

Vinnie lay in Julian's arms in the large double bed and thought of Adam Turner. For a few brief moments she had felt like a young and carefree girl again, instead of a young matron with responsibilities. She tried to remember her youth, but her thoughts wandered as she hesitated on the edge of oblivion. Love-sick, she thought. She had been love-sick once. She had been infatuated with the slim fair son of Colonel Lawrence from the big house. Was that love, she wondered.

'Julian,' she murmured. 'Do you love me, Julian?'

'Mmm,' he answered sleepily.

She thought of Edward, her third child. One day he would marry. And Louise and James also. They would all marry and leave Foxearth and she would be alone with Julian. Love-sick, she pondered drowsily. Was it a good thing to be? Was Adam Turner love-sick? Did he really wish he could marry her or did he say that to all women?

'Julian, do you still love me?'

This time there was no reply and Vinnie felt abandoned and lonely. Did her husband still love her? Why did she need to ask such a question? Bert's sister . . . she smiled up into the darkness. It's all right, she consoled herself. You are safe here. You have given Julian three beautiful children. How could he not love you? Love you . . . Love-sick . . .

'Julian, I love you,' she whispered. 'Oh, please God, make it all right.'

And then her eyelids fluttered, her head rolled on the pillow and sleep claimed her.

*

The New Year was seen in with the usual optimism and celebrations. The first three months of 1905 were cold and there was some snow in February. April, however, held back its showers and the temperature rose to nearly sixty degrees. The doctor allowed Vinnie and Edward to venture out into the sunshine and thus she found herself one afternoon sitting in the high-backed basket chair with a heavy shawl over her shoulders and a fur tucked round her legs. Edward slept in the crib beside her as she lay back against the pillows, eyes closed, enjoying the early Spring sunshine. If only the harvest was a good one, she thought wistfully. The previous year had been successful, but already this year's hops were badly infested with wireworm despite the women's efforts. For the first time Foxearth was reducing the acreage under hops and Vinnie had not protested, being more aware with each passing year of the risks involved and bowing at last to Julian's superior judgement. Julian was unusually pessimistic and the threat of imported hops, still untaxed, gave rise to discontent bordering on anger. The Government was slow to act and there was widespread campaigning among the growers for positive action to draw attention to their desperate situation which was now almost out of control. Several more farmers in the Weald had gone over to fruit growing, one or two had gone out of business altogether. Vinnie knew that Julian was becoming increasingly involved with the more militant growers and could not visualize where it would all end.

But now the three children and the household management took up most of her energies and she was happy to leave farming matters to Julian. She had ceased agitating on behalf of the pickers, because it caused unwanted friction between herself and Julian and she knew that there was little spare money for costly new accommodation for the hoppers. If she had analysed her feelings, she would have admitted to a certain amount of guilt at thus 'betraying' the people whose meagre background she had once shared. But she did not enquire too deeply into the workings of her mind, preferring to concentrate on matters more directly her concern. Julian wanted it that way, she knew, and for the moment she was content to play out her new role.

The children were her greatest joy and Julian took second place – that much, at least, she admitted to herself. To some extent the children had come between them, dividing their areas of interest more sharply than before. Julian's protective period had given way

to one of acceptance. Vinnie could manage home and family
without his help; she was a good mother and the household ran,
on the surface at any rate, like oiled clockwork. He now knew that
she could conceive and give birth without too great a disruption of
the home, which left him free to concentrate his energies elsewhere. He spent very little time with the children, but he loved
them in his own undemonstrative way.

On the surface, they were a happily married couple. That,
thought Vinnie, is the impression Eva would form. Only to herself
would Vinnie acknowledge that their love-making was not all she
had hoped for. As the years passed the close, intimate moments
grew less frequent, but neither remarked upon it. Perhaps it was
the natural course of events. Had she expected too much? The
possibility that Julian was not the man for her was one she would
no longer consider. He had given her three beautiful children and
a secure home and she was grateful. Her life was immeasurably
richer than she had any right to expect and she gave thanks in her
prayers for her good fortune.

However, Vinnie wondered sometimes if she was the sort of
wife Julian wanted and if not, where did she fail him? She was
faithful, affectionate and she could entertain his friends without
causing him any embarrassment. She could be a Lavinia when
she made the effort, but more often than not she remained a
Vinnie. She had given him the sons he wanted and a daughter.
She was attractive and had kept her figure and knew that he
considered her to be a credit to him. Was that enough? Very
occasionally the thought of Mary Bellweather still rankled, but
now Mary was engrossed with young Alexander and there
appeared to be no room in her life for romance, although Vinnie
knew that William le Brun renewed his attentions from time to
time . . .

'It's good to see you out and about again.'

Vinnie opened her eyes to find Adam Turner beside her, a rake
in his hand. She smiled up at him, shielding her eyes with her
hands.

'It's nice to be here,' she told him. 'What do you think of my
little Edward? Isn't he beautiful?'

Adam leaned over the crib. 'He looks like a monkey,' he
grinned. 'They all do.'

'They don't!' cried Vinnie. 'At least, mine don't.'

'Let's hope he grows up with the Harris good looks.'

'Thank you, kind sir, although the Lawrences aren't exactly ugly.'

'A very handsome family,' he agreed. 'I'm longing for Bert to come home and see you all.'

To Vinnie's dismay, Bertie had written twelve months earlier to say that he had married one of the English nurses from the hospital and they would stay on in India for a 'year or two' before coming back to England. He wrote regularly and sent photographs of himself – wearing a rakish patch over his right eye – and his wife Beatrice; she was a tiny dark-haired girl with a serious expression. So far they had had no children. After her initial disappointment, Vinnie had eventually recovered from this shock but had never quite forgiven Beatrice, whom she secretly blamed for her brother's prolonged stay in India.

Now she sighed. 'If he ever does come home,' she said. 'He seems quite happy where he is.'

'He'll come back, you'll see.'

'You've been saying that for nearly two years now!' she reproached him.

'I don't like to see you so miserable,' said Adam.

Vinnie was surprised. 'Do I look miserable?' she asked.

'Sometimes, when Bert's name crops up. He's very important to you, isn't he?'

'He's all the family I've got left.'

'There, you see! Now your eyes have darkened. I hate to see them like that.'

Vinnie stared up into the good-natured face under its unruly mop of brown hair. She was flattered that he should notice the expression in her eyes. Now he was looking at her with a level gaze that was slightly disconcerting and Vinnie felt a small stirring of excitement. Abruptly his expression changed.

'I have the answer,' he cried. 'You are lacking a brother and I am lacking a sister. Why don't I take Bert's place until he gets home?'

'Take his place?' Vinnie's eyes widened.

'Yes. Look on *me* as a brother. If you want someone to laugh with, a shoulder to cry on, or whatever you need a brother for, I'm willing and able.' He snapped to attention and swung his right arm up in a salute. 'Volunteering for brotherly duties, ma'am!'

Vinnie began to laugh.

'Sir?' he said, assuming an injured expression, his hand still to his forehead.

'Oh Adam, stop it! You look so ridiculous. Put your arm down, for heaven's sake! Someone will see you.'

'Would it matter?' He dropped his arm. 'You take life too seriously, Vinnie. You should laugh more – it suits you.'

His gaze was frankly admiring and Vinnie found it exhilarating. 'If Bert was here, he'd tell you to laugh more, young Vinnie,' he told her. 'It's a great tonic. Keeps you young at heart.'

Vinnie protested. 'I'm not supposed to be young at heart. I'm supposed to be a sedate matron, mother of three.'

'Permission to disagree – sir! You should always be young at heart. Look at the Colonel – he's still game and he's getting on for ninety. We have some good laughs together. He can still enjoy a naughty joke; in fact he thrives on them! *And* remembers plenty of his own! We have to be careful Janet isn't hovering too near, though. I suspect she likes to take them back to the kitchen.'

Colonel Lawrence and Adam got on well together, both being what the Colonel described as 'true military men', and they spent many happy hours comparing notes on the army. Fortunately Janet also enjoyed the young man's company, otherwise she might have resented their friendship.

Vinnie hesitated. 'No one could ever take Bertie's place . . .' she began.

'I wouldn't dare to try,' said Adam. 'I merely offer myself as a proxy Bert until he comes back to you in person. I don't think he'd mind at all, do you? Probably appeal to his sense of humour.'

'Well then, I agree,' she said breathlessly, because it did seem for some reason to be a momentous decision. 'I appoint you Bertie-by-proxy.'

He dropped to one knee, letting the rake fall to the grass and with a flourish took off an imaginary hat. Vinnie made a pretence of knighting him and he replaced the hat and jumped to his feet.

'I vow undying brotherly love,' he said lightly, and before she realized what he was doing, he leaned forward and kissed the top of her head.

'Now I must do some gardening,' he said quickly. 'Even brothers have to earn an honest crust.'

And he strode away before she could think of a tactful protest. Her thoughts were still confused when Edie appeared a few minutes later with a tray set for two people and looked round in surprise.

'Where's Mr le Brun gone, ma'am?' she asked.

'Mr le Brun?' Vinnie exclaimed. 'What are you talking about – and who ordered refreshments?'

Edie looked at the tray as though seeing it for the first time, then she screwed up her face in concentration.

'He was here, ma'am,' she said at last. 'Mr le Brun was here. I showed him out into the garden and I asked him if he'd take some refreshment, like you always tell me to say, and he said "Yes" and Cook says to—'

'Edie, please! When was Mr le Brun here? I haven't seen him. Are you sure you didn't dream it all?'

The girl looked aggrieved. 'I'm quite sure, ma'am. At least, I think I am. He was here, ma'am, when you was kissing Adam Turner and Cook says to take tea and sandwiches for—'

'*Edie!*' Vinnie swallowed hard. 'What are you saying! I was *not* kissing Adam Turner. Do you understand? It was just a silly joke; it was not a real kiss.'

Edie looked at her helplessly. 'No, ma'am?'

Vinnie muttered 'Damnation!' under her breath. Clive le Brun had called and he, too had seen that foolish kiss. He had then left without speaking to her – it was obvious he thought the worst, she realized angrily. He had no right to make such a judgment on her without understanding the full facts. She did not want him to think badly of her and was mortified to discover how much she cared about his good opinion.

Edie set down the tray on the grass beside Vinnie, then changed her mind and picked it up again with an anxious look at Vinnie's face.

'Oh, leave it here!' cried Vinnie. 'And go away!' She sighed heavily. Why was life so difficult, she wondered.

The tray was set with a silver teapot, jug, sugar bowl and water jug and there were two tea plates and a plate of wafer-thin sandwiches. Vinnie opened one. Tongue. She put it into her mouth whole and began to pour herself a cup of tea, but just at that moment Edward opened his eyes and began to cry. Vinnie looked at him dispassionately for a moment.

'He's right,' she told him crossly. 'You do look like a monkey!'

CHAPTER SEVENTEEN

The salesman, a Mr Benjamin Todd, was very brisk. 'The Humberette, sir, is a fine motor, precision built to the highest specifications. We have sold four already – one in February and three in March – and hear nothing but praise from their owners. No complaints whatsoever. Inexpensive, lightweight – it's the smaller version of the Humber. A nice ladies' car, sir. Tubular chassis, you see, like the de Dion. Not much to choose between them, except that this is British made.'

Julian watched with some trepidation as the salesman, a middle-aged man with a Kitchener moustache, walked round the vehicle, slapping it affectionately from time to time. He paused to glance at Julian, weighing up his customer. Rightly deducing from Julian's expression that he knew nothing about motor cars, he continued with growing confidence.

'Take you anywhere, this will, sir. Five horse-power engine. Even take you up hills, this will. Don't be deceived by its size. It's got pull, sir. Imagine five horses and their combined pulling power. It's got all that under here!' He slapped the bonnet. 'For a lady friend, did you say?'

'No, no,' Julian corrected him. 'It's for my wife. A surprise present for her birthday next week. The fifteenth, in fact. I said your firm was recommended by a lady friend, a Miss Bellweather, who bought a car from you some years ago.'

The man shook his head. 'Don't recall the name, but never mind. So, it's a present for your wife? A most fortunate woman, if I may say so.'

'I hope she'll be pleased,' said Julian. 'She has been trying to convince me that we need a motor ever since she first saw Miss Bellweather's Wolseley.'

The salesman nodded. 'Well, the little Humberette will make a perfect gift,' he said. He took off his curly-brimmed bowler, smoothed his rapidly thinning hair and replaced his hat, giving it a final tap to settle it more precisely on his head. 'But you'll drive it, too, I take it, sir?' he asked.

'I imagine so, though I confess I have never been very enthusiastic about the sport.'

'Ah, but you will be, sir,' Mr Todd assured him. 'You will change your opinion as soon as you get behind the wheel. I guarantee it. The motor car is going to revolutionize travel. No doubt about it, sir. Oh, you may shake your head, but in ten years' time it will no longer be looked upon as a sport. Very soon now people will start to take the motor car seriously as a means of travel. Do you understand the combustion engine at all, sir?'

Julian shook his head. 'I thought I would hire a chauffeur to—'

Mr Todd raised a warning finger and wagged it at him. 'A chauffeur-*mechanic*, sir, if you'll allow me to offer a word of advice,' he said. 'A chauffeur will drive you around and teach your wife to drive. A chauffeur-mechanic will do both those things *and* he will understand the motor. He will know what to do if the car won't start and what to do if it stops. He will teach you all about the engine, how to maintain it, everything. Take my advice, sir, and don't rely on your local blacksmith or cycle-dealer. What they know about the refinements of a motor car could be written on this!' He held up a well-manicured thumbnail.

'I take your point,' said Julian.

'It would break your heart, sir, to see what the uninitiated will do to a decent motor. The things I've seen! But there – I could recommend a reliable young gentleman if you wish, but that comes later. First, we have to decide if this is the right motor car for you. The price – well, you could call it a round £131 and you won't find another motor to touch it at the price.'

Julian was impressed, both by the man's manner and the vehicle itself. He did not understand the intricacies of the coil ignition or column-mounted gear levers, but he liked the smooth grey leather upholstery, the sober green paintwork and the cycle-type wire wheels. He could imagine Vinnie driving it. He could even, with a stretch of the imagination, visualize himself at the wheel or bent knowledgeably over the engine, assisting the chauffeur-mechanic in a piece of delicate motor surgery.

'Sit in it, sir!' cried the salesman suddenly. 'Nothing like getting the feel of a motor, I always say.'

Julian climbed up gingerly and settled himself on the squeaky leather seat, and Mr Todd climbed in beside him. 'Now, you've got the single-spoke steering wheel, sir. Hood extra. Doors, well, they come on the dearer model but most people find them quite unnecessary. The mudguards protect you from road dirt, you see, and the ladies always wear veils against the dust. Motoring clothes are becoming quite fashionable already. Gauntlet gloves, a smart scarf. I like to see a smart man at the wheel of a motor. If you're going to do a thing, then do it properly, I say. Spend a few pounds extra and look the part.'

Julian nodded and he went on, 'No, you can't go far wrong with this little motor. The electric car may be quieter, but it hasn't got the range. The steamers? Well, who wants to spend thirty five minutes starting her up!' He shook his head fiercely. 'The Humberette is a joy to own. I tell you, sir, that the horse is on its way out. You mark my words! All we need now is decent roads for the motor car to run on.'

Julian nodded. 'Do you own a motor car?' he asked.

The salesman threw back his head and his booming laugh rang out. 'I should say I do!' he replied. 'The poor old horse is obsolete! I drive a twelve horse-power Lanchester, but I wouldn't recommend it for a beginner, or a lady motorist. For you, sir, the Humberette is the perfect choice.'

He saw from Julian's expression that the likelihood of a sale was imminent and knew better than to give his customer time to reconsider.

'You'd like a spin in it, no doubt? No trouble at all. We'll soon have it topped up with fuel . . .'

*

Two-and-a-half hours later Julian was seated beside Sebastian Smith, a young man of twenty-one years who was steering the Humberette through the congested streets of Peckham Rye, heading in the general direction of Maidstone. The drivers of horse-drawn traffic gave them as wide a berth as possible, not out of any feeling of courtesy but out of deference to their horses who, blinkered or otherwise, were liable to take fright when confronted by such unfamiliar and exceedingly noisy vehicles. It was a Saturday afternoon and the streets were thronged with horse-drawn vehicles of every size and description – some drawn by one or two horses, others by as many as six. Railway parcels vans, trams, buses and delivery vans all mingled with the fast private carriages and the slower waggons bringing in produce from the country. For pedestrians, crossing the road required both courage and determination. Crossing it safely was often achieved more by good luck than good management.

Sebastian did not make conversation with his new employer. In fact, he hardly registered Julian's presence beside him on the seat. He was still dazed by the extent of his good fortune. Mr Lawrence had hired him for one month to teach him and his wife to drive the motor, and to impart a working knowledge of the engine to Mr Lawrence. There was a possibility that the month might be extended by one or even two weeks. He would be lodged and fed and paid handsomely – all for the pleasure of driving and maintaining the beautiful Humberette! Great concentration was required to handle the motor while still enjoying the interested stares of passing pedestrians and the envy which he fancied he saw in the eyes of every other driver. He was also fighting a rising frustration, for the density of the traffic restricted their speed to a mere ten miles an hour whereas the promised top speed was twenty-five!

A light drizzle was falling, which made the going less comfortable than it might have been and blurred their goggles. The road was filthy. Soot from thousands of winter fires was brought down in the rain to mingle with the horse-dung which lay everywhere, and the resultant stinking slush was spattered over them in fine droplets by the hooves of every horse they passed. Julian clung on grimly as they swerved round corners, narrowly avoiding huge coal-carts and brewers' drays whose drivers swore volubly at them and shook their fists.

Policemen were controlling the traffic at various junctions and only when they were in sight did the Lawrences' new chauffeur-mechanic see fit to slow down, unwilling to risk a brush with the enforcers of law and order at such an early stage in his career. Julian glanced at him and was amazed to see the young man smiling broadly, while he himself felt uncomfortably damp and dirty and extremely apprehensive. The passing traffic towered over them, seeming likely to crush them at any moment. The Humberette, whatever else one might say in her favour, was certainly not large and was easily dwarfed by the giants of the road – even by the little horse-buses – which shared the highway with them.

Julian was beginning to think that his earlier opinion of motoring had been the correct one and wondered uneasily if he *had* done the right thing in buying Vinnie a motor car. No one in his right mind could pretend that present conditions were pleasurable or in any way comparable with the elegant comfort of a brougham. Even the train offered a more civilized way to travel. He, too, was conscious of the stares of passers-by but, unlike Sebastian Smith, saw only amusement in their eyes.

His companion leaned towards him and shouted above the din. 'We'll take the Maidstone road through Farningham and then go down Wrotham Hill and out through Mereworth.'

Julian nodded his approval. He took off his goggles, gave them a quick wipe with his handkerchief and then put them on again. The handkerchief was already very muddy and there was very little improvement in his visibility. He marvelled that Smith could see to drive, but he obviously could. It was obvious, too, that he was a capable driver; he managed the gear changes with dexterity and used the brakes in good time, so that apart from the inherent vibration and noise the movement was smooth enough.

'You'll have to watch her starting-handle,' Smith shouted. 'It turns *anti*-clockwise. Unusual, that. You just need to remember, that's all, or you'll hurt your wrist when you crank her . . .'

He sounded the horn suddenly, in order to alert a small grimy boy who was weaving his way erratically through the traffic. The boy made a rude gesture, at which Smith laughed. 'These wheels,' he continued, 'will give you two thousand miles! Incredible, isn't it?'

Julian shouted, 'Yes, it is.' He felt inadequate, like a child on its first day in a new school. The fact that this was an unfamiliar role added to his general discomfort.

'She'll need good maintenance,' Smith continued. 'Wipe down the paintwork after every trip. Repaint her after a twelvemonth. Clean the brass regularly – these lamps will come up a treat with a bit of polish. It's the acid. It's everywhere – in the air, in the road dirt. Eats away at a car. You'd be amazed.'

'Does it? Yes, I see,' Julian shouted back.

It seemed an age before the traffic began to thin and they left London behind. Julian breathed a sigh of relief as the streets gave way to country lanes and he recognized the outskirts of Farningham.

'The worst is over,' grinned Smith. 'How are you enjoying your first ride, Mr Lawrence?' He rushed on without waiting for an answer. 'Are you a competitive man, sir? You could compete in this motor, you know. Enter her in hill climbs. I could drive her for you, if you like. She'd do you credit, Mr Lawrence. Heart like a lion, this little motor!'

Julian could only nod. His relief was giving way to a feeling of nausea, brought on he suspected by the noise, smell and constant motion. He took off his goggles and laid them in his lap. They were tight around his head and the constriction was giving him a headache. Tiredly he rubbed his eyes, then closed them.

'How much further?' he asked.

'I'm not quite sure. Ten or fifteen miles, maybe. Are you all right, Mr Lawrence?'

'I'm tired, that's all.'

'Not car-sick, then? Some people do suffer that way, I'm told.'

'Do they? No, I think I'll be fine.'

Sebastian glanced at him with kindly concern. 'You look a bit pale, sir. We could stop if you like and give your legs a stretch?'

'No thank you. I'd rather we pressed on, if you don't mind.' Julian pulled out his watch. 'Nearly four-thirty. I'm longing to see Mrs Lawrence's face when we arrive.'

Smith's answer to this remark was drowned by the rattle of wheels and clatter of hooves as they were overtaken by a heavy army waggon, its load sheeted against the rain. As he drew level the driver grinned, shouted something unintelligible and waved his whip. Smith waved cheerfully back. At the same moment a dog-cart drawn by a small pony emerged unexpectedly from a side turning on the left. The pony, terrified by the sudden confrontation, reared in fright and the elderly lady driver lost control. Julian screamed a warning, but it was too late. The pony lunged to the left, swinging the cart directly in the motor's path and Smith, in turn, swung the car to the right in an effort to avoid them. There was a terrible, juddering crash as the little Humberette smashed into the rear wheel of the waggon and overturned, flinging Julian and Sebastian out on to the road.

For a moment all was pandemonium until the waggon driver, a young Army corporal, managed to rein in his four horses and scramble down. By a miracle he was unhurt, though badly shaken. Apart from the three vehicles involved in the accident, the road remained empty, so there was no immediate help at hand.

'Oh Christ!' muttered the corporal and, fearful of what he would find, he made his way round to the dog-cart which had turned over on its side. The pony had broken free and was cantering back along the lane from which they had just emerged. Incredibly, the elderly woman was sitting up in the road, nursing her left arm. Her hair was dishevelled and her clothes were dirty, but otherwise she appeared unharmed.

'My spectacles!' she told him. 'Look for my spectacles; they can't be far. And don't stare like that. I've broken my arm, that's all.'

The corporal blinked at her stupidly for a moment, unable to marshall his thoughts sufficiently to make any kind of reply. She was alive, he thought. That made two of them. It was very quiet though. Too quiet, thought the corporal as, with a sinking heart, he moved round to inspect the motor car and its occupants.

Sebastian Smith was dead. The rear wheel of the army waggon had passed over his chest, which was crushed and bloodied. The young corporal had only been in the Army for five months and he had never seen a dead man before. The sight made him shiver.

'Jesus Christ!' he whispered and left the body exactly as it lay. The face was peaceful and the eyes were closed. The corporal hoped death had been instantaneous.

Three yards away, Julian lay on his back. He was still breathing but his face was grey and his open eyes stared sightlessly into the sky. The corporal knelt beside him and gently shook his arm.

'Sir? Can you hear me?'

The slight motion disturbed Julian's head, which lolled suddenly to one side. His mouth fell open, but he made no sound. A movement caught the corporal's eye and he turned to see the rear wheel of the motor whirring slowly to a stop. The front half of the vehicle was a mass of splintered wood and twisted green metal. Slowly the corporal stood up, a hand to his head. He moved out into the road and stared desperately in both directions. The rain had stopped and overhead the clouds parted to let an incongruous ray of sunshine bathe the scene with a warm, gold light.

'My spectacles!' cried the elderly woman again, but now her voice trembled and its pitch was higher than before. Shock had set in and feeling had returned to her broken arm, which was very painful. Somewhere to his left, the young corporal heard the welcome sound of voices and turned to see three farm labourers approaching at a run across the field.

'Thank Christ for small mercies!' he muttered and hurried forward to meet them.

*

The walls of the hospital corridor were tiled in dark green to a height of about five feet; above that was a line of patterned tiles and from there up to the ceiling the tiles were ten rows of dark green, one of patterned, eleven rows of white. Vinnie counted them again and again in a vain effort to distract her thoughts and subdue the black despair that rose within her. The bench on which she sat was of polished wood. The floors were of a highly polished heavy-duty linoleum. The nurses whisked past like efficient nuns in their white head-dresses, their shoes tapping out their urgent business, their uniforms crackling with starch They wore calm expressions and were kind but firm. An hysterical relative further along the corridor was being treated like a fractious child.

'Now then, Mrs Wood, we can't have this sort of behaviour, can we? You will upset the other visitors and you wouldn't want to do that, would you? Just sit down again and someone will fetch you a nice cup of tea . . .'

Vinnie sat upright because the tiled wall was cold to her back and she did not want to start shivering again. Being upset was frowned upon and she did not want to be given a cup of tea. She looked at Clive, who sat beside her, and he gave her a half-smile which twisted his face and made him look vulnerable. She looked down at her feet and then began to count the tiles again.

A trolley was wheeled past with someone lying on it – a woman with grey curls matted with blood. Vinnie tried to swallow but found her mouth dry and unco-operative. A door opened and a nurse stepped out into the corridor, a white medical card in her hand.

'Mrs Wellington?'

Heads turned. People on benches turned enquiring looks upon people on other benches, but nobody answered. The nurse repeated the name a little louder and her manner hinted at disappointment. She consulted the card and tried for the last time.

'Mrs *Ivy* Wellington?'

Slowly a young woman raised her hand. 'I'm Mrs Ivy Wadding-ton,' she ventured nervously.

The nurse frowned at her and re-read the card. 'Waddington, is it?" she said. 'Come with me, Mrs Waddington, please.'

They both disappeared through the door, which closed behind them with a discreet click. Vinnie tried to imagine what was happening to her and then sighed deeply without knowing that she did so. She felt a pressure on her arm, saw Clive's long fingers and smiled at him with fear and misery in her eyes. He had been at the house when the news of the accident had reached Vinnie and had insisted on accompanying her to the London hospital where Julian had been taken, following an initial investigation at the local cottage hospital.

Ten rows of dark green, one of patterned and then eleven rows of white. Clive and Vinnie had been sitting on the bench for more than three hours, but to Vinnie it seemed an eternity. When a doctor appeared at the end of the corridor and strode swiftly towards them, her stomach churned with fear as she tried to read his expression. A sister met him half-way down the corridor and they whispered together for a moment. Clive's fingers tightened on Vinnie's arm, but then doctor and nurse moved towards Mrs Wood who was sipping a cup of tea. The doctor leaned over her, his voice low; as he spoke the cup and saucer fell to the ground and smashed. The nurse supported her as another nurse appeared and ran to assist them.

That will be me soon, thought Vinnie dully. They will tell me soon that Julian is dead and will ask me not to make a noise or upset other people. She made up her mind to be very quiet and was glad she had no cup and saucer to drop. Julian was under-going an operation. He had sustained severe damage to his head and had gone into a coma. The surgeon was hoping to 'relieve the pressure', but Vinnie did not quite understand what that meant. A nurse had told her not to worry, but she could not help it. She worried in case he died and she worried in case he lived with a damaged head and a brain that did not function properly.

'I'm cold,' she whispered.

Awkwardly, Clive put an arm round her shoulder and pulled her towards him so that her head rested on his thin shoulder. He said nothing, but she knew that was because there was nothing he could usefully say and he was not a man to waste words and certainly not able to make meaningless comforting noises. Over the past three years he had become a regular visitor to Foxearth and the business relationship had developed into a personal friendship. Vinnie liked and respected him and she was beginning to understand that behind the brusque manner was a man of integrity. She wondered that he had never remarried but continued to lead a bachelor existence with his son William. There seemed to be no real bond between father and son, which puzzled her whenever she bothered to think about it. He was a lonely man, yet she dared not pity him the lack of affection in his life. Pity, she knew, he would resent, for Clive le Brun was a proud man and self-sufficient. He did not suffer fools gladly. She thought perhaps that was why he did not choose to share his life again.

The street door swung open just then and a man came in, carrying a screaming child in his arms. More bustle. More running to and fro of doctors and nurses before they once more disappeared behind closed doors.

'Don't let him die,' Vinnie prayed. 'Let him live and let him be the same as he was before. Don't let him lose his sight or hearing – or his wits. How could he bear it? How could *I* bear it?'

'I suppose it was going to be a surprise?' she said. 'The car, I mean.'

'Don't blame yourself.'

'But when I think how often I have hinted and teased him about getting a motor. This would never have happened if I—'

'That's foolish talk,' he told her. 'It was an accident, not an act of God.'

'But if he dies . . .' Her voice faltered to a stop and she began to shiver.

'You need a hot drink,' he said. 'I'll get you a cup of tea.' He started to rise but she cried out, 'No! Stay with me, please, Clive,' and he did not insist.

Eventually a door opened at the far end of the corridor and Vinnie *knew* that this time Julian was the subject of the doctor's concerned expression.

'Mrs Lawrence?'

She stood up quickly. 'Yes?'

The doctor looked at Clive. 'Mr le Brun is a family friend,' said Vinnie.

The doctor nodded to him politely. 'Will you both please come with me?'

They followed him along the gleaming tiled corridor into an office painted in green and white, where he indicated two chairs and they sat down. The doctor sat down on the opposite side of the desk, rested his elbows on it and pressed his fingers together thoughtfully.

'Mrs Lawrence, the operation on your husband has now been

completed and he is as well as can be expected. How successful it
has been we cannot say at this stage.'

'Is he still in a . . . ?' She could not bring herself to say the word.

The doctor pursed his lips. 'We think so,' he said, 'but until the
effects of the anaesthetic wear off we cannot be certain. It is
disappointing but not disastrous. We can operate again – in fact I
am sure we will have to do so. All we have been able to do so far is
remove broken bone fragments and lift some of the area that has
been compressed. What damage – if any – has been done, we
don't yet know. When he is stronger – in a day or two – we will
undertake certain tests. Until we have these results, I am afraid we
cannot tell you very much. It may be a long process and we must
all be patient. The brain is a very delicate instrument and we like
to move cautiously, one step at a time. Your husband is very lucky
to have survived such a severe blow. He must be very strong and
that is all to the good, of course. It puts his chances of recovery
quite high.' He smiled at Vinnie and shrugged lightly. 'Who
knows? He may come round from the anaesthetic and ask for egg
and bacon!'

Vinnie smiled obediently.

'Oh, some do, you know, Mrs Lawrence. Stranger things have
happened. The human will is astonishing. If a man has the
will-power, he can fight his way back to normality against
tremendous odds. Do you think your husband has the will to live?'

'I hope so . . . I mean yes, I think so.' She glanced at Clive who
nodded. 'Yes, he does,' she said.

'Good. Then we can be hopeful, Mrs Lawrence.'

'For a full recovery, do you mean?'

The doctor hesitated. 'We can hope so,' he said. 'We can also
pray.'

The colour left Vinnie's face. 'I want to know the truth,' she
said. 'I think I can bear anything, if only I know the truth.'

The doctor hesitated. 'Tell her,' said Clive.

The doctor was slightly annoyed by this approach. He had
taken great pains to soften the blow and give the wife some hope.
Now they had rendered his efforts valueless. He stood up
abruptly, gathered a few random papers into his hands and
shuffled them so that the corners were neatly aligned.

'*If* your husband recovers consciousness,' he said, 'there is
every chance of a full recovery. If he does not, then I must tell you
that there is very little we can do for him.'

'Then the tests . . .' Vinnie began.

'We can only carry them out if he is conscious.'

'I see.'

'But please don't give up hope. A comatose condition could last for five weeks or five hours. He could open his eyes at any moment.'

Vinnie nodded, then turned to Clive. 'I want to see him,' she said.

Clive looked at the doctor. 'Is that possible?'

'Just for a moment, then.'

A small brisk nurse led them up interminable stairs and into a ward where thirty or more beds were arranged in rows against the walls. Some had the curtains pulled round them; in others the occupants were clearly visible, peering curiously at the newcomers. Vinnie averted her eyes, reluctant to invade their privacy.

Julian lay flat on the bed, his head swathed in bandages. He had one tube in his arm and another in his nose. His eyes were open and he stared up at the ceiling. A large purple bruise covered the left side of his face and his lips were puffed up to twice their normal size.

'Julian!' Vinnie whispered. She moved closer to the bed and touched one of his outstretched hands. 'Oh, my dear Julian, what have they done to you!'

She blinked back the tears as she raised his limp hand and kissed it, but as she let his hand fall back on to the coverlet they began to course down her cheeks, scalding her eyes.

'Now, don't take on, Mrs Lawrence,' said the nurse. 'Your husband's going to be all right.'

'He's not,' said Vinnie. 'I know he's not.'

Clive took hold of her shoulders and turned her away.

'We will go now,' he said. 'You have had enough for one day.' He nodded to the nurse as they went out. 'We shall be back tomorrow,' he told her as he led Vinnie out of the room.

*

Rose kissed the children goodnight, assured Mrs Bryce that she would not be late home and let herself out of the front door. The neat blue jacket and skirt flattered her figure, which was less plump than it had once been, for grief over Tom's death, worry and a diminished appetite had all contributed to a considerable weight loss over the past three years.

She walked thoughtfully along the lane, her head well down for there was a strong wind blowing. Her mind was busy with an urgent problem, but her eyes noted the changes which had taken place in the countryside. Tom had made her aware of her surroundings and now young Tommy did the same, informing her gleefully when the cuckoo first sounded and bringing home what old Mrs Bryce called 'bits and bobs to litter up the place' – fir cones, oak-apples or a spray of wild pear blossom.

Rose saw the hawthorn in blossom and the buttercups and red campion in the hedgerows, but her thoughts were on Andy Roberts, who had asked her to marry him. Tonight she would meet him at the 'Horse and Cart' as she did most Saturday evenings, but tonight he would want an answer and she was still undecided. It was three years since Tom had died and, as Andy rightly said, no one expected her to stay single for ever, not even for Tom. Andy was offering a good home for her and the five children. Many men would think twice, she knew, about taking on a ready-made family, but he was a generous man. But – and to Rose it was a big 'but' – he would want children of his own and she had hoped she was done with childbearing. She had borne six, counting the baby who had died, and did not relish starting all over again. Her youngest, Sam, was already ten – where had the years gone, she asked herself. Would the children take to a new father, she wondered. The boys certainly needed one, for they were growing up fast and Tommy was almost more than she could manage with his rebellious manner and wild talk. Three growing boys were a problem for a woman to bring up single-handed.

Climbing over the stile, she made her way along the edge of the hop-garden where the beech tree was coming into blossom and the horse-chestnuts were already candled with white flowers. Tommy did not like Andy Roberts and that was another reason why she hesitated to say 'Yes' to his proposal. Andy had assured her that they would 'rub along together' and told her not to worry, but she did. A resentful son would be a constant source of friction, she thought; yet she knew that Tommy's dislike for Andy stemmed mainly from his fierce loyalty towards his father's memory, and she could not find it in her heart to censure him for that.

A small movement caught her eye and she saw a very young featherless bird in the grass. It was much too young to be attempting flight, so presumably it had fallen from its nest – pushed out by a cuckoo, perhaps. Its ugly yellow mouth was opened in a demand for food and it squawked shrilly. Rose looked up into the trees, but could see no sign of a nest.

'Silly baby!' she said. 'It's no good screaming at me. I can't help you.'

Gently, she lifted it further into the hedge where it might at least avoid being trodden on by unwary feet. Then, immediately in front of her she saw another one – and then a third!

'Oh lordy!' said Rose. 'I suppose the wind's blown your nest down, is that it?'

Carefully she gathered them together and hollowed out a rough shape in the long dense grass. Three yellow mouths opened and three trebles shrilled for attention. She shrugged. 'Wait there for your mother,' she advised them, 'and keep quiet or a cat will find you first.'

The nearer Rose drew to the 'Horse and Cart', the more troubled she became. Andy was a good man and she had known him for a long time. The other children were fond of him. Grace worshipped him! And Rose herself? If she was honest, she did not yet love him because her feelings for Tom were still too strong to allow it, but she was realistic enough to admit that as time passed her pain grew less and there was no way she could keep Tom's memory alive for ever even if she wanted to. Tom was dead and she need not reproach herself for anything. She had loved him for all his faults and had done her best to cherish him. She had been a good wife and mother and felt none of the guilt and remorse which afflicted many widows.

Would Tom wish it, she wondered for the hundredth time. Would he expect her to bring up his family with no thought of love or companionship for herself? She found Andy attractive and sometimes he roused her to half-forgotten passions. He wanted her and he loved her and she knew she could make him happy.

Sighing, she pushed open the door of the 'Horse and Cart' and Andy at once stood up to call a greeting. He was sitting with Tim Bilton and Adam Turner, watching Jarvis and his wife Joan playing darts.

'Hey!' cried Tim as one of the darts bounced off the wire and fell perilously near. 'Watch what you're doing, Jarvis! Trying to kill me, are you?'

'That's not a bad idea,' said Jarvis. 'Put you out of your misery, like.'

'Well, I'm not in any misery, so you just watch what you're

doing with those darts. My dog could throw better'n that!'

There was a ripple of laughter in which Jarvis joined.

'That's it,' cried Joan. 'You put him off, then maybe I shall win for a change.' She saw Rose come in and waved a hand. 'Here she is, Andy. Been pining for you, he has, love.'

Rose smiled and said 'Hullo' all round as Andy kissed her and pushed his jacket along the seat to make room for her to sit down beside him. He went to the bar to order her a stout. Maisie was wiping glasses and Ted was laboriously printing a notice to the effect that the 'Horse and Cart' would be closed the following Sunday.

'"Due to a family bereavement?"' said Andy, reading it upside down. 'Who's died then, Ted?'

Ted looked rather sheepish. 'The wife's cousin,' he said. 'Hardly knew her actually, but Maisie's set her heart on going to the funeral.'

Maisie leaned on the counter, her manner confidential. 'She's a very rich woman,' she told Andy. 'Spent her life in Australia. Gold, you see. Her husband got gold fever and off they went. When he died she came back to England and now she's followed him. We were close as children. Violet, her name is, but of course I always called her Vi – we all did – and she hated it.'

'Aha!' said Andy. 'So you reckon there might be some . . . ?' He rubbed his fingers together.

'You never know,' said Maisie. 'At least I want to be there when the will's read out. She had no children to leave it to.'

Joan called out, 'What about Rose's stout then, Maisie? Poor girl's dying of thirst here.'

Rose protested that she was in no hurry, but then Tim decided it was his round and it took another few minutes before they were settled down once more. Jarvis and Joan finished their game – to Jarvis's satisfaction – and inevitably the talk turned to Foxearth and Julian's accident.

'It's quite broken the old Colonel up,' said Adam, shaking his head. 'Knocked all the stuffing out of him, poor old boy. He keeps saying, why should he be still alive and useless and Julian in the prime of life and lying at death's door.'

'Bad as that, is it?' asked Andy.

'Well, he's been like that for nearly three weeks now and never moved a muscle! Being fed through a tube – Ugh! You might as well be dead and done with it.'

'Three weeks?' said Rose. 'Is it really as long as that? It only seems like a few days ago we heard about it. Poor Julian – and poor Vinnie. What must it be like for her? Up to London every day and all for nothing. If he can't recognize her or speak to her or anything—'

'Just like a vegetable,' said Tim. 'I'd rather be dead.'

'But he could come out of it,' said Jarvis. 'It's a coma, you see. People can come out of a coma and be as right as rain again. He just might do that one of these days.'

'And again he might not,' said Tim, determined to look on the black side. 'And where will we all be if he goes? The Colonel's past it, poor old boy, and the mistress can't run the place. I reckon we'll all be looking for work if he dies. Not a cheerful prospect, but you've got to face facts.'

'He won't die. He *can't*,' said Rose. 'It would be too awful for words. Vinnie with those three little ones.'

Joan shrugged. 'It does happen, though,' she said. 'Look at poor old Tom.'

Andy gave her a warning glance and she hastily took another sip of her port and lemon.

Adam drained his glass. 'They're thinking of arranging for Vinnie to stay in a hotel,' he told them. 'That way she'll be near Julian in case anything happens and she won't have to keep travelling to and fro. It's wearing her out.'

'So soon after the new baby too,' said Rose. 'I should think she's exhausted. And what a sad homecoming for Eva – to find her brother like that.'

'When are they due at Southampton?' asked Joan.

They all looked at Adam. 'Ten days' time,' he told them. 'Mr le Brun's offered to go down to meet them.'

'He's been a tower of strength,' said Tim. 'Leastways, that's what Janet says and she doesn't miss much, that one.'

Adam was silent. He did not like Clive le Brun and was aware that the feeling was mutual.

'Well,' said Andy, a little too casually. 'Shall we go then, Rose?'

There was an immediate chorus of meaningful comments and loud laughter.

'Hullo, Rose! You watch out!'

'Going already? What are you up to, Andy?'

'Never trust a man who leaves a pub before closing time!'

Rose blushed furiously but Andy pulled her to her feet,

grinning broadly. She buttoned her jacket, not meeting anyone's eye and aware that Joan watched her curiously.

Outside, she put her arm in Andy's and they began to walk back in the direction of Brook Cottage, leaning into the wind which whipped Andy's hair into his face and threatened to dislodge Rose's hat. Nervously, Rose chattered about the baby birds she had found and about Mrs Bryce's cough. She was just starting a story about the goat when Andy interrupted her.

'It's no use, Rose,' he said good-humouredly. 'You're going to have to give me an answer sooner or later and I'd rather it was now.'

She was struck dumb in the face of a need for an instant decision.

'I don't know, Andy—' she began.

'That's no good, Rose. You've been thinking it over for nearly a twelvemonth. What's it to be, love? Do you think you could put up with me, because I could put up with you and what's more I'd *like* to.'

'It's partly Tommy—'

'He'll come round, I've told you. He can help me in the forge and I can teach him to shoot. He'll be no problem.'

'But if he *is*, Andy, you'll lose patience with him and I'll be between the pair of you, pulled in both directions.'

'That's how it could have been with Tom, Rose. It's a fairly normal sort of problem – part of a boy growing up. I was at loggerheads with my father when I was his age. My mother had a real rough time of it, bless her. But it wasn't the end of the world. We both lived through it and were friends again.'

He stopped and leaned back against the trunk of a large chestnut tree, pulling her with him. 'We're not going another step until it's settled, see? I mean it, Rose. We can stay here all night if you like – in fact it might be fun!'

'You'll get me a bad name, Andy Roberts!'

'No, love, I want to make an honest woman of you. *Then* we'll have some fun! What d'you say, eh? Take a chance with me? You'll never regret it, Rose, I promise you. You're a lovely woman and you deserve a good husband. I'll treat you well and I'll help you with the kids. I'll make you happy, Rose, make up for all the bad times you've had.'

She sighed deeply. 'I know you'll do all those things,' she said slowly, 'but is it fair on you, if I don't love you enough? There are a lot of women in Teesbury who'd give their eye-teeth to marry you.

Would I make you happy, Andy? I couldn't bear it if you ever thought you'd made a mistake in asking me.'

'How will we know if we don't try it?' he challenged.

Rose was silent and at last it was Andy's turn to sigh. 'Look, Rose, life's never perfect. I'm not pretending it would be a perfect marriage. I reckon there will be times when you think you made a mistake and times when I think *I* have. But that happens in every marriage, even the ones where neither of them have any doubts. We can't expect miracles. People are funny. The most we should expect is to be happy some of the time and not so happy the rest of it. But we'd be together and look after each other as best we know how.'

Rose was staring at him. 'I've never heard you talk so much,' she marvelled. 'You really have thought it all out.'

'And you haven't?'

'I've tried, but I couldn't see anything straight,' she told him. 'Nothing was black and white.'

'Is it now?'

'I think it is.'

Andy was filled with sudden hope. 'What d'you mean? That you've made up your mind?'

'Sort of.'

'Rose! For pity's sake!' he said and then had a rare flash of inspiration. 'Look, Rose. Suppose you say "No". Suppose you turn me down and I accept that and you walk away and suddenly the wind blows this tree down. Crash! You turn round and I'm trapped under it, dead!'

'Andy, don't!'

'What would you think?' he insisted. Rose was silent.

'I'll tell you,' said Andy. 'You'd think, "Oh God, why didn't I say 'Yes'. He was right. We could have been happy together." And you'd be sorry for the rest of your life. I'm still talking, you see. I can't seem to stop. Oh hell, Rose! I love you, dammit!'

Rose looked at him. 'Well, then,' she said, 'I'd better say "Yes" or you'll never stop talking!'

He held her at arm's length, staring into her face, looking for proof that he had heard her right. 'You mean it, Rose? You're sure?'

'No,' said Rose. 'I'm not sure, but you are and that's enough for the time being. It was what you said about the tree – it was true.'

'Perhaps you *do* love me?'

'I'm sure I will, Andy.'

'Oh God, Rose. Now you've said "Yes", I don't know what to say.'

She laughed. 'What a time to run out of words! Just say it again, that you love me, will you?'

He pulled her close and held her so tightly that she protested he was breaking her ribs.

'I love you, Rose Bryce, soon to be Roberts.'

'Rose Roberts,' she said. 'I hadn't thought of that.'

'Then you start thinking,' he said, 'and I'll start kissing.'

CHAPTER EIGHTEEN

Clive le Brun finally persuaded Vinnie that she should stay in an hotel near to the hospital and he made all the arrangements for her. She was at first reluctant to agree, protesting that Eva and her family were due home and she must be at Foxearth to look after them. Clive, however, was adamant that Mrs Tallant was quite capable of dealing with visitors and that no one would expect Vinnie to exhaust her strength by daily travel to London and back. They would expect her to want to be as near as possible to her husband, in case she was needed urgently 'for any reason', as he expressed it. At last Vinnie saw the logic of these arguments and, grateful that someone else had made the decision for her, gave in gracefully. In fact she was thankful that the arduous twice-daily train journeys would be at an end.

The hotel was a small one, only two streets away from the hospital and it was run by Mr and Mrs Arnold Riley on friendly family lines with breakfast and evening meal provided. Vinnie moved in, after a long talk with Julian's consultant, on the strict understanding that if Julian made no progress in the next four weeks she would take him back to Foxearth and nurse him there. Nurse Ramsey could be recalled if necessary.

Her small bedroom contained a bed with a creaking spring and a feather mattress; a washstand with a marble top and a matching set of bowl and jug in lilac-coloured china; an oak chest of drawers and a tall narrow mahogany wardrobe. The floor was covered in a highly polished linoleum and the bedside rug was home-made from bright strips of material. It was comfortable, nondescript and perfectly adequate for Vinnie's needs. Unfortunately, the large sash windows which let in plenty of light also let in noise. The traffic in the road outside and the rowdy customers at the nearby pub made sleep virtually impossible until nearly midnight, and each morning she was woken soon after dawn by the clatter of hooves and rattle of wheels as the horse-buses plied the streets, taking the workers to Bryant and May's and the cycle factory for the early shift.

Mrs Riley was a motherly soul who did her best to ease Vinnie's burden by the only means at her disposal – over-feeding. She gave her an extra slice of bacon at breakfast and an extra potato with the evening meal, assuring her that 'one must feed grief to avoid a breakdown'. On Vinnie's third day she was just sitting down to dinner when Mr Riley hurried over to her.

'Mr le Brun is here,' he told her. 'I thought you might wish him to join you for dinner?'

'Oh yes, please,' said Vinnie. 'Please show him in.'

Clive looked taller than Vinnie remembered as he made his way between the seated diners, unaware of the curious glances and whispered comments which his unexpected appearance provoked.

He greeted Vinnie with an embarrassed peck on the cheek and sat down opposite her.

She smiled. 'You're like a breath of country air,' she whispered. 'At least you have a healthy colour – everyone here seems so grey. The whole of London seems grey.'

'It's your mood,' he said. 'How's your husband? Is there any change at all?'

'Almost none,' she told him. 'Today I fancied his eyelids flickered, but it was so brief and it wasn't repeated. I didn't tell the nurse in case I had imagined it. But at least he's no worse,' she added.

'I'm so sorry.'

'It was nice of you to come up, Clive, but I feel I must be taking you away from your work. It's selfish of me to allow it.'

'I only come when it's convenient. You need not worry on my account.'

Mrs Riley came to their table with a notebook and pencil. 'It's chump chops or a nice bit of liver,' she told them. 'Greens, carrots and boiled potatoes, followed by a jam sponge with custard. I'd have the liver if I was you.'

'The liver, then,' said Vinnie obligingly.

Clive chose the chops and also asked for a bottle of champagne. Mrs Riley looked confused.

'There's not a lot of call for that,' she said anxiously, 'but I'll talk to my husband and see what we've got. Most people drink either red or white you see. Red with beef, isn't it? And liver, I think. Oh dear, I don't know. It's not my department, the wine, and Arnold's busy at the moment.'

Vinnie caught Clive's eye and he said, 'Well, bring us a suitable wine, moderately priced.'

'I will, sir. And that's one liver, one chops. Thank you.'

'Is it bearable here?' Clive asked when she had moved on to the next table.

Vinnie nodded. 'Very bearable,' she said, 'and I can't thank you enough for all your help. The Rileys let me use the telephone and I keep in touch with Foxearth. Oh, what a sad homecoming for Eva! I haven't told them of the accident because the news is so bleak, but she will have to be told when they get home. It will be such a shock.'

'The news might be better by the time they arrive,' he said.

'Do you think so?' asked Vinnie.

'Not really, no,' he said with disconcerting honesty. 'I'm trying to cheer you up, that's all. You look so wretched and I feel so helpless.'

The food arrived promptly and for a while they ate in silence. 'You're only toying with that,' said Clive. 'Eat it, Vinnie, or you will be the next invalid.'

Meekly she obeyed, although she hardly tasted anything and had it not been for his eagle eye, would have left much of the dish untouched. As it was, she forced it down and a claret helped a little.

'What do you do in the evenings?' he asked her, as they waited for the sponge pudding to arrive. 'I wondered if we might engage a hansom and take a look at the river. The fresh air and a walk might do you good.'

'I think it would,' she agreed. 'I don't like to walk the streets on my own, so I usually sit in the lounge and read a magazine or *The Times* and try to avoid catching Miss Emily Walford's eye.'

Clive raised an eyebrow enquiringly and Vinnie smiled and lowered her voice.

'She's sitting behind me. The one with the braids round her head. She has a very loud voice and repeats everything you say. The most telling remark sounds idiotic when it echoes round the lounge. She's almost a resident here, it seems, and takes her position very seriously.'

Mrs Riley bustled up with the puddings. 'Now, Mrs Lawrence,

you tuck that away and it'll put new life in you. It's light but nourishing and you need building up. She's too thin, sir, to my way of thinking. Oh, was the wine to your liking, Arnold says?'

'Very nice indeed,' said Vinnie quickly, for Clive had in fact expressed his disappointment.

'Ah, that's good!' She was evidently relieved and carried the good news back to the kitchen.

'You're too kind to people,' said Clive and she saw the amusement in his eyes. 'It wasn't very nice at all, so why tell a lie?'

'Because they're nice people,' said Vinnie.

He laughed, genuinely delighted by this illogical answer. Vinnie tried to feel affronted, but she was too weary and it seemed very unimportant.

'Julian's a—' Clive began, then left the sentence unfinished.

'A what?'

'Eat up your light but nourishing sponge,' he said.

'You're changing the subject.' She looked at him. 'You were going to say Julian's a lucky man. I know you were, so you needn't deny it. Why didn't you say it, Clive? Because he's lying ill not a mile away from us and not at all lucky?'

He hesitated, then said slowly, 'No. I decided not to flatter you at such a time. It seemed inappropriate. Eat up – Mrs Riley may not allow you to leave the table until your plate is empty!'

Later, they took a cab to Westminster Bridge and walked along the embankment. It was a clear night and as the sky darkened the stars appeared, cold and clear above the rooftops and spires that made up the skyline. The lights along the embankment were reflected in the placid water of the Thames which ran slow with the turning of the tide. Boats moved up and down at a leisurely pace, black shapes against the glittering water: sailing barges with their rigging taut; a string of squat coal barges from the Midlands, steam-engine clanking; a paddle-steamer coming alongside to put down the last passengers of the day.

Vinnie said suddenly, 'I went to Margate once when I was fifteen. Eva and Julian took me for the day. I rode a donkey and it ran away with me. When I fell off, Julian was there to catch me. It was the first time he held me in his arms.'

There was a catch in her voice which did not go unnoticed.

Clive said, 'Vinnie, please don't raise your hopes too high. You do know, don't you, that Julian's chances lessen with each day? I think it's important for you to be realistic. The doctors do you a disservice with their constant evasions.'

Tears threatened as she nodded. 'I know, Clive. I don't want to stop hoping, but I think I understand what's happening. It's so sad for him. Such an undignified way to be – helpless and with all those tubes. Worse than a baby. It haunts me at night when I'm in bed and I think he might stay that way for months. He wouldn't wish it, Clive . . . if he knew, I mean. I would rather he was dead than stay like that. Is that a wicked way to think?'

Clive considered before he spoke. 'No,' he said at last. 'It's the compassionate way.'

They looked across to the far bank, lost in their own thoughts. The breeze that rippled the water disturbed their hair, but lightly – a caress, almost. Somewhere down river a ship's horn sounded two short blasts and a small boat passed them, close in, with a hissing wash which lapped rhythmically at the bank below. A young flower-seller approached, a bunch of violets in her out-stretched hands. She wore no shoes and her arms were bare beneath the ragged shawl.

'Buy some flowers for the lady, sir. Penny a bunch!'

Vinnie looked at her and saw the wariness in the girl's eyes as she steeled herself for a refusal.

Clive fumbled in his pocket and tossed her a sixpence.

'Crikey, sir, how many d'you want?' she asked.

'Just one bunch.'

'Bless you, sir! 'Ere, take a bunch with a ribbon round it.'

He took the proffered flowers and she turned aside to accost another couple.

'For you,' he said to Vinnie. 'For the lady!'

She tried to answer, to thank him, but the simple gift brought a rush of unwelcome tears to her eyes and it was some time before she could gain sufficient control of her emotions to stammer out a 'Thank you'. He did not attempt to comfort her but leaned on the parapet of the embankment wall, looking out across the river.

'I'm sorry,' said Vinnie, wiping her eyes. 'I don't know why I did that.'

'You need to cry sometimes,' he said. 'It's a relief. I would rather you cried here with me than alone in your room at night.'

Vinnie wondered why, but did not ask. Suddenly she said, 'You never talk about your wife, Clive?'

'No I don't,' he said, his tone uncompromising.

She held the violets to her nose and inhaled deeply. 'They're lovely,' she said. 'Bertie was always promising to buy me a bunch of flowers, but he never did. I didn't mind because I knew he hadn't any money. It seems strange now, not to have enough money.' She paused. 'You should talk about her, Clive. It's not natural. I'm a good listener and I really want to know – besides, it's easier talking in the dark.'

He made a small annoyed sound in his throat, but Vinnie settled herself beside him against the parapet and looked sideways into his face, waiting.

'I don't often care to think about it,' he said, 'because I made her unhappy and then she died and that's a waste of a life. I didn't mean to make her wretched but I obviously did – and she turned to another man for affection. It was his child she was carrying. She died giving birth to it and it was born dead.'

Vinnie sighed deeply, her own sad memories revived by his words. She looked at him out of the corner of her eye and saw that he stared straight ahead, his hands tightly clenched.

'I was glad when she died,' he said. '*Glad!* Not because I didn't love her, but because I didn't know how I could live with her, seeing her with another man's child. I loved her very much, but I don't think she ever knew it. I don't even think she meant to hurt me. She was just looking for the love she didn't receive from me – or thought she didn't. Communication between people can be so very difficult. Do we ever say what we mean? Or do we say only what we *think* we mean? I wonder if we ever understand ourselves, let alone another. Poor Katherine! It was a high price to pay for affection. William was just thirteen when she died and it took us both a long time to recover from her death.'

'Do you think you have recovered?' Vinnie asked him gently and he shrugged wordlessly. 'Perhaps you don't want to?' she insisted.

'I don't know,' he said. 'I just don't know. I live from day to day and I find it's the best way.'

Abruptly he straightened up and began to walk away, so that Vinnie had to hurry after him.

'Was it hard?' Vinnie asked. 'To talk about it to me?'

'Yes.'

'I'm sorry, Clive. Maybe it was wrong of me to insist but . . .' She stopped.

'But you were curious?'

'Yes, I was, but it wasn't idle curiosity, Clive. It was—'

'I don't think we need to discuss it any more,' he said. 'It's getting late. I'll take you back to your hotel and then catch the last train home.'

'And will you come up to London again?'

'Probably, in a day or two perhaps.'

He raised his hand as a carriage approached and the driver reined the horse to a halt. Clive helped Vinnie in and gave the address before climbing in beside her. Neither of them spoke on the way back. Clive took her into the hotel and then bade her a curt 'Goodbye'. Vinnie, with a slight frown, watched him until he was out of sight. Mrs Riley beamed at her from behind the reception desk.

'A very pleasant gentleman,' she said. 'Relative, is he?'

Vinnie shook her head. 'He's just a good friend,' she replied.

*

They had moved Julian into a private room and now Vinnie sat close to his bed, her knees pressed into the mattress. She held his right hand between her own and leaned forward to be as near to him as possible, so that she need not raise her voice. It was impossible to know whether or not he heard anything and, if he did, whether or not he understood what was being said. But, dismayed by the lack of any apparent improvement in his condition, Vinnie had spent the last week at his side, all day and every day, entreating and bullying him by turns to come back to her. The nurse had argued with her in vain and even the doctor warned her that she was merely exhausting her own resources to no good purpose. For Vinnie it was the only way she could think of to contribute towards Julian's recovery. She felt it was her determined will against his failing spirit.

The nurse and the doctor might well be right, but Vinnie knew she would never forgive herself if he died and she had made no effort to save him. How did they *know* he could not hear or understand? How could they be *sure*? The doctor had told her that the test results proved conclusively that he did not respond to stimuli. Vinnie was not prepared to accept these results, however, and told the doctor so with a firmness that surprised even herself. In the end they gave in gracefully and left her alone. Now, as she spoke to Julian, she kept her eyes firmly fixed on his face in case there should be the smallest tremor in the closed eyelids or a flutter of movement on the passive lips. While she talked to him, her hands were kneading the knuckles of his limp fingers, curling and straightening them, stroking and sometimes scratching the palm. If he could not hear, perhaps he could see. If he could not see, then maybe he could feel.

'I want you to pay close attention,' she was saying. 'Don't worry if you miss some of what I say, because I shall say it again and then again. I know you're very tired and I know you're very ill, because they tell me so. I hope you're not in any pain. They tell me you're not and I hope it's true. But, Julian, you look just the same dear man to me. Just as handsome as ever! Oh yes, I have to watch the staff nurse! I think she's taken a shine to you!'

She smiled and patted his hand to show that this was only a joke. 'But she can only have you while you're her patient. As soon as you are well I shall take you home with me, back to Foxearth where we shall all be together again. I have made up my mind to it – you and me and our three little ones. Oh yes, you *will* get better, Julian.' She laughed again and kissed his hand gently and then more fiercely, then she shook it.

'Julian!' she cried. 'Are you listening to all this? I want you to understand that no matter how ill you feel or how near to death, you are *not* to die. Do you hear me, Julian? I say, you are *not* to and I can be very determined. This is not your old Vinnie talking – it's a new, strong Vinnie. This is a *Lavinia* talking to you, so you must pay attention. Julian! Do you hear me?'

She sat back, momentarily defeated by the inert figure of her husband and releasing his hand, stood up to ease her stiff legs and arch her back. As she stood there, the door opened quietly and the nurse looked in at them.

'Everything all right, Mrs Lawrence?' she whispered.

'Oh, please don't whisper,' Vinnie begged. 'If he can't hear us, then it doesn't matter how loudly we talk but if he can, then let him hear our voices. So much the better. Perhaps we should play loud music, clap our hands and stamp our feet.' She looked wearily at the nurse. 'I don't know,' she said.

The nurse treated this 'flight of fancy' with a tolerant smile. 'Anything I can get you?' she asked, as though Vinnie had not spoken. 'Cup of tea? A bun? You must eat, you know. We don't want another invalid on our—'

'He's not an invalid,' interrupted Vinnie. 'He's a patient. It's not the same thing – is it?'

'Sister's very worried about you,' said the nurse. 'She says you don't eat enough to keep a flea alive. Let me get you a cup of tea and a Chelsea bun. They're lovely and sugary and—'

'Yes, thank you,' said Vinnie. 'That sounds nice.' Anything, she thought, to get rid of her.

Once the nurse had departed, Vinnie resumed her monologue. 'Now listen, Julian, because this is the exciting news. Listen to me carefully. You're going to be so thrilled. Eva is coming today! Your Eva! Your sister Eva is coming *here* to the hospital to see you. Do you hear that, my love?' She raised her voice a little. 'Eva is coming here today to see you. Clive went to Southampton to meet them and he will take them all back to Foxearth and then bring Eva up to London to see you. Isn't that wonderful news? You and Eva together again after all these years! But, Julian, you don't want her to see you like this, do you? She will be so upset and I know you don't want to disappoint her, so I want you to try especially hard to open your eyes – just the tiniest bit. Will you try to do that, my love? To please me? Oh, I know you will. Don't worry if you can't manage it, Julian. We can't always do what we want to do, but I want you to *try*.'

She turned away as the nurse came back with a small tray and set it down on the bedside table beside her.

'I got the girl to butter it for you,' she told Vinnie with a smile. 'That's the best way with a Chelsea bun. My grandmother always did them like that – split them open and buttered them. Now, how is your husband today?'

She took the notes from the end of the bed and scanned them briefly. 'No deterioration,' she said. 'That's a good sign, anyway.' She replaced the notes briskly. 'Now do try to eat that bun. It will do you good.'

'His sister is coming today,' Vinnie told the nurse, who paused on her way to the door. 'They haven't met for nearly eight years. She's been in India with her husband. I was hoping . . .' Her voice trailed into a hopeless silence.

The nurse looked at Julian doubtfully. 'Well, there's no knowing,' she said. 'It could do the trick, meeting his sister again after all this time. The shock, you see.' Then, seeing Vinnie's expression change, she added hastily, 'But don't set your heart on it, Mrs Lawrence. Let's just wait and see, shall we?'

With another smile she rustled out of the room. 'Bertie's wife is a nurse,' thought Vinnie. 'She must be a good person. And Bertie must love her so I shall too, whatever she's like, for his sake. Beatrice . . . it's a nice name.'

She stirred the tea and watched a single tea-leaf whirl in the cup. When it slowed down, she gave the tea another stir. The bun was very fresh and buttery and coated with sugar. 'It's delicious,' she thought, surprised, took another bite and sighed. 'At any moment now there will be footsteps in the corridor, the door will open and Clive will be there with Eva beside him. Poor Eva!'

She froze suddenly in mid-bite at a sound from the bed. It was half-way between a sigh and a moan and Vinnie's heart leapt with something akin to fear as she looked at her husband. A small scream escaped her lips as she saw that Julian's lips were now parted instead of closed. So she *had* heard a sound! He had made a sound and she had not been watching! In a panic, she leaned over him.

'Julian! It's me, Vinnie. I'm here, darling! Oh Julian. You can move! You moved your lips. You did! Try again. Oh no, wait!' She stared round her, too confused to think what she ought to do next. Ring for the nurse! Yes, that was it. Her hand stretched out to press the bell three times and then she was leaning over Julian once more.

'Again, Julian!' she urged. 'Try again! Oh, you *can* hear! You are going to get well again. I can hardly believe it. Do you hear me, my love? Do you understand, I wonder? You are going to be well and Eva is coming today. She'll be so delighted. Can you imagine? Oh, I wish I could hug you, but I daren't. You look so frail but' – she snatched up his hand – 'I can kiss your dear hand.' She smothered it with passionate kisses. Where was the nurse? Would she never come? Then the doctor must be summoned and then the consultant . . .

There were quick footsteps outside and the nurse ran into the room. Vinnie turned towards her, her face radiant.

'He spoke!' cried Vinnie. 'He did – at least, he tried to. He made a sound and, look, his lips have moved. They were shut before. They have been shut all this time. They—'

She broke off. The nurse seemed surprisingly calm, almost too calm and she did not speak as she examined Julian. First his eyes, lifting the lids one after the other, then his pulse. There were more footsteps and the doctor hurried in. Vinnie saw the nurse give him a significant glance, then he almost pushed Vinnie to one side as he, too, leaned over the still figure on the bed. She stumbled back, a hand to her throat. Why were they behaving this way? She had told them . . . She swallowed painfully and for a few seconds the room swam crazily. She tried to speak, to attract their attention, but they were conversing in low whispers across the bed. Then the nurse came towards Vinnie and took a firm hold of her arm. Incredibly the doctor was drawing the sheet up over Julian's face.

'No!' screamed Vinnie. 'Don't do that!'

She pulled herself free of the nurse's restraining grasp and ran back to the bed. Tugging the sheet from the doctor's hand, she threw herself across her husband's body.

'Julian, I love you!' she whispered. 'Do you hear me? I love you. You did your best and it doesn't matter. We can't always do – what we . . .' She took a deep agonized gulp of air as the tears blinded her. 'We can't always do—'

The nurse was at the bedside, saying the comforting things that nurses say at such times. Vinnie heard the door close quietly as the doctor went out.

'Now Mrs Lawrence, it's all over,' said the nurse. 'He's at peace now. Your husband is at peace. You must try to see it that way.'

Gently she coaxed Vinnie to her feet.

'Oh Julian!' whispered Vinnie. She looked at the nurse. 'He tried to speak. I know he did.'

The nurse nodded. 'Very likely,' she said. 'It happens like that, sometimes. They rally suddenly at the last moment.'

Vinnie shook her head dazedly, then the door opened again and the room was suddenly filled with people – the doctor, Clive and a young woman who was at once a stranger and yet familiar. She wore a dark travelling suit and her face was very pale.

'Eva!' cried Vinnie.

Julian's sister was very pale and there were unshed tears in her eyes as she ran into Vinnie's arms. They clung together for a moment, then Eva drew away and moved towards the bed and Vinnie watched, stricken, as she dropped to her knees beside her dead brother. Vinnie turned towards Clive with a look of bewilderment. His face was grim but he said nothing. She moved to stand beside him and he put an arm round her shoulders. The sound of Eva sobbing somehow gave Vinnie strength; she was shivering, but she no longer wept.

Clive said quietly, 'I'm sorry we were too late. We were

downstairs with the doctor when you rang the bell. He was explaining that there was no hope at all, that the brain damage was massive.'

Vinnie raised her head. 'What, none at all – ever?'

'No, but he didn't want you to be without hope. He says he thought it best but I think he was wrong.'

Vinnie nodded slowly, then went to her sister-in-law and knelt beside her, putting an arm round her shoulders.

Eva looked up, her eyes full of remorse. 'If only we had come home earlier . . .' she began. 'Now he doesn't even know I'm here. He'll never know.'

'He knew you were coming,' Vinnie assured her. 'I told him and he understood. It was your name he said, just before he died. He said "Eva". Very clearly.'

It was a lie, but one which Vinnie felt was justified. She herself had lost a husband. Eva had lost a brother. Eva was staring up at her, her beautiful face ravaged by grief, a glimmer of hope in the large eyes.

'Did he?' she stammered. 'Oh, Vinnie, did he truly?'

'Cross my heart,' said Vinnie.

Then the tears began again for both of them and they clung together, hugging each other amid their mutual sorrow.

*

Colonel Lawrence took the news of his son's death better than anyone had dared to hope, for in his wisdom he had expected it and had not been buoyed up by the false promises despite pretending otherwise. The arrival of Eva, untimely in one respect, went some way towards softening the loss of his only son, and the three grandchildren whom he had never seen provided an extra interest for him. The children spent several hours each day in the old man's bedroom, talking about their life in India, bewailing the loss of their beloved Indian ayah and reminiscing endlessly about the two Highland terriers they had left behind in Calcutta. The Colonel told them fantastic stories, real and imagined, about his exploits as 'a military man' and, watching him surreptitiously, Janet breathed a sigh of relief. She had expected the news of Julian's death to kill him.

Gerald Cottingham was obliged to spend several days in London on his company's business, while Vinnie and Eva coped with the funeral arrangements with the help of Clive le Brun. To

Vinnie, the days passed in a whirl of activities and decisions which, for the time being, dulled her pain. The household continued to function, meals were prepared and linen was changed. Dead flowers were replaced by fresh ones and the carpets were beaten daily as before.

Vinnie felt guilty about this air of normality. It wasn't that no one cared, she told herself, or that Julian's passing made no difference. It was simply that the trappings of everyday life demanded attention and it was easier to continue the routine than neglect it. And the familiar routines were somehow soothing. She hoped Julian would understand.

The church was booked for the service, flowers were ordered, the undertaker came and went and Julian's body was finally brought back to Foxearth in an oak coffin lined with white velvet. Relatives and friends were notified and invited to the funeral. The solicitor was visited, the bank manager called at the house and the local stonemason was instructed to add Julian's name to the Lawrence family head-stone. Hymns were chosen and a menu was prepared for the funeral supper. The funeral itself was to start at four o'clock and the meal, for about thirty people, was planned for five o'clock. The cousins from Dorset were coming, as well as a few distant relatives of Christina's and the Colonel's cousin. Also Clive and William le Brun, of course, Mary Bellweather and Roland and Emily Fry.

Mrs Tallant was at her wits' end to know how to accommodate and feed so many people, but Cook was calm and reassuring. They had been through it all before when Christina Lawrence died, she reminded the others, and it would be no different for Master Julian. One sad, mad scramble and then it would all be over and the family would settle back and discover just how unhappy they were.

'The funeral's the easy part,' she told them. 'It's the afterwards that's so miserable. All the rush and hurry is over and you're left with a great big nothing that goes on and on for weeks and months.'

'Oh, do stop it,' said Edie.

'I'm only telling you how it is,' said Cook. 'It's part of life, folks dying. One day it'll be me you're all crying over, then it'll be you. There's no point in fighting it. Folks get born and then they die and the ones that are left learn to live without them. It's the way of the world and always has been.'

'They're going to sing "Abide with Me",' said Doll. 'That's a lovely hymn. One of my favourites – but I won't be there to sing it, more's the pity.'

Edie said, 'Why not? We're all invited, Cook said so.'

Doll shrugged. 'Someone's got to look after all the little ones,' she said, 'so it will have to be me.'

'You sing it all by yourself then,' said Cook. 'He'll hear you all right.'

'Who will?' said Edie. 'God?'

'No, silly. Master Julian. He'll hear Doll singing a hymn if it's meant for him, special.'

Doll looked dubious. 'I've got a lovely little hat, too,' she said. 'With black crêpe flowers and a bit of veiling. I wore it once when the old girl died at my last place.'

'I haven't got a black hat,' said Edie. 'It's not fair.'

'Nothing in this world is fair,' said Janet. 'That's what the poor old Colonel said to me when he heard the news. "It should have been me, Janet. I've had my life. It's so damned unfair." Those were his exact words.'

'Poor old fellow,' said Mrs Tallant. 'We're very lucky to still have him, if you ask me. Many men of his age would have gone out like a puff of wind with a shock like that.'

'Well, he hasn't,' said Janet, 'and I don't intend that he will.'

'Adam Turner says we should all have a day off, to respect the dead,' said Edie unexpectedly.

They all looked at her in astonishment and Mrs Tallant snorted. 'Adam Turner said so? Well, who's he to tell us what should and shouldn't be done? He's only the gardener. He should remember his place, same as the rest of us.'

'But he's not like us, is he?' said Edie. 'He's different 'cos of being Bert's friend.'

Mrs Tallant's expression hardened. 'I suppose he told you that, too, did he?'

Edie nodded. 'He's more like a friend of the family because of Bert.'

'I never heard such nonsense in all my life!' said Cook. 'The very cheek of the young cub! He's no more a friend of the family than—'

'He kisses Miss Vinnie!' cried Edie. 'I've seen him!'

There was such a long shocked silence that Edie wondered anxiously if she had said something wrong.

'Well, he *did*,' she whispered as Mrs Tallant seized her by the arm.

'Don't you – *dare* say such a thing ever again,' the housekeeper told her. 'That's a wicked slander, that is, and I've a good mind to box your ears. If anyone should hear you, I reckon you would be out of a job and serve you right. Whatever's got into you, to say such a thing?' She shook Edie hard.

'But it's *true*!' Edie wailed. 'I saw him kiss her, but Miss Vinnie said I wasn't to tell no one because it was only a joke.'

'A joke?' said Janet. 'Miss Vinnie and Adam Turner?' She shook her head. 'You've got it all wrong, Edie,' she said 'You just forget it and don't ever say such a thing again. Don't clout her, Mrs Tallant, you know what a daft ha'porth she is!'

After another shake, Mrs Tallant released Edie reluctantly. Doll finished cutting the children's tea-time sandwiches and arranged them on a plate.

'Mind you,' she said thoughtfully, 'he does have some claim on Vinnie's affections. Edie's right there. And I've seen them giggling together like a couple of children. I thought it harmless enough—'

'Of course it's harmless,' cried Mrs Tallant. 'Don't *you* start!'

'But he *is* a bossy-boots,' Doll insisted. 'Told me the other day that I shouldn't give the children cucumber in their sandwiches.'

'He never did?' cried Cook. 'Cheeky whelp! What does he know about cucumber – or children – or anything else, come to that? All he knows about is the Army. Parading up and down and banging off rifles! That's about all he knows. And as for gardening! He can hardly tell one end of a rake from the other! Look, Janet, I know you've got a soft spot for him but—'

'I haven't – not any more,' said Janet, with an effort at nonchalance. 'Say what you like about him, I don't care.'

'Well, now I've heard *everything*!' cried Cook. 'I thought he was your golden boy?' Her eyes narrowed. 'What's he done to upset you? Come on, cough it up!'

Janet shrugged. 'Nothing in particular,' she said uneasily. 'It's just the way he talks to the Colonel sometimes. As though, like Edie says, he's one of the family. Criticizing people behind their backs. Not much, but a word here and a word there. I don't like it. I pretend not to hear.'

'What d'you mean, "people"?' Mrs Tallant demanded. 'Us, d'you mean? Criticizing *us*, is that it?'

Janet nodded and Cook let out a whistle of pure rage.

'Not me,' said Edie. 'He didn't criticize *me*, Janet?'

'Yes, you and all.'

'Ooh!' She began to wail.

'Oh hold your noise!' said Doll. 'You really are a big baby. We shall just have to keep our eyes and ears open where Mr Adam Turner's concerned. At least we're all in this together.'

*

The funeral, which took place on Vinnie's birthday, proceeded without a hitch. The sun shone and the promise of an early summer was everywhere about them as the mourners followed the coffin into the packed church. It seemed that all of Teesbury was there. Vinnie was moved to see that Rose and Andy Roberts, with Mrs Bryce and the children, sat towards the back of the church. Rose's eyes met hers with compassion and Vinnie thought back to Tom's death and wondered fleetingly what life was all about if it could be snatched away so easily and buried in a wooden box.

She sat down in the front pew and stared dry-eyed at the floral tributes piled high over the coffin, trying to remember Julian riding or playing croquet or even sitting writing at the big desk in the study. The only image she could raise was of Julian lying stiff and straight in his coffin, the white velvet tastefully arranged around his head to hide the crushed skull and ragged hairline that had so appalled her.

Poor Mr Smith, she thought suddenly. The young chauffeur-mechanic had a mother and father, maybe sisters and brothers also. His funeral had been held in Peckham some weeks previously and she had sent a wreath and a letter of condolence.

They all knelt to pray, then stood up to sing. Vinnie would not look at the Reverend Parsloe. She did not like him and had tried unsuccessfully to arrange for another vicar to take his place. Beside her stood Eva and Gerald and their oldest child. Then the cousins from Dorset. Behind them the le Bruns and various of Julian's business friends. She sighed and blinked hard and wondered if Julian was somewhere in the air above them, watching, with them. 'Dear God,' she prayed, 'was Julian's life mostly happy? I do so hope it was!' She wished she had answered the telephone the night he rang from Mary Bellweather's house – and had not sided so determinedly with the hoppers – or flouted his wishes over the Bryces. Remorse enveloped her darkly and she felt as though she was suffocating. She had made his life less happy than it might have been, but now it was too late and nothing could be undone. It was all so horribly final. If only she could begin to understand. They rose again to sing the final hymn and Vinnie realized she had not heard a word of the service. She tried to sing but her voice wavered ridiculously and she gave up the attempt.

When at last, in the churchyard, they began to lower Julian's coffin into the cold dark earth, a Red Admiral butterfly descended from the air above them and settled on the polished lid. Slowly it was lowered down with Julian's body into the grave. Vinnie waited in an agony of apprehension for the butterfly to reappear, but it did not do so and only then did her dry eyes melt into tears.

CHAPTER NINETEEN

Mary Bellweather and Alexander returned to London the following day and on Monday he went to school as usual and Mary
continued to wear her black gown. Mrs Markham fussed over
Mary, concerned to see how much the funeral of Julian Lawrence
had affected her. The housekeeper had seen the way Mary had
looked at him on his last and only visit and her heart had warmed
to the sight of Mary with a man on one side and a child on the
other. To her way of thinking it was 'downright unnatural' for a
beautiful woman like Mary to have no family of her own, a quite
scandalous waste in fact. That evening she had watched Mary
proudly as she served the three of them at table, recognizing at
once how *right* it looked. She still remembered Julian's side of the
telephone call he had made to Vinnie on that near-fateful evening
and heard his delight as it dawned on him that Vinnie was at last
with child. Mary's congratulations had held the falseness that
only one woman can detect in another's voice and Mrs Markham's kind heart ached for her still. Although she had met
Vinnie only rarely, she could neither like her nor forgive her for
the havoc she had unwittingly caused in Mary's life.

Many years ago Mary and Roland Fry had been very close
friends and Mrs Markham had confidently looked forward to a
wedding. Then Roland's interest in Vinnie and her misfortunes
had caused a rift between him and Mary which was never healed.
Still, Mary had Alexander now and he partly filled the gap in her
life; Mrs Markham's joy in their relationship was only marred by
the fear that one day Mary would lose him, too. He was twelve
now, a robust child, not tall but well-proportioned. His suspicious
manner and habitually sullen expression had gradually disappeared over the past three years, to be replaced by an almost
eager friendliness, having discovered the world to be less hostile
than he had thought and now being prepared to risk close

relationships. Mrs Markham secretly adored him and spoilt him whenever she could, but she would never have admitted to a need for affection in her own life although her days were long until he returned home from school each day and her spare moments were taken up with knitting socks, pullovers and gloves for him. She even knitted him a bright red waistcoat, but he teased her unmercifully about it and it was never worn.

On the afternoon following the funeral, Mrs Markham was therefore horribly dismayed to open the front door to an over-painted woman who announced herself as 'Alex's Ma'. The housekeeper's first instinct was to slam the door and lock it, and she struggled for some seconds before she could overcome this instinct and recover her poise. Judging by the triumphant grin on the woman's face, she was not hiding her feelings very well.

'Say it's Mollie Pett come for the boy. What's the matter, cat got your tongue? You don't look very pleased to see me.'

'I – of course, I . . .' Mrs Markham stammered, opening the door reluctantly and retreating into formality. 'Please come in. I shall tell the mistress you are here.'

'Oh I *am* obliged. She'll be that pleased to see me!'

Mollie Pett laughed mockingly as she swept past the housekeeper into the hall. Mrs Markham felt an overpowering desire to strike her and was appalled to discover such primitive emotions surfacing within her. She closed the door so clumsily that the brass knocker jumped and a moment later Mary looked up from a letter she was writing to gaze in astonishment as the housekeeper rushed into the morning room without so much as a knock.

'Mrs Markham—!' she began.

The housekeeper was obviously greatly disturbed. 'It's *her*, ma'am!' she burst out. 'Mrs Pett! Alexander's mother. In the hall as cheeky as you please and looking like a trollop! Oh ma'am, what are we to—'

'Hush!' cried Mary, trying to hide her own agitation. 'She mustn't hear you. Mollie Pett! Oh, let me think a moment.'

Mrs Markham watched helplessly as Mary, a hand to her head, thought desperately. 'I half expected it,' she told the housekeeper. 'I should have given it more careful thought, but I so dreaded the prospect. Oh heavens, what's best to do, I wonder . . .'

'I could tell her you're out, ma'am,' Mrs Markham suggested. 'Or gone away. How would that be? Gone away for a week – or a month – to the country and taken Alexander with you.'

Mary was shaking her head. 'That won't do,' she said. 'It would only delay matters. No, I must deal with it today if I possibly can.'

'But supposing she wants him back! Oh, ma'am, if Master Alexander was to see that awful creature! You can't let him go with her, Miss Mary. He'd never survive that sort of life after all this.' In her anxiety she had grasped a handful of her apron and was crushing and squeezing it into a thousand creases. Mary, seeing this, nodded towards it and the housekeeper gave a gasp of irritation at her own folly and tried ineffectually to smooth out the tell-tale marks.

Mary suddenly made up her mind.

'Keep her in the breakfast room for five minutes,' she ordered, 'and then show her in here. I may be wrong, but I think I know how best to deal with her. I pray to God I'm right.'

With these words she sat down at the desk and drew a sheet of paper towards her. She looked up as the housekeeper hesitated. 'I may need you later as a witness,' she said. 'If I *do* ask for your signature, show no surprise and do as I say.'

Mrs Markham nodded and a slight feeling of relief warmed her. Miss Mary sounded efficient. Miss Mary knew what to do.

She went out and five minutes later, to the minute, showed Mollie Pett into the morning room where Mary waited, silhouetted against the light from the large window with a hand outstretched towards her visitor.

'Mollie, how nice of you to call,' she said. 'I'm so pleased to see you have escaped from that dreadful place where we last met. Do sit down and accept my apologies for keeping you waiting.'

Mollie ignored her hand and, with a toss of her head, announced firmly that she had 'come for the boy'.

Mrs Markham, at a look from Mary, went out, closed the door quietly and, for the first time in her life, applied her eye to the keyhole.

'I was expecting you, of course,' Mary smiled. 'You'll find him very well. He's quite an intelligent boy and making good progress at school although he missed such a lot of schooling in the early years. Will you take some tea with me, or coffee and cake? Mrs Markham makes a very good walnut and date slice.'

'You can cut out the smarmy talk,' said Mollie. 'All I want is Alexander. I've a right to him! He's old enough to earn a few bob and it looks like I'm going to need him.'

Mary glanced at the small carriage clock on the mantelpiece.

'I'm afraid he doesn't come out of school until three,' she said. 'But no doubt you can come back later. I'll have all his things packed and ready. But please tell me how *you* are faring. They told me at the prison that you had been released a week early. I had meant to call and see if we could help you in any way when you came out.'

'We?' said Mollie. 'Who's "we"?'

'The Brothers in Jesus.'

'Oh, that lot!' She snorted derisively, then seemed to notice for the first time Mary's reddened eyes and black gown.

'You're not looking exactly perky,' she said. 'Someone died?'

Mary stiffened and averted her eyes. 'A friend of the family,' she said shortly.

'Oh, sorry to hear it, but we've all got to go sometime.'

'Yes.' With a determined effort Mary brought her thoughts back to the present. 'How are you managing, Mollie? And how are your two little girls? I did hope at one time that you and Amos . . . he was a good-hearted man.'

'He was a pig!' snapped Mollie. 'Wanted to keep me under lock and key. "That may suit your gipsy women, but it don't suit me," I told him. Couldn't so much as look at another man without him ranting on at me. "If you want me, you'll have to marry me," I said, but he was too scared of his folks. They took a dislike to me and made up lies about me, to scare Amos off.' Her face had settled into a scowl as she recalled their real or imagined duplicity. 'Told him I was making up to this other chap and then Amos give me a hiding. I don't take a hiding, I don't – not for something I haven't done – leastways, not really done. I mean I did fancy him, he was a real looker, but I never done nothing.'

'Don't you want to see your daughters?'

Mollie shrugged. 'What's the use?' she said. 'I've got no place of me own, but I *will* have. I'm saving up.'

Mary hesitated. 'You're not . . . on the street again, are you?'

'I certainly am, *and* making better money than I ever did sweating my inside out all hours God sends at Lena-bloody-Tulson's! I can still catch a man's eye. All I need is a few decent togs and then I could pull a better sort of client.'

Mary took a deep breath. 'How will you manage to entertain your clients if Alexander is living with you?' she asked.

Mollie shrugged. 'He'll have to wait out until we're through,' she said.

'Wouldn't it be easier for you if you lived alone?'

' 'Course it would,' said Mollie, 'but his bit of money will come in handy.'

'I expect most of it will go on feeding him. And buying his clothes.'

'We'll manage.'

'I don't think you will, Mollie,' said Mary in a quiet, level voice. 'I think he would be more trouble to you than he's worth and you know that. I think – no, let me finish – that you'd rather he stayed on here with me and I have a proposition to make to you. If you allow Alexander to remain here – that is, you legally relinquish your rights to him – I will pay you a sum of money which will set you up in a room somewhere and buy you some new clothes.'

Mollie opened her mouth to speak but Mary ignored her and continued, 'Whether you find yourself honest work or carry on in your present miserable occupation is entirely up to you. I shall be in no way responsible. If you let yourself go downhill, it will be no good bleating to me. Alexander will be my legal ward, do you understand?'

Mollie nodded speechlessly.

'Good. Then what do you say?'

She glanced at Mary. 'And suppose he doesn't want to stay with you?'

'Then he comes back to you. We can ask him, of course, but – and this is very important – I don't want him to see you like this.'

'Like what?'

'I don't want him to know what you have become,' said Mary. 'His last memory of you was in the hop-garden, when you were younger and times were happier. If he stays with me, I should like his memory of you to be a pleasant one.'

Mollie heaved a deep sigh. 'Look, I'm no bleeding saint' she said, 'but I'm no worse than a lot of people, believe you me.'

'I do believe you,' said Mary. 'Please try to understand, Mollie. My only concern is for Alexander. You deserted him and I have given him a new life. If you insist on taking him back, it will be hard on him—'

'And you!'

'Oh yes,' Mary admitted. 'It would be very hard for me to part with him, but I would have to do so if you insisted.'

'And you wouldn't give me any money if I take him, is that it?'

'None at all,' said Mary firmly. 'None at all.'

'How very Christian! Brothers in Jesus, my arse! It's bribery.'

'You don't have to accept. No one is forcing you. It will be your decision entirely. Take the boy and go – or leave him here and I will make you a lump-sum payment to compensate you for the loss of his earnings – *and* I will continue to pay the Hearns for the maintenance of your two little girls.'

Mollie adjusted her tattered hat more firmly on her head while she struggled with her greed. Mary waited.

'How much?' Mollie asked.

'Fifty pounds!'

In spite of herself, Mollie gasped, 'Strewth!' Then she said hastily, 'It's not enough.'

Mary looked disconcerted. 'Not enough?' she repeated. 'Well, how much do you want? Fifty pounds is a great deal of money.'

'A hundred!' said Mollie and it was Mary's turn to gasp.

'A hundred pounds!' she cried. 'That's a fortune. That's ludicrous! A hundred—'

'Or else the deal's off!'

Mary stared at her, seeing the excitement mount in Mollie's face, giving it some of her earlier prettiness.

'One hundred pounds! Not a penny less,' cried Mollie. 'Then I'll make myself scarce.'

'You're sure?' said Mary.

Mollie nodded, hardly daring to breathe, unable to believe this new and glorious twist of fate. She watched as Mary opened a small drawer in the desk and took out a bulky sealed envelope.

'Count it, please,' she said, watching as Mollie ripped it open and counted out a hundred one-pound notes.

'You knew!' she gasped. 'You crafty bitch! You knew all along!'

Mary handed her a sheet of paper. 'Please read this carefully and then Mrs Markham will witness our signatures. It's a rough document I have drawn up giving me your permission to become Alexander's legal guardian. In due course it will go before the courts and become legally binding. There are one or two points on which you must help me, however. I know his date of birth but not his father's full name and occupation ... Is something wrong?'

Mollie's face was screwed up and she drummed her fists against her forehead. 'You bitch!' she whispered. 'You rotten, stinking bitch!'

Mary sighed softly and laid down the pen, waiting while Mollie controlled her temper. Outwardly she was cool but inwardly she felt a sickening fear that even now something was going to go wrong. Mollie's defeated fists fell into her lap and for a while longer she neither could nor would meet Mary's eyes.

'Bertram Harris, soldier,' she said, and did not see Mary's shocked expression and the way her hand began to shake. Bertram – Bertie – Vinnie's brother? Was it possible? If so, it could ruin everything.

'Dear God,' thought Mary, 'if she guesses, the trump card will be hers and I shall have lost Alexander. Mollie could take the boy to Vinnie; she could "sell" him to the highest bidder. If Vinnie knew that her brother had a son . . .' Even as her mind grappled with this unforeseen danger, she was rallying arguments. It need not be the same Bertram Harris; it was a common enough name. She turned away and filled in the details on the preliminary document she had drawn up with such optimism only twenty minutes earlier. It did not *have* to be the same Bertram Harris, but she knew with a dreadful certainty that it was. Yet Vinnie had told her of Bertram's marriage! She clutched at the straw. If Bertram Harris was already married, he was unlikely to want to claim an unknown twelve-year-old son whom he did not yet know existed. 'Dear God, help me,' she prayed. 'Don't let me lose Alexander.'

'Does this Bertram Harris know about his son?' she asked, trying to appear calm and businesslike.

' 'Course not!' said Mollie scornfully. 'He didn't stick around long enough to find out! Just two young soldiers come up to London on a weekend's leave. No address for me to write to, nothing. I should have had an allowance, I reckon. Soldiers get allowances for their wives and children. Well, I wasn't his wife but Alex was his kid. I wished afterwards I'd gone for his mate, Adam. Better looking, he was – and he fancied me. But Dora, that's my girlfriend that was, she took a real shine to this Adam, so—' She shrugged. 'I got Bertram, bless his cotton socks!'

It *was* the same man. Mary could no longer pretend otherwise. She breathed deeply to calm her wildly beating heart. Then another thought suddenly struck her.

'But can you be so sure that this child—'

'Oh, it's Bert's kid, all right,' said Mollie. 'I knew the moment I opened my eyes the next morning. You can tell, can't you? At least, you wouldn't know that, not being married, but some women can tell straight off and I'm one of them. I had this funny fluttering feeling down here – and my bosoms were all tingly. Real strange, it was, how quick it happened. Oh, I knew all right, but the blighter had gone by then, hadn't he?' She laughed.

'Do you have an address for him?' said Mary. 'Where did he live at the time you met?'

Mollie laughed. 'Oh Lord, he wasn't going to tell me that, was he! It wasn't like that at all. Just what they call a one-night-stand. Two soldiers out on a spree. These two lads picked up us two girls. End of story. Anyway, what's it matter? It was years ago.' She remembered the money she held in her hand and began to count it again, licking her fingers carefully as she pulled out each note.

'Oh, and one thing more,' said Mary. 'You're to move right away from this area. I don't want Alex to ever discover your whereabouts. If he ever asks, I shall tell him you were too poor to look after him and asked me to do so. Will that do? Or I could say you're married – I don't know.'

'Tell him I'm dead,' said Mollie. 'That way he'll give up asking and if he ever should meet me he'll never put two and two together.'

Mary looked up, humbled suddenly by this generous suggestion. Mollie read her thoughts and shrugged.

'Nobody's all bad,' she said. 'You're a Christian, you ought to know that.'

All Mary's scheming threatened to collapse around her as last-minute doubts crowded in. Mollie saw that too and stood up abruptly, cramming the money back into the envelope and thrusting it into her pocket.

'Well, is that the lot?' she demanded. 'No more questions? Then give me the bloody pen and let's get it done with.'

Mary rang the small brass bell and after a decent interval Mrs Markham came into the room.

'Will you act as witness to a document, Mrs Markham?' Mary asked her. 'There's no need for you to know the content of the paper. You will merely sign your name to say you witnessed our two signatures – Mollie's and mine.'

'I will, ma'am, yes.'

With a sheet of blotting-paper obscuring most of the wording and all of Bertram Harris's name, Mary signed. Then Mollie signed and Mrs Markham witnessed both signatures with scarcely veiled excitement.

'I will show Mollie out,' Mary told her and the housekeeper

withdrew, this time to apply her ear to the partially opened kitchen door. Mary and Mollie stood on the doorstep and Mollie, fiddling to readjust her hat, snatched it off suddenly and hurled it across the street.

'I think I'll go and buy meself a new hat,' she said with an attempt at bravado. 'Well, look after him!'

'I will,' said Mary. 'You have my promise on it.'

'Thanks.'

She walked away, her head held high, her bright ginger hair glinting in the sunshine. Mary closed the door as Mrs Markham rushed back into the hallway.

'Well?' she demanded.

'He's ours!' Mary whispered.

It would not be easy. She must keep Mollie out of his life and she would pray that Vinnie never discovered the boy's true identity. But for the present, at least, Alexander was hers and she would fight tooth and nail to keep him.

*

Three-year-old James closed his eyes in a thrill of anticipation as the swing arced higher and higher. Although he knew he was, in fact, quite safe – Nanny Doll would never let any harm come to him – there was always the remotest chance that his podgy hands would involuntarily relax their grip on the ropes and he would go flying up into the air, up over the bushes and trees and over the chimneyed house-top! But he did not allow so much as a squeal to pass his lips as his movement through the air flattened his blond curls to his head and breathed on to his eyelashes. He hoped Louise was watching him, but more probably she was absorbed with her doll. Teddy, he knew, was asleep in his large round-bottomed pram and unconsciously James envied him the security of that small world of the bouncing rattling rides. The swing began to slow down as Doll smilingly stepped aside to watch him, her hands on her hips. When it stopped, James wriggled impatiently on the seat.

'More, Nanny, more!' he demanded.

Doll assumed an air of great astonishment. 'More?' she cried, fanning herself with one hand. 'Glory be, Master James! You'll wear me out with your "More Nanny, more." I can't keep pushing you on that old swing. I'm worn out, honest I am. You've quite worn me out!'

This delighted him. It was one of their favourite games. 'More!' he cried. 'More and more and more!'

Doll put a hand to her heart and staggered towards the trunk of the tree, leaning against it in a state of apparent exhaustion.

'Oh, I can't, Master James. Don't ask me for more swing. You'll be the death of me, you really will!'

'I want *more*, Nanny! More swing!' His voice rose to an excited squeak.

'Oh, you dreadful boy!' He giggled as she levered herself slowly away from the tree and tottered towards him.

'Just one more go, then,' she said. 'But then no more. I'm quite puffed-out with all this pushing. You and your swing!'

Briefly two-year-old Louise looked up from the doll she was nursing to watch Doll set the swing in motion again. She was fair too, but a pale silver blonde with striking dark brown eyes. Of the three children, she was the only one with a birth weight of less than six pounds and she had never been plump. Even at two she was a dainty child, beautifully proportioned and finely boned with an exquisitely shaped head and doll-like face. Her hair clung wispily to her head and neck and curled into a halo when the weather was damp. Women already envied her her looks and men's admiration was open and inevitable. Yet she was not beautiful. Her features, though individually perfect, combined in an obscure way so that her small almond-shaped eyes set close to the narrow nose gave her face an almost feline quality and her cheeks were flat and very pale.

'Up you go! Up you go! Up, up and UP you go!' chanted Doll. Her beloved James kicked his legs and leaned backwards and forwards as his contribution to the required effort.

Adam said, 'A sight for sore eyes – a pretty young nanny and her three little charges!'

'Oh, it's you,' she said, continuing to push the swing.

He raised his eyebrows. 'What sort of greeting is that?' He leaned back against the tree, one hand in the pocket of his breeches, the other holding a long grass which he nibbled. He knew his best profile was towards Doll and he did not underestimate his good looks.

'Those little'uns think the world of you,' he said, changing the subject, slightly disturbed by her indifference.

'I should hope they do,' she said, giving the swing a final push and retreating from it to watch, one hand shading her eyes, as

James swooped to and fro with his eyes tightly closed. 'That's what I'm here for.'

'What, to be adored?' he asked, his tone gently teasing. 'You should have a man to adore you, not three kids.'

'If that's what I wanted, I'd have one by now,' she told him.

'It's never too late. I know someone who could be very interested. Very best references. First-class qualifications. He's got a degree in adoration.'

She had to laugh. That was the trouble with Adam Turner – he had a very clever way with words.

'Don't bother to tell me his name,' said Doll. 'I've enough to think about with my three charges, as you call them.'

'What do *you* call them?'

'My Jumbo James, my Fairy Fay – that's Miss Louise – and my little Teddy Bear, asleep, bless him. They're all my pets and they're all I want.'

Adam spat the chewed grass from his mouth. 'But they're *not* yours,' he reminded her, 'and they'll grow up and leave you. Move on to a governess or go to school. Who will adore you then?'

She shrugged. 'That's my worry,' she said lightly. James began to kick his feet. 'More!' he cried. 'More, Nanny!' He caught sight of Adam and saw that he held Doll's attention.

'More swing!' he cried again.

'Oh no!' Doll exclaimed. 'You slave driver! You awful boy! I can't push you any more, I'm much too tired. Oh dear! Please don't ask me.'

James wanted Adam to see the game. He wanted Adam to see how high he could go and how brave he was. His father used to clap his hands and call out 'Splendid!' but his father was dead. Uncle Gerald had admired his courage and so had the cousins. Now they too had gone away to their new house.

'Push me again! More and more!' he cried.

Doll shook her head doubtfully. 'I don't think I can, Master James. I've not an ounce of energy left in me,' she told him. 'You've worn out your poor old Nanny.'

Adam stepped forward suddenly. 'I'll give you a push, young-'un,' he said, seeing from the corner of his eye a spark of alarm in Doll's expression. Before she could intervene, and before James could decide whether or not he wanted Adam to push him, he grasped the ropes and began to twist them so that the swing spun.

'No!' cried James.

Adam laughed cheerfully. 'Don't say "No",' he said. 'You haven't tried it yet. This one of my very special twisters and you'll love it. You'll go round and round like a Catherine wheel and then fly away up to the moon.'

'Don't,' said Doll. 'You'll make him dizzy.'

James began to squeal with alarm and Louise looked up again, a slight frown on her face.

'I said *don't*!' snapped Doll, and she tried to push him aside but his hands still held the twisted ropes. They were very close and a gleam came into his eyes.

'What's it worth?' he whispered. 'Give me a kiss and I'll let him go.'

'I will not!'

'Right then – one more twist, Master James and away you'll go. Up into the sky and—'

'He'll do nothing of the sort,' cried Doll, struggling to prise Adam's hands from the ropes. 'Take no notice of him, Master James. He's only kidding you.'

'I'd like to be "kidding" you!' said Adam. 'Come on. Take a chance. Kiss me – you might even like it. One kiss to save your precious Jumbo James from a terrible fate. What sort of Nanny are you if you won't make such a small sacrifice?'

'You save your kisses for the mistress!' snapped Doll desperately as his large hands defied all her efforts to remove them from the ropes. She regretted the words as soon as they were out. Adam at once released the swing and she let it unwind slowly and carefully, soothing James as she did so.

'Oh, you know all about that?' said Adam. 'So that's it. You're jealous!'

'Jealous!' she answered. 'Don't flatter yourself. Surprised, that's all I am. Surprised that she bothers with someone like you.' She helped James down from the swing and sent him off to pick her some daisies.

'Oh, she bothers,' said Adam. 'And can you wonder? She needs someone to cheer her up. Nobody laughs round here.'

'The master's not been dead a month,' cried Doll. 'What d'you expect? Fun and games? Some of us cared and some of us miss him, you know.' Her eyes flashed dangerously.

He shrugged. 'Still in black after three weeks. It's not right.'

'If it's what she wants . . .' said Doll. 'Who are you to say what's right for her? You're just the gardener around here, remember?

You're not the privileged guest any longer – you've a job to do, same as the rest of us.'

His smile persisted but his eyes were hard. 'Call that a job? Pushing a swing all day? I'd like a job like that.'

'My job is to care for these children and that's what I do,' cried Doll. 'I feed them, wash them, dress them, play with them, nurse them when they're sick . . .' Her breath came quickly. 'You're a fine one to talk. You do next to nothing. Oh yes, we *have* noticed! Walk around with a rake over your shoulder or hide yourself away in the potting-shed, sat on your backside reading Cook's *Daily Mail*. Not to mention creeping up to the Colonel's room for a so-called "quick chat". More like an hour-and-a-half, and Janet worried sick that you'll tire him out.'

He smiled lazily. 'Have you finished?' he asked.

'No, I haven't! Cook sent me out for some marjoram last evening and I couldn't even *find* it! The herb garden's like a jungle! All overgrown and chock-a-block with weeds. It's a disgrace. You could try weeding it one day, if you could spare the time and it's not too much effort!'

Adam leaned down and pulled another long grass which he examined carefully before he spoke. 'You *are* jealous,' he said. 'You all are – and you really should be more careful what you say. For your information, I am *not* just the gardener and you might be very sorry one day for that spiteful little outburst.'

He leaned forward to tap the grass stem against her chest. 'I'm eating with "the mistress" this evening, only to me she's "Vinnie". Think on that, Miss High-and-Mighty Dorothy! She's alone now and needs a man about the place. Might pay you to give me that kiss and keep me sweet for the future.'

'You flatter yourself,' Doll snapped, trying to hide her uneasiness. She was not to know that Adam had not been invited to eat with Vinnie, but that he now intended to see that she did invite him. Three weeks was a long while and maybe now was the right time to make the first move.

'She'd no more think of marrying you than fly!' cried Doll angrily. 'Young William le Brun is more her match and *he's* been over several times. As for me kissing you – no thanks! Not now and not ever. You're a sly devil, Adam Turner; I wonder how Vinnie's brother ever picked you for a friend and that's the truth.'

Without warning, Adam's smile faded. He pulled her towards him and kissed her hard on the mouth, his tongue trying to force a

way between her closed teeth. As she opened her mouth to
scream a protest, it slid in and one hand went round to the back of
her head so that she could not wriggle free. She flailed at him with
her fists and suddenly, to her amazement, he released her with an
oath and she saw that young James had sunk his teeth into Adam's
thigh.

'Don't you hit him!' screamed Doll as she saw the large hand
raised against the boy. 'Don't you dare! Jumbo, lovey, stop! It's all
right, little love. Come to Doll, that's the way! There's nothing to
cry about.' She knelt on the grass and drew the trembling,
frightened child into her arms where he clung, his plump little
body shaking with fright.

'It'll be your word against mine,' said Adam.

She looked up at him.

'Get out of my sight,' she said.

*

Vinnie sat at her writing desk in the study. Her elbows rested on
its dark polished surface, her head was in her hands. She felt
drained of emotion, tired and ill. The doctor had told her to rest
each afternoon, but she dare not. Only frenzied activity could
keep her sombre thoughts at bay. She had been invited to the le
Bruns' for dinner that evening and had accepted, but now she
could not face the prospect. The effort required to bathe, change
her clothes, force herself to converse and be a 'guest' was too
daunting. She would telephone Clive and make her apologies; he
would understand. William would be disappointed, she knew. He
had been very attentive since Julian died. If only everyone would
leave her in peace, but it seemed they must all be fussing over her,
coaxing her to eat, urging her to rest, commiserating with long
faces and talking round the house in lowered voices.

Vinnie longed for life to get back to some kind of normality. It
could never be normal again, she knew, for Julian was dead. The
nights were agonisingly long and the days sad and grey. She felt
listless and indifferent to what went on around her. Planning the
menu was a meaningless chore, for she had no appetite. The
Colonel's attempts at cheerful encouragement were embarrassing to her. He meant well but she had no wish to be 'jollied'
along. The children were happy enough with Doll, she knew, and
she would pay them more attention when her depression lifted. It
was surely natural, she told herself, to be depressed after the

death of a loved one. Mourning was a process to be suffered after a bereavement. Surely they could allow her that much. She had told the doctor she did not need him, but still he made a point of seeing her for a few moments every day on the pretext of visiting the Colonel.

In front of her on the desk was a letter from the solicitor asking her to call in at his office or offering to call on her. There was a bill from the butcher and another from the vet, for there were now two foals in the new paddock and a yearling. It was an expensive hobby, she thought, and money might be a problem in the not-too-distant future. She assumed she would have to take on a farm manager. Ned Berry was a good pole-puller, but he had no head for business. She sighed. There was so much to think about and so much to be done.

Her thoughts returned to William le Brun and she wondered if his interest in her was entirely platonic. He had, she knew, been paying court to the daughter of a local councillor; the girl was no doubt greatly distressed by William's sudden attention to Julian Lawrence's widow. Vinnie could not understand it – men were fickle too, it seemed.

She thought about Rose and Andy and the children. Rose was expecting another child and the blacksmith's pride and delight were well-known. Vinnie remembered Julian's excitement when he had learned that James was on the way. It all seemed another world, another life in a far distant past.

There was a knock at the door and Adam Turner came into the room. His face lacked its usual smile and Vinnie wondered wearily what *his* problem was. Guiltily she thought that she had neglected him lately and wondered whether or not an apology would be in order.

'I had to see you,' he began. 'I didn't want the others to know.'

Vinnie frowned. 'The others? Whatever do you mean? Is something wrong?'

'I hate to bother you,' he said, 'when you've so many troubles of your own, but—'

Vinnie motioned him towards a chair and turned to face him. 'If it's me,' she said, 'you must understand that I'm just not seeing anyone at the moment. I don't enjoy company. I—'

'No, no,' he said hurriedly. 'Of course it's nothing you have done. It's just that – well, I hardly know how to put this without upsetting anyone but . . . I think perhaps I should go away.'

'Oh no, Adam!' she cried. 'Why should you?'

He shrugged miserably. 'I feel I don't rightly fit in here any more,' he said. 'It's no reflection on anyone, don't think that for a moment, but at one time I felt close to you and I thought I was some comfort to you in Bert's absence.'

'Oh, you were! I mean, you *are*,' said Vinnie. 'I don't understand what you're driving at. Please Adam, just tell me what's wrong.'

After a little more coaxing, Adam explained haltingly that he felt his presence at Foxearth was resented by the other members of the staff. When he had been Vinnie's guest, they had accepted him as such. Now he was the gardener, but still a friend of Vinnie's, they were uneasy in his company and fearful perhaps that he would 'carry tales'.

'Oh, but that's absurd!' cried Vinnie. 'No one would accuse you of anything underhanded. I can't believe it, Adam. You must be mistaken.'

He wished he could think so, he told her, but that was the only explanation for their coldness towards him. He did his work as well as he could and he only wanted to be friendly, but he could no longer pretend that they thought of him as anything but an interloper.

Vinnie listened in silence to the sorry tale, secretly appalled. How could she have been so blind? Whatever would Bertie think if he knew his closest friend had been made to feel unwelcome in his sister's home? It was hard to believe that such a genuine, kindly person as Adam could possibly arouse so much animosity. She had not thought Mrs Tallant capable of small-mindedness – to snub him repeatedly, as he had asserted. Vinnie was ashamed. And Doll – to reject his friendly overtures as though he were some sort of pervert! None of it made any sense. What on earth had inspired them all to unite against him, she wondered. Were they jealous? She had seen no sign of anything untoward, but then she had not been aware of very much at all since Julian's death.

'Poor Adam,' she said. 'I'm so sorry that you have been unhappy and I've had my head in the sand. Whatever must you think of me?'

He smiled at her. 'I think you are a very sad, beautiful, lonely woman,' he said softly. 'I want so much to help you – I feel Bert would expect me to offer some kind of support at a time like this –

but we seem to have lost each other, you and I, somewhere along the way.'

As she made no answer, he stood up and crossed the short distance between them, then in the most natural way he fell on to his knees beside her and took hold of her hands. 'Dear little Vinnie,' he said softly. 'I don't want to leave you, but I feel so useless. So helpless. I feel unwanted and—'

Vinnie was horrified. 'No, Adam! Don't say that, I beg you,' she cried. 'It's all my fault; I've neglected everything. I've lost interest in it all and there's so much to be done – so many decisions to be made. I just shrink from it all. I seem to fill my days with household matters and ignore the important things going on around me. No, Adam, don't you dare say again that you are unwanted or that you should leave Foxearth.' She smiled. 'A proxy brother shouldn't desert his sister in her hour of need.'

Adam gave a slight shrug and she thought he looked a little happier at her words. He gave her hands a little squeeze.

'I just want you to be happy,' he told her. 'I want to make up to you for all your unhappiness. Look at this!' He touched the stuff of her black gown. 'Still in black! I can't bear it, Vinnie. Julian wouldn't want it, I'm sure. Wearing black doesn't bring him back; it doesn't make you remember Julian more clearly or more often. And it casts a gloomy shadow over that sweet face. If Bertie was here, he'd be where I am now – I know he would – pleading with you to change into something lighter and come back into the land of the living. The doctor's worried about you. I overheard him saying so. "Too withdrawn," he said. Now, we're going to make a big effort, you and I, for your sake, for Bert's, for everyone's sake.' She looked at him doubtfully. 'Oh, yes we are, my poor little Vinnie. Now come along. Stand up and pay attention to your brother. I suppose you are dining alone tonight?'

'I've been invited out to the le Bruns',' Vinnie began, 'but I was going to make my excuses.'

'Cancel it,' said Adam. He put a finger under her chin and his eyes were very soft. 'You go upstairs now and rest, then change out of your black and come down to dinner in – let me see, now? Ah, I have it – the apricot taffeta. The colour will give your face a warm glow. Then we will dine together, just the two of us.' She hesitated. 'Just to please me,' he said. 'And then I won't leave Foxearth.'

'Oh Adam, don't speak of it!'

'Then you agree?'

Vinnie nodded. 'That's my girl!' he whispered, hiding his relief with an effort. He kissed the tip of her nose. 'A kiss from Bert for his own good little Vinnie,' he said softly. 'Now, off you go and I'll tell Mrs Tallant to telephone the le Bruns – no, off you go and take a nap. I can deal with it; it's about time someone took you in hand.'

Smilingly, he shooed her out of the room and waited until she was upstairs. Then he sat down at the desk and read through the day's mail. When he had finished he sat for a while enjoying the novelty of his situation. His fingers drummed ceaselessly on the desk-top and his lips curved in a satisfied smile. Then he rang the bell and turned slowly in his chair to meet Edie's astonished gaze.

'Please ask Mrs Tallant to telephone the le Bruns,' he told her. 'Say that Mrs Lawrence is unwell and will not be dining with them this evening. Make her apologies. And tell Cook there will be two at dinner tonight. I shall be eating with Mrs Lawrence. That's all. What are you staring at, girl? You can go.'

*

It was nearly ten o'clock that evening when Clive le Brun was announced. Adam had told Edie to telephone and suggest that he might care to join them for coffee and liqueurs.

Clive walked into the room and stopped short in shocked surprise. The maid's call had puzzled him, for he had received an earlier message that Vinnie was unwell. Now he found her not only in what looked like perfect health, but dressed in an apricot taffeta gown which threw a soft glow on to her already flushed cheeks. Her eyes wore the drowsy look of someone who has drunk a deal too much wine. And she was sharing her meal with Adam Turner, who looked exceptionally pleased with himself and was obviously deriving great enjoyment from Clive's reaction.

'Clive!' said Vinnie. 'How lovely of you to call. Will you—'

His words cut short her invitation. 'I'd like to speak to you privately,' he said, his tone very level.

'Oh, you can talk in front of Adam,' said Vinnie. 'He's an old friend of the—'

'I said privately,' insisted Clive. 'Perhaps the morning room or the study?'

'Perhaps I'm in the way,' said Adam, making as though to rise.

'No, Adam, of course you're not,' said Vinnie, putting a hand on his arm. 'Clive and I will go into the study. We won't be long.'

She stood up and crossed the room carefully. Clive made no comment but his expression was grim. Once in the study he faced her coldly.

'I'm sorry if I have interrupted your little *tête à tête*,' he said with heavy sarcasm. 'I understood you were unwell?'

Vinnie tried to concentrate on what he was saying. 'No,' she said. 'At least, I don't think so.'

'Then why didn't you come to dinner as arranged?'

'Adam thought we should eat at home,' she said. 'No, that's not right. Adam thought I should change out of my black ... No, Adam—'

'What has it got to do with Adam?' His questions were ruthlessly blunt to the point of rudeness.

Vinnie began to consider her answer, then forgot the question and sat down heavily on a chair. Clive towered over her. 'You turned down our invitation so that you could stay at home and have dinner with Adam Turner.'

'Did I?' Vinnie shook her head in a troubled way. 'No, I don't think that was it,' she said. 'It was for Bertie's sake . . . to please Bertie.'

'Your brother is in India.'

'But Adam is my brother, in his place. He's my brother by proxy. Yes, that's it,' she said eagerly, pleased to have sorted out the problem so clearly. 'Adam is my brother until—'

'Don't talk such rot, Vinnie!' Clive snapped. 'You're behaving like a child.'

Vinnie's lips trembled as she struggled to retain the wonderful aura of well-being brought about by the wine. Clive pulled up a chair and sat down opposite her, his manner uncompromising.

'I came over tonight because I thought you were ill and might need me,' he said. 'I now see that I was wrong. You are perfectly well and you have Adam Turner to advise you. He seems a very odd choice but that is your business, not mine. I also have to tell you that I am going to London at the end of next week. An uncle of mine died about six weeks ago and I am one of the executors. I delayed attending to the estate until I thought I could safely leave you.'

His manner was having a sobering effect on Vinnie. It dawned on her slowly that he was going away. 'But where are you going?' she asked. 'How long will you be away?'

'It's difficult to say how long these things will take,' he told her, 'but I will leave a telephone number with William where you can reach me if the need arises. I'm sure it won't be necessary, however.'

She looked at him helplessly. 'Why are you being like this?' she whispered. 'Please don't be angry.'

'I'm not angry, Vinnie. I'm disappointed in you, that's all. I thought you had more sense.'

'But Adam said—'

'Adam Turner is hardly the ideal judge of what is best for you, Vinnie. Being a friend of your brother's does not automatically render his judgement sound.' He stood up and held out his hand. 'Remember that William will have a number where I can be reached, and try not to make too great a fool of yourself over that young upstart. Don't bother to ring for Edie – I'll see myself out.'

Before Vinnie could think of a way to delay him, he strode out of the room and a moment later she heard the front door slam behind him.

'Damn!' she whispered miserably. Her head was clearing. She glanced down at the apricot taffeta with sudden distaste and wished she could make just one decision and get it right. Her confidence oozed away as she sat there feeling angry, dejected and confused.

Adam came into the room. 'I heard all that,' he said. 'I listen at keyholes! Pompous old fool! Don't let him spoil our evening.' He held out his hand. 'Come on, your coffee's getting cold!'

Vinnie gave him her hand and allowed herself to be pulled up from the chair. 'Can you play chess, Adam?' she asked suddenly.

'Chess? Good heavens, no! And I don't want to. We've better things to do with our time.'

CHAPTER TWENTY

The clock on the mantelpiece ticked steadily for almost twenty-four hours a day, but just occasionally it missed and whenever this happened Mrs Bryce smiled, remembering the time her husband had dropped it. They were on their honeymoon and the clock had been a present from one of her favourite uncles. Her very new, very young husband blushed and stammered his apologies and she tried hard to pretend it did not matter, when in fact she was very upset. She considered it a bad omen because the glass had cracked and she had expected seven years' bad luck. Fortunately, in the novelty of her newly-married state she had soon forgotten the incident.

The ticking clock missed now and Mrs Bryce, who was knitting, smiled, putting aside for a few moments her thoughts about Rose and the children. In spite of her loyalties to Tom, she was the first to admit that Andy Roberts was doing his best for Rose and the children. Even little Tommy – *not* so little Tommy now, she amended with a smile – was beginning to show him signs of affection. Not often, but it was a start. And the boy loved to 'help' in the forge. As soon as he got home from school he changed his clothes and joined Andy and Martin, enjoying the noise and bustle and learning fast. He would make a good blacksmith one day.

Of course Andy had no sons of his own yet, although Rose was expecting again and it might be a boy. Secretly Mrs Bryce hoped for a girl, for she wanted Tommy to take over the forge. She thought Tom would wish it to – to see his first son a 'man of substance' in the village. She shuddered when she thought how close they had all come to the workhouse. If it had not been for Vinnie . . .

At the end of the row she paused, took off her spectacles and rubbed her eyes tiredly. One of the three candles was burning low and she had no more. She took up a pencil from the table beside her and added 'candles' to her shopping list. She would pop down to the store before she went to work in the morning. Critically she considered the sock she was knitting, measuring it against its fellow. They were to be a present for Andy, for his birthday. He was good to Rose and the children and for that she could forgive him any faults he might have – and he must have some, for no one was perfect, although Rose had nothing but good to say about him. She was very loyal, Rose was. And dutiful. She sent Tommy over once a week to chop her firewood and invited her to lunch on alternate Sundays. And, of course, she and Rose were together in the hop-gardens most days, so she was never short of company or behind with the news.

Mrs Bryce had long ago learned how to be content. Now she thanked God for Rose's good fortune and for the joy the grand-children brought her – and not least for Brook Cottage, which Vinnie had told her was hers for as long as she wanted it. Beside her the dog jerked in sleep and twitched her nose.

'Make the most of it,' Mrs Bryce told her with a smile. 'You'll not have a moment to call your own when those pups arrive – *and* it won't be long now, by the size of you!'

The little Jack Russell had blown up like a balloon. It had been her first time on heat and Mrs Bryce had tried to keep her in, but the wretched mongrel from the 'Horse and Cart' had somehow evaded her eagle eye and the deed was done. God alone knew what the puppies would be like! Not that it was an ugly mongrel; it was quite handsome as mongrels go but there . . . ! She had resigned herself to a funny-looking brood and hoped Vinnie would not mind too much. Vinnie had given her the little bitch when Rose and the children moved out – 'to keep you company'. She was a thoughtful girl. Always had been, thought Mrs Bryce, and now she'd lost *her* husband . . . There was a knock on the door and she put down her knitting and went to the front door. She had three different locks on the door and would never open one of them until she was sure who it was.

'It's only me – Vinnie!' All three locks were immediately undone and the two women hugged.

'What on earth are you doing at this hour?' Mrs Bryce asked her as Vinnie came into the room, throwing off her heavy shawl.

'I was lonesome,' said Vinnie. 'I thought I would just walk down and see if your light was still on. If not, I would have gone home again.'

Mrs Bryce bustled round. 'Sit yourself down, Vinnie. Talk of the devil! I was just thinking about you. Good job you came when you did – another few minutes and I'd have gone to bed. Oh, stop your barking Trix, it's only Vinnie. She knows you've brought something for her.'

The little terrier pranced round Vinnie's feet as she bent to fondle her.

'I was just thinking I'd done enough knitting for one night,' said Mrs Bryce. 'Only a few more inches to go. Andy's feet are that big. Size eleven. I'm always pulling his leg.' She looked at Vinnie keenly. 'Fancy a cup of tea? I'm always ready for one, as you well know.'

Vinnie nodded and handed over a small parcel. 'Her ladyship's bone,' she said. 'We had a nice piece of pork on Sunday, big enough to feed an army. I don't know why Mrs Tallant is so extravagant when there's only me to eat it.'

Vinnie reddened slightly as she spoke, for she *did* know. Mrs Tallant had made several passing references to the fact that Adam frequently shared Vinnie's evening meal and Vinnie suspected that her extravagance was by way of protest.

Mrs Bryce unwrapped the bone and called Trix into the scullery to eat it. Vinnie sat down in the armchair opposite the old lady's favourite rocker and looked round the room, while Mrs Bryce clattered spoons and cups and tea-caddy in the scullery.

The room itself had never been her home, but some of the furniture had surrounded the five-year-old Vinnie when she first went to live with Mrs Bryce and Tom. The table, with one leg still wedged on a small pebble to make it match its fellows and keep the table steady. The armchair in which she sat was as hard and unyielding as ever, stuffed to bursting, its back covered with an antimacassar, its arms protected by crocheted squares. Vinnie remembered the first time she had sat in it, her short legs stuck out in front of her, while Christina Lawrence persuaded Mrs Bryce to give her a home.

'Don't scowl so, child,' Mrs Bryce had said. 'No one's going to bite you!'

Tonight the familiar old chair, the ticking clock and the warmth of the welcome she had received were like a balm to Vinnie's bruised and battered spirit. She hardly knew why she had come to Brook Cottage – had not meant to come, in fact. At dinner she had picked at her food without interest and repulsed Adam's attempts at conversation. Almost rudely she had cut the meal short, telling Edie they would not be wanting coffee or liqueurs. Adam had raised his eyebrows and Vinnie had said, 'There will still be plenty of coffee in the kitchen.' She had feigned a headache and left him looking angry and hurt. In retrospect she was ashamed of herself, but it was too late now.

Mrs Bryce came back into the room with a tray in her hands.

'I was just counting my blessings when you knocked,' she told Vinnie. 'This little cottage is just right for me and quite near Rose and the children. There's hardly a day passes but one or other of them doesn't pop their little heads round the door. I keep a few biscuits or a barley sugar handy in the tin, same as I always did. There's a bit of coconut cake here, so help yourself. I can't get out of the habit of cooking for a family and I'm eating too much. Look at the size of me! I don't know what my husband would say if he could see me now. Never did like fat women, he didn't. "You could fall off and hurt yourself," he used to say.' She giggled. 'He could be really saucey at times. I didn't know what to make of him at first, I wasn't used to it. Young and innocent in those days, I was.'

Vinnie had heard it all so many times before, but she smiled obligingly.

Mrs Bryce frowned. 'You all right, Vinnie?' she asked. 'You're very quiet. Not much to say for yourself.' Vinnie took a large mouthful of cake. 'And don't answer with your mouth full,' said Mrs Bryce automatically, whereupon they both grinned.

Mrs Bryce poured milk and tea into the cups, carefully shaking the tea-strainer so as not to drip it on to the tablecloth.

'You embroidered this cloth,' Mrs Bryce told her. 'For Christmas that year I had the neuralgia so badly. D'you remember? You were eleven then. Washes beautifully, although the silks have faded just a bit. Not much though.'

'I remember,' said Vinnie, pushing the last of the cake into her mouth and discovering suddenly that she was hungry.

'Well, that didn't last long,' Mrs Bryce laughed. 'Help yourself, love; there's penty there. Every slice *you* eat means less round my middle, because if it's there I shall tuck in. You look a bit peaky still, but it's not surprising. It takes a long time to get over a loss like that. "Feed a sorrow," isn't that what they say?'

She chattered on, waiting, while Vinnie ate a second and then the last slice of cake. She refilled the teapot, then took down her tin full of curling rags.

'I'll do it.' It had always been one of Vinnie's favourite jobs. Now Mrs Bryce moved on to a straight-backed chair with the tin of curling rags and Vinnie stood behind her. First the brushing

with the wooden bristle brush, now minus most of its bristles, then
the combing with the large tortoiseshell comb with the wide teeth.

'There's still only one tooth missing,' Vinnie marvelled.

Mrs Bryce nodded complacently. 'That's been a good comb,
that has,' she said. 'Mind you, I gave a lot for it and you get what
you pay for. I've always said that. Pay that little bit extra if you can
and you'll be well satisfied.'

Vinnie measured out each lock of hair and folded the ends into
a strip of cloth. Then she rolled it up with deft practised movements, gave it a twist and tied it securely. The hair-curling was Mrs
Bryce's nightly ritual. Tom had teased her about it and she had
told him, 'When I forget my curlers, you can send for the undertaker!'

While Vinnie was thus engaged Mrs Bryce chattered desultori-
ly, deliberately leaving longish silences in which Vinnie could tell
her, if she wished, why she had come. Something was wrong and
it was not only Julian's death.

'Ouch! Not too tight, you'll scalp me!' she cried as Vinnie
distractedly twisted one curler too far.

'Sorry! There, that's the last one.' She sat down abruptly as
though exhausted.

'Another cup of tea, dear?'

'Yes, please.'

Vinnie sat staring into what was left of the fire, waiting for
words to form in her mind. The dog got up suddenly and trotted
over to the door; Vinnie let her out into the garden and waited for
her to come back again.

Mrs Bryce came back into the room with a plate of sandwiches.
'There you are, love,' she told Vinnie. 'You tuck into these. You
look as though you need a bit more flesh on those bones. There's
one lot of cheese, and anchovy paste in the other.'

Silently Vinnie began to eat. Fatigue and despair showed in her
eyes. She drank two cups of tea and ate her way through all the
sandwiches. Then Mrs Bryce brought her the apple pie and cold
custard she had been saving for her lunch next day and Vinnie set
about it as though she had not eaten for a month.

'Little ones well, are they?' asked Mrs Bryce.

'Yes, thank you.'

Vinnie scraped the dish clean and sucked the last morsel of
custard from the back of the spoon. Then she looked at Mrs
Bryce, who was knitting again.

'How did you know,' she asked, 'that your husband was the

right man for you – or didn't you know?'

Mrs Bryce checked her row, turned the needles and tugged more wool from the ball.

'I didn't know he was the right one,' she said, 'but I did think all the others were the wrong ones. I suppose that meant it had to be him. I don't know, Vinnie, really I don't.'

Vinnie stared down at the worn carpet and said, 'I don't think I made him very happy and now he's dead I want to make it all up to him, but it's too late and I don't know how I can bear it. If only I hadn't married him, he might have been happier with someone else.'

'But Vinnie, love, it was him wed you the way I heard it, not the other way round. Maybe if he hadn't wed you, he'd have been *more* unhappy wishing he had! Folk are funny, Vinnie. You must think about all the good times you had and try not to brood. You gave him three lovely children.'

Vinnie nodded, wanting to be convinced.

'Look Vinnie, maybe Julian Lawrence wasn't the man for you, but it doesn't matter. I'm sure you did the best you could for each other and that's what matters. That's all anyone can do.'

A long deep sigh escaped Vinnie's lips and she stood up, leaned over and kissed the old woman's cheeks. 'I've eaten you out of house and home,' she said.

'I like to see someone enjoy their food,' said Mrs Bryce, 'and I was glad of a bit of company. You pop in whenever you've a mind to. You may be Lavinia Lawrence of Foxearth, but to me you're still young Vinnie and always will be.'

She followed her to the door, arranging the shawl more snugly round Vinnie's shoulders.

'Mind how you go,' she said. 'Give my love to all the little ones, bless them! That Doll is a real sweet girl. You can see they're fond of her.'

Vinnie kissed her again and Mrs Bryce kept the door open as long as she dared to light her on her way down the lane. Then she called in Trix – who had sneaked out again – and locked and bolted the door once more.

'Well, Trix, what do you make of all that, eh?' she said. 'I'm sure I don't know – but I'd better stock the larder in case she comes again!'

*

Vinnie discovered that Julian's life had been insured for a very large sum of money – an amount that decreased with the passing years. It was intended, the solicitor explained, to protect a woman with a young family. The older the children were, the less time remained for them to be dependent on their mother's estate. Vinnie's children were very young and the policy itself had only run for four years of the twenty-five for which cover was provided. There were also bequests for each child, maturing when they reached twenty-one years of age. In Julian's will he had also left Foxearth to James, with the proviso that Vinnie should live there for as long as she wished.

She asked the solicitor if there were any restraints on how the insurance money could be spent and his answer was in the negative. She wanted, she explained, to modernise the farm in various ways. That, apparently, was not only acceptable but far-sighted. He explained that if she did not want to tie up her capital the bank would be only too pleased to make her a loan, since she was able to offer such impressive collateral. He seemed to approve Vinnie's plans wholeheartedly and she left his office with a lighter step and a growing feeling of self-confidence.

At last, it seemed, she had made a wise decision. All that remained was to carry out her plans, and although that in itself was a daunting prospect, she knew Ned Berry and Clive le Brun would willingly give their support and the benefit of their considerable experience. She had determined on two main areas of improvement – the hoppers' accommodation – now long overdue – and the new form of stringing hops. The first involved the largest financial outlay; the second depended on Ned Berry's co-operation. It was almost June now, too late in the year to put either plan into effect, but at least Vinnie felt she could begin negotiations. She was longing to do something positive. James's inheritance was in her hands and times were bad in the industry. Vinnie meant to do all in her power to preserve the estate intact for him and that meant a full-time involvement in affairs of which she knew very little.

Too late she regretted that the arrival of the children had distracted her from the management of the farm. Yet Julian had not encouraged her interest and only now was she beginning to understand his view. She still did not entirely concur, but she did have an inkling of his attitude and the reasoning behind it. Vinnie was no longer 'one of them'. She was 'the guvnor' and the overall picture looked rather different.

She returned to the house feeling very pleased with herself and found a letter on the hall table. It contained Mrs Tallant's resignation.

'But why?' Vinnie demanded, as soon as the housekeeper answered her summons. She waved the letter angrily. 'All you say here is "matters beyond your control". *What* matters? I don't understand. At least if you are determined to leave, I should like to know why you are going.'

Mrs Tallant drew herself up to her full height and clasped one hand inside the other. 'It's not my place to say, ma'am,' she said. 'I should like to leave at the end of the month, if that's convenient.'

'Well, it's not,' said Vinnie. 'Of course it's not convenient. It will never be a convenient time for you to go, because you belong to Foxearth.'

'I'm sorry, ma'am, but there's no other way round it,' she answered. 'And I venture to say, if you'll forgive me, that I shall not be the only one leaving you.'

Vinnie gasped. All her new-found confidence evaporated as she looked at the housekeeper.

'Not the only one? Now you *will* have to explain yourself,' cried Vinnie. 'Something must be very wrong – and all these hints are not making anything easier. I tell you, I cannot understand what is going on and I insist on an explanation. If you will not give me one, then you can hardly expect me to furnish you with a reference.'

Only Vinnie knew that she was bluffing. After so many years of faithful service to Foxearth, she would not dream of letting the housekeeper go without a glowing reference – but Mrs Tallant did not know that and it was her turn to go pale.

'That's entirely up to you, ma'am,' she said stiffly.

'Yes, it is,' said Vinnie. 'Where will you go without a reference?'

'I'll manage somehow, ma'am.'

Vinnie's composure deserted her and she stood up. 'You will tell me *at once*,' she shouted, 'the reason for this monstrous letter. Otherwise you will pack and leave within the hour! I mean it. Don't push me too far, Mrs Tallant. You have upset me terribly and I am in no mood for any more arguments.'

She screwed the letter into a tight ball and threw it across the room. For a moment she thought the housekeeper was going to defy her, but then Vinnie saw her expression change.

'Very well then, ma'am,' she said stiffly. 'If you must know the truth, I am not prepared to take one more order from Adam Turner. I was engaged by the other Mrs Lawrence and I stayed on to serve you and the master. I do not expect to take my orders from the gardener. And neither does any one else on this staff, believe me!' Her eyes flashed. 'You wanted the truth and that's it. To us, Adam Turner is an upstart nobody and if you care to make a pet of him, that's your business. Me, I hate to see you and the Colonel being made fools of, but that's your choice. *I'm* not under his spell and no more is Janet nor Doll nor Edie. None of us like him, you see, because we've seen through him—'

Vinnie held up her hand to quell the flow of impassioned words, but now that the housekeeper had been provoked into having her say she intended to say it all.

'No, ma'am,' she cried. 'I *will* speak. The others won't dare to tell you, but I'm leaving so I don't care. That Adam may be your brother's friend, ma'am, but he's a rogue. A smooth-talking, double-crossing rogue. Oh, I can see how he's deceived you. He deceived us at first. But lately we've seen through his little game. We've put our heads together and it's plain as the nose on your face what he's up to. He's tried to play us all off, one against the other, with his sly little digs, and I don't doubt he's done it to you. Putting doubts into your mind about all of us—' Vinnie's guilty look betrayed her instantly. 'Oh, he has? I thought as much. I said so to Cook only last week.'

Here she ran out of breath and stood in front of Vinnie, her chest heaving, her eyes blinking, flecks of spittle forming at the corners of her mouth.

'Please, Mrs Tallant,' said Vinnie faintly. 'Please do sit down for a moment. You look terrible – you will make yourself ill.'

'Ill? It's a wonder I'm not ill already with the worry of it all,' said Mrs Tallant. She remained standing, however, and for a moment the two women looked at each other helplessly.

'I had no idea . . .' Vinnie began, then faltered to a stop.

'Oh, we don't blame you, ma'am. It's a very sensitive time for you, with the master gone and everything. We know that and we sympathize. But, ma'am, he is not to be trusted. I wish I could make you believe that. He behaved very badly towards young Master James and when—'

'What?' cried Vinnie. 'What do you mean? What did he do? I've heard nothing of this.'

'No, you wouldn't, ma'am, because Doll was scared to tell you. But he frightened Master James on the swing, trying to make him dizzy and then when Doll protested he . . . well, he made certain unpleasant advances to her which she hated—'

'Oh, dear God!'

'And then he said he was going to be master here one day and we'd all better watch our steps. I've seen him, ma'am, sitting at that very desk, reading your letters.'

'Mrs Tallant! Stop this!' cried Vinnie. 'I don't want to hear it.' She clapped both her hands over her ears and sank down on to the sofa, her head bowed. She was so still for such a long time that the housekeeper became worried that her revelations had been too great a shock.

'Are you all right, ma'am?' she asked timidly.

Vinnie opened her eyes. 'I'm all right, Mrs Tallant, but – forgive me for asking you, but do you swear to the truth of all this? On your honour?'

'I do indeed, ma'am,' said Mrs Tallant fervently. 'Talk to Doll yourself, ma'am, and she'll tell you. Mr Bilton, too.'

'Tim Bilton?'

'Yes, ma'am. Trying to tell him how to run the stables! Mr Bilton says he can't stand much more of his interference. But he's so cunning, ma'am, that Adam Turner. He's got the poor old Colonel eating out of his hand. Takes him whisky, ma'am, and you know what the doctor said.'

'Whisky!' Vinnie groaned, then she took a deep breath. 'Mrs Tallant,' she said, 'I appreciate what you have told me and I would like you to reconsider your resignation. I would also like to see Doll immediately and I shall want to speak to all the staff individually before I go to bed tonight. Except Mr Turner. I shall talk to him in the morning.'

The next two-and-a-half hours were harrowing ones for Vinnie. She went to bed that night exhausted and disillusioned, only to lie awake rehearsing what she would say to Adam in the morning.

She spent a sleepless hour sifting and resifting the evidence about Adam's treachery, for that is how his behaviour appeared to her. She had taken him trustingly into her home, a perfect stranger, on the grounds that he was Bertie's friend, and he had betrayed that trust. He had been charming and devious and she shuddered when she thought how near she had come to disaster. Master of Foxearth! That he would never be – but could it have happened? Vinnie hoped not, but she acknowledged her own vulnerability and confessed that she had found his open, friendly manner reassuring. He had a warmth which she needed, but warmth in a husband was not enough. In a friend it was sufficient, but Adam had not intended to remain a friend. That much was painfully obvious now.

She sighed, tossing restlessly in the large bed as she remembered the frequent occasions when she had drunk just a little too much wine. Was that design on Adam's part, she wondered miserably, or her own foolishness? Had he hoped one night to take advantage of her? Would she have allowed it to happen? The idea terrified her. She had come very close to another grave error of judgement and she could only thank God – and Mrs Tallant! – for her reprieve. In turn angry and remorseful, she muttered furiously into the darkness and longed for the release of tears, but this was denied her.

What would Adam have to say for himself, she wondered. Could he somehow justify his behaviour? In one way she hoped he could, because then she would not have to send Bertie's friend away. Yet if he stayed, one by one the staff would leave. Was that part of his plan? Maybe he would replace them with people of his own choice – people of whom she could not approve. Lying alone in the darkness Vinnie's imagination ran away with her and the whole affair took on the dimensions of a hideous nightmare.

Trembling, she sat up and lit her bedside candle. The feeble light showed her the familiar room and she took comfort from it. She told herself she was being ridiculous, allowing the incident to assume unwarranted importance. The servants could not all be wrong. There was no conspiracy. If Adam could not give her a satisfactory answer to their complaints, then she would ask him to go. But supposing he refused? A fine perspiration broke out on her skin at the prospect. Could he refuse? No, of course not. She was being ridiculous again. But how would he react, if he *was* guilty? He might show a side of his nature which she, at least, had never seen. He might become abusive; violent, even. Vinnie shrank from the thought. She longed for sleep and oblivion, but was afraid to rest before she had covered all the likely ramifications of tomorrow's confrontation.

After another restless hour, she had just decided to go downstairs and make herself a hot drink when the door creaked and she saw it opening. Thinking it might be one of the children, she waited, but to her horror it was Adam Turner who came into the room. He was barefoot and wore only a dressing-gown. His finger was pressed to his lips.

'We don't want to rouse the whole house, do we?' he whispered as he crossed to stand beside the bed, smiling down at her.

Vinnie's heart pounded with fear. He *knows*, she told herself. He's aware of what's happened here this evening. But what can he possibly hope to achieve by . . .

She put out a hand to reach for her own dressing-gown, thankful that at least her nightgown covered her, but his hand closed over hers.

'You don't need that,' he whispered.

To her horror, he sat down on the side of the bed and she realized that under the dressing-gown he was naked. Fine brown hairs covered his chest and the soft light flattered him. To the right woman he would appear an attractive mate. But not to her!

'For God's sake!' she said, her voice low. 'What do you think you are doing here – and at this hour of the night? Are you mad?'

'I've come to put my case,' he mocked, his hand still round her arm in a painfully firm grasp. 'I don't see why these hysterical old biddies should have it all their own way. Oh yes, I told you – remember? – that I listen at keyholes! I don't think you are stupid enough to listen to the tittle-tattling of a pack of stupid women. You have more sense than that, Vinnie. You're like Bert. You've got your head screwed on the right way and an eye to the main chance.'

Vinnie tried to tug her arm free. 'Don't you speak about my brother like that!' she hissed. 'And let go of my arm. You're hurting me.'

'Then stop fighting me,' he said. He still smiled and his voice was so calm. 'Just listen to me.' He saw her eyes go to the bell beside the bed. 'I shouldn't ring that,' he said. 'That *would* be a mistake. Then they would find us in bed together. Oh, I'd jump in as soon as look at you; I've thought about it often enough. You and me, Vinnie, in that lovely big bed.' His tone changed slightly, almost caressing her. Vinnie watched him with the fascination of a rabbit for a snake.

'It could be so wonderful,' he whispered. 'I wager you have never known true delight in your marriage bed. I could show you that, Vinnie. That's no idle boast. And it would be so right – the two of us, brought together by Bertie. He'd be so happy for us. Can you imagine the letter you would write? Between us we'd make Foxearth our heaven. I'd make you laugh – I'd show you how to enjoy life. No one else would matter. Just you and me. We'd laugh all day and make love all night. It's the perfect answer for us and in your heart you know it.'

'And the children?' Vinnie asked, her mind racing, wondering how best to handle this man. She did *not* want to attract the attention of the household and she did not for a moment doubt that Adam would carry out his threat to climb into bed with her. Then doubtless he would claim she had enticed him.

'The children? I'd be a good father to them—'

'You made James cry,' she said.

His smile did not falter. 'Did James say so? Or was it Miss Slyboots Doll? She's a wicked little liar, but you won't realize that. You're so honest, Vinnie, you believe the best of other people. You don't want to believe ill of her, so she can easily dupe you.'

He found her other hand and held both to his lips. 'Dearest Vinnie, don't let them spoil our love. I know it's early days, but I do know I love you and that you could learn to love me. I've loved you ever since I first saw you.'

'You tried to kiss Doll,' said Vinnie, her tone as steady as she could make it.

His eyebrows went up and he shook his head gently. 'Doll *told* you I tried to kiss her,' he corrected her. 'Doll would like it to be that way. She's an attractive woman and she needs a man, but I'm not for her. I'm for you, Vinnie. Why don't you admit it and let the rest of the world go hang!'

'You do realize,' said Vinnie, 'that if you stay they will all leave? *All* of them!'

'Good riddance to them, then! We don't need them,' he said. 'The world is full of cooks and grooms and kitchen-maids.'

'And gardeners,' said Vinnie. 'Don't forget gardeners.'

For a moment Adam's charm nearly deserted him. She saw the involuntary tightening of his lips, but she was no longer frightened. He recovered his composure almost at once.

'Vinnie! Dear little Vinnie, do be careful,' he said softly. 'Don't send me away. You will regret it all your life and Bert will never forgive you.'

'I shall write to him,' said Vinnie, 'and tell him how it happened. You are wasting your breath, Adam. You see, I do believe these hysterical women you so despise. And in spite of your denials, I think I can prove to myself that *you* are a liar.'

His eyes narrowed and for a moment Vinnie was frightened. Then, before she could lose her nerve, she snatched up the bottom edge of Adam's dressing-gown – and saw the two semi-circular bruises half-way up his thigh which James's small teeth had made when he bit him.

'I thought so,' she said quietly. 'Doll *was* telling the truth.' She dared not look at his face, but heard him suck in his breath.

'Damn you, you cunning bitch!'

In his anger, Adam abandoned all thoughts of caution. His left hand caught Vinnie a stinging blow across the side of the head, knocking her sideways. Unfortunately for him, she fell towards the bell-rope and clutched at it as she went down.

Adam sprang to his feet and she saw the indecision in his eyes. Even now, she thought incredulously, he is *still* prepared to try to turn this to his advantage.

'Keep out of this bed,' she warned him. 'If you lay so much as a finger on me, you will regret it. And if you are not out of this house and off my property when I get up in the morning, I shall telephone to the local constabulary and have you charged with assault.'

As they faced each other across the bed, Vinnie saw a burning anger suffuse his face and wondered how she could have misjudged him so totally. She prayed that someone would answer the bell before he did her some physical harm. The air was charged with a terrifying tension and Vinnie's heart seemed, literally, to stop beating.

'I won't ever forget this!' He spat the words venomously as footsteps sounded along the passage. 'I'll make you pay—'

There was a knock on the door and Mrs Tallant's voice said, 'Mrs Lawrence, ma'am?'

Vinnie waited, but Adam made no move.

'Come in, please!' Vinnie called and was relieved to see him turn on his heel. As the housekeeper came into the room he strode past her, almost knocking her over.

'It's all right, Mrs Tallant,' Vinnie said shakily. 'Mr Turner is leaving tonight.'

'Leaving? Oh, I'm glad to hear it, ma'am,' she said. 'But you look white as a ghost. Has he – I mean, if he's dared to—'

'No, no,' Vinnie assured her. 'I'm not really hurt. But I would like a mug of hot milk to help me sleep.'

*

In the morning Adam Turner had gone, and the livid fingermarks on Vinnie's face told the curious staff all they needed to know.

CHAPTER TWENTY-ONE

Mary Bellweather had not spoken to Alexander about her talk with his mother. She fully intended to do so, but the days passed and she could never quite bring herself to broach the subject. She had applied to the courts and the wheels of the interminable legal process had been set in motion. Now her conscience racked her that Alexander was still unaware of the moves which affected him so deeply.

One day, at the beginning of August he raised the matter himself.

'I saw my mother yesterday,' he said calmly.

They were sitting together over dinner. Mrs Markham had cleared away the plates and brought in the dessert – a fluffy sponge and jam sauce. Mary, panic-stricken, waited until she had gone out of the room, then cut a generous slice of pudding for Alexander and pushed the plate clumsily towards him. So much, she thought bitterly, for Mollie's promise to disappear. So much for her own story that Mollie was dead. She wanted to scream with shock and disappointment, but before she could decide what to say he went on.

'She was outside the school, on the other side of the road. I've seen her there before.'

Mary managed to say, 'Have you?' but to her ears, at least, her voice sounded unnatural and she was sure the boy would notice.

'I don't think she knows which one is me,' said Alexander, staring fixedly at his plate. 'She hasn't seen me for such a long time. I wonder how she knows I go to that school?'

Mary was wondering the same thing. Had it slipped out in her conversation with Mollie? She did not think so, but Mollie must have guessed that the school he attended would be reasonably near his home.

'You didn't speak to her, then?' said Mary.

'No.'

Mary waited, unsure how to follow this. Should she seize the opportunity to tell him, now, of the arrangements made for his future? Or wait for a lead from the boy? He seemed remarkably calm and she envied him.

'She was all dressed up,' said Alex. 'Very smart, in new clothes, but some of the older boys laughed about her. They said she was a whore waiting to pick up a young client.'

He was not eating the food, only pushing it around his plate.

'I should have stuck up for her, but I didn't. I didn't look at her again. I didn't let her know it was me. I thought today I would speak to her but—' He laid down his spoon and fork with a sigh. 'She wasn't there today, she didn't come. I think perhaps she'll go to another school and look for me there.'

Slowly Mary lifted her eyes. 'Perhaps that's for the best,' she said. 'I don't know.'

'I didn't want her to find me,' said Alex, 'and I think maybe that's wicked of me. My own mother! And why didn't she ask at the school if she wanted to see me? Do you think she was just curious?'

Mary gave a slight shrug, but could not answer. She was angry with herself for not taking command of the situation, but fear paralysed her and she could not think coherently.

'Mary?' he insisted. 'Do you think my mother was just curious or is she looking for me?'

'Just curious,' said Mary, with an effort. 'She came here a few weeks ago and said she wanted to take you away with her, but she could not keep you because she had no money.' The boy showed no surprise. 'I said that you were happy here with me and doing well at school and – oh Alex! I asked her to let you stay. Do you mind, Alex? I thought it best for you – and' – she lowered her voice until it was almost a whisper – 'I could not bear for you to go away. Maybe that was wicked of me. She had no money, nothing; she had been in prison. I asked her if she really wanted you and your sisters, but she said, "No". She is not going to marry Amos Hearn. I did hope she might. It would have been a good home for her and a better life.'

'So you gave her some money,' he prompted. 'And she bought all those new clothes?'

Mary nodded, choosing her words carefully. 'She wants to make a new life for herself,' she told him. 'When she had you and

the girls, she was very young and she could not cope. She is still
very young at heart. It would be a struggle for her to bring up three
children and she knows you and the girls are better off as things
are. I shall go on sending the Hearns money for your sisters, and
your mother has agreed that I should be your legal guardian –
unless you object.'

Alexander looked at her and he seemed so much older than his
twelve years. 'If I thought she wanted me back, I would have to
go,' he said, 'but I don't think she does. Do you?'

'No,' said Mary, 'I don't think so. She loves you all very much,
but she doesn't want you with her. She wants what's best for you.'

'That's what I thought.' He sighed deeply. 'Do you think she'll
be happy now?' he asked.

'I think so,' said Mary. 'Yes, I think she will be – in her own
way.'

He nodded and was silent for a while, finishing the food on his
plate. When the plate was empty, he set his spoon and fork side
by side and looked up.

'We had a spelling test this morning,' he said. 'I came fourth
out of sixteen!' A slow smile of triumph spread over his plain face.
'I was seventh last time,' he added.

*

For Vinnie the next few months passed in a whirl of activity –
anything to dull the pain of her loneliness. From morning to night
she filled her time so that there was no opportunity for thought.
The doctor watched her with alarm, aware of her motives but
afraid that she would overtax her strength. The children were a
comfort to her, although the two youngest were too young to
register the loss of Julian's presence and James, with the resilience of a three-year-old, soon came to terms with the fact that he
would never see his father again – Vinnie found this hurtful,
although she could not wish it otherwise.

There was so much to do. Architects to be consulted regarding
the plans for the hoppers' huts which would be built for the 1906
season. There was the Bank Manager to be encountered and
finance to be negotiated. Then she made several journeys up and
down the country to see for herself the pros and cons of the new
method of hop-stringing – journeys which convinced her of the
value of the innovations. She collaborated with Roland Fry and
the Brothers in Jesus in providing a day's holiday for thirty

deserving London children, giving them a fine lunch and entertaining them with a Punch-and-Judy show, donkey rides and a treasure hunt. She sent all of them home with an apple and a shilling each, as well as a present – skipping ropes for the girls and a whip-and-top for the boys.

She and Doll took her own children to Margate for a week's holiday and it was judged an outstanding success with perfect weather and a friendly landlady.

Vinnie and William le Brun attended the Merryon shoot together, Clive having been confined to bed in London by an attack of pleurisy which also delayed the completion of his work on the estate and his subsequent return to Kent.

Eva and her children came to stay for two weeks at the beginning of August, while Gerald supervised the redecorating of their house at Bromley. Foxearth echoed with the shrill cries of children, while the two women talked endlessly together.

One of Trix's litter of six joined the Foxearth household – a leggy dog puppy with creamy fur who went by the name of Skipper and was adored by the three children and hopelessly spoiled by the kitchen staff.

Colonel Lawrence never fully recovered from the shock of his son's death, but the various excitements carried him along and Janet and the doctor kept him as healthy and comfortable as possible.

Before Vinnie had realized it, the summer was nearly over. It was the end of August and the hop-pickers would soon be arriving. She threw herself headlong into the preparations, assisted by Ned Berry and Steven Pitt but relying more and more on William le Brun, for without Julian she was quite unable to deal with all the various issues involved.

At last the hop-picking season was upon them and the gipsy caravans arrived in twos and threes from all parts of Kent. Vinnie went to Wateringbury station in the middle of the night to meet the Londoners and see them installed with their luggage in the various carts and waggons which would carry them from the station to Foxearth.

Hop-picking began and the next four weeks passed in a whirl of activity. To Vinnie's surprise, she thoroughly enjoyed it.

William le Brun was there in his official capacity as factor. He helped her to decide on a price per bushel for the hops and he intervened at once when the local carter tried to overcharge her for the haulage of the hop-pockets to the station. At the end of the month he double-checked Vinnie's accounts for her and stood by to see that there were no arguments at the last Saturday's pay-out.

On the final Sunday, after the fair had closed down and the last of the pickers were packing their belongings, William stayed to dinner to celebrate the end of the hop-picking. He and Vinnie lingered over the meal – Cook had excelled herself with *boeuf en croûte* and a meringue – and Vinnie, buoyed up by the satisfaction of a job well done, was in excellent spirits. As mistress of Foxearth, albeit with William's help, she had seen through her first harvest. Julian would have been proud of her. Next year, she told herself, she would see it through alone. *And* improve the accommodation.

The new-found self-confidence suited her. She held her head proudly and her expression was tranquil. Her earlier doubts and regrets had been swept away and there was a radiance about her of which she was unaware. It was not lost on William, however, and at that moment he made up his mind that he wanted to marry Vinnie Lawrence. He almost blurted it out, but he bit back the words while his heart hammered with excitement.

Vinnie laughed suddenly. 'You're giving me what Mrs Bryce calls an old-fashioned look,' she told him. 'Have I spoken out of turn or something?'

'No, you haven't. Vinnie, I shall be going up to London tomorrow, to see my father.'

'Oh?' She thought it rather odd that he had not mentioned this before. 'Well, give him my kind regards – no, my love. That dreadful job must surely be nearly over. He's been away for weeks. Thank goodness you have been around, William. I don't know how I would have managed without you.'

William looked at her shining eyes and prayed that she would never have to manage without him again.

*

Miss Garret fiddled with the inkwell on her desk, shuffled the completed letters and glared pointedly at the clock on the wall. Another late day! It was beyond a joke, she thought angrily. It was most inconsiderate, to say the least. *He* might choose to work late every evening, but *she* was not being paid for the extra time and ten minutes here and a quarter of an hour there soon added up. Her small mouth was pursed disapprovingly and her rather heavy brows met in a frown above her thin nose. Mr Wainwright had never kept her late, knowing that she had a fifteen-minute journey by horse-tram to her home in Wood Green. Mr Wainwright had been a true gentleman, she reflected, but his nephew was not of the same mould. She glanced across at him, regarding the bent head with disfavour. 'Taciturn' was probably the best word to describe him. He was not a happy man either, she reflected. And whenever his son telephoned, his mood worsened. Miss Garret dreaded young William le Brun's calls. Whatever he said to his father – and Miss Garret would not dream of listening in – it did nothing to lighten Mr le Brun's sombre mood.

Poor Mr Wainwright might have been corpulent and bald, she thought, but he was a cheerful man and he made little jokes to brighten her day. Working for him had been a pleasure. No, she amended cautiously, it had been her greatest pleasure. She would never admit to herself that she had adored her late employer.

At home she had been merely Olive Garret, with a querulous elderly mother who was both demanding and unappreciative. To Mr Wainwright she had been an efficient and highly-valued secretary. One of a new breed of women. She sighed heavily; her employer had died 'of his heart' at the age of fifty-four and her secretarial post would end when Mr le Brun finally settled the estate.

She glanced across at him and thought without compassion that he looked drawn and ill. The pleurisy had been unfortunate, but he should have gone to a convalescent home as the doctor suggested.

He seemed to sense her scrutiny and looked up. 'Oh, Miss Garret, are you still there?' he said. 'I'm so sorry. You'd better go home now. I'll lock up when I leave.'

'These letters, Mr le Brun. You haven't signed them.'

He did so, scrawling his large signature across the bottom of the page, so unlike Mr Wainwright's small neat hand.

'I have been writing a reference for you,' he said. 'Here, read it and tell me if I have missed out anything. I don't know you very well and I want to be fair.'

Surprised, she took the sheet of paper. So this was what he had been working on so assiduously for the past half-an-hour. The reference was a good one and she was flattered, but . . .

'You've got my age wrong,' she said reluctantly. 'I'm not thirty-three, I'm thirty-eight.'

'You look younger,' he said. 'It was just a guess. Let's leave it at thirty-three, shall we?'

'Yes, Mr le Brun. Thank you.' She hesitated. 'And could you say how long I worked for Mr Wainwright – for twelve years?'

He amended the draft. 'Type it up first thing in the morning. I shall be finished here by the day after tomorrow. I shall pay you a generous bonus out of the estate for your invaluable assistance. I'm sure my uncle would have wished to show his appreciation for your legal survice.'

'A bonus! Oh, Mr le Brun! What can I say? That's most unexpected but—'

At that moment there was a knock on the street door and it opened to allow a young man into the room. Before Miss Garret could say anything, Mr le Brun spoke.

'William!' he said. 'What in the world are you doing here?'

'Hullo, Father.' The young man smiled at Miss Garret. Mr le Brun looked confused, but said, 'That will be all then, Miss Garret. Thank you. Please post the letters on your way home as usual.'

Miss Garret was very impressed as William, with a cheerful smile, helped her into her coat while Mr le Brun glanced at some papers on his desk. He did not seem at all pleased to see his son, she thought. This puzzled her, but it was none of her business. He had written her a good reference and was going to pay her a bonus. That would be a pleasant piece of news for her to carry home to her mother. She gave them both a brisk nod and said 'Goodnight'.

As the door closed behind her, father and son regarded each other warily. 'An unexpected pleasure!' said Clive. 'What brings you here, William? I'm rather busy, so if you could come to the point—'

'I want to ask your approval,' said William.

'Oh? Approval of what?'

'I think I want to get married, Father,' said William. He thought irritably that his father must surely know what he was talking about. 'No, what am I saying? I *do* want to get married and I want to ask her as soon as possible. I thought I should tell you first, in case you have any views on the matter – not that I shall change my mind about her, but I'm hoping you will give us your blessing and – and your approval.'

'Aren't you rather young to be thinking of marriage?' asked Clive.

'No, I don't believe I am. I do a good day's work – more than most others of my age – and I could support a wife. Not that—' He let the sentence go unfinished. It would not sound at all well to suggest that money was not of great importance because Vinnie was a wealthy widow.

'You are only twenty-one,' said Clive. 'That is too young in my opinion. I really don't think you should take on such a commitment just yet. In another year, perhaps.'

William stared at him, astonished. 'Father! Aren't you curious to know who it is, this lady I want to marry?'

'I assume it is Mary Bellweather.' Clive pushed some papers into a folder, put the folder into a drawer in the desk and locked it. 'You and she seemed to be—'

'Of course it's not Mary. It's Vinnie Lawrence! For heaven's sake! Father, you *can't* pretend you haven't guessed?' William exploded. 'I don't understand you. You say I'm too young, yet you were married yourself at the same age. Then you pretend you don't know who I am talking about. Of course it's Vinnie Lawrence. You've absolutely no reason to think otherwise.' William's disappointment was painfully obvious. 'It's Vinnie Lawrence I want to marry and I thought you would be pleased. Obviously I was wrong, although I can't imagine—'

'Has she given you any encouragement?' interrupted Clive.

William hesitated. 'She hasn't discouraged me,' he said. 'I believe she is very fond of me. In fact, yes, I think in her own way she is encouraging me, but it is still not so long since she lost her husband.'

'Exactly.' Clive stood up abruptly. 'It's much too soon, William. I think you're fooling yourself if you think that Vinnie is ready to marry again. Wait! Don't fly off the handle! Let me finish. I don't deny she could make you a good wife, but I *do* think this is the wrong time to ask her. If you're asking for my advice, then—'

'I'm not, Father. I'm asking for your approval,' said William, trying hard to remain unruffled by this unexpected reaction to his news. 'I was hoping you would say "Go ahead" and wish us well, but it's pretty clear you are not going to. What is your objection to her? Isn't she good enough for me? Is that it? Does her East End background make her unacceptable for me but acceptable for the Lawrences? It doesn't make sense, Father.'

Clive reached for his coat, pulled it on and carefully buttoned it before he spoke again. Then he looked directly into his son's eyes which smouldered with ill-suppressed resentment and with an effort spoke more gently. 'I'm sorry, William. Forgive me if I wasn't very encouraging. I have nothing against Vinnie Lawrence as a wife for any man, but I think your timing is wrong. Vinnie may well accept you—'

William's face brightened. 'Then you don't object to my asking her?'

'No, I don't object and if she says "Yes", then of course I shall be pleased for you both and I'll wish you well and help you in any way I can. As for me marrying young, it was a mistake, quite frankly, and one I had rather hoped you would not repeat. Your mother and I . . .' He shrugged. 'Don't misunderstand me, William. We were very much in love and we were very happy for some years, but the relationship – well, there is no point in going over the past. Let us just say that there were problems which we might have solved had we been older.'

Clive sighed deeply, then put a hand awkwardly on his son's shoulder. 'I'm sorry, William. Let's start this conversation again. You're a new generation and things change. My father warned *me* against marrying so young, but I didn't take a damned bit of notice.' They both laughed rather self-consciously as he went on, 'We'll go back to where you ask me if I approve of Vinnie as a wife for you. Yes, I do. She's charming and intelligent. Do you love each other?'

'I love her, Father. I think perhaps she loves me.'

'Ah! Well, ask her then, William,' said Clive, 'and we'll all go on from there.'

*

At nine o'clock the next morning Janet opened the door to William le Brun. One look at his face told her why he had come at such an unusually early hour.

'Is your mistress at home?' he asked, his manner as formal as his clothes.

'Yes, Mr le Brun – at least, she is and she isn't. She's gone out for a walk, probably down to the river.' Seeing his surprise, she added, 'She's taken to walking early, sir, when no one's about. She likes to be alone with her thoughts – leastways, that's what she told Doll.'

William hesitated. 'How long will she be, do you think? Has she been gone long?'

'About fifteen minutes, I should reckon, sir. Would you like to wait in the drawing room, sir?'

'I don't know.' Janet watched him curiously as he tried to hide his nervousness, then he repeated, 'I don't really know.'

'Why not go after her?' Janet suggested. 'You might meet her coming back. She doesn't always go far, although sometimes she's about an hour.'

'An hour! Oh, then I will walk down and try to find her. Thank you, Janet.'

As he turned away, she said, 'Suppose you miss her, sir. Do you want to leave a message?'

William frowned. 'No, just say that I went to look for her and I shall be back.'

'I'll tell her, sir.'

With an effort, she refrained from adding 'Good luck, sir!' but she did hope Vinnie would marry Mr le Brun. They all did. He was young, reasonably good-looking and, more to the point, he was not likely to sell Foxearth and whisk Vinnie and the children away to a new home. Tim Bilton had reconnoitred Harkwood and assured them that the le Bruns' town house in Tunbridge Wells, even with its elegant façade and long garden, was no match for Foxearth. No, if William married Vinnie he would move into Foxearth and would, they felt sure, prove a good and fair man to work for. More important still, the future security of the household staff would not be imperilled. Janet crossed her fingers for him, closed the front door and rushed back to the kitchen to pass on the news.

*

Vinnie was sitting by the river, leaning against the old bridge. Her eyes were closed as she listened to the water breaking softly against the stonework and slipping among the reeds below her, while the morning sun warmed her face. She believed herself unobserved and William, moving silently across the grass, was able to study her. This was the woman he loved, the woman he hoped one day to marry. She seemed so very young and vulnerable, he thought, and he longed to take her in his arms and protect her from the harsh world. She sat childlike, hugging her knees, her long skirt tucked decorously round her legs, although she had thrown off her shoes and her bare feet were pale against the green grass.

'Vinnie?' he said.

He spoke gently but Vinnie was startled and her eyes snapped open.

'William!' she said. 'You made me jump! Oh, my heart's thumping away!'

He hurried forward. 'I'm so sorry,' he said. 'I didn't mean to startle you.'

She relaxed and smiled, patting the grass beside her. 'Sit here with me,' she said. 'The sun's so warm. This is my favourite spot; it's sheltered from the wind but it catches the sun. It should have sad memories for me, but I find it strangely comforting to hide myself away here.'

'Sad memories?' he asked.

'Of my mother,' Vinnie explained. 'She was drowned in this river when I was five. They found her body right here,' she pointed, 'washed up against the bridge. I try to imagine it sometimes, but it doesn't make me feel sad.' She glanced up at him with earnest grey eyes. 'I feel that she's close to me here. It's very odd. In the churchyard beside her grave I feel nothing at all. I remember as a child being taken there by Mrs Bryce and thinking, "That's a lump of grey stone, that's not my mother." I felt cheated somehow.'

William nodded. He was disconcerted by Vinnie's mood and unsure how to turn the conversation along more appropriate channels.

'She was pretty, my mother,' said Vinnie, 'in a tired sort of way. I only have a hazy picture of her, but Bertie told me. She had a hard life and I often think that if only she were alive now I could help her – make her life easier for her. But then, if she hadn't died I wouldn't be here now. It's as though her death saved me from a life like hers.'

'A strange twist of fate,' said William. 'I'm sorry if I've disturbed you in your favourite hideaway.'

'It doesn't matter.' She sighed. 'She was looking for me, you see. There was a row, I remember, and I had run off somewhere and couldn't be found. She sent Bertie to look for me, then they all started to look for me. My mother thought I would be down here because I had kept on about wanting a picnic by the river.'

'And were you?'

'By the river? No, it turned out that I was asleep in an old gipsy cart. Bertie remembered it all so clearly. Somehow she must have tripped and fallen in.'

'Poor soul!' he said.

'It's very strange,' said Vinnie. 'I tried talking to God in the church but I was never at all sure that he was listening. Really, I could never see how he had the time to listen to my problems when he has the whole world to worry about. But if I talk to my mother I feel she's always there, listening carefully.' She gave a little laugh. 'Does that sound crazy to you?'

'No Vinnie, it sounds possible.' He smiled at her, then on a sudden inspiration said, 'Do you think she can see us here together? Do you think she approves of me?'

Vinnie looked at him in surprise. 'I suppose so,' she said. 'I don't see why not. You're a very nice person. Oh William, what am I saying? Of course she would approve of you.'

William had felt his courage ebbing away and now he was suddenly fearful that if he delayed his proposal, he might not make it at all.

'I mean, would your mother approve of us together,' he stammered. 'Vinnie, what I'm trying to say is—'

Vinnie was staring at him astonished, her mouth already opening in protest.

'No, Vinnie, please don't say anything,' he said. 'Please let me finish what I want to tell you.'

'Oh no, William!' she protested, suddenly aware of his purpose.

'Vinnie, you must listen,' he insisted. 'You must know that I love you. That—'

'William, I *don't*!' cried Vinnie. 'Oh, please!' But nothing could stop William now that he had made up his mind.

'I love you Vinnie; I suddenly knew it the other evening, I suddenly realized. All these months that we've been together, it was not just friendship. It was much more. Vinnie, say you felt that too – that you felt it was more than friendship?'

She stared at him, utterly dismayed. 'Oh William, no,' she whispered.

He held up his hand. 'Don't, Vinnie. Let me go on. I love you and I want to marry you more than I've ever wanted anything. I'll love you Vinnie, always. I swear it! And the children too, I'll love them. I think they like me, don't you?'

'Yes . . . I'm sure they do, William, but—'

'So I'll be a good father to them, have no fears about that.' He was looking at her with such earnestness that if she hadn't felt so sorry for him, she might have found it funny. She wondered how he could possibly have thought that she loved him – she had given him no encouragement, had never thought of him as anything but a friend.

'It's been so wonderful, Vinnie,' he was saying. 'These past months have been so happy and I want it to be like this for ever. It could be, Vinnie, I promise you it could. Only say you will marry me, Vinnie, and everything will be—'

'Stop it, William, I beg you!' she said. 'I can't let you go on. Let me explain why I must say "No" to your most generous proposal, because it *is* generous and I appreciate what you are offering.'

'It's not generous, Vinnie,' he cried. 'How can you say that it's generous to make me the happiest man alive? Because that is what I would be!'

Vinnie was looking at him with an expression of deep regret and he scrambled suddenly to his feet. Holding out her hands, she allowed herself to be pulled up beside him and he stared at her in an agony of apprehension.

'Don't turn me down, Vinnie!' he pleaded.

Hopefully Vinnie said, 'I thought you were fond of Mary? I always thought you and she had so much in common.'

He had the grace to look embarrassed. 'I do admire her,' he said, 'but she can't hold a candle to you! I suppose I turned to Mary because you were unattainable. I mean . . . you were Julian's wife.'

Slowly they turned and began to walk in the direction of Foxearth.

'I wasn't a very good wife,' Vinnie said suddenly. 'I wasn't right for Julian, although I wanted to be right. I have thought about our marriage a lot over these last months, and I'm not very impressed with my part in it. I wanted to do the best for so many people and it didn't – couldn't – work. I should have realized, but I didn't. Now I would like to go back and start again, but it's too late. It's always too late.'

'We all make mistakes, Vinnie,' he said, trying to comfort her. 'I expect you and I would make a few, but if we loved each other enough—'

'No, William, it wouldn't work,' said Vinnie. 'Not if I didn't love you. It's hard enough when you do love someone, believe me! Even if I did love you I wouldn't marry you. I shan't marry anyone just yet. I need time to sort myself out and come to terms with the past. I should never have married Julian, but it wasn't all bad. We were very happy at first and then later the children gave us both a lot of joy.'

Vinnie sighed heavily and then glanced at the young man walking beside her. His brown eyes, pale and flecked with gold, looked into her own from beneath the unruly mass of ginger hair which he had tried unsuccessfully to smooth into some kind of order. 'Is any of this making sense, William?' she asked.

He shrugged, his face set in lines of deep disappointment. 'I think I understand,' he said, 'but may I wait for you, Vinnie? I don't mind how long it takes you to feel that you are ready. I could wait a year and then ask you again. How would that be?'

'Well, I may not know my mind even then,' she told him. 'And I may never love you as you deserve to be loved. Love doesn't come to order, I'm afraid. You are still young, William. I should feel happy if you would think of us as good friends. Later, if I ever should love you . . .'

It was his turn to sigh. They walked in silence for a while, then he grinned ruefully.

'My father will say "I told you so",' he observed.

'Clive?'

'Yes. I asked him for his approval of my proposal and he said it was too early.'

'He was right,' said Vinnie. 'Poor Julian has been dead less than a year. Sometimes it seems such a long time ago that he died, at other times it seems like yesterday. We will still be friends, won't we, William, the way we were before?'

'Of course.'

'I shall look on you, whatever happens in the future, as one of my dearest friends.'

A smile lit his face and Vinnie thought, 'He's so young, so vulnerable.'

'I will always be at your service,' he said.

'How terribly formal!' she teased. 'But I thank you, kind sir.'

He laughed and she went on, 'And what will you tell your father?'

William thought about it. 'That I asked you and you said it is too early to think of remarrying – but that I may ask you again.'

She looked at him, wondering if she would ever love William le Brun. It seemed unlikely . . . It seemed unlikely that she would ever love anyone again. The words of the old country saying rang through her head: This year, next year, sometime—

'I'm a patient man,' he told her. 'At least I will try to be!'

Suddenly he took her face in his hands and kissed her gently. 'I love you, Vinnie,' he whispered. 'I hope you will come to love me.'

Vinnie felt a great sadness for him as he took her hand. The word 'Never' finished the old saying and to Vinnie it had a prophetic ring to it. But the future was a long way off and at present she felt she would never again be certain of anyone.

They stopped under the big chestnut tree at the far end of the garden and she thought William was going to speak again. Instead he looked at her wordlessly, then bent his bright head to kiss her hand in a half-mocking gesture that was at once tender and full of hope. Then together they left the shadow of the tree and walked back through the October sunshine towards the house.